INNER

CITY

BLUES

"[AN] ENERGET

"A sharp, insightful look at the multi-dimensional, multi-ethnic stew of L.A. cops and robbers, saints and sinners. Charlotte Justice is a heroine for the nineties—tough when she needs to be, tender when she wants to be, and on the case 24/7! I look forward to her next adventure."

—BARBARA NEELY
Author of *Blanche Cleans Up*

"Paula Woods got the goods on all the crooks and thieves. / In *Spooks and Spies and Private Eyes* she brings them to their knees. / So when you want to get serious / to the point of delirious / about things quite mysterious / tune in to those *Inner City Blues* / which will bring you the good news / that justice is still in the race / to close the book on another case."

—NIKKI GIOVANNI

"Paula L. Woods's debut novel crackles with originality, grit, and fine writing. LAPD homicide detective Charlotte Justice is a wonderfully complex and realistic heroine, and *Inner City Blues* is an important and gripping novel. Paula L. Woods is definitely one to watch."

—HARLAN COBEN
Author of *One False Move*

"LAPD Detective Charlotte Justice, heroine of Paula Woods's debut mystery *Inner City Blues*, is a sleuth to be savored, smart, tough, funny, and brave. Woods has crafted a marvelous, touching, sassy, superb novel. Don't miss this one."

—CAROLYN G. HART
Author of *Death on Demand*

"Detective Charlotte Justice is just what the world of crime fighting ordered. Sassy, smart, streetwise, and sexy, Detective Justice makes an unforgettable debut in *Inner City Blues*. . . . From the opening page, the author hits the reader right between the eyes with her sharp prose and on target dialogue. . . . Woods has done an exceptional job of weaving in the intricacies of a homicide investigation while peppering it with a cast of suspects, dead ends, dead bodies, and a dose of gang violence and philosophy. . . . [Her] character development sparkles, with her secondary characters giving outstanding performances."

—*Mosaic*

Please turn the page for more reviews. . . .

INNER CITY BLUES

A CHARLOTTE JUSTICE NOVEL

PAULA L. WOODS

ONE WORLD
THE BALLANTINE PUBLISHING GROUP • NEW YORK

A One World Book
Published by The Ballantine Publishing Group
Copyright © 1999 by Paula L. Woods

Library of Congress Catalog Card Number: 99-69500

ISBN 0-345-43793-4

Cover design and collage by Kristine V. Mills-Noble based on photos courtesy of The Stock Market and Definitive Stock

This edition published by arrangement with W.W. Norton and Company.

Manufactured in the United States of America

First Ballantine Books Edition: February 2000

10 9 8 7 6 5 4 3 2

FOR FELIX

Never judge a book by its cover.

—Cecilia "Grandmama Cile" Justice (1908–   )

CHAPTER 1

MESSING UP
MY CHA-CHA

Twelve years, eleven months, and fifteen days into living out my *Top Cop* fantasies—Christie Love with a better hairdo—my Nubian brothers down on Florence and Normandie had to go and pitch a serious bitch and mess up my cha-cha. Since May of '79, when I stood in the graduating class at the Police Academy, I had survived my years with the LAPD with little more than a few bruises, a shoulder prone to dislocation, and a couple of badly torn fingernails.

Survived the early years in patrol cars with partners whose every joke began "There was a white man, a Mexican, and a nigg . . . uh . . . *black* man . . .'' Survived my first assignment as a gang detective in Southwest, where I learned more about L.A. homeboys in the first three months than I had in three years of graduate study in criminology. And let me not forget the edu-mo'-cation I got when I went over to South Bureau Homicide, where I saw more dead bodies in five years than detectives in other parts of the country see in their whole careers.

I had survived stun guns and choke holds; Afro puffs and Jheri curls; floods, fires, and medflies; the '84 Olympics and the Whittier quake. At thirty-eight, I weighed thirty pounds less than I had in high school, had all my teeth, and had never, until getting caught near ground zero on a fine spring day, seriously been in fear for my life.

But thanks to twelve decent, Gates-fearing residents of Simi Valley and its pro-cop environs, I spent the days leading up to my thirteenth anniversary in the Department back in uniform dodging bullets, new jack Molotov cocktails, and more Pampers tossed through broken grocery store windows than I care to remember.

As I watched the city I loved go to hell in a handbasket, I kept reminding myself that the Los Angeles I wanted to protect and to serve was basically composed of law-abiding citizens, not mad looters dragging microwaves down Pico Boulevard—near *my* house, no less.

There was a deadly carnival atmosphere in the air. Gang members and grandmothers, who usually gave each other a wide berth, were united in their rage over the verdict and the stench of despair that had hovered in the air since Watts blew up in 1965. But unlike the Watts riots, which were confined by segregation to a much smaller area, the alliance of the poor and the befuddled yearning to live large was everywhere, of every color and economic class, all wanting to bring down some particularly offensive part of the system in their corner of the city. So it didn't matter if it was beating Reginald Denny in South Central or looting a jewelry store in Long Beach—anything and everything was fair game.

I had to do something to keep the peace, so even though it was against Department policy, I'd finagled a way to stay on duty almost forty-eight hours. And while it was the most stressful thing I'd done since joining the force, I was getting through it okay. But it was Friday, May 1, the day after the National Guard set up housekeeping in shopping centers all over the city, that the last straw, blown in on a warm Santa Ana wind from a most unexpected direction, broke this camel's back.

A motley crew of twenty of us—street cops and desk jockeys from Parker Center, South Bureau, and a couple of the divisions—had been deployed by bus to a strip mall on Rodeo Road. Spelled exactly the same as Rodeo (as in Ro-day-o) Drive in Beverly Hills, the running joke in some parts of town was how far apart the two streets really were. Rodeo Drive's sleek boutiques and Mercedes-Benzes epitomized the Southern California good life, and the chief of police and residents there made damn sure everyone knew Beverly Hills was *not* in the City of Angels. I bet most of the tenants on Rodeo Drive didn't even know about their poor relations that runs through what black folks call "the Westside," less than five miles southeast as the crow flies.

My Rodeo—although pronounced the way the cowboys do—was no less treasured than Beverly Hills's. Shopping centers and moderately priced planned communities on the western end of the street gave way to soul-food joints, strip malls, and solidly middle-class homes to the east. At the corner of Rodeo and La Brea was a busy commercial district. I bought my first forty-five (record, that is)—Fontella Bass's "Rescue Me"—at the record store that sat on the corner, and down the street on La Brea was the Baldwin Theater, where I went on my first real date.

Rodeo forked to the left at Dorsey High School and through a neighborhood of postwar tract houses whose identical twins in what white folks call the Westside would command at least a hundred thousand more. A little farther east were blocks of vintage Spanish homes, including the original residence and beautiful rose gardens of Mayor Tom Bradley and his wife, Ethel.

Two streets separated by a few miles and lot of money, in those days the Rodeos were competing in a grimly fought battle to see who would survive the hell of the last forty-eight hours. With a chief of police who served as a former aide to Chief Gates, I was betting well-staffed and well-patrolled Beverly Hills's Rodeo would be the hands-down winner this time around.

That day my Rodeo looked more like a war zone than a major thoroughfare through middle-class black L.A. Its smoldering rubble was a symbol of the largest civil insurrection in modern American history, and I had been powerless to stop it.

I couldn't stop the torching of my record store, up in flames that first night along with several black-owned businesses.

I couldn't stop the multiracial looters who scrambled for

merchandise at the Fedco store, giggling like kids fighting for candy from a piñata.

And I couldn't stop what faced the score of us who pulled up in our armored bus, a day late and a bullet short, to another devastated strip mall whose windows gaped at us like a toothless drunk and whose erstwhile customers were removing their and everybody else's dry cleaning without presenting a ticket.

It was a little after three in the afternoon when we arrived, and by four we had apprehended and restrained a rainbow coalition of looters with the plastic handcuffs we were using faster than Kleenex in flu season. After the suspects were transported by prison bus to the emergency holding facility, I threw myself onto our bus and stretched out in the first row.

Opposite me was my new partner/trainee and the only other female on the bus. Genoveva Cortez was an entry-level detective—a Detective I or D-I, we called them—and a recent transfer to headquarters from South Bureau. Cortez was a lot like me when I got my first assignment at Parker Center, the LAPD's headquarters, over eleven years ago—intelligent, assertive, naïve as hell. But my first assignment at Parker Center was as a grunt in Press Relations, not the LAPD's renowned Robbery-Homicide Division. And my baptism by fire came by assisting the Press Relations commander with the media on a VIP homicide, not trying to work homicides while the whole city went up in smoke at the rate of three fires per minute.

Cortez was dealing with it, though. Made me understand why they chose her to be the second woman to join RHD's homicide unit, which up until my arrival was a very exclusive—as in white-only—boys' club. But homicides—even the demanding, high-profile ones RHD handles—have a way of ignoring gender and color lines. And female homicide detectives had made contributions everywhere else in the Department—why not RHD? So it was finally determined, after much gnashing of teeth and wringing of hands, that even the LAPD's crème de la crème had to change to keep up with the times, ugly as they were.

But the kind of thing Cortez and I were doing during the

riots was without precedent, even if we were of the right "persuasion" for the job. That was because there were so many riot-related murders to investigate that the homicide detectives in the Bureau and divisional operations were completely overwhelmed. And so it was somebody downtown's bright idea to loan out Robbery-Homicide Division detectives—including Cortez and me—on a temporary basis, to provide detectives to process as many homicides on the scene as we could safely and quickly manage.

I guess it's like the song says—some girls have all the luck. Shopkeepers murdered in their burned-out stores. Looter-shooters killing each other over CDs. Gang members whacking their rivals, *High Noon* style, just because they could get away with it. In forty-eight hours, Cortez and I had personally investigated nine crime scenes in what is usually the South Bureau's jurisdiction, more than we would usually handle in RHD in a year.

And we weren't getting much sympathy from our bus mates, either. "You downtown divas work so many celebrity cases you forget what it's really like in the streets," Mike Cooper snorted. "This shit is what we gotta deal with all the time."

He suggested we cruise King Boulevard. "Bound to be some more 'bidness' for you ladies over there," he said with just a hint of sarcasm in his voice.

As the bus made its way east, Cortez and I sat staring at each other across the aisle, our heads propped up against the windows. My reflection played back to me in the glass behind Gena's head gave the illusion we were cheek to cheek. Gena was darker than I, the deep sheen of her hair and eyes marking her as a Latina much quicker than my pale skin and light brown hair would tip some people off that I was black. And while I knew Gena was a full seven years younger than I, you wouldn't have known it that day. We were too tired to talk, too tired even to acknowledge each other. We looked more like chimney sweeps than cops.

At first I only half-heard Mike Cooper's voice. A detective out of South Bureau, Cooper worked what used to be called the gang detail, before some acronym-happy police administrator christened it CRASH—Community Resources Against Street

Hoodlums. As he droned on, I looked behind me to see what all the hoopla was about.

Despite his religious devotion to weightlifting, Cooper was still a rodent of a man, weasel-eyed and mousy-haired, who reminded me more of the before than after pictures at Gold's Gym. He was whining about how he hadn't seen his family for two days, as if it were any different for the rest of us. Cooper was clearly exhausted, but something in the tone of his voice had the hairs on the back of my neck standing at attention and straining to whisper urgent warnings in my ear.

"Goddamn it, I'm sick of this shit! These fuckin' bangers out here might as well have been the V.C. some of us saw in 'Nam, the way they ambushed Denny. These animals don't give a fuck about human life, so why should we?" The supportive murmuring drifted toward Cortez and me like a foul wind, carrying Cooper's words with it. "We're supposed to be the best-trained law enforcement agency in the world, not some fish in a barrel for these mud-brown niggers and spics to pick off. I'm telling you, I don't give a shit about no fuckin' prime directives—the first little jungle bunny who looks at me cross-eyed is gonna get a cap in his ass! I *know* how to get this city in order!"

We were all tired and a little crazed, but Cooper was having a bona fide out-of-body. It wasn't his anger or racism that surprised me, but the fact that the fool had the nerve to be this open about it.

Although Chief Gates had proclaimed after the Rodney King beating that the LAPD saw no color except blue, every black or brown-complexioned cop knew otherwise. It was a part of their job, so went the thinking of some of our paler brothers in blue, to provide a running commentary on the race of every suspect we ran in. Or to type out gorilla-in-the-mist jokes on their mobile digital terminals (as in "What do you get when you put Mike Tyson in a steam room?"). And a comment on how they'd love to see Anita Hill's pubic hairs (or mine, or Cortez's) in their Coke cans was always good for a laugh—theirs, not ours.

Women and minority officers knew that to protest the casual racism and sexism of our co-workers singled us out as difficult, opening the door to an even more rigorous dosage of fun and games at our expense. If you complained of racial or sexual harassment to the Internal Affairs Department, it would automatically trigger an investigation and no one would work with you. And without a partner you could trust at your back, your ass would be grass, left out to dry in the Santa Ana winds.

But even with the built-in protection the system gave him, for Cooper to go this far in mixed company was way, *way* over the line. Cortez and I both came out of South Bureau. Cooper had known and had worked with both of us there. Besides, there was no mistaking Cortez as a Latina, and despite the fact that my coloring could be misleading to some, Cooper knew damn well I was black.

Still pointedly ignoring us, Cooper ranted and raved while a few others, some of whom I could trace back to my days in the Academy, grunted their approval and nodded their heads like newly saved sinners at a tent revival. Cortez's eyes darted between Cooper in the back and me; our Latino driver's eyes were fixed icily on the road ahead.

The encouragement from the choirboys in the back of the bus made Cooper all the bolder. "You split tails *think* you're makin' a difference in the Department with all that community outreach you do," he called out, slipping into the derogatory terminology too many of our colleagues use for female officers, "but I'm tellin' you, these bastards out here will kill you just as quick as they would me. Maybe quicker. And them penny-ante Berettas you're carryin' ain't gonna make a fuckin' bit of difference against the firepower they've got out here."

He damn sure was right about that. We had all heard that morning about three officers, including the brother of Dodger player Darryl Strawberry, who were ambushed by a gang-banger with an AK-47. Luckily the shooter was brought down and the men weren't badly injured. Still . . .

The sinews in Cortez's neck tightened as Cooper strode up front and sat on the edge of my seat. I didn't move my feet to accommodate him or even look at him directly. He pushed my feet aside and gestured out the window. We had just passed the burned out hulk of Aquarius Book Center, the first and oldest black bookstore in the city. I had just bought Toni Morrison's latest novel there a few days before the world went crazy.

"Tell me, Justice, do you think these homies and pachucos give a rat's ass about you?" His whispering breath bore the sour surprise of stale whiskey. "Do you? Do you think if we put you off this bus right here you'd make it to the end of the block without these fuckin' animals rippin' you to pieces? They won't even *see* you; they'll just see the uniform and those gray eyes you got and figure you for one more honky bitch cop out to oppress their lazy asses."

Cooper's eyes lingered over my body. "Or maybe they *will* recognize their sistuh"—he ran his tongue over cracked lips and drawled out the word in his own version of redneck-from-the-hood—"and get themselves a little piece of that sweet-cream ass before they put a bullet through your head."

Sergeant Burt Rivers, a veteran I'd known since joining the Department, called out for Cooper to lighten up. We were under Burt's direct command, so Cooper should have listened. But he was too far gone to turn back now.

I gently put my left hand on Cooper's shoulder, easing him back so I could look him in the eye and he could see my hand on my gun. Said as calmly as I could, "Mike, I know you're tired. So am I. But if you don't get off my bra strap right now, I'm going to aim this gun at Mister Willy there and change that Waco twang to a West Hollywood falsetto. So why don't you save the drama for your mama before somebody gets hurt?"

The bus reverberated with catcalls and "She sure told you's," in four-part harmony. Cooper glared at the chorus in the back and then leaned in a little closer toward me.

I unsnapped my holster. I could have smoked him right then and there if he pushed me.

Cooper's beady eyes had taken on a new gleam, but I realized he was no longer looking at me, but through the window behind me. "Pull over, Guillermo," he called out to our driver. "Looks like we got us a curfew violator."

By that time the gaze of everyone on the bus had shifted

starboard to take in a male the color of café au lait sprinting west on King Boulevard. Sporting three days' worth of beard on his angular face, a Raiders cap, black leather jacket, and wrinkled dark green cotton pants, the man appeared skittish and agitated amid the graffiti-covered apartment buildings and lengthening shadows.

He approached an Infiniti Q45 parked mid-block on the almost-deserted street. With its glistening, white metallic paint job and gold rims, the car was an easy target. The man peered through the car's window, peeled off his jacket, and wound it around his fist. He looked around as if he were trying to determine who would notice if he smashed the passenger's window.

"Looky here, Justice, we got us a 487.3 in progress." Cooper sounded almost gleeful to be quoting the California Penal Code number for grand theft auto. "Let's wait 'til he makes a definitive move." As if on cue, the man dropped to his knees, feeling around for something underneath the car. He stood up with a smile, one of those magnetic key holders in his hand. "Now ain't that a bitch?" Cooper exclaimed to the guys in the back. "Some poor bastard's dumb enough to leave his keys under the car for this nigger to find. Come on, fellas."

Cooper, a pimply-faced boot named Amundsen, and four others clambered off the bus, their riot helmets snapped into place, rifles in hand. A little older and slower off the mark, but at six-six and in his early fifties more commanding in stature and presence, Sergeant Burt Rivers brought up the rear, John Wayne with a mustache.

Gena slid across the aisle to my side of the bus. "*Es muy peligroso.*" She glanced at the apartment buildings on either side of the street. A tic hopped in her left eye.

Very dangerous was right. I watched as Cooper and Burt approached the car; Amundsen and the others stood back about ten feet and waited, rifles clasped across their chests. The man, tall, trim, and younger-looking than I suspected he actually was, didn't run or back off but started gesturing toward the car. He seemed vaguely familiar, but I couldn't place him. The Raiders cap he wore rang a bell—a football player coming from the Coliseum? If so, he must've had some kind of shock; the stadium was being used as an emergency jail facility. Besides, the team's practice field was fifteen miles away in El Segundo, and it was the off-season. This would be the last place you'd expect to see a football player.

A camera was slung over his shoulder. A news photographer? Or maybe just a Looky Lou, one of a score we'd seen since the riots started, capturing the fiery moments on everything from video cameras to disposable thirty-five-millimeter Kodaks and Fujis.

I slid the window down in time to hear, "Gentlemen, I'm Dr. Lance Mitchell. I just finished my shift over at California Medical Center's Emergency Room, and I locked my keys in the car. I came over here to drop off some medication with a patient."

He started patting his pockets. "I know I've got my ID somewhere . . ."

"Hold it right there!" Amundsen bellowed. The boot eased up to the man, patted him down nervously. "He's got no ID, sir," he told Rivers.

The man looked up with what tried to be a charming smile. "Maybe I locked it up in the car, too."

Something about that smile clicked in my head—this was the doctor who treated me in the hospital's ER last fall! I struggled to get the window down farther, to warn Cooper and company to ease up.

"Sir, step away from the vehicle!" It was Sergeant Rivers, polite but firm. I was probably the only one to see his mustache twitch.

When Mitchell didn't move Cooper shouted, "Goddamnit, nigger, get away from the car! You ain't no fuckin' doctor and you know it! You were tryin' to cop a G-ride, just like you probably stole that fancy camera you're carryin'."

Now why, I remember thinking, did Cooper have to go there? I started banging on the windows, but no one heard me. I might as well have been screaming underwater for all the good it was doing.

"But you ain't stealin' this car, you Mandingo-assed motherfucker!" Cooper said. "Now put your hands on the hood of the car."

Cooper prodded Dr. Mitchell on the collarbone with his baton. The doctor's hand flew up reflexively, batting the baton away from his face. Amundsen stepped forward and put the butt of his rifle in the doctor's gut before Rivers, his training officer, could stop him. My stomach churned in response and I anxiously fell in line behind Cortez and the others rushing off the bus.

Please, God, not this. Since Rodney King, black men from all walks of life had risen up to complain about their treatment at the hands of the LAPD. It had caused the Department a lot of embarrassment. We didn't need to go through it again, especially not now. I had to do something to stop this.

When people watching from the nearby apartments saw the first blow, they could have reached for their Uzis or their video cameras, but most of the stream of thirty or so Latinos and blacks being disgorged from the buildings were brandishing forty-ounce bottles of Schlitz Malt Liquor, lengths of lead pipe, and brooms. They stood jeering at the officers, who by then were arrayed in a half circle around Dr. Mitchell and the car, facing the oncoming crowd. Cortez and I joined them and started ordering people back inside.

We stood that way for some time—cops yelling at citizens, citizens cursing at the top of their lungs. The stalemate was broken when a shot echoed from somewhere nearby. In the second of hush that followed someone threw a bottle at Amundsen, who, rookie that he was, impulsively waded in before anyone could stop him. After that, it was on—tire irons and empty forties crashing and clanging with aluminum police batons and riot helmets.

I was hoping Guillermo had radioed in for backup because things had gotten completely out of hand; if it persisted, somebody was going to get killed. A smaller group of men, women, and more than a few kids broke for the bus and tried to rock it. A half dozen officers headed back across the street to secure it and Guillermo's butt.

Cooper was only partially right about my people trying to rip me to pieces. I could have been any color from sunshine white to shoeshine black, could have been their mama's best friend, but it was the dark blue uniform that made me a target that day. Despite their best efforts to kick my ass, though, I still managed to find Mitchell and drag him to his feet.

But I could have sworn it was a fellow officer who grabbed my right arm and gave it a gut-wrenching twist as I strong-armed my way through the surging crowd of my black, brown, and blue brothers, Mitchell in tow. Cortez saw us from the other side of the crowd and moved in to watch my back. Somehow we made it past Cooper and the others, who had just about stabilized the situation with help from a couple of extra patrol cars from the nearby Southwest Division station and an air unit thrumping overhead.

We had moved Mitchell away from the melee, past the boarded-up taco stand at the corner, past the McDonald's, and almost to the intersection, when my arm got too heavy for me to carry and my back began to spasm. Dr. Mitchell hustled me into a storefront's recessed doorway while Cortez went around the corner to see if she could flag down some help.

We stayed crouched in that doorway, amid the empty wine bottles, forties, and the smell of urine, for what felt like forever. But probably only a few minutes elapsed before Cortez returned, tailed by a redheaded reporter I recognized as Neil Hookstratten from the *Los Angeles Times*. Riding with him was the also-redheaded but dreadlocked Fred "F-Stop" Stoppard, a former LAPD crime scene photographer who now worked for the paper.

Cortez explained Hook would transport us to the temporary jail facility at the Coliseum. "To hell with jail," snapped Mitchell. "You've got an officer here who needs medical care!"

My partner ignored him and continued to confer with the reporter.

"This is ludicrous," Mitchell broke in. "I'm a doctor, god-damn it, and I'm telling you your partner needs medical attention and she needs it now!"

I was in no shape to argue, but we had a suspect to consider. Cortez was watching the melee we had just left behind us, finger-ing her handcuffs like a rosary. Finally she returned them to her belt and asked Hookstratten to drive us to the hospital.

Dr. Mitchell was visibly relieved as he got into the backseat of the Taurus to attend to me. Cortez got in back, too, her eyes on our suspect. "Let's get her over to California Medical Center,"

Mitchell suggested to Hook. The reporter turned on the car's emergency flashers and whipped a U-turn on King, turned left at the corner, and flew north on Vermont like a bat out of hell.

Mitchell was fighting a losing battle to make me comfortable as we were jostled about in the back of the car. "Haven't we met before, Officer . . . ?"

"Justice . . . *Detective* Justice," I corrected. "Out of Robbery-Homicide Division downtown." The puzzled expression on the doctor's face only intensified. "Everyone's in uniform and on the street until this thing is over," I explained.

"No . . . no . . . that's not it." His face scrunched up in concentration. "We've met before. Was it the Vineyard last summer? Were you a patient at California Medical Center? I'm sure I remember . . ."

"This isn't about Detective Justice, it's about you, Doctor," Cortez interrupted. "What in God's name are you doing here?"

Mitchell ran his fingers through what looked to me like chemically straightened hair. "I hadn't heard anything on the radio about any trouble in this part of town. So I assumed it would be safe to run some extra hypertension meds over to one of the elderly women I treated yesterday."

" 'Assume' makes an ass of you and me," I reminded him. "How could you 'assume' with a riot going on that there wouldn't be trouble everywhere, especially in South Central? Just because you didn't hear it on one of the all-news radio stations doesn't mean ain't nothing going down."

Cortez was equally testy. "And acting like you were about to break into that car only made matters worse."

"It was *my* damn car! I just locked my keys in it." The words slipped out of Mitchell's mouth before he could catch himself. He apologized quickly, his words tumbling over themselves in his haste to make us understand. "You have no idea what kind of madness we've been dealing with at the hospital. Mrs. Rucker's pressure was one sixty over one ten yesterday. She should have been admitted, but we didn't have the beds. Didn't even have enough antihypertensive medication to give her—so many nonpatients had been begging to get prescriptions filled, the pharmacy had run danger-ously low. And with all the local pharmacies burned down and our suppliers afraid to send trucks into the area, what was Mrs. Rucker going to do?"

"Are we missing something here?" Hookstratten's eyes widened into the rearview mirror. F-Stop, who got his nickname for the near-artistic precision of his crime scene photographs, turned in his seat, dreadlocks bristling, and looked, puppy-alert, at the three of us in the back.

"Not a thing," I warned the redheaded duo. They both caught my drift, hunkered down in their seats, and pretended not to listen.

Mitchell inhaled deeply and let the air shudder out in a rush. "I'm sorry. I've been on a forty-eight-hour shift at the hospital. I guess I'm not thinking too clearly." He looked down at his hands, then defiantly at me. "But that was *my* car! Didn't you see the license plate?"

How could I miss it? It was one of those notice-me vanity plates in a red frame that proclaimed, "ER doctors do it STAT."

I avoided answering his question by asking the fellas up front for their cell phone. They were making such a show of not listen-ing to our conversation that I almost had to say it twice before F-Stop responded. As he passed the phone back to me, he noticed the Nikon that Mitchell was carrying, and the two began a sotto voce pantomime about the model they both evidently used.

Whatever mercy mission he'd been on, Lance Mitchell was probably also on a little expedition to take pictures of the war zone to show off to his buppie friends on the golf course or his summer house in Oak Bluffs at the Vineyard. I had seen that kind of behav-ior all day, mostly from whites who drove in from the Valley or the Westside—*slumming*, my Aunt Winnie in Harlem would call it—but to think of a brother doing it really fried my ass.

I dialed the unlisted land line for the com center and told the radio telephone operator we had two officers-need-help situa-tions. I gave her the location of the altercation and made sure that adequate backup had been dispatched to the taco stand. It had—

five more patrol cars with four men each and a National Guard unit were already en route. Then I told her my status, our present location and destination. I also gave her the license plate to get the DMV status on the Q45 Mitchell claimed was his.

"I know my driver's license number, too, if you need it," Mitchell offered.

I motioned him to be quiet. "Never mind, Doctor. I remember . . . you reset my shoulder last fall."

And the way it was feeling, he might be doing it again.

CHAPTER 2

BACK DOWN
MEMORY
LANE

Since Wednesday night, I'd seen things and made arrests I thought would have been impossible just the week before. A black-owned savings and loan on the Eastside, the one my Grandmama Cile told us had been greeted with cheering in the streets when it opened forty-five years ago, burned so completely only one exterior wall was left standing. Five white women in FMPs—fuck-me-please pumps, as the working girls call them—we arrested in front of a Foot Locker, where they'd formed a human chain to pass Reeboks and Nikes from the store's broken windows to a Jeep Cherokee waiting at the curb.

There was the junkie who stabbed a neighborhood pharmacist for refusing to give him the key to the cabinet where *las drogas* were kept. Then there was the elderly black man with an aluminum walker we jammed but didn't have the heart, or time, to arrest. Caught leaving the same drugstore, he was accompanied by his wheelchair-bound wife, who obligingly carried in her lap enough Depends and other high-ticket items to last the both of them a month.

But no matter what I'd seen on the streets the last few days, it was clear when we got to California Medical Center's Emergency Room that we had crossed into some twilight zone of pandemonium.

Not that we didn't bring a certain amount of chaos with us. It started with the officers-need-help call, which drew available units from all over the area to our reported route to the hospital. By the time Hook and F-Stop dropped us off, we were surrounded by a phalanx of LAPD cars from South Bureau and Southwest Division who had picked up the dispatch and fallen into line.

As our entourage pulled up, I noticed an elderly Korean man in the back of a pickup. Evidently brought in by a couple of passersby, he looked as if he'd been hit by a car and left for dead. A pregnant Latina in full labor was trying to make it through the ER door, helped along by her panicked husband and two small children. They were almost knocked over by a young white man carrying a bluish-skinned young woman, wheezing from inhaling the ash-laden air.

Mothers with sick infants who hadn't been able to get to *las clínicas familias* jockeyed for position at the triage desk with old people, all pleading to have their prescriptions filled. In the examination area, the riot-injured vied for attention with the heart-attack victims. I heard the sounds of six different languages coming from behind the curtain of every exam cubicle except the one at the end of the hall. It was being used as a makeshift morgue; the three silent bodies covered with bloody sheets spoke a language all their own.

While Cortez accompanied Dr. Mitchell to the back so his injuries could be treated, I made two phone calls. The first was to Lieutenant Tony Dreyfuss. The lieutenant was in charge of homicide investigations that went on in South Bureau's jurisdiction, including our bus and its inhabitants that night. Fatigue and my aching back made me wrap my upper body around the receiver in an effort to focus on what he was saying; Lieutenant Dreyfuss's stutter was a sure sign that he was madder than a wet hen. After he got finished figuring out what the hell a physician was doing over on King Drive, he told me to have Cortez check out Mitchell's medication story and call him back.

My second call was to my brother, Perris. My father had told me when I called to check in the day before that Perris had decided to close his law office and do pro bono work for curfew violators and looters, so I wasn't surprised to find him still in court, despite the late hour. In the background I could hear a judge pounding his gavel for silence and roaring about who had the audacity to bring a cellular into his courtroom.

"Char! Is that you?" Surprise made my brother's voice a tenor rather than the characteristic bass of the Justice men.

"I'm over at California Medical Center. I caught a little hell in a situation over on King . . ."

Just then a blood-spattered, nut-brown baby was rushed by me in the arms of a similarly injured, darker-skinned man. At the sight of them, I was overwhelmed by the unwanted memory of jacaranda blossoms. A wave of nausea consumed me as I was drawn back almost fourteen years to the sight of bluish-purple trumpets drifting down from the tree in front of my house, into the growing puddle of blood in which my husband, Keith, and six-month-old baby, Erica, had lain. I could see as if it were yesterday the blue-gray barrel of a gun glinting at me from the passenger's side of the black car. The injured father's cries for help for his baby in the ER reminded me of how I had screamed and cried over my family, laying in our driveway, until my neighbor gathered me up and took me away into the dark coolness of my house, into the dark days and months that followed.

The dull ache that had taken root in the middle of my back branched out to my shoulders, enlivened by electric leaves of pain in my right forearm that brought a line of a psalm to mind, one I used to get on my knees and pray every night through most of my twenties: *Unto thee will I cry, O Lord my rock.*

All I remember on my slow-mo descent to the floor was a tattoo-embellished right arm as it simultaneously grabbed me and then the phone. Soon there were softer, less hairy arms under mine as a nurse's aide got me into a wheelchair and took me to a cubicle near the nurse's station. I managed to get onto the gurney and had just closed my eyes—wishing the room would stop spinning and the pain would go away, wishing I was back on the street instead of here, wishing I was back in the day when life was a whole lot simpler—when my past walked in and reminded me how bad the pain was, even way back when.

Aubrey Scott parted the plaid cubicle curtain and stood smiling down at me. "Charlotte Justice! I thought I recognized you when they brought you in."

Despite the world coming apart at the seams outside, Aubrey Scott stood before me like he just stepped out of a GQ spread, all six feet *fine* of him, notwithstanding his grizzled face and less-than-fresh dark green surgical garb.

Wincing as I tried to stretch out, I caught myself wondering if I smelled as bad as I thought I did and if my underwear was cotton or something a little more feminine. "I . . . I . . . heard you were living in San Francisco," I stammered.

"Our medical group won contracts to run eight emergency departments down here last year. We decided to move our administrative offices south, so here I am."

And not a moment too soon, from the look of things in that ER. Aubrey's smile faded as he examined my shoulder, gently holding my right arm as he tried to rotate it in the socket. "How did this happen?"

I gave him the short version of my adventures in hell.

Shaking his head: "God, Charlotte, I don't know how you do it."

I thought about the thirty or more people I had seen in the waiting room and the dozens more in exam rooms and in the halls: "I *could* say the same thing about you."

"Oh, I'm usually just a paper pusher," he explained. "I came down here last night to relieve Dr. Mitchell and the others. They're the real heroes." He manipulated my arm a little more. "Did I hear Dr. Mitchell say he'd reset this shoulder for you before?"

"Last fall. Altercation at a Raiders game."

"Still a sports junkie, I see. Why don't you get out of that vest and shirt so I can get a better look?"

His matter-of-fact tone caused an immediate conflict between my mind and body, both of which were saying, "Take it off, girlfriend!" for vastly different reasons.

God knows why, but as I loosened my holster and gingerly

undid my shirt and bulletproof vest, a Minnie Riperton song, "Memory Lane," started going through my head. As much as my aching body was in that cubicle, seeing Aubrey again took me back to when I was twelve and I would hide my chubby self in the shadows, watching him playing basketball in our driveway, wishing I was the sweat rolling down his not-yet-hairy, sixteen-year-old chest. Back to when I was seventeen and decided to lose thirty pounds to surprise him when he came home from Yale for summer vacation. Back to that fall when I cried my eyes out after we received the unexpected announcement of Aubrey's wedding to Janet Murphy, a pixie-faced rival in high school who had trapped him at the altar and then mysteriously "lost" the baby two months later.

Back down memory lane.

And now, twenty-odd years later, I was painfully aware of the road not taken, of the innocence of those days. Great joy—and even greater sorrow—made me forget the way Aubrey's perpetually tanned brown legs would uncoil from a chair, making me wish I could climb every delicious inch of him. I had forgotten the incredible butter softness of his long, squared-tipped fingers, how they felt on my back when he slow dragged with me at a fateful, blue-lights-in-the-basement party, the dim lights making his honey-colored eyes barely visible as he . . .

. . . flashed a penlight in my eye. "Charlotte . . . Charlotte . . . look directly into the light this time."

I returned reluctantly to the present, wishing for the protection of my Kevlar vest to cover my nipples, which I feared were standing up and winking "hello" to Aubrey through my hospital gown.

Aubrey averted his eyes, mumbled something to himself. To me he said, "Let me send someone else in here to take a closer look at that shoulder." He was outside the cubicle curtain, calling for a nurse before I could respond. Easing back on the examination table, I was grateful when a young Filipina nurse named Santiago came in with a blanket to cover my telltale flesh.

I was surprised to see Dr. Mitchell part the cubicle curtain a few minutes later, Cortez still close on his heels. As he swept into the cubicle in fresh surgical greens, I noticed his hands were pretty badly scratched up. A purple shiner and a butterfly bandage over his left eye only substantiated my original suspicion that he should have been on a gurney instead of me.

While Mitchell was washing his hands and putting on gloves, Cortez whispered in my ear, "His story checks out. A pharmacy technician said that around three thirty he picked up a prescription for a patient for a hypertension medication called Cardura."

"Call Lieutenant Dreyfuss," I whispered back, "and see what he wants to do on a 243." I knew Cortez would remember the California penal code for battering a peace officer; I just didn't want to telegraph my intent to Mitchell.

Her eyes told me she was with me. "I'll get right on it," she said.

So Mitchell *was* the good Samaritan he made himself out to be. But there was something about this guy that still didn't jibe for me. For starters, he should have been dead on his feet. But for Mitchell, it seemed the past few hours on the street hadn't happened. If anything, he appeared energized by it, all hyperkinetic, Hawkeye-Pierce-in-the-MASH-unit efficiency as he examined my shoulder and forearm. "Does this hurt?" he asked.

My cursing convinced him it did.

"Sorry, but we're going to have to get this shoulder back in." He gave me a local anesthetic and returned later with Nurse Santiago, who held my uninjured hand and tried to distract me while he went to work.

He might as well have let me bite down on one of my bullets for all the good the local did me. After he finished I lay gasping for air on the gurney while Ms. Santiago stood shaking her hand, trying to get the feeling back in her fingers. I apologized, and she smiled weakly, said something in what sounded like Tagalog, and left me alone with the doctor.

"You know, you can't be a black man in this city and not have your share of run-ins with the cops," he said grimly, pausing to check his handiwork. "But you're the first cop who ever helped me *avoid* an ass whipping."

I started to protest, to explain the stress everyone was under out there, but sank back on the gurney beneath another wave of pain that managed to slip past the local anesthetic. "You don't have to explain," he said. "You got me out of there, and, as much as I hate cops, I *am* grateful."

"That's very nice, but I don't want your gratitude, Dr. Mitchell . . ."

"Please, call me Lance."

He gave me a boyish smile that I'm sure he thought was charming, but it wasn't cutting any ice with me. "What we did was against Department policy for handling suspects, so your gratitude ain't gonna do diddly-squat for me, okay?"

I rewound in my mind the tortured conversation I'd had with Dreyfuss; getting my ass kicked trying to save this sightseeing, I-hate-cops-but-have-the-nerve-to-be-flirting Negro; Cooper's crazy anger on the bus. This whole thing smelled like trouble, something I definitely did not need.

If only I had known how much trouble it would be.

Shortly after Mitchell left, a middle-aged black male nurse in psychedelic green scrubs and blond-tipped, close-cut hair bustled in and outfitted me with a sling. He must've conferred with the first nurse about my killer grip because he very gingerly held my hand while he fastened the contraption into place.

A lab tech was next, a big-legged, caramel-colored, round-the-way girl sporting an intricate set of braids that must have taken two days to put in. "You Charlotte Justice?" she chomped around her Double Bubble. "Dr. M ordered some blood work on you."

She tied the rubber tourniquet around my good arm. Airbrushed fingernails gleamed at me in shades of red, black, and green, disappeared in latex gloves. She gave me a soft-handled grip to squeeze. "It'll help your vein stand out," she explained.

"So how come you're so special?" She threw me a sideways glance as she tapped on the vein in my arm. "The order was to draw you stat. You a friend of Dr. M's?"

"No, I just helped him out a few hours ago. Maybe he's returning the favor."

I squeezed the grip harder and she checked the result. Satisfied, she got out the needle and released the rubber cord. "He's like all of that, y'know what I'm sayin'? He helped me get this job. A bunch of us got jobs here because of Dr. M."

"That's really . . . ouch! . . . nice." I tried not to look, but my vein seemed to have slipped from under the needle.

She frowned and bit her lip. "Nice don't even begin to cover it, girlfriend." She tried the stick again. "I mean, Dr. M works with kids on the street, helps us with scholarships, then hooks us up with jobs afterward. He's all that and a bag of chips far as I'm concerned."

Despite all her diversionary chatter, Hometta was making a mess of my arm. After the third time trying to find my vein, I peeked at her name badge. It *said* she was a phlebotomist, but you couldn't prove it by me. "Have you been doing this long, Ms. . . . Brown?"

Ms. Brown pushed the braids away from her face and gave a proud smack on her gum. "Uh-huh, I graduated from Drew University last winter." Pride turned to frustration on her fourth attempt. "Dang, you got them rollin' veins. Lemme see if I can get Dr. Mitchell to help me out."

She came back a few minutes later, all smiles, with Mitchell in tow. Confided to me, "He's really good at this." Said to him, "Remember, Dr. M, when you helped me with that junkie . . ."

"This is really getting old, Ms. Brown," Mitchell snapped. "Don't you think I have enough to do with fifty patients out there without doing your job, too?" He moved her aside, deftly inserted the needle into my vein and attached the vial to collect the blood. Two more vials were quickly filled and passed to the embarrassed lab tech. He capped the needle and threw it in a disposal box on the counter. Said over his retreating shoulder, "Get it together, Jamilla, or you won't be around here much longer."

Jamilla Brown was stricken. It even seemed a little harsh to me, and I was the one with the Swiss cheese arm. I tried to console the young woman. "Don't worry about Dr. M. He's had kind of a hard day."

She craned her neck, made evil slits of her eyes. "Like I'm supposed to care."

As the radiology clerk wheeled me back to the ER, I could see my brother, Perris, had arrived and was standing in the hallway, talking to Aubrey and Mitchell. Seeing Perris and Aubrey together again reminded me of how inseparable they used to be. Of how, with their letterman's jackets and good looks alone, they could stop conversations cold just by strolling down a hallway at our high school. Perris was the shorter of the two—a muscular six-two to Aubrey's more slender six-five. My brother's walnut-toned skin still bore the faint traces of his six-year bout with drugs and alcohol. He won the decision but was left with a crescent-shaped scar that rode just above his left eyebrow, a memento from when he blacked out in '84 and wrapped my mother's new Cadillac around an Olympic-bannered light pole. But, scars aside, you couldn't deny my brother was still good-looking, still the not-so-Dark Prince of the Justice clan.

The clerk told Dr. Mitchell the radiologist wanted to talk to him about my X rays. Mitchell excused himself and walked back the way we had come.

My brother was careful hugging me, but his kiss on my forehead transmitted a concern and affection I was always seeking in my family but felt too rarely coming from his direction. "Char, what am I going to do about you and this Top Cop thing?"

We all laughed but there was a familiar edge to his words that let me know Perris wasn't playing. He turned to Aubrey. "She hasn't changed much, has she, man?"

In a voice that made me press my knees together, Aubrey said, "Actually, Perris, she has."

Aubrey squeezed my good shoulder reassuringly as he wheeled me into an enclosed treatment room. "You two can wait in here, where you'll have a little more privacy. Dr. Mitchell should be back with the X-ray results soon."

He and Perris gave each other the Omega Psi Phi handshake,

which always reminded me of a cross between arm wrestling and a bear hug, and promised to get together real soon. "Maybe shoot some hoops," Aubrey suggested.

Perris gave him a card with his home address and number on the back. Aubrey gave us cards, too. *CaER—California Emergency Medical Group,* it read. *Aubrey M. Scott, M.D., M.B.A., Chief Executive Officer.* Their offices, the card informed me, were in Marina del Rey.

"Keep in touch, Char." Aubrey drawled out my nickname a little, *Sha-a-r,* the way only my family and close friends do. I was surprised he still remembered.

I could still feel the warmth of Aubrey's hand on my shoulder. Perris's words weren't nearly as comforting.

CHAPTER 3

MORE THAN
MY ARM
IN A SLING

"**C**har, we've got to talk." Perris's voice was low. "I don't know what happened out there, but this thing with Dr. Mitchell could be a big problem."

"He told you what happened?"

"Yeah, and I think he needs representation. But I thought I'd get clear on your involvement before I decided what to do."

Well, I'll be damned. Perris was always searching for an angle to bring down the Department. He'd been like this since he got shot in the line of duty and left the Department fourteen years ago—critical, harping, on a one-man search-and-destroy mission to trash the LAPD.

Falling back on the home training my parents instilled in all their children, I gave Perris a tight-lipped, edited-for-the-public version of the situation on King Boulevard. My brother's left eyebrow shot up, the scar above it making him seem doubly suspicious. "That doesn't quite fit with what Mitchell told me. Was there anything else?"

"Not really." I tried to erase my face, remove the traces of truth I felt sure were staining my cheeks.

Even though I'd been a detective for years and was used to

lying when necessary, Perris's big-brother eyes could read me like a book. "Char, don't even try it. Mitchell told me about the name-calling, the batons, the whole thing." He pointed his finger at me. "What you're doing right now is no better than those cops who covered for Koon and his boys on the Rodney King beating."

Anger beat truth to my lips, rose above my throbbing shoulder. "Then why the hell did you ask me, if that's how you feel? And how dare you compare me to Koon and that gang of idiots! You don't know what goes on out there anymore, Perris, and to accuse me of covering for bad cops is completely out of line!"

He was quiet for a beat, then said, "Char, look at me." He dropped down on his heels and squared up the wheelchair so I was forced to look him in the eyes. "I know the Department has been your life. Maybe too much so . . ."

Here we go.

". . . but I'm telling you, what's going on in these streets right now is showing a side of the LAPD that frightens me, for the city's sake as well as yours."

I called on a technique I had learned years ago in one of those stress management classes: *Breathe in . . . stay calm . . . breathe out . . . stay focused.* Instead of letting the pain and anger flood your senses and leak out of your eyes, you relaxed until you could float above it, finding some corner of hurt you could cut away from the rest and objectively analyze, turning it over in your mind like an interesting piece of evidence at the scene of a crime.

Why was Perris trying to turn me against a job I loved? Imposing order on a crime scene, sifting through the evidence and statements to discover the hard kernel of truth, had become as natural to me as breathing and, over the years, just about as essential. It gave me a deep sense of satisfaction when I broke a case and made a bust, then calmly presented the long and sometimes intricate trail of evidence in court that helped put another criminal behind bars and gave the victims' families a sense of closure I never got from the criminal justice system. And while I wasn't on the streets anymore, I even felt that rush in the struggle to get Dr. Mitchell out of that situation. I had been successful and more; I had stopped a situation on the street from turning ugly, one that could have literally fanned the flames and brought a lot more heat down on the Department than we already had or needed.

My youngest sister, Rhodesia, the psychology student, keeps telling me I suffer from the Supersister Syndrome, while my Grandmama Cile says I'm just like every other black woman she knows—trying to keep the solar system in order by juggling the planets herself. If anybody had asked me that day, I would have merely told them I was good at my job and was needed out there regardless of the sour grapes the antipolice branch of my family kept trying to throw in my face.

Perris hadn't stopped talking, hadn't noticed I had stopped listening. "I wish you could have walked in my shoes these last two days. I'm representing a sixty-two-year-old Guatemalan who's been detained in a county holding cell, half-naked and without benefit of counsel. And you know what he did? He left his insulin in his car and went out after curfew to get it."

"He should have known the rules. They've been broadcast on every television and radio station in L.A., including KMEX."

"For God's sake, Char, the man's car was just parked in front of his apartment building! What does the city have to gain holding a sick old man like that on eight thousand dollars' bail?"

"There had to be more to it than that."

He tried again. "What about the brothers on Loyola Marymount's b-ball team who happened to be driving through Beverly Hills the afternoon of the twenty-ninth? They got spread-eagled on Rodeo for playing their music too loud! When Louise saw what was going down, she called me from her cell phone to go over there and represent them."

"I'm sorry, Perris, but you know as well as I do that they don't play in Beverly Hills. I also know your wife is an overzealous community activist who, God bless her, can go round the bend on these things pretty quickly . . ."

Perris's hand sliced the air. "Do you hear yourself? You're stonewalling me at every turn. Don't you get it? Gates and his cronies in this county are setting up a police state, damn the Constitution, and you're part of the occupying forces!"

"That's it!" I shouted. "I don't need the big-brother lecture! Just because you got out when you did and have a high-profile law practice in Beverly Hills doesn't mean everybody else who stays in the Department is stupid. I *know* I'm needed out there, so I don't have to take this crap off of you!" I jerked the wheelchair back. "Hand me my vest . . . I gotta get back out there . . ."

"I don't think so." Lance Mitchell had returned and slid the X rays up on a wall-mounted light box. He pointed to a disconcertingly angled mass of bones I was surprised to learn was my right shoulder. "You don't have any broken bones, but this chronic dislocation problem you have concerns me. I'm recommending you go home and get some rest." He backed me down with a bandaged finger. "And don't even *think* about going back out there until you get this shoulder checked out by an orthopedic surgeon."

A throat cleared behind us: "Sorry to interrupt." I hadn't noticed that Cortez had entered the room, stood shuffling from foot to foot by the door. "I just got off the phone with Lieutenant Dreyfuss." Her words were directed to me, but she was staring at Dr. Mitchell. "The ID on the Q45 car checked out; it's Dr. Mitchell's car all right. But it got trashed pretty bad after we left."

"Isn't *that* just great!" Mitchell slapped the X rays down on the counter.

The tic dancing in Cortez's eye told me there was more. "And?"

"But his wallet and keys weren't in the car like he said. While Rivers and Cooper were securing the scene, they found the wallet behind Mel's Tacos."

Mitchell looked ill. "Was there any money in it?" he asked. He got even sicker when Cortez shook her head. "I had just borrowed two hundred dollars from Dr. Scott," he explained glumly. "What about my keys?"

Cortez shook her head again. "Even the registration was gone."

Alarmed, he started for the door. "I've gotta get out of here."

In the hallway beyond Mitchell were Chip LeDoux and Darren Wright, the team of Southwest uniforms who'd brought up the rear of our police escort, standing by the nurses' station. One of the nurses had set up a makeshift first-aid station there and was putting a four-by-four gauze bandage on LeDoux's beefy arm while Wright, a stocky brother with a bald head as shiny as a lowrider's hubcap, looked on. They were half-listening to the nurse's friendly chatter about the cases they'd seen in the ER but had moved instinctively to block the doorway when they saw Mitchell make his move.

By the way she was standing, I knew there was something else on my partner's mind. "What is it, Detective?" I asked.

Cortez was watching Mitchell intently, a cat at the goldfish bowl. "You want to tell her, Doctor, or should I?" As soon as Mitchell turned to say something, she pounced. "They found his wallet all right. But it was underneath a body. Preliminary ID is of a . . ." She checked her notepad. "I may not be saying this right . . ." She struggled over the first name, settling on a halting, phonetic pronunciation: "Sin-kay Lewis?"

It was as if someone had dimmed the lights and asked me to make a wish on a birthday cake. But it wasn't my birthday, and I suddenly couldn't catch a breath, could barely nod my head.

Perris put an unsteady hand on my shoulder. "You're kidding! Robert 'Cinque' Lewis of the Black Freedom Militia? He and that gang haven't been seen or heard from in years!"

In thirteen years, eleven months, and nineteen days to be exact, the working part of my brain reminded me. Since I saw him behind the barrel of that gun, May 10, 1978.

"Rivers made him." Cortez's voice seemed far away. "Even though the corpse had been beaten up pretty badly, Rivers said it was hard to mistake him what with the . . ." I could hear her consulting her notes, " 'scarification marks on his face and a missing left arm.' " She slapped the notebook shut. "I have no idea what he's talking about, but Rivers mentioned something about you would remember him, too, Charlotte."

Always—in my dreams.

I could feel myself slipping away, into that midnight-blue place I thought only existed in my hellish dreams. What had helped pull me out of the hole then was the Twenty-eighth Psalm. It was given to me by Grandmama Cile after I had hidden in my house for so long I thought I'd never see the light of day or feel the sun's warmth in my bones. The Twenty-eighth, as I grew to call it, became my lifeline, dragging me to the surface to breathe in the life that seemed so far out of reach. I could recite it at will, especially in times of trouble:

> Unto thee will I cry, O Lord my rock
> Be not silent to me:
> Lest, if thou be silent to me,
> I become like them that go down into the pit. . . .

Help me, God. Don't let me fall. "So he's dead?" a voice I barely recognized as my own asked.

"As a doornail."

Through the haze in my brain, I could make out Officers Wright and LeDoux moving in, providing silent yet ominous backup.

Fear danced in Mitchell's brown eyes. "Wait a minute . . . what are you guys looking at me for? You know I didn't kill anybody!" He appealed to Perris. "Don't let them take me, man! You gotta help me!"

Cortez's tone was soothing: "No one is accusing you of anything, Doctor. But we do need to get your statement."

"Can't you do it here?" Mitchell's voice had become strident.

Cortez shook her head. "We'd prefer to do it downtown."

Mitchell started sweating like a trapped animal, and I knew why. Infamous cases of blacks dying "in custody" had become the stuff of community conspiracy theories and put the fear of God into a lot of black folks—including some of the professional ones—that they'll "go downtown" and never be heard from again.

Perris must have smelled Mitchell's fear, too. Patting him on the shoulder, he told the nervous doctor, "They don't have enough to arrest you or they'd do it right now." To Cortez: "I assume you're not charging him with a 243."

Cortez was careful. "Not at this time."

"See?" Perris said to Mitchell. "They're not going to charge you with assaulting an officer. I think you should go on downtown and give them your statement."

Mitchell was about a 7.0 on the Richter scale. "I'm not going anywhere alone with these guys! And I didn't see anything! Can't you just go down there with me?"

He appealed to Perris, who had moved in a little closer to me. "I'd like to, but under the circumstances, I'd better stay here with my sister."

I stared in utter but grateful disbelief at my brother: he chose me over a chance to do battle with the LAPD. If my father had been there, he would have said, *Close your mouth before you catch a fly.*

"But I'll page a colleague of mine. She should still be at the courthouse." Perris flipped open his cell phone. "Her name is Sandra Douglass, and she's an excellent criminal attorney. I'll have her meet you at Parker Center."

I could see a few of the hospital's employees gathered outside. Aubrey Scott broke through the congested doorway, positioned himself between Cortez and Mitchell, bellowed, "What the hell's going on here?"

"Man, they're trying to stick me with some kind of murder rap!"

"Step aside, Doctor!" Cortez warned Aubrey.

The uniforms moved in a little closer. So did the group of employees gathering outside the door. Perris stepped in between Aubrey and Cortez. "Dr. Scott's just a little upset, Detective," he explained, pushing Aubrey toward the door.

Cortez considered the crowd in the hall, took a deep breath, and, in her best community-relations voice, explained the situation to Aubrey and the agitated knot of hospital staff.

"So take his statement here," Aubrey demanded. A chorus of heads nodded and mumbled behind him.

"We'd prefer to talk with him downtown." Cortez turned to

Mitchell, forcing herself to sound more friendly, less official. "Would you mind helping us out, Doctor? Officers Wright and LeDoux can give you a ride downtown and back if you'd like."

Panic-stricken, Mitchell backed up against the far wall and looked to my brother for guidance.

"Why don't you have someone here drive you, Dr. Mitchell?" Perris suggested. "I'll ask Attorney Douglass to meet you there."

Jamilla Brown stepped forward, chewing. "My shift is over. I can take you, Dr. M."

"I'll have the administrator on duty get the hospital's legal counsel out of bed, too," Aubrey told the shaken physician. "Don't worry, Lance, we'll straighten this mess out."

"Cinque Lewis." Even though the others were gone, Perris was whispering as if it were a secret only we shared. "I never thought I'd hear that one-armed, rhetoric-spouting sonofabitch's name again. And just a few days from the day he . . ." He caught himself and glanced furtively at me. "Are you all right about this, Char?"

I was and I wasn't. "It's going to take some getting used to."

"Maybe we should talk about it."

My brother's suggestion hit me like a ton of bricks. Perris was one of the main members of my family who tried to sweep "the horrible business with that hoodlum" (as it was euphemistically called) under the rug from the moment Cinque Lewis tore into our lives. In that regard, Perris was cut from the same cloth as my mother. As far as Joymarie Curry Justice was concerned, "Let sleeping dogs lie and maybe they'll choke before morning" should have been the motto on the family crest. So much so that when I tried to talk about Cinque Lewis, I was counseled by my social-worker mother to set it aside and get on with my life. Or what was left of it.

Getting on with my life meant I rarely discussed Cinque Lewis with anyone or acknowledged the void he'd caused in my life. I didn't discuss it on my job, didn't discuss it with my friends, and, above all, I didn't discuss it with my family. To talk about it now, after all those years of silence and evasion as if it were nothing, was inconceivable, like trying to change the planets in their orbits.

Not even Supersister could pull that one off.

I think Perris knew that what he was asking me to do was outside of the natural order of things, could sense the fears it raised in me. It must have scared him, too, because his hands were cold as they took mine. "Char, if it's true, if they've really found Lewis, it's only going to be a matter of time before somebody starts digging around, asking questions. You may end up with more than your arm in a sling."

Pain and a growing uneasiness battled for control of my body. "Yeah, I know what you mean."

But Perris wasn't saying what he really meant. What he meant was that he knew Cinque Lewis stole my life. Stole it as sure as if he'd pumped the bullets into me that May day instead of my husband and baby girl. And now he had finally gotten his just desserts. And the fact that he had and I was within twenty miles of where the deed was done meant I would immediately be suspect.

Suspected of trying to help his killer get away. Or killing him myself.

But I couldn't be concerned about that right then. Couldn't be concerned about the professional implications, but above all couldn't let my emotions get the upper hand of my intellect. Couldn't fall apart in my brother's arms in the middle of that ER, no matter how much he may have been trying to encourage me or how much I may have wanted to. Which, mind you, I didn't. What I wanted more than anything at that moment was to see the bastard, to see for myself the still, lifeless face of the cold-blooded killer I knew Cinque Lewis to be.

By the time I was discharged at ten that night, my arm in a most unbecoming and unnecessarily loud blue sling, I was trying to talk my brother into driving me by what had become the scene of a murder. He argued with me—naturally—citing the curfew, the dangers of going back over there, Mitchell's orders to go home, and the amount of painkillers I had been given as logical reasons to stay away. He gave me every reason under the sun except the one I knew he'd better not say to my face: *I don't think you can handle it.*

"I'm a uniformed police officer, and you've got a judicial pass in your windshield, so that curfew excuse is weak, Perris. Plus, it's better for me to go there now while I've still got an adrenaline rush than later when the painkillers they gave me really kick in. And besides, Mitchell could have his own motives for keeping me away. He *knows* I work in Robbery-Homicide."

Perris rolled his eyes. "You don't honestly think Mitchell had anything to do with this, do you?"

"I won't know until I've investigated the scene, read the field interview cards, and seen the results of the post." I poked him in the arm. "Until there's been a complete investigation."

He shook his head, pointed the car south, warned, "Twenty minutes, then I've got to get home myself."

We rode without speaking, although Perris grumbled a lot to the windshield about folks needing to know when to give things a rest.

I didn't want to hear it. Cinque Lewis had been at the center of my life for a long time, since the day he showed up, ranting and raving, in my husband Keith's office. There was a time when hating Cinque Lewis was the only thing that got me out of bed in the morning. No way was I not going back to the scene, even if I was the only one there, and I didn't care if Perris approved or not.

CHAPTER 4

WHO'D A
THUNK IT?

The Department's priority during the riots had been restoring law and order and protecting property. Murders were the unfortunate by-products of the violence we barely had time to process as we fought block by block to reestablish some semblance of order in the city.

But the significance of Cinque Lewis turning up dead after so many years must have given the case VIP priority from downtown because when Perris and I got over to Mel's Tacos, we found Rivers and Cooper had stayed behind to set up the crime scene and had been joined by some very jumpy National Guard troops. They were standing in front of the hastily erected crime scene tape at the east end of the block, trying to keep a log of the arriving personnel, and guarding the perimeter. My LAPD comrades jerked their heads toward me in recognition but were being kept busy by the curious who had come out of the woodwork to view the latest neighborhood drama and the misguided few who still thought they could provoke a confrontation with the law.

The high-profile status of the case was confirmed when I saw Steve Firestone, my supervisor from RHD, on the other side of the crime tape. He loped his way over to Perris's black BMW when he saw us drive up. Helped me out of the car. "Charlotte—Detective Justice. I heard what happened. You okay?"

Perris had gotten out of the car and was standing next to us. A moment passed before I remembered my manners and introduced them. Perris shook Steve's hand slowly, trying to divine beneath Steve's fair skin, Airedale-wiry brown hair, and hawklike nose some telltale sign, some flicker in his hazel eyes, that said, *Yeah, I'm a brother, too.* Steve, however, wasn't giving any signs of recognition or acknowledgment, not even in that surreptitious way light-skinned black folks have of connecting with each other sometime.

I explained to Perris that Detective Firestone was a working supervisor in RHD—a Detective III or D-III—for the Homicide I unit that included Cortez and me. Perris nodded acknowledgment but held his tongue. He'd seen—and crucified—plenty of guys at Steve's level on the witness stand over the years, so he could not have cared less about this one. Especially if Perris suspected he was trying to pass for white.

I tried to fill the lengthening silence: "I see they called you out on this one."

Steve shrugged. "I was about to go off duty, but when the Bureau called and I found out who it was, I volunteered to lend a hand."

Steve, I knew, had been working in another part of South Central. But because Cortez and I had left with Mitchell and missed being on the scene when the body was discovered, there was probably no one else to send. I tried to find a judgment on Steve's face about our action with Mitchell but only saw exhaustion rimming his eyes, making them seem older than their forty-five years. "What've we got?" I asked.

"You know you shouldn't be here, Detective Justice."

"Tell her, man." This from my suddenly vocal brother.

"Look, I'm not going to touch anything. And you can note in the log that I was not out of your sight and direct observation the whole time. Have Rivers act as a witness if you think there'd be a problem. Hell, ask one of the Guardsmen."

"I just don't want no shit landing in my lap." Steve knew having an officer on a crime scene who knew or had a close connection with a victim was against LAPD policy and could jeopardize a case. And while he was respectful enough not to ream me out in front of my brother, I knew what he was implying. Not so much that I had known the victim, Cinque Lewis, personally, but my husband, Keith, definitely had.

The coroner's aquamarine-blue—coveralled mortuary attendants were finishing up their work. Given the danger on the streets, I'd heard the coroner's officer hadn't been able to do more than scoop and scat since the rioting started Wednesday, the metallic-blue morgue vans sometimes loaded up three and four deep, so I was kind of surprised they were able to get to this one so fast. Nothing like word of an infamous victim to bring everybody running. But there were no photo ops to be had on this gloomy street. The only flashes of light were from the strobe on the LAPD photographer's Nikon as he recorded everything of interest around the body. Everybody worked rapidly, aware that despite the National Guard cover, they could be picked off any minute by a shot from one of the surrounding buildings.

"Are you sure you wouldn't rather go home?" Steve asked.

"No, I need to see this." Needed to put this to rest once and for all.

The attendants had started to wrap the body up in heavy plastic sheeting and a pink sheet that looked for all the world like it had been borrowed from a Doris Day movie. Mikki Alexander, the newly hired coroner's investigator in charge of the body, stopped them so I could see.

When I think back on it now, what surprises me was how completely detached I became when I was finally face to face with Cinque Lewis, a man I'd been obsessed with finding most of my adult life. I eased up on the body, feeling like I was having one of those dreams that plagued me for months after Keith and Erica were first killed. I was seeing everything through a long, dark tunnel, only this time there was light at the end of it, courtesy of Steve Firestone's flashlight.

I closed my eyes for a moment, summoned up a line of the Twenty-eighth: *The Lord is my strength and my shield; my heart trusted in him, and I am helped.*

When I opened my eyes I could barely make out in the darkness where the bullet had entered Lewis's head from the right side, leaving his left eye blown out like a whitewall tire and a ragged gaping hole in his left temple, but remarkably not a lot of blood. He had aged a lot since the mug shots I'd seen and appeared much older than he should have. What little hair he had was close-cropped and stark white. His face was speckled in *Miami Vice*–length stubble, also white, that went a long way to obscure the marks on his face. The marks themselves, so vivid in my mind from staring at his image on Department and FBI notices, appeared to be more like a bad case of acne than the ritualistic scarification I knew from the reports were part of the Black Freedom Militia's initiation ceremony.

I pulled the plastic bag back a little farther. Steve's flashlight revealed Lewis was wearing expensive, triple-pleated gray gabardine slacks and what was once a white Polo shirt before little rivulets of blood gave it a pink-and-white tie-dyed effect. Poking out of the sleeve wasn't the flipperlike vestige of Lewis's left arm I'd read about, but an expensive-looking plastic and metal prosthesis with a finely detailed hand that matched the victim's brown-paper-bag color precisely.

I knew then how Cinque Lewis could have disappeared for so long. This distinguished-looking, conservatively dressed man was a hundred and eighty degrees from the wild-eyed revolutionary police in five states and the FBI sought in connection with Keith and Erica's slaying. But if anyone could have seen through his disguise, it would be a veteran like Sergeant Burt Rivers.

Mikki Alexander leaned in, a hurried urgency in her tone that underscored the danger around us. "The body was found face down under the awning over there, head facing due west." Steve's flashlight caught the scorch marks at Lewis's right temple. "As you can see from the powder burns, he was shot at close range. The bullet was a through-and-through, in and out the cranium, then lodged in the wall back there." She pointed to a gouged-out spot marked "A" in the dim light, near the stand's graffiti-covered back door.

"We've got the slug," Steve explained. "Recovered the casing, too. Looks like a .38, but I'm hoping ballistics can confirm that when they analyze it on Monday."

As if SID, the LAPD's Scientific Investigation Division, would be willing to bump this case ahead of the hundreds of others they had backlogged for ballistics testing.

"He was probably robbed," Alexander continued, pointing toward the body in the dark. "There's a mark on his neck that looks like a chain-snatcher got to him."

Firestone handed me a Polaroid he had taken of Lewis's face. I frowned at it and looked at the buildings nearest the scene. "Have the field interviews produced anything?"

"It's too dangerous for Cooper and Rivers to be trying to interview anyone," Steve explained.

"What about the female Mitchell was taking the medication to?"

"They did go over there. West end of the block. Older woman named Doxie Rucker told them Mitchell dropped by there about four with the pills, stayed about fifteen minutes, and split."

I was beginning to feel a little light-headed, and it was getting hard to concentrate. "There was a gunshot while we were out here with Mitchell. Anyone in the buildings around here see anybody leaving the scene?"

"Not that they're willing to admit," Steve said. "And outside of interviewing Mrs. Rucker, I'm sure as hell not asking anybody to go into those buildings on a door-to-door." The battered, stuccoed apartments surrounding us leaned in crazily, mocking Steve's uneasy gaze. "Besides, with all the other gunfire in the neighborhood plus the mess this afternoon, I'd be surprised if anyone noticed or could get through on nine one one if they did."

Alexander flicked back a strand of honey-streaked hair. A gold bangle clanked against her clipboard. "Not to worry." Her accent was Midwestern WASP, full of nasal Chicago twangs. "I can get an ETD from the liver and the degree of po-mo lividity. But

I'm gonna wait until we get back to the morgue. I'd rather not take the chance out here."

Liver temperatures and the degree of postmortem lividity, the way a body stiffens after death, is a very precise, if ghoulish, method to determine the estimated time of death. Under normal circumstances these measurements are taken at the scene. But the riots of 1992 were no ordinary circumstance, and nobody was going to ask Alexander and the other coroner's staff members to risk their lives to do it right then.

As she click-clacked her way toward the blue coroner's van in some absurdly high heels, I roused myself to ask Steve if they found a weapon.

"We've combed the immediate area as best we could and came up empty. They've dusted the Dumpster for prints, but this is it for tonight."

Herman Wozniak, a latent print specialist from SID, was standing about twenty feet away near a wine-colored Dumpster, sorting through the trash and lifting prints faster than the Tasmanian Devil on crack. I was surprised anyone from SID would have even ventured out that night, but Woz was there, all six-two, two-fifty of him, huffing and puffing from the effort and, I was betting, the fear. A baby-faced Korean Guardsman stood in a half crouch inside an empty big-screen television box someone had left nearby, his young eyes alert for a potential sniper in one of the buildings.

We moved away from the immediate crime scene, on the other side of the second set of yellow tapes. Steve lit a Camel. "You were here, Charlotte," he said, exhaling the smoke out of the corner of his mouth. "Could Mitchell have disposed of the weapon away from the scene?"

I coughed and made a show of waving the smoke away, stalling a little while I reconstructed in my mind our route down King Boulevard. I could visualize the ride in Hook's car. Entering the hospital's ER. Cortez dogging Mitchell's heels while he was being treated. "Cortez or I had him under direct surveillance almost the whole time from the moment we left the scene."

"*Almost?*"

"Well," I hedged, "there was a moment when I got faint on the street, and Cortez went to get some help. But Mitchell stayed with me."

"Could he have dropped the gun without you knowing it?"

"I would have noticed." Given how much pain I had been in, it was more a statement of belief than fact.

"And at the hospital?"

"Cortez was with him the whole time, except for when he showered and changed clothes. . . ."

"Shit!" he exclaimed. "She let him shower? There goes our chances to do a gunshot residue test!"

"Steve, how was she to know there'd been a shooting? Give her a break, she's new to RHD!"

"And was *supposed* to be the hottest thing to come out of South Bureau Homicide since a certain Detective Justice." Exasperation made his voice tight, his breathing ragged. "And now look at the two of you! The guys are gonna start calling you the Lucy and Ethel of Homicide I!"

"That's pretty low, Steve." I hoped the moniker didn't find its way onto the bulletin board in the office.

A pause; then, "Any other time he was out of your sight?"

"He went to radiology with a transport clerk to consult on my X rays. He could've hidden it along the way, but I doubt it."

Steve took another drag on his cigarette, counted. "That's at least three opportunities."

I knew right then and there I hadn't heard the end of Cortez and me removing Mitchell from the scene. Much to my relief, though, Steve let it go and turned his attention to the corpse. "He put up a pretty good fight," he noted. "Blood and skin under the nails of his good hand. Nothing on the prosthesis—which you'd expect—but Alexander's got both of 'em double-bagged anyway so she can get samples once they get him back to the morgue."

I had a flashback to the scratches on Mitchell's face and hands I saw in the ER, which I had assumed he had gotten in the fight on the street. "Did you tell this to Cortez? She's downtown with Mitchell now."

"Yeah, I talked to her. His lawyer says he had a legitimate reason for being in the area, which Cortez had to admit she corroborated herself at the hospital." He hocked and spat on the ground. "His attorney is balls to the walls on this one . . ."

I winced at the characterization, but Steve didn't even notice.

". . . won't allow him to give skin or blood samples without a warrant. Says we got no probable cause, that he got those scratches in the fight with our officers. Hinted that if we continue to harass her client they may file a civil suit for *our* attack on *him*. The hospital's attorney's no better—said he could get a restraining order to keep us out two minutes after we got a search warrant to get in. Way Cortez told it, the silk-suited prick said he could make a pretty convincing case that a bunch of LAPD storm troopers tearing up a hospital would be disruptive to patient care and might start a riot *inside* the hospital."

"Cortez mentioned they found Mitchell's wallet under the body. Isn't that enough probable cause?"

"You would think so, but not according to that wuss brain of a deputy D.A. I think this Douglass bitch has his balls in some kind of vice grip."

I gritted my teeth. Even though attorney Sandra Douglass was not one of my favorite people, Steve's ball-buster rhetoric was getting next to me. I unclenched my jaw, took a deep breath, and asked where exactly was the wallet found.

Steve ducked under the crime tape and walked over to the spot on the pavement where Lewis's body had lain. A small puddle of blood glistened darkly on the blacktop. "Cooper spotted it here, under his right shoulder." He indicated a marker labeled "1" on the ground, then went to retrieve the wallet from his car. "They've got pictures that show its exact location," he said when he returned.

I took the package in my free hand. "And there was no money in it?"

Steve shook his head. "They left the plastic, though."

"Too bad. Mitchell said he had just borrowed two hundred dollars from his boss."

"Well, it's in somebody else's pocket now."

I started to squat down to take a closer look at where the wallet had lain on the ground. Dizziness was my reward. I dropped the package. Steve scooped it up and grabbed me by the elbow. "You okay?"

The others were watching me closely. "Maybe I will go on home," I whispered.

"Good idea, Detective," he whispered back. "We're almost through here, anyway."

Steve stood holding me lightly by the elbow, not making a big deal of it, talking while I took a minute to let the dizziness pass. "Cooper, Rivers, and I were just going to canvas the bystanders, see if they saw anything, before we wrap this one up."

I rubbed my temple and tried to focus. "Most of the folks out here now were probably involved in the situation earlier and just didn't get arrested. So I don't know who you're going to find willing to talk to you tonight."

"At least we'll get some names. Maybe we can get statements later, when things cool off."

Yeah, maybe by 2012.

We walked slowly in the direction of Perris's car as the mortuary attendants were putting the body in the van. While Steve went back to ask Alexander a question, Burt Rivers, off in the distance talking to Perris, started walking briskly in my direction. He rubbed a gloved hand over his silver crewcut. "Who'd a thunk we'd ever see that lowlife again?"

"Yeah, who'd a thunk it," I said into the darkness, my mind still trying to take it all in, to grasp something just out of reach. "Burt, did you notice whether Mitchell had any scratches on him when you approached him?"

"Not that I can remember. You see any scratches on that doctor?" he asked Cooper, who had just joined us.

"Maybe." Cooper unsnapped and removed his helmet. "But

that jungle bunny damn sure had a bunch afterward." He smiled, revealing a freshly chipped tooth in his overbite.

We watched Cooper walk away, the unsettled look on Burt's craggy face mirroring what I imagined was etched on my own. "Cooper's always been a badge-heavy loudmouth," he apologized, "always throwing his weight around." He put a huge hand on my shoulder. "Try and forget about him, Charlotte. Go on home and get some rest. This has been a long night for you."

Burt Rivers was always doing the mother hen on me, ever since we first met at Southwest Division and he found out I was Keith Roberts's widow and Perris Justice's sister.

"Hope I did the right thing out here today," I said.

"I'm glad you got that doctor out of here." Burt's brown eyes were almost swallowed by the wrinkles in a quick smile, quickly gone. He watched Cooper talking to the crowd behind the yellow crime scene tape, whispered, "It allowed us to get control of the situation a lot quicker."

Coming from one of my former training officers, Burt's opinion meant a lot. Burt Rivers was the best T.O. a boot could ever hope to have, a seasoned veteran who had the street in his blood. There were rumors that he even gave up a desk job downtown and a spot on the fast track to keep doing what he loved best.

"I'm just sorry you got hurt out here." I could read affection and real concern all over his face.

Steve rejoined us, walked with Burt and me back to Perris's car. "What went down here shouldn't have happened, Burt. You know that. Cooper was out of control."

Burt nodded his head thoughtfully, then exchanged glances with Steve before saying, "Up until we found Lewis, I would have agreed. Now I wonder if Cooper wasn't following his instincts all along."

"What instincts?" I asked. "Mitchell was a half a block away from the taco stand when we saw him."

"But he *was* coming from the direction of the stand," Burt

reminded me, "the *opposite* end of the block from that patient, Mrs. Rucker."

I stole a glance at Steve, who replied, "Cortez said Mitchell claimed he'd gone to the stand hoping to get a burrito, found it boarded up, got nervous being out on the street, and ran back to his car." Steve gave an elaborate shrug. "It may sound a little shaky, but without a witness to place him behind that stand, we're shit out of luck for now."

Perris was sitting behind the wheel of his Bimmer. He raised a thumb in Burt's direction in silent acknowledgment. Once upon a time, when Perris was on the force and stationed at Southwest, he and Burt had been co-workers and good friends. But they had fallen out when Perris left the Department—"went over to the other side," as Burt put it—and became a criminal defense attorney. Burt would never understand that, for an upwardly mobile family like mine, policing would never be tolerated as more than a means to an end, especially for Perris, an only son and black American prince of the realm. And Perris would never understand how it hurt an old war horse like Burt Rivers to see a cop with talent leave the Department, how he would consider my arrival as a boot the next year as a second chance to keep a Justice in the LAPD family.

But they had evidently talked tonight, for the first time in years as far as I knew. And for my money, it was a step in the right direction.

Burt smiled as he closed the car door: "Take care of your little sister, Justice."

My brother's voice was strained: "What does that mean?"

Maybe the hatchet wasn't completely buried. I shook my head. Men. "You guys stay safe out here," I said.

"You, too," Steve replied and stood watching us pull away from the curb.

CHAPTER 5

THE MAN
WHO STOLE
MY LIFE

It was almost midnight when we finally pulled up to my house in the Fairfax District. A white, Spanish-style, one-story stucco with a blooming jacaranda tree in the front, the house Keith and I bought fifteen years ago sat on a rising knoll in the middle of the block, a blue-shuttered oasis in the still-smoky night.

My neighbor, Odetta Franklin, stood barefoot in her front yard, an African head wrap covering her short, graying locks, looking for all the world like a Ghanaian woman going to market or like she was still in her native Beaumont, Texas. In her left hand she gripped a leash. My tan-and-white boxer strained the other end. "Hey, Miz Charlotte," she drawled across the street. "This here dog was worryin' me to death, barkin' and yelpin' his ass off in yo' yard. I finally brung him home t'sit with me."

Beast jumped and strained against the leash as she walked him over. She stopped when she caught sight of my arm. "Darlin', what happened t'you?"

"Just a little situation over on King," I explained as Perris helped me maneuver out of the car and open the front door.

"The one at Mel's Tacos? Child, I seen that on *The Scene at Six*. Was you hurt bad?"

"Just this damn shoulder again." I decided not to tell her about Cinque Lewis right then.

"These fools out here have lost they minds. Son, give this dog some a them peanut butter biscuits in the kitchen and lemme get her inta bed."

Mrs. Franklin had been my neighbor for almost fifteen years and was the one who found me in the driveway the day that Keith and Erica were killed. Later, she was one of the few who supported my decision to join the force, and she had been the only one from the neighborhood to come to my graduation from the Academy. Even my own brother and mother didn't come, but Mrs. Franklin was there with my father, Grandmama Cile, and my two younger sisters, cheering as if it was a Grambling/Alcorn football game.

Perris came to the doorway with the dog just as Mrs. Franklin was settling me into bed and I was putting my notebook on the nightstand and my Beretta in the drawer. I patted the comforter. "Up, Beast." The dog bounded onto the bed, licking my face and snuffling my immobilized arm. As I hugged him around his thick neck, I could smell the smoky residue of a thousand recent fires that permeated his coat.

I turned on the television news and was instantly sorry. If one more white newscaster called black and Latino rioters "those animals" without showing the numerous white rioters I'd seen on the streets, I was going to throw a brick through the screen. The rebroadcast of Brett Stewart's *The Scene at Six,* despite the comfort of having a handsome black man as a co-anchor, wasn't much better; the station seemed to be as obsessed with intercutting images of Watts burning in '65 with footage of armed Koreans on store rooftops and blacks beating up Reginald Denny as everyone else. The situation at the taco stand got barely a mention.

I kept flipping channels, hoping to find something with some black folks in it that was positive. My choices were *Yo MTV Raps* or *'Round Midnight,* video gangsters versus junkie jazz musicians. I settled for an ESPN roundup show.

Mrs. Franklin had gone to the kitchen and reappeared with her hands on her hips. "Baby, you ain't got nuthin' in there but shrimp fried rice tha's growin' hair and frozen food," she declared. "Lemme go next door and get you some pound cake; I made it myself yesterday." My objections were scattered like chicks before Mrs. Franklin's waving hand. "You'll be glad you got somethin' sweet in the house when them painkillers wear off."

My brother and I chuckled after we heard her close the front door. It was the first time we'd laughed together all night. Before it died away, I figured I'd better head off any more big-brotherly lectures. "Perris, I'm really beat. Can we just call it a draw and take it up again tomorrow?"

He nodded, patted Beast's head, then came around to squeeze my good hand. "Char, I know I've not been the best of brothers to you, but I hope you know I love you and I've always been concerned about you. We *need* to deal with this."

His worried brown eyes let me know he wasn't talking about restoring order to the streets of L.A. But I wasn't ready to talk about it . . . not yet.

"Thanks, Perris" I said softly. "I appreciate your concern. Really. But I'm going to be all right. Don't I always pull through?"

Perris had finally left and I was just getting into the NBA scores when I heard the door open again. I eased opened the nightstand drawer, felt better when I put my hand on my gun. "Mrs. Franklin, is that you?"

"Yeah, baby, don' shoot me. I'm just puttin' the cake on top a the refrigerator." A few minutes later she reappeared in the bedroom doorway, leaned on the jamb. "Is your friend coming by?"

"What friend?"

Her eyes became round brown and white saucers. "Now I don' know his name. I calls him 'Vette Man. You know," she prompted, "the white-lookin' fellow who comes by here in that black Corvette?"

Odetta Franklin should work surveillance for the Department. Annoyed, I picked a flea off Beast's ear and popped it between my fingernails. "Him? He's just my supervisor, Mrs. Franklin."

Mrs. Franklin nodded, eyes narrowed and her mouth pinched. "I figured him for a cop—always sittin' in the car for a few minutes 'fore he gets out, like he's lookin' for somebody in the bushes. A lotta times he don' even go up to the porch, just sits outside starin' like he lost somethin'. "

How odd. Steve had only been inside my house twice that I knew of. But I didn't have much time to consider the implications of what she said because Mrs. Franklin, who offered psychic readings at a storefront around the corner under the name of Sister Odetta, stood at the foot of my bed, squinting at me over her cheaters and trying to penetrate my soul. If she was hoping I'd add a little more information to her data bank, she was sadly mistaken; I let her last comment hang in the air longer than a Michael Jordan three-pointer.

Finally, she gave up. "It's none a my business anyway. I just figured you might want the comp'ny."

"I'm fine, Mrs. Franklin. Thanks for checking up on Beast."

"He ain't no problem. In fact, it was good to have some comp'ny these last coupla days."

Beast's furiously twitching stump said he'd enjoyed it, too.

I didn't really relax until Mrs. Franklin dead-bolted the door and dropped the key in the mail slot, and even then I couldn't calm my mind. The ESPN program was over, so I channel-surfed some more, then picked up a magazine by the bed. It was hard to get into *Essence*'s article on "Your Summer Look" when my world was up, down, and sideways. Ditto for reading the May 1 meditation from the *Daily Word,* a recent gift from Mrs. Franklin, part of her well-meaning attempt to put me in touch with what she called my Higher Self. "*As we rest in God's healing presence,*" the little magazine told me, "*we experience freedom from fear, anxiety, and tension.*"

I wished.

I checked the messages on my answering machine; there were several from my parents and siblings, one from my Uncle Henry, a couple from my girlfriend Katrina. The clock on the nightstand glowed 12:30, too late to call anybody back. I started to call Steve to talk about the Lewis case but thought better of it, especially given what Mrs. Franklin had said about his clandestine visits. But my curiosity got the better of me, and I dialed his house anyway. When his answering machine picked up after the fourth ring, I hung up without leaving a message. I didn't want him to get the wrong idea about the reason for my call.

When Steve split up with his third wife in March, he was so shaken by the young woman's sudden departure with their three kids that I found myself commiserating with him over a glass of wine after work or dropping a "cheer up" card on his desk. Once he followed me home in his Corvette after a particularly grueling murder scene and hung around for an hour, reminiscing about his Jewish grandparents, who had, in the sixties, lived in a house very similar to mine just a few blocks away. How Grandfather Feuerstein would mutter "shvartzes" under his breath when little Steve and his black mother would go with his father for excruciating Thanksgiving dinners or Seders. I remember him examining the door frame for evidence of the nail holes that meant a mezuzah once kept the house's inhabitants safe. His excitement when he found the putty-filled, painted-over markings was sad and touching in a way that's unusual for a cop.

About a week later he was back at my house again, wired up from something he'd discovered on a case we were working but at the same time depressed about being separated from his family. I felt sorry for him, but when he tried to kiss me, I was frankly taken aback, even more so when I found out that wasn't all that was on his mind.

My girlfriend, Katrina Timms, had expounded many times about the limitations of what she called the sympathy fuck. But, as she would also be quick to say, getting your account serviced halfway is sometimes better than not at all. Katrina works in a bank, so I guess she knows about such things. All I knew was it had been a long time since anyone had made a deposit in my account. But I also knew it wasn't going to be Steve Firestone.

And it wasn't because Steve was a cop that I avoided getting into a relationship with him. Cops dating each other, or even being married, was not unheard of in the LAPD. But seeing someone who was my immediate supervisor, technically still a married man, not to mention confused about who and what he was? Not in this lifetime. Besides, I knew a few cop wives who shopped at the local Vons, and I didn't even want to *think* about them confronting me in the frozen-food section over some rumor they heard about me breaking up an allegedly happy cop home. Not to mention what my colleagues or my lieutenant at RHD would say.

After the situation on King Boulevard, they would probably be closing ranks anyway. And while I credited myself with averting "Rodney King: The Sequel" by getting Mitchell away from that taco stand, at least one of my colleagues on that bus acted as if I had crashed his own private lynching party. The fact that he was a physician didn't make any difference; for Cooper and some of those other guys on that bus, Lance Mitchell just happened to be a nigger in the wrong place at the absolute worst time.

But now with the Cinque Lewis murder, Mitchell's presence near the scene raised even more questions than it answered. Maybe Mitchell *was* just looking for a bite to eat after his mission of mercy. Maybe he was out there playing Rambro, stumbled across the body, and fled the scene. But common sense would have dictated he would have admitted to seeing the body when Rivers and the others first approached him.

Unless he did the deed himself. Maybe Lewis had tried to rob him. It was possible, but surely a man like Lewis, who'd managed to avoid the law all these years, had more sense than to pull such a poot-butt crime. Or maybe Lewis was a hype, rousting folks for money for a fix. But that prosthesis and the clothes he was wearing were expensive and suggested Lewis had some kind of means, or did at one time.

Had Mitchell gotten into a fight with Lewis over the wallet, struggled over Lewis's gun, and shot him in self-defense? Rivers and Cooper didn't seem to remember any scratches on Mitchell when they first approached him, but that didn't mean they weren't there. And I didn't notice any powder burns on his hands either, but maybe he had worn gloves. But why would he?

And if Lewis had robbed him, where was Mitchell's money now? In the pocket of another rioter who went through Lewis's pockets after the fact?

I could help Steve retrace our steps and try to figure out if Mitchell disposed of the gun somewhere. Mrs. Franklin could drive me back over there tonight.

I tried to get up, but just the thought of putting my clothes back on made me dizzy, and I gratefully sank back into the pillows. But I had to do *something*. Maybe I would be able to turn my brain off if I made a few informal notes. I reached for the little notebook I always carry and began to write some quick notes:

1.	Vic/Cinque Lewis	Any wits see him arrive on scene?
		Check the toxicology report for drug usage
		Where'd he get that arm?
		Where's he been for 14 yrs?
2.	Mitchell	Good Samaritan, Looky Lou, or both?
		Why look for fast food in a war zone?
		Any wits see him behind stand? See him talk/fight with Lewis?
		Scratches on face—when acquired?
3.	Scene	Apartment buildings—any wits in sight lines of stand?
4.	Weapon	Where is it? Retrace route in daylight, look for outdoor hiding places
		Check with F-Stop—hidden in his car?
		Does Mitchell have a gun permit?

But the one question that remained, that gnawed at me like a ghetto rat on a baby's crib: Why wasn't I the one to find Lewis behind that stand? Better yet, why couldn't I have been the one to pull the trigger on the man who stole my life?

The more I thought about it, the more I could feel myself losing it; my chest was getting tight, it was hard to catch a breath, and my headache was coming back. I felt like I would explode if I didn't get myself under control.

Breathe, I told myself. *Stay calm*.

It wasn't working. I rummaged through the nightstand, trying to find my Alupent or the Xanax my doctor prescribed for times like this, times when I needed to shove the memories back into the little corner I'd allotted them in my well-ordered universe.

I couldn't find the asthma inhaler or the tranquilizers. Finally I went into the kitchen. I kept the good stuff in the back of a cabinet above the stove—a hiding place I started using back when my brother was drinking heavily. Standing on a chair, I could see a half a bottle of Cragganmore up there. I strained to grab it and stuck it under my good arm while I hopped down.

I cut back from my usual two fingers to one in deference to the painkillers, pouring the fragrant single-malt Scotch into a brandy snifter. I reached for Mrs. Franklin's cake on top of the fridge, cut myself a healthy slice, and put it on a paper towel. Beast, who had trailed me into the kitchen in the hopes of more peanut butter biscuits, tried begging for some cake. When he saw he wasn't going to get anywhere, he snorted in disgust, padded down the hardwood hallway, and flopped onto his futon in my bedroom.

I sniffed the Scotch again as I sat on the edge of the bed and let its ribbon of fire work its way down my throat. I eased back into the pillows, took a big bite of cake, and tried to let my mind drift. It worked for a while, until I caught myself wondering about Steve's assessment of the crime scene.

I never tired of Steve's ability to draw the right conclusions about a case from seemingly unrelated bits of evidence. I knew why he made D-III so fast. In turn, his more experienced listening ear gave me a chance to work through the theories that rattled around in my head, talking to each other.

My conversations with Steve about race were usually much murkier. He could unravel any mystery but that one—was he black, white, or other? His confusion showed at the office. Whenever I saw him around Parker Center, he was usually with whites, talking and laughing just a little too loud. The brothers at Parker Center had taken to calling him "incognegro" for his unwillingness to socialize with black folks. And even when I did see him talking with a black person, he seemed uncomfortable, like he didn't quite know how to behave, didn't want anyone to think he was one of us.

But he was still a good detective, one of the best. I drifted off trying to imagine Steve's face, to read his reaction to the night's events, but was jolted awake by the image of my husband's instead. He would have been able to put all of this in perspective even better than Steve. Keith Roberts was the most perceptive man I ever knew. Even after all these years, just the thought of him could wake me up from a sound sleep, make my heart start hammering. I lay there, feeling a strained ache in my chest, as if my heart were covered by heavy scar tissue that kept it from beating freely.

That's how Keith and Erica's deaths felt to me, like an old scar. Healed over but an ugly, raised scar nonetheless. To touch it was to remember just how you got it, just what you were doing when you were injured. And I didn't want to go there, didn't want to relive the way Cinque Lewis cut down my husband and baby in our driveway, virtually in front of my eyes. I burrowed down deeper in the bed and tried to block out the image with a pillow over my head.

But I couldn't block out the sound of my brother's voice. It's always easy for someone else to say, "You should talk about it" or "You need to deal with this." But these well-meaning people are never around at two in the morning to put the pieces back together once you do, once you start picking at old scars. And if you happen to open up around them, to let it out—and there are no words for the feelings, so you howl—they're the first ones to start reaching for their hats. "Better let her have some time to herself," they whisper as they tiptoe away.

I tried to talk to Grandmama Cile right after it happened. That's when she copied out the Twenty-eighth Psalm and recommended regular church attendance.

I tried to talk about it with Perris a long time ago, but all he ended up doing was getting drunk on Rémy Martin and crying over Keith and Erica as much as I did.

I tried to talk to my parents about it. While my father was willing to listen, my wild grief made my mother uneasy. "Tearing yourself up like this for so long is unhealthy," she warned as the first anniversary of their murders approached, and I had fallen into a deep blue funk. "You act as if you're the guilty one, instead of that wretched piece of trash. Don't let him have his victory over you. You've got to get on with your life."

So I stopped talking about it. I took my anniversary grief and my everyday pain home. And there I was, left in the middle of the night with demons I hadn't even summoned, with only a prayer copied from the Bible in my grandmother's ornate hand, the eerie glow of a television set, and a bottle of something to ward the evil off. Something the color of rich amber that would slide down my throat, a liquid barrier against the blue-black nightmares that glowed darkly on the other side of the crime tape and threatened to eat me up alive.

When they began shortly after Keith and Erica were killed, the nightmares had been like both an alarm clock and a three-day drunk—waking me up but making it almost impossible to get out of bed. I couldn't finish my dissertation. I was so numb it felt like my heart and lungs had been ripped from my body, and I cried so much those first few months a good puff of wind could have knocked me over. I found myself on my knees a lot, something I hadn't done since nightly prayers at Grandmama Cile's house when I was little. By that August I was making a bargain with

God, or maybe it was a deal with the Devil: all my future joy in exchange for getting rid of the nightmares for good. I sealed the bargain with a half a bottle of Cragganmore.

I didn't know how to hold up my end of the deal until I entered the Academy that September. But instead of it being penance, I found at twenty-five a mission in policing, a calling, a life if not of joy then a certain dry-eyed satisfaction that I could protect other families better than anyone had protected my own. And the nightmares stopped.

Breathe in . . . stay calm . . . breathe out . . . stay focused. I would not cry, I would not fall apart. There was too much to be done.

Think about something more pleasant would be my mother's advice. I took my glass, wandered down the hall and back to the kitchen. Another piece of Mrs. Franklin's cake would certainly be more pleasant than thinking about Cinque Lewis. Two fingers of cake and one of Scotch. Or maybe it should be the other way around.

I had to laugh as I stood there, with my crystal brandy snifter and paper towel shedding crumbs: my vices had become so adult. Nothing like my response when I found out Aubrey had married Janet Murphy. It was 1970 then, and I was only seventeen, too young to drink legally and too proud of my newly found figure—courtesy of a freshman-year crash diet—to eat anything as verboten as pound cake. Back in those days the only thing I could do to ward off the blues was lose myself in my studies.

Studying had gotten me into college at sixteen and a 3.8 GPA, so it couldn't be all bad. And it wasn't as if I didn't date *any*one after Aubrey broke my heart. But a relationship, a serious one-on-one, boyfriend-girlfriend thing, maybe even a little jazz-radio-playing-in-the-background-while-we-have-sex-in-his-apartment kind of thing—I didn't even get close.

Professor Roberts—Keith, as he insisted his students call him—was one of the few bright spots in my life in those unhappy days after Aubrey got married. I signed up for his Introduction to Criminology class, thinking it the perfect place to plan the murder of the new Mrs. Aubrey Scott, but once I went to a few classes I was hooked. Keith had an uncanny ability to make lectures about the constitutional underpinnings of our criminal justice system seem like the most exciting thing in the world. I was fired up for the first time in my college career. I aced my midterm, wrote a blistering term paper on the significance of the Miranda ruling, and began to think for the first time that maybe there were other careers besides teaching high-school history.

My change of heart regarding a teaching career had a lot to do with Keith. He was intelligent, caring, completely in my corner. So much so he wouldn't let me coast through undergrad with a History/Black Studies major. While my mother considered it perfectly acceptable for me to pass my time teaching high school history until I got married, Keith argued it was the career of least resistance for a girl child of what he disdainfully called the L.A. niggerati. He believed I could do much better if I just put my mind to it.

Part of our assignment in Keith's class was to observe a trial. While everyone else in class chose the sensational murder trial of a black sportscaster, I chose the first-degree murder trial of a Nestor Avenue Deathstalker accused of killing a rival Mudtown Royal. Keith testified as an expert witness for the prosecution, and I was fascinated to see another aspect of what a criminology professor does. The picture Keith painted on the stand of the Compton-based gang and their sworn enemies in Watts—their origins, how they had their roots in the Slauson gang of the sixties and even before—opened up a new door on the world for me, one I didn't get to see in View Park, the golden ghetto where I'd spent most of my childhood.

Keith's expert testimony helped the D.A. establish a motive in the killing, one based on territorial boundaries between gangs that law enforcement was then only beginning to understand. And got me turned on to a field of study that would take me as far away from teaching in the L.A. Unified School District as I could possibly get.

The Cragganmore tasted good, unlike the first time I tried it. I was eighteen then, and the occasion was to celebrate the conviction of that Nestor Avenue Deathstalker. Keith and I were at his apartment in the then-middle-class Jungle, a maze of apartments just north of my parents's house in View Park. Keith was so sophisticated and so different from me. Ten years my senior, a product of New York City's down-and-dirty Harlem versus L.A.'s sheltered View Park, Cragganmore versus the Boone's Farm Strawberry Hill wine my classmates and I drank.

By that time I had a crush on Keith that was stronger than dirt, and I was just old enough to think I could do something about it. But as he sat next to me on his sofa, Keith made it very clear we were going to be colleagues and friends, not lovers. "Girl, you're practically jailbait," he teased and took my glass when I turned up my nose at the bitterness of the single-malt Scotch.

So we were friends and colleagues until I entered graduate school. By then I was more mature—a very grown-up and filled-out twenty before he even kissed me and almost twenty-one when we finally made mad love one night at his apartment. Since at that point we were so much in tune with each other's work, aspirations, and dreams, getting married seemed the next logical step. So we did it, jumped the broom, on an unseasonably warm November Saturday in 1974.

From the balcony of our honeymoon hotel on Maui, Keith predicted we could be as influential as Will and Ariel Durant, the famous husband-and-wife historians. "I'd prefer Ossie Davis and Ruby Dee," I had countered and dragged him to bed, determined it was time to do something other than talk shop.

For the three and a half years of our marriage we were a team—friends, lovers, independent parts of a strong whole. Our research and fieldwork on gangs complemented each other but allowed each of us room for our own professional achievement and recognition. Our life together gave us rock-solid love and unquestioning support, someone who always had your back. Our daughter, Erica, an acorn-colored angel with the widest smile on earth, gave us joy.

My glass was empty again. I allotted myself one more finger of Scotch and another of cake and went back to bed. As I moved down the hall, I passed the closed door of the bedroom that had once served as a combination of Keith's office and Erica's nursery. I started to go in, but figured I'd strolled down memory lane as much as I dared in one night. As my mother would say, let sleeping dogs lie. I took another sip of Scotch, hoping it would help me have a long, dreamless sleep.

CHAPTER 6

THE NUT HOUSE

I wish. Nightmares and the sound of helicopters tracking looters kept me up until dawn, and I was still struggling to get dressed when my sister-in-law, Louise, glided into the middle of my living room about noon, a sable-toned contradiction in a wide-legged designer pantsuit, tiny dreads, and tortoise-shell eyeglasses. She had awakened me earlier that morning and offered me a ride to pick up my car and brunch, an offer that saved me having to call a cab or bother Mrs. Franklin, and spared my taste buds the indignity of a microwave breakfast.

I told Louise my father had called earlier and wanted me to pick up some seafood for a family barbecue that afternoon. "That doesn't keep us from going to brunch" was her reply. No one could accuse my sister-in-law of not enjoying a good meal or two, or of being a timid eater. As we headed up the coast to her favorite Malibu restaurant, I realized I could have said Daddy was barbecuing yak and Louise Boudreaux Justice would gladly offer to bring the Trappey's hot sauce. For me, anything was a Happy Meal as long as I didn't have to cook it.

It was just the two of us that day; the twins were at my parents' house, and Perris was still in bed. "He didn't sleep well last night," Louise explained as we took our seats at an oceanside table at the trendy restaurant. "He talked in his sleep all night long and didn't settle down until the sun came up. He's really been through the wringer."

I could understand *that*. The first sip of my Electric Lemonade was a soothing blue balm for my jangled nerves. I gazed out at the famous and usually fabulous Malibu coastline, choked today with seaweed and garbage, and wondered what was on my sister-in-law's mind besides a good meal out.

She didn't keep me in suspense very long. As soon as our salads arrived, she said, "Perris told me they found Cinque Lewis, but he just about bit my head off when I asked him for details."

So that was it. My family's foolish secretiveness about that whole time period was something my cut-to-the-chase, bare-your-soul sister-in-law did not suffer gladly. The two of us going to brunch alone gave Louise a chance to get the uncensored Cinque Lewis story straight from the horse's mouth. But I wasn't any more eager to spill my guts with Louise than I was with Perris, regardless of how close my "sister-in-love" and I had become over the years.

"I didn't want to know anything confidential," she was saying. "I was just asking Perris if this Cinque Lewis brother and his Black Freedom Militia were related to the Symbionese Liberation Army, and he practically jumped down my throat."

I explained to her that the Militia and the SLA were totally different. "Both full of hot air, but different."

"But both of their leaders were named Cinque," she noted. When she had something on her mind, Louise could be more stubborn than my boxer. Maybe humor would throw her off the scent.

"You know how people in L.A. are," I began. "Changing their names, trying to shrug off their past like a cheap suit. If it's not Jews like my boss's father Anglicizing their name from Feuerstein to Firestone to be more 'American,' it's Hollywood hopefuls going from Norma Jean Baker to Marilyn Monroe."

Louise pointed her fork at me, chewing and nodding in mute agreement.

"Then in the late sixties and seventies," I added, "black folks got into the act—every third Negro I knew was changing his name to Kwame . . ."

". . . or Kareem . . . ," Louise, the UCLA graduate, chimed in.

". . . or Keisha, for that matter. Even my own parents were into it—who ever heard of naming a child Rhodesia?"

"Now you leave Matt and Joymarie out of this!" Louise was laughing and wiping the tears from her eyes with a napkin. "Rhodesia is a *lovely* name!"

"Yeah, if you're an African colonialist. It's like everyone had some kind of virus. Still does—look at Queen Latifah. Now you *know* her mama didn't name her that!"

Louise laughed along with me but, damn her, would not let it go. "So Cinque Lewis named himself after that guy in the Symbionese Liberation Army . . ."

"Donald Defreeze," I nodded, "who named *himself* after the nineteenth-century African captive who mutinied aboard the *Amistad*. After Defreeze was killed in that Patty Hearst shootout, Robert Lewis adopted his name in 'memory of his fallen comrade,' and his girlfriend started calling herself Sojourner Truth after the abolitionist, whose original name, by the way, was something else, too."

"What was her real name?"

"Who, Sojourner Truth?"

She swatted at me playfully. "No, silly, Cinque's girlfriend!"

"Her?" I drained my glass, signaled our waiter for another. "Candy something or other."

"Umph, umph, umph," Louise sighed. "Not much better. Was the girlfriend shaking and faking, too?"

"Keith said she was one of the most dedicated sisters he ever met—running the Black Freedom Militia's alternative school, that kind of thing. Then she got squeezed out in some sort of power struggle. That must have been the last straw, because shortly after that she went to Keith and spilled her guts about the Militia's drug dealing."

Louise's face went still for just a moment, reminding me she and Perris had both had drug problems at one time. "When did they get into drugs?"

"When the Colombians started waving huge amounts of cocaine under their noses—no pun intended. Before you could say 'Power to the people,' they started buying small quantities of coke to sell, allegedly to fund their community programs. Pretty soon the money got so good that their mobile libraries, free health clinics, and the rest just fell by the wayside."

"And that's what this girlfriend told your husband? *That's* why he and your baby were killed?"

My neck and jaw tightened so quickly I unintentionally cracked the ice I was sucking. Like magic, our waiter appeared with another drink. I took a sip, let it play over my tongue until the blue sparks reached and calmed my brain. It was one thing to play the Negro name game or dish about the politics of the Black Freedom Militia but quite another to talk about what happened to Keith and Erica.

Louise caught my drift, shifted uncomfortably in her chair. We both finished our salads in a prickly silence. It wasn't until they had delivered our desserts that she ventured to ask me what became of the girlfriend and Cinque.

"The Department didn't really think she was involved, so when she came up with an iron-clad alibi, they kicked her," I explained. "She faded into the woodwork after that. And Cinque had been long since in the wind. My guess would have been Cuba or Algeria until yesterday."

Louise leaned forward in her chair. "What I still don't understand is why your family is so hush-hush about all of this."

"I went through a real hard time when Keith and Erica were first killed. Stayed closed up in the house for months. So when I finally came out of it, I think everyone was only too glad to sweep the whole thing under the rug."

"But why wouldn't Perris talk to me about it? I'm his wife!"

"I think he felt responsible. He and some buddies had been unofficially patrolling the house, but he wasn't there when it happened. I think he always felt guilty about letting me down."

Louise stared in my direction, a frown creasing her dark face. "But wasn't that the same day he got shot on duty? He certainly couldn't help that. Yet Perris and your mother act like what happened is some kind of scandal they can't talk about. They were all huddled up on the phone talking about it last night, and now he's all grumpy. I don't get it."

I remembered my mother counseling Perris before he got married: "Louise is a nice girl. Don't burden your relationship with a bunch of old family mess." Looking at my sister-in-love's pained expression, I could see the mess was about to hit the fan.

"I think it goes back to when Perris left the Department, then couldn't pass the bar, and started drinking heavily. My mother kept covering for him, saying it was just a phase he was going through, as if it were puberty or something."

"As you say, he *is* his mother's child."

There was a daughter-in-law edge to Louise's voice that I wasn't going to touch with a ten-foot pole. "Another reason Joymarie doesn't talk a lot about Cinque Lewis," I hurried to add, "is that street violence was something she never thought could touch our family. That's why she insisted we move from the old neighborhood to View Park—so she could say she still lived among black folks, but not the everyday, garden-variety ones. For my mother to talk about Perris getting shot or Cinque Lewis and what he did to me is a painful reminder that evil can touch her family. And, despite her best efforts, one of her children still insists on dirtying her hands with it."

"But Perris was a cop for six years . . ."

"That was different. Perris joined the Department to avoid getting sent to Vietnam. He was in law school at night the whole time he was on the force."

". . . and he's a criminal defense attorney now. How's that any better?"

"Emphasis on the word *attorney*," I reminded her. "Attorneys are always acceptable to my mother and her crowd, as are doctorate-level educators like my sister, Macon. Even Rhodesia getting her Ph.D. in psychology is okay."

Louise pointed out psychologists talk about their feelings all the time.

"But they *are* called 'Doctor.' " I laughed. But the way I felt about my mother's niggerati pretensions and judgments about the work I chose to do wasn't funny.

After Louise had all but licked the crumbs from her plate, I asked her if she still had time to take me downtown to get my car. "Sure. I figured last night you'd need a ride. That's one reason why I offered to meet you for brunch."

"And the other?"

Louise's eyes locked into mine. "I figured you needed to talk to someone."

I exhaled into the salty air. "I don't know, girl. Sometimes, when I think about all the high achievers in our family, I feel like a cloth coat in a room full of mink."

Despite Louise's protests to the contrary, I knew it was true. My mother was a pedigreed, third-generation Angeleno, the highest-ranking black social worker in the county before she retired, and Negro club woman of the century. And despite all that down-home talk, my father Matt was a brilliant chemist, a successful businessman, and one of the West Coast coordinators of the '63 March on Washington. Perris had his upscale Beverly Hills law practice, and besides my mercurial sister Rhodesia, currently pursuing a Ph.D., there was my other sister, Dr. Macon Justice, headmistress of a chichi private school up north. Not to mention my UCLA M.B.A. sister-in-love, Louise, who worked as Perris's part-time office manager, ran around behind four-year-old twins, plus was on the board of I don't know how many civic-minded, nonprofit organizations.

But Louise wasn't having it. "Didn't you tell me one time you became a cop because you took the LAPD motto literally?"

" 'To protect and to serve'? That's right."

"Well you know that's the definition of the Greek word *hero*. And, from my standpoint, that's exactly what you are, just as much as anyone else in the Justice family. So why should what everybody else does or says prevent you from pursuing what you know is your calling and what I've heard from Perris you're pretty damn good at to boot?"

"He told you that?"

She held up her right hand. "If I'm lying, I'm flying."

I sighed again and signaled for the check. "Thanks, Louise. It's been kinda hard to keep that in perspective these last few days."

She reached out to squeeze my hand. "I know, honey. But you know what I always say . . ."

"*Illegitimi non carborundum?*"

"You got it," she laughed. " 'Don't let the bastards get you down.' "

Everyone can remember where they were when a major tragedy happened. I was sitting in my sixth-grade class reading a love note from the boy who sat behind me when the principal's voice scratched over the loudspeaker, broken up from the system's feedback and his own emotions, to tell us President Kennedy had been shot. My father was barbecuing near our swimming pool when we saw the fires burning in Watts that first August evening in 1965.

I was finishing up the paperwork on a child homicide we had just cleared when I got a call that the verdict was in on the King beating. By three, all of us who could get away from our desks were huddled around the televisions in Press Relations up on the sixth floor of Parker Center. Cops of every race, creed, and color were standing shoulder to shoulder in that room. In their nervousness, many of them had lit up cigarettes, forbidden in the building as one of the Press Relations officers tried vainly to remind them. I wondered if my godfather and mentor, Deputy Chief Henry Youngblood, was watching the verdict on TV from his office upstairs, chomping on a Macanudo his doctor forbade him to light.

When the verdicts were read and the LAPD Four were acquitted of the charges against them, as "not guilty" flashed across the screen of every local and national special-bulletin newscast, I was flabbergasted. It didn't matter that they were my brothers in blue—those guys were all the way wrong and should have been convicted.

The eye contact I made with some of those in the Press Relations office that day told me I wasn't the only one disgusted by the verdict, but more than a few of my fellow brothers and sisters in blue—including some of the black ones—were breathing a sigh of relief and slapping each other on the back like it was a three-peat for the Lakers. But their smiles turned to grim stares of disbelief when the black-and-whites and Channel 4's news helicopter reported on the angry crowds at Fifty-fifth Street and Normandie, then, an hour later, at that infamous intersection a few miles south.

Around seven, the brass finally got it together and ordered us to move out to City Hall, where a mob had already gathered, shouting "No Justice, No Peace," and trashing everything in sight. After an agonizing wait of what felt more like three days rather than just three hours, I had put on my uniform and was good to go. And had been going ever since. But unlike that pink bunny on television, I was having trouble beating the drum. Pulling up to Parker Center that Saturday afternoon with Louise reminded me of just how tired I was.

The building looked worn out, too. A vintage design, the LAPD's headquarters was named after William H. Parker, the legendary chief of police who modernized the force and turned it into the widely respected and imitated organization it was pre-Rodney King. It was Parker, Uncle Henry told me, who came up with the concept of a "thin blue line" of LAPD officers standing between civilized society and the scum and vermin Angelenos were led to believe would overrun the city. It was a lot easier to hold the line in the Communist-obsessed fifties, but as time went on there were some noticeable cracks in the LAPD-drawn blue demarcation line between them and us, cracks that threatened to split the city apart as dramatically as the San Andreas Fault.

The first came after the Watts riots in 1965, when then-Chief Parker warned of a city that was projected to be 45 percent Negro (as we were called at the time): "If you want any protection for your home and family," Uncle Henry remembered Parker saying, "you're going to have to get in and support a strong Police Department. If you don't, come nineteen seventy, God help you."

And most people did, making the LAPD the most powerful—and in some quarters, feared—department in the city through most of the seventies and eighties. Chief Darryl Gates, who as a young officer had once served as William Parker's driver, was at the helm during the current civil unrest, although he had been noticeably out of sight in its beginning hours, choosing instead to make an appearance at a fund-raiser to defeat a police reform initiative. Some in the Department, my godfather included, believed Gates intentionally decided to let the City Council members—some of whom had loudly shouted down his offer to put a thousand cops on the street as a precaution—try and hold down the fort without us while the minority community blew off a little steam. Little did Gates know that steam would blast a hole in the middle of the city.

Louise guided her Volvo around the front of the monument to Gates's mentor, which was where I was officed along with the scores of detectives in the Robbery-Homicide Division and several hundred other members of the various Operations Bureau departments and administrators, including the lame-duck chief himself.

"Can you manage driving with that sling?" Louise asked.

"It's an automatic," I replied. "Piece of cake."

Thirty minutes later, my trunk laden with ten pounds of shrimp, oysters, and salmon I bought for Matt to barbecue, my ancient Volkswagen Rabbit and I were struggling along Crenshaw Boulevard toward my parents' house. I passed the offices of KJLH, the FM radio station owned by Stevie Wonder which had switched from its regular urban contemporary format to let the community vent their feelings about the last few days. It reminded me of the sixties soul station KGFJ and its most popular disc jockey, Magnificent Montague. His innocent tag line "Burn, Baby, Burn" took on an ominous meaning when Watts went up in flames. The station was never the same after it, either.

But KJLH was trying, albeit belatedly, to do the right thing. After awhile, though, I got tired of listening to the same anger, complaints, and fear; I switched off the radio and slapped a cassette in my tape deck. Marvin Gaye's *What's Going On* reminded me that the inner city blues I was feeling had been defined more than twenty years ago.

As I crept through block after block of charred buildings and rubble of what used to be a thriving business district, I knew how I'd respond to the commercial that ran after big sporting events: *Charlotte Justice, you've just lived through seventy-two hours of pure hell. What are you going to do next?*

I'm going to the Nut House.

The name we kids gave our house had its origins in a family story of how, when my walnut-toned father was introduced to my fair-skinned mother, he said: *I'm just a nutty Negro, but would you be my Almond Joy?* Matthew Justice was a freshman at UCLA at the time, running track and moonlighting as a janitor at Max Factor in Hollywood. Joymarie Curry was just fourteen, a sophomore at Jefferson High School, and too young to marry. So they carried on a perfectly proper courtship for five years until my father established himself as a chemist and could provide for my mother in the style to which her family, the silver-spooned, painfully proper Currys, had made her accustomed.

Daddy had learned from his experiences in the shadows at Max Factor a thing or two about makeup, and had struck out on his own after the war to manufacture cosmetics—war paint, Grandmother Cile called it—for Negro women. Sales were brisk in beauty shops, bridge clubs, and sorority meetings on the Eastside and across the country. Matt's blood, sweat, and tears earned him a colored man's fortune—and put us firmly in what everyone else in America would probably call the middle class.

But it was good enough. Good enough to get my father some plum assignments from the big white cosmetics companies, which meant he didn't have to be away from home so much, traveling door-to-door with those makeup cases. Enough to move my mother, Perris, and me in the late fifties from our house on

Fortieth Place on the Eastside to the newly integrated Negro Mecca of View Park, on what colored folks called the Westside.

And into the house on the hill came the inhabitants of Justice's Nut House. Although my parents named all four of us after our family's ancestral homes—Daddy believed it was a way of honoring the Negro's place in the world—until I was ten and Perris was fourteen, there was just us and we were the Nutty Buddies.

Perris, a walnut-toned facsimile of my father, was named not after ritzy Paris, France, but rural Perris, California, where Daddy's parents had a vacation house. Perris was doted on by my mother, who saw in him the color she could only obtain with my father's Foundation #6 or a summer sweating her hair back to its not-quite-straight roots in L.A.'s unforgiving desert sun.

Then there was me. A half shade darker than Joymarie, I felt simultaneously adored by my father and envied by my mother. My mother's colorstruck relatives, on the other hand, exhaled a collective sigh of relief that "that Charlotte (not-even-North-Carolina-but-*Arkansas!*) Negro's blood" wouldn't prevent another member of the Curry clan from joining their cherished blue-vein societies, an unofficial Los Angeles Negro Social Register of formal clubs and informal social connections where admittance and upward mobility were dependent on having skin pale enough to see the venous blood coursing beneath.

But Mother gave most of her attention to Perris, her first-born and only son. To me she gave grapefruit diets, drilled into me that I had to be twice as smart and three times as tough as whites to get half their salaries, and warned of the paradox of being too black to be white and too white to be black in a world that made you choose and then, regardless of the choice you made, gave you hell about the decision.

The lessons of my mother's life colored my own. I knew—and usually found a way to rebel against—most of the Nut House rules. Rule #1: Don't marry anyone too light or too dark—for the sake of the children. So I married Keith—brilliant, kind, loving, but with a melanin count that put him squarely in the Brazil nut to roasted chestnut range. Rule #2: *Common* is a word that should only be applied to stocks, not people. So who's my best friend? Katrina Keikilani Timms, my half-Hawaiian, straight-outta-Compton girlfriend who could and would say "Fuck you" in five different languages at the drop of a hat. Rule #3: Don't even *fix* your mouth to say you were in love with some white person. As if, just by looking at her, you couldn't tell a fair amount of white blood flowed in Joymarie's too-blue veins.

Most of all, I learned from my mother's experiences that life in America was a game called Pigmentocracy, color a card you played. If you're black, step back. If you're brown, stick around. If you're yellow, you're mellow. And if you're white, you're all right. So if my "high yellow" color lulled my white superiors in the Department into thinking I was somehow safer and less militant than my darker sisters and brothers, then that was their mistake, not mine.

I let myself in with my old house key. Perris and Louise's twins, Ebony and Ivory, were watching Nickelodeon in the den, and my mother was standing ramrod straight at the kitchen sink, every naturally auburn-colored hair in place, wearing makeup and pearls while she peeled vegetables.

I kissed her on the cheekbone, caught a heady whiff of her Chanel No. 5. "Child, don't scare me like that!" Joymarie Justice looked at me over her shoulder, her smoke-gray eyes zeroing in on my sling. "Perris told me you were hurt, but he didn't say it was bad!" She rinsed off her hands and dried them on a towel. She walked toward me with a frown, stopped and flicked some lint off the sling. Then she stood before me, hands on slim hips, awaiting my report.

Maybe my good arm was raised up a little, half-expecting a hug, or maybe I looked like the motherless child I sometimes felt myself to be in Joymarie's critical presence because a tumbler seemed to click belatedly somewhere in my mother's brain. "Come here, baby." She gave me an awkward back thumping as if she were burping me and murmured, "No one can hurt my babies anymore, I won't let them," just like when Perris and I were little and afraid of the bogeyman hiding in the closet.

She was right—Cinque Lewis was dead, and I could finally give up my search for Keith and Erica's killer and really get on with my life. The possibility made me almost giddy, but just as I felt the light shine on my long-buried feelings, the hug was over and my mother was back at the sink, making what I guessed she considered better use of her hands.

"These blessed onions always make my eyes water." She brushed furiously at her perfectly made-up face.

The cabbage she was shredding for coleslaw, and I wondered what she was talking about. I sighed and went to the freezer in search of the vodka to make a screwdriver. "Where's Daddy?" I asked. "I need him to get the grocery bags out of the car."

"I'll take care of it. Your father's always in that confounded lab of his," she fussed on her way to the car. "I don't know why I put up with him and that mess out there."

Mother had been complaining about my father's lab, situated at the rear of our double lot, for as long as I could remember. But she never complained about the cruises, couture clothes, and new cars his hard work afforded her.

I grabbed my drink, exited through the kitchen door, and made a beeline for the lab. On the way I paused for a moment to gaze at the swimming pool, which my father and the famous black architect Paul Williams had spent many hours designing.

In the thirties, as part of a magnificent estate he designed in Bel-Air for a white client, Mr. Williams had created a pool that included the twelve signs of the zodiac, done up in custom-made tile, similar to the Hearst mansion in San Simeon. When Williams designed our house, my father asked if he could create a slightly different pool for us, with the symbols of the zodiac replaced by twelve famous blacks in history. So instead of Cancer the Crab, there was abolitionist Harriet Tubman; Martin Luther King, Jr. replaced Aquarius the Water Bearer. There was even a tiled mosaic of the hair-care genius Madam C. J. Walker, Daddy's role model. I always had the eerie feeling whenever we swam in the pool that we were being held afloat by their somber faces and high expectations.

The familiar clash of chemicals and perfumes greeted me at the laboratory door. My father stood hunched over a device I knew from experience measured the amount of elasticity in hair strands. He saw me out of the corner of his eye and immediately came over to the door. "Char! How you doin', baby?"

No matter how old I got, the world always felt safer in my father's arms. Part of it was his height—although age and bending over workbenches had stooped him a bit, Matthew Justice was still a solid six-one—but it was also the gentleness of my father's spirit, his ability to give the unconditional love I craved, a welcome contrast to my mother's angles and edges and judgments.

"It's been pretty rough, Daddy," I whispered into his chest.

"I know. Your Uncle Henry called earlier to give me the four one one."

In addition to being my godfather and a deputy chief in the Department, Henry Youngblood was my father's best friend, going back to their days at Jefferson High. There was hardly a week that went by without Matt Justice and Henry Youngblood seeing or talking to each other.

My father held me for a while, then broke the embrace and wandered over to the yellow Formica table, a relic from our old house on Fortieth Place. "I tole Henry how this uprisin' reminds me of what happened to me and him in the Zoot Suit Riots in forty-three."

"I don't think you ever told me about that one," I said, sitting on an old sofa, a castoff from one of my mother's redecorating binges. My father was my first and best history teacher, and probably the main reason I even considered teaching as a career. I loved nothing better than learning the history of Los Angeles through his eyes.

"Sure I did," he insisted. He plopped down next to me, delighted to tell me again. "It was in June. Henry and I had got draped in our best threads—the fine vines with the reet pleats—to take your mother and her sister downtown to a movie. That's where the mob caught us. Bunch of white navy boys from the radar base at Chavez Ravine, came downtown whuppin' on the Mexicans—and more than a few coloreds, quiet as it was kept—supposedly for attackin' white women. It was all a bunch of lies, of course, cooked up by the newspapers and small-minded bigots. We had to run like hell to get the girls out of there that night—those boys assumed they was white women! We never did tell Joymarie's parents about it."

My father's nostrils flared, and he made a noise that might have passed for a laugh if you didn't know him better. "But, bottom line, it was just hate—hate for our flashy suits, hate because they believed colored and Mexican boys weren't enlisting like they should, just hate pure and simple." He shook his head in disgust. "Henry said this time the riotin' was a hundred, maybe a thousand times worse. Hate flyin' every which way. He's takin' it pretty hard, too."

"He must be beside himself," I agreed. "He was one of the few who pushed for contingency planning in the event something jumped off following the verdict."

My father shook his head slowly, dismissing the world's craziness with a sly smile. "But you know Henry—he ain't gonna COSM."

"Well, normally I wouldn't cry over spilled milk myself." I couldn't help but smile too, pleased I wasn't so tired that I couldn't decipher one of my father's numerous acronyms. He had so many, Uncle Henry had been threatening to make him an honorary cop for years.

He turned to face me. "How are you holdin' up, Charlotte?" Using my given name was always a sign my father wanted the truth—straight, no chaser.

"I'm fine, Daddy. Especially since that bastard Lewis turned up dead."

"Your brother called to tell us last night. He was pretty upset. Talked to your mother for the longest about it, so I can only imagine what it was like for you. Did they find out who did it?"

"They took a physician in for questioning who had been near the scene."

"You don't mean Aubrey Scott?" Daddy must have heard from Perris that his favorite lab assistant was back in town.

"No, this guy works for Aubrey at California Medical Center. That's how we ran into Aubrey, when Dr. Mitchell and my partner took me downtown to be treated."

"Hmph," Daddy snorted, "I remember when that was one of the few big-time hospitals in town that would treat black folks. So you think this Mitchell dude had somethin' to do with Lewis's death?"

"I'm not sure. But he had a camera with him, which really bothered me for some reason. It was like he was sightseeing or something."

Matt shook his graying head and sighed. "I'm not surprised. Folks from all over town, black, white and otherwise, have been cruisin' up and down Crenshaw, snappin' pictures as if all this destruction is just so many floats at the Rose Parade. So if it's not this Mitchell fella, where does that leave you for suspects?"

"Nowhere really. I went by the scene last night on my way home; they hadn't found any witnesses. But the detective assigned to the case works with me, so I'm sure I'll find out more when I get to work on Monday."

"Well, I cast my vote for you takin' care of yourself." He smiled and wrapped his arm around me. "I'm sure it hasn't hit you yet, but you've had quite a shock, little lady."

I think my father was waiting for me to cry, but I had used up all the tears allotted to me in this life when Keith and Erica were killed. There was no emotion left other than that scarred-over spot in the middle of my chest, a wasteland where nothing bloomed.

After a few minutes my father sighed, hugged me closer, and kissed my hair. "Char, you know I'm here for you." His voice was so soft I almost didn't hear it. "Whenever you're ready, your old man is here."

CHAPTER 7

SO BLUE

I didn't hear from Steve at all on Sunday, which I chalked up to the caseload—he was probably working overtime just to keep up. Still, considering I got injured in the field and almost passed out at a crime scene, you'd think he would have called. Did refusing to sleep with him mean I was now entitled to less than common courtesy?

The more I thought about it, the more irritated I became. Rather than stew about it, I channeled my anger into writing out an informal chronology of the events of Friday afternoon in anticipation of the paperwork blizzard I knew awaited me at the office. It was amazing how much of Friday and the days preceding it had hardened like cement in my mind.

But it was the parts I didn't record that tore at my dreams that night. After battling the covers until the rising sun called a halt to the fight, I got up on Monday, agitated and bone-tired at the same time, and decided to head in to work early. As I made my bleary-eyed way downtown, I saw little ones being escorted to grade school by federal troops and wondered for a moment if I was in Little Rock instead of Los Angeles. An exhausted-looking young Guardsman popped a packet of coffee granules into his mouth, then washed them down with a double-caffeinated cola. Despite my aversion to his brand of poison, I understood the need.

Parker Center was still heavily guarded, but with the cleanup under way and the rioting down to a few isolated incidents, life was approaching something akin to normal. My lieutenant usually came in early, so I figured I'd catch him before the day got too busy. I could see him in his corner at the far end of the bull pen that housed the twelve detectives in our Homicide I unit, a DARE mug full of coffee and a slew of reports stacked up neatly on his desk.

During my tenure in the LAPD, I'd watched Lieutenant Kenneth Stobaugh, Jr., rise through the ranks like a hot-air balloon. In his early fifties, he was tall, lean, taciturn—sort of a latter-day reincarnation of Gary Cooper. Like me, Stobaugh had a master's degree in criminology. But while I was ABD (all but the dissertation, as my father called it)—permanently sidetracked from finishing my doctorate in criminology by Keith and Erica's deaths—Stobaugh had completed his doctorate in public administration. He was one of the new breed of professional police administrators springing up in the Department—well educated, focused, committed. And very ambitious.

With his father, an uncle, and two older brothers in the LAPD and a black-sheep sister with the Sheriff's Department, policing was a calling in the Stobaugh family. His father, Ken Senior, was a former star homicide detective in the Department with a reputation of closing almost 90 percent of his cases thirty years ago. RHD legend had it that Junior's first words out of the womb were, "Drop the scalpel, Doc, and put your hands up!"

But things had slipped a lot since Ken Senior's glory days. Murders were increasingly committed on the street, not in the home, and therefore much harder, if not impossible, to solve. But since 1990, when Lieutenant Stobaugh took command of RHD's Homicide I, our unit's clearance rate had improved, even as those handled by the divisions and bureaus declined, garnering Captain Armstrong's attention and signaling Lieutenant Stobaugh's status as a man on the move. Even his sparsely decorated desk looked as if it could be packed up and relocated to greener pastures at a moment's notice. And it just might be; I'd heard rumors Stobaugh was being discussed as successor to Captain Armstrong, if and when Armstrong retired.

I dropped into a brown vinyl-covered side chair and waited until my lieutenant came up for air. When it looked like it might take awhile, I slid some Oreo cookies under his tanned nose as an inducement.

"Oh, I'm sorry, Justice. I thought you were someone else. How's the shoulder?" Stobaugh didn't wait for my answer, gesturing instead with the cookie toward the papers on his desk. "I've been poring over some of the death reports we've been getting over the last five days. Did you know these riots have resulted in over fifty deaths? Most of them are probably going to be chalked up to 'casualties of the rebellion,' but there are a good number here that I think we can close."

Stobaugh's eyes sparked and his mouth inched up a little at the corners. He looked like he would have welcomed the challenge of going out there and solving every one of those homicides himself if he could. His face assumed an expression of concern as he refocused on me. "I read Firestone's preliminary report on the Lewis homicide. Pretty damn rough on you, I'd say."

This was as close to empathy as I was going to get from my iron-jawed lieutenant. Still, he was a marked improvement over a supervisor I once had in West Bureau named Lieutenant Curtis Skirk, known there as "Skirk the Jerk" for persistently and rhythmically rubbing female detectives' knees while we related particularly difficult vice cases.

"Lieutenant Dreyfuss over at South Bureau is about to shit a brick over what went down on Friday," Lieutenant Stobaugh continued. "He's left three sputtering messages for me since Friday night. I thought I would get your report before giving Tony a call back."

"I haven't written it up yet . . ."

"In your own words then. Firestone's report said you have a personal connection on this one."

My heart sank as I tried to calm myself enough to devise a coherent response to the inference behind Stobaugh's words. Although I tried not to draw attention to it and label myself as an obsessive, everyone in the Department knew about my special interest in finding Keith and Erica's killer. For years I had followed the case, dogging Uncle Henry for information and begging him for copies of the investigating detective's reports. The Department's conflict-of-interest policy prevented me from getting any closer to the case, much less being assigned to it, so the scraps of information I could pull together were like strands of a loved one's hair, carefully preserved in my own reconstructed murder book, a royal blue, three-ring binder I kept at home that mimicked the LAPD's official homicide paper trail. When I got to RHD myself in '90, my bootleg murder book was finally liberated from Keith's office and moved downtown with me. It took up most of the bottom drawer of my desk, where I camouflaged it beneath a pair of old tennis shoes, a box of Tampax, and an extra pair of panty hose.

My interest in the unsolved murders had taken on the trappings of a holy quest, and, even though they pretended not to, everyone in RHD knew it. So Stobaugh's comment, filled with innuendos and assumptions, raised my hackles but made me grateful I had made notes the night before. I would not be caught flat-footed. But as I related my account of the events of Friday night, I could sense Stobaugh wanted something more.

"That's all in Firestone's report," he said impatiently. "And while I've got him and the new girl, Cortez, assigned to the case, I doubt if anyone misses that shithead Lewis, excuse my French. But we've got ourselves a bigger problem, Justice."

"What's that, sir?"

Stobaugh's green eyes reached out to me across the small space separating us and brought me up short. "Your reasoning for removing the physician from the scene."

"I'm not following you, Lieutenant."

"From the report filed by Officer Cooper, the suspect was behaving suspiciously when he was spotted. Under the circumstances, he should have been arrested and detained on the spot."

"The full degree of the circumstances wasn't known until *after* the situation was over," I replied. "If by circumstances you mean the discovery of Cinque Lewis's body."

"Not just that, Justice. The report Cooper filed indicates the suspect attempted to attack him."

I chose my words carefully. "I'm sure Cooper would say that, sir, but some might disagree with his characterization of the situation."

A twitching eyebrow told me I had my lieutenant's attention.

"When Rivers and Cooper approached Dr. Mitchell, Cooper was already highly agitated himself."

"What are you trying to say, Detective?"

"Not trying, *am* saying, sir. Mike Cooper used racial epithets on the doctor, provoked him through the use of his baton, and in essence fostered a volatile climate that resulted in Amundsen's use of excessive force and us almost having another Rodney King situation out there. We moved Mitchell from the immediate scene to defuse the situation and prevent another riot."

Stobaugh was visibly displeased with what he was hearing. If I forced the issue and made him take my 181—LAPD-ese for a Personnel Complaint—it would get back to Cooper, Dreyfuss, and Internal Affairs, too. After the worldwide transmission of members of the Department doing the Fred Astaire on Rodney King's head, I don't think anyone at South Bureau wanted Internal Affairs checking into Cooper's hotheaded remarks or actions. Nor would my ambitious lieutenant-on-the-move want to be the one who forced the misconduct into the light of day.

"Well, emotions have been running unusually high out there," he reasoned. "Isn't it possible that Cooper or this boot were merely overreacting to an extreme circumstance? Or that you're overreacting?"

Stobaugh's voice had taken on a patronizing boys-will-be-boys tone I didn't appreciate one bit. So much so, I decided to let the other shoe drop. "Dr. Mitchell clearly identified himself out there. Cooper wasn't listening because he was already around the bend. In fact, just prior to us pulling up to the scene, he'd been making offensive racial remarks on the bus about black and Latino suspects."

"Such as?"

"Such as calling them 'animals' for one . . ."

My lieutenant waved a hand vaguely. "Calling people animals is hardly a racial slur, Detective."

"How about calling the rioters 'mud-brown niggers and spics' or threatening to put a cap in the ass of the next 'little jungle bunny' to look at him cross-eyed? Cooper had that bus so whipped up, I'm surprised they didn't kill that doctor."

Stobaugh regarded me for a long moment, before getting out a notepad. "Did he say anything else?" he asked, pen poised but his green stare a million miles away.

"Other than calling Cortez and me 'split tails,' there wasn't much more to say," I replied sarcastically. "But when Cortez and I didn't respond to his little jokes at our expense, Cooper came up to the front of the bus where we were sitting and started getting up in my face, talking quite graphically about how some looter would like to get a piece of my 'sweet-cream ass' before tearing me apart." Thinking about being on that bus with that fool made my jaw tighten all over again.

Stobaugh dropped his pen, closed his eyes, muttered, "Jesus H. Christ! He actually *said* that?" and started rubbing his temples. "Was there anything *else*?"

"Not unless you want to talk about the Jack Daniels I could smell on his breath."

Stobaugh swore sharply and jerked around in his chair as if he'd been stung by a bee. "Are you *absolutely* sure about this, Justice?"

"Ask Cortez. She was right there and can verify everything that I just said—except maybe the part about his breath. Lucky for her she wasn't as close to him as I was."

Stobaugh started rummaging through the stacked reports

on his desk. He unearthed one, removed a blue Post-It note and began to read, then looked up at me. "We'll get to Cooper. But in the meantime can we get back to your actions at the scene? From what I can understand from Tony's note on Cooper's report, he seems to feel you didn't consider other options for handling the suspect."

It was an effort to keep from grinding my teeth. "That's a bunch of crap! Burt Rivers told me he was glad we got Mitchell out of there, and he was senior man out there."

"Well, Dreyfuss says here you could have secured Dr. Mitchell in the bus . . ."

"Inasmuch as the bus was almost tipped over by the mob, I don't think that would have been too wise."

"Well, what about securing him away from the immediate area until backup arrived?"

"That's exactly what we attempted to do, but when Mitchell realized I was injured, he convinced Cortez to take me to the hospital instead of taking him to jail."

He flipped through the report before him. "Cortez's 51 report says *you* asked to be taken to the hospital."

"No way!"

He slid it across the desk. "Read it for yourself."

I settled back to read Cortez's Investigating Officer's Chronological Record but soon sat up with my mouth hanging open. Although she was sitting not more than ten feet from me on that bus and saw the same thing go down among Cooper, the boot, and Mitchell that I did, Gena Cortez's chron record of that afternoon was as pristine as the streets of Beverly Hills. And as much of an illusion. There was no mention of Cooper's behavior on the bus, she left out his provocation of Dr. Mitchell and the first blow struck by the boot. And for some reason, she had noted *my* insistence on being taken to the hospital despite her reluctance to remove Mitchell from the scene.

With the spin she put on the events of Friday afternoon, maybe Gena Cortez would have been better placed in Press

Relations than RHD. "I see Detective Cortez left a few things out of her report." I slid it back to Stobaugh, already planning what I was going to say to the latest addition to the Homicide I unit. "Look, Lieutenant, I'm not going to call another member of this Department a liar, but I was so out of it I was in no position to make that call. Mitchell convinced Cortez to take me to the hospital. What do you think I did—hold a gun to her head?"

"But you were senior in the situation, Justice. You're expected to provide the leadership, help Cortez make the right call."

"I'm sorry, sir, but you seem to have forgotten the officer down out there was *me!*"

Stobaugh held up his hand in a plea for peace. "I can see we're not going to resolve this right now. Tony Dreyfuss's message asked me to speak with you about the incident, which I have, and while there are some issues that are still a little cloudy, I think we can keep Internal Affairs out of this."

An alarm went off in my brain. "I can handle this myself, Lieutenant. I have no intention of filing a report."

The silence at that moment reminded me of another of my father's sayings: *so quiet you could hear a rat piss on cotton.* Looking at Stobaugh in the sudden stillness, I could hear the rats relieving themselves all over my shoe. And feel the color rising in my cheeks. "You mean Dreyfuss and Cooper want to file a 181 on *me*, don't you?"

Stobaugh's averted eyes spoke volumes.

"Lieutenant, you know I'm up for promotion! Something like that in my jacket could ruin my chances."

"I'm completely sympathetic to that, Justice. I'll speak with Tony again; I'm sure once he hears the other side, we can make this whole mess disappear and get back to work."

The implications of what Stobaugh was saying weren't lost on me. I'd accused the boot of exerting an excessive use of force while Cooper had sexually harassed me and engaged in misconduct, which by departmental policy required an Internal Affairs investigation and possible reprimand. But to put such an investigation in motion might result in an equally strenuous investigation of my actions at the scene, possible reprimands for me, and the loss of working relationships I had nurtured for almost a decade. And hurt my chances for promotion, not to mention my lieutenant's. I didn't want Internal Affairs in my business any more than Stobaugh did.

I watched Stobaugh watch me. I could see why my lieutenant would go far. He appeared to be doing me a favor by smoothing things over with Dreyfuss, but the bigger favor was the one I'd be doing for him by making it unnecessary for him to drop a dime to Internal Affairs on Cooper and Amundsen. And Burt Rivers, too—I had almost forgotten the boot was under my old training officer's direct command.

Stobaugh gathered up some reports and placed them on the battered file cabinet behind him. "How's the arm? Have you seen a doctor yet?"

"Not yet, sir." My response came out a little too sharply, but I was still angry at the box I felt he was forcing me into. "I feel fine."

"That may be, but you know you need a medical clearance before you can come back to work full time."

"It shouldn't matter; I can shoot left-handed. And even with the injury, can't I pull desk duty? How active do I need to be to push some paper around and interview some witnesses? I could be a real help on the Lewis case. I know the file . . ."

When Stobaugh wrinkled his nose like he just smelled a mess of chitterlings, I realized I was trying too hard. "Call the medical liaison's office, and tell them I said to get you a referral to an agreed medical examiner ASAP. If he clears you, then we can talk about it. My biggest concern is that we don't compromise an investigation by having your conflict of interest get in the way. You get the clearance and then we'll talk."

"Understood." I rose from the chair, sensing the dampness left behind in the vinyl chair by my anger and fear.

reathing fire, I stalked over to the part of the Homicide I bull pen that I called home. It was composed of mismatched sets of wooden and metal desks that faced each other in clusters, echoing the long wooden "tables" of Department history. A few detectives from our section were already there and in motion on the worn blue carpet, typing up reports, making phone calls, taking bets on who would make it to the NBA finals.

I called the medical liaison's office to get the name of an agreed medical examiner to do my return-to-work evaluation. They gave me Dr. Mostafavi, an orthopedic surgeon I'd seen for a previous shoulder injury. I shoved his number in my jacket pocket to call later that day.

While I was leaving a message on Steve's desk, I saw Gena Cortez walking in with a civilian employee. I could barely discern the soft lilt of their voices as Cortez said something in Spanish. Resisting the urge to charge her right then and there, I waited until she got to her desk facing mine.

"Can I speak to you for a minute, *partner*?" I asked through clenched teeth.

"Charlotte, I'm surprised you made it in." Cortez seemed genuinely glad to see me. "Could it have been any worse out there?"

I walked around my desk and stood next to hers. "Gena, I've been talking to Stobaugh. From what he tells me of the chron record you filed, you forgot to mention a few things about last Friday."

Cortez got busy aligning the papers on her desk and reading the messages on her desk. "I really don't have time to talk about this right now, Charlotte. I've got to try and scare up some wits on these 187s that we pulled on Friday. And with you out . . ."

I sat down in a vacant chair next to her desk and leaned toward her so only she could hear. "You need to hone some of your observation skills before talking to any witnesses, Gena. Why did you put in your report that it was me who wanted to be taken to the hospital?"

"Did I?" she said.

Yeah, heifer, you did, I didn't say.

An expression flitted across Cortez's face too fast for me to read. "That must have been an oversight on my part. I'll get it back from Stobaugh today and make a correction."

That was a little too easy. "And while you're at it, you better take a look at some other parts of your report. You were a little sketchy about what really happened out there."

"Really? What'd I miss?" Suddenly she got all wide-eyed and innocent.

"The part about Cooper provoking that whole situation with Mitchell, for starters." I tried, and failed, to keep the bite out of my voice. "You know damn well he was out of line, Gena!"

She stilled her hands on the desk and considered them for a moment. "Look," she said calmly and faced me squarely, "after I interviewed Mitchell, I got a call from Tony Dreyfuss. He said that Cooper was a little stressed out but that he had talked to Cooper and straightened it out. Dreyfuss asked me to let them handle Cooper as an internal disciplinary problem and not to mention it or what happened with the boot in my report."

"Did you stop and think that maybe Cooper's on the Christopher List of Forty." The Christopher Commission report, released a few months ago in the aftermath of the Rodney King debacle, had identified a number of "bad apples" in the department, cops with a history of violence that should be monitored. Some were justifiably on the list, some not. It wouldn't surprise me if Mike Cooper's name was on it, and, from what I'd observed, for all the right reasons.

Cortez frowned, and her eyes glazed slightly. "I hadn't even considered that."

"Well, if he is, then I'm doubly pissed because he's hood-winked Dreyfuss over at South Bureau into covering for him big time—squealing like a stuck pig about a lack of judgment on my part in how *I* handled Mitchell at the scene. Without Dreyfuss knowing the whole story of what went on out there, it makes you and me look like some kind of estrogen-crazed females. That's about the *last* thing we need!"

Cortez's shoulders twitched up and down and her words came out strained. "Okay, Charlotte, maybe I was wrong, but I didn't think what happened was worth making into an intradepartmental beef. I worked with these guys at South Bureau. I don't want them thinking now that I'm downtown, I'd rat them out."

"Don't you think I feel the same way? I worked over there for five years, but wrong is wrong. And your first loyalty should be to the truth, not to your old bowling buddies. You know what's been going on out there in the streets, Gena. What if some wits come forward with a videotape? Your report is gonna look like a whitewash!"

"And what am I supposed to do?" Cortez's tight whisper had risen in pitch to a near-wail. "Rat out a man with more years in the Department than I've got fingers and toes? What would that get me? Ostracized, that's what. At least this way I've made a reasonably truthful report and got a couple of guys in the field who owe me big time."

"And you think having them in your debt is worth you jeopardizing your career? Don't forget, Gena, we're the only women who work Homicide up here who don't have 'coffee making' as part of our job description! Don't *think* that some of the boys in South Bureau have forgotten we made it ahead of them, and you shouldn't either. This is Parker Center, their precious Glass Palace, and there are gonna be those who try and throw a rock at you and hide their hand. The sooner you figure that out, the better off you're gonna be!"

Cortez shifted in her chair and studied her hands some more. "I'm really sorry, Charlotte. I was so pissed after Mitchell's lawyer got through with us and then the call from Dreyfuss . . . I'll get the report back from Stobaugh and correct it. Honest."

Was I seeing things or did a big cartoon balloon suddenly mushroom over Gena Cortez's head, saying, "She's lying?" I didn't know for sure, but I *did* know I was going to have to keep an eye on my new partner. "What happened when you questioned Mitchell?" I asked.

"Just about what you'd expect; he denied everything."

"Couldn't you convince the D.A. to make a case of probable cause out of the wallet?"

"Mitchell swore he left it in his car. Remember, he mentioned it at the scene *and* the hospital."

"Yeah, but he could have been setting us up."

She agreed but told me that right after we left the scene, one of the rioters took a baseball bat to the Q45's windshield and several suspects made off with everything in the car that wasn't attached. "Anybody could have stolen Mitchell's wallet and dropped it behind the stand, even Lewis himself, for all we know. That's his lawyer's contention, and she made a convincing enough case that the deputy D.A. who was supposed to file the case advised us to back off."

"Did anyone consider that maybe Lewis tried to steal the wallet from Mitchell and Mitchell shot him before we arrived?"

"Sure, but we can't find a weapon, and I didn't see any powder burns on Mitchell's hands when we had him in the car. Did you?"

"No," I had to admit, "but there *are* such things as rubber gloves. And if we had arrested him on the 243, we would have had his clothes to do a gunshot residue test."

"But Dreyfuss advised me when I called in not to pursue it!"

"As they say, hindsight is a mother."

We sat for a moment while I let my anger subside. When I could do it calmly, I asked her if anyone had surfaced who could place Mitchell at the scene.

She shook her head in disgust. "Which really bothers me. Even in all of the madness, you would think someone would have seen something." More relaxed now, Cortez reached for a couple of cookies from the pack I put on her desk and chewed one thoughtfully. "Which is why Stobaugh thinks this is gonna end up being a low-probability case for us. He wants us on some of our more productive cases, which, given as much as I've got to do, would be fine with me."

Good old Stobaugh. Always playing those percentages. "Did Firestone or the uniforms out there find the weapon?"

"Not that I know of." Cortez checked her watch. "Look, Charlotte, I gotta make some phone calls."

"I won't keep you then. Just one more thing." I paused on my way to my desk. "What if that had been a Latino physician out there Friday night, Gena? Would you have glossed over Cooper's behavior as easily in your report?"

Cortez paused with the last cookie halfway to her mouth. I took it out of her hand and held it up for her to see. "In my community, when people forget who they are, we call them Oreos." I crushed it slowly in my fist, letting bits of brown cookie dust fall on her desk. "Don't let them make one out of you."

I went back to my desk, unearthed my Cinque Lewis binder, and tucked it under my arm. As I left the Homicide I bull pen, I could see Gena Cortez out of the corner of my eye, still red-faced at her desk, brushing the cookie crumbs away.

CHAPTER 8

I Prefer My Oreos with Milk, Thank You

O n my way back home, I decided to stop by the supermarket to restock my empty freezer and refrigerator. A quick drive to my local market quickly showed me the error in my thinking; the store's parking lot was still littered with debris, the building's wide glass facade blinkered by plywood from one of those board-up companies whose stock I wish I'd been smart enough to buy a week ago. It wasn't until I got to the white folks' Westside that I found a fully functional supermarket, its aisles teeming with customers playing sudden-death bumper carts, baskets piled high with their personal version of emergency supplies—everything from powdered milk to prosciutto.

I felt as if I were in a bad Fellini movie, watching the crowd of Fairfax mensches and Westside Wandas practically duking it out in the aisles. That is, when they weren't glaring at me—the only black person in the store—like they were afraid I was going to club them to death with the baguette in my cart. I gave them all a wide berth, wandering around until I saw my reflection in a freezer case—pale face, bloodshot eyes, fingers laced through the front of the shopping cart like one of the homeless women downtown. I hadn't done anything like that since Keith and Erica were killed and I haunted our local Vons for months, aimlessly filling the cart with food for two and baby formula when there was only me to feed. That quick glimpse of myself brought me to my senses, and I left my cart in the aisle and got the hell out of there.

Once I got home, I started to make a halfhearted attempt at straightening up in preparation for Marisol, my housekeeper. With bus service still interrupted in parts of South Central and her phone out of order, I couldn't be sure she was coming. But after a few minutes I realized the day's activities had taken their toll on my shoulder and arm. The pain reminded me to call the doctor's office. I was surprised to be able to get an appointment for Tuesday afternoon.

Marisol arrived just as I was dozing off on the sofa. I napped while she worked around me. After she left, I poured myself a glass of juice, popped a painkiller, and opened up the paper. There was an article about the death toll during the riots, with a map of locations throughout South Central and other areas and brief details on each of those killed. The LAPD didn't play it up, and evidently the Metro editor wasn't up on his L.A. history, so there was no mention of Lewis's connection to the Black Freedom Militia, just his given name, Robert Anthony Lewis, age, and place of death on King Boulevard.

I turned on the television in time to catch the tail end of *The Oprah Winfrey Show*. It was a special show, broadcast from L.A. Oprah had flown in over the weekend, seemingly as motivated by a need to do something as I had been these last few days. But the show, while well intentioned, only exposed the tip of the iceberg.

As Oprah recapped the seething anger that had burst into the fiery destruction of the last six days, I sat in my bedroom and marveled at the irony: God made the world in six days, but the anger of His children was threatening to undo it all in the same amount of time. I tried to think of an appropriate prayer, but, of the dozens I had recited in Sunday school or on my knees at night with Grandmama Cile, the only one I could dredge up was "Father, forgive them; for they know not what they do."

Around six I was in my kitchen, pouring myself a second glass of wine and opening up the pizza that I had picked up, when Beast issued a warning bark and marched to the front door. The way the hairs stood up on his back, I was guessing it might not be a friend and instinctively reached for the gun in my purse. I eased up to the carved wooden door's peephole, hoping it was Mrs. Franklin checking up on me but taking no chances.

I yanked the door open to find Steve Firestone, in a pair of khakis and a navy blue windbreaker, jiggling the screen door. "Good God, Charlotte, you scared me!" He made a move to nuzzle my neck as he moved past me, but I jerked away in time. "I wasn't sure you were here."

"Didn't we agree that we'd only see each other in the office?" I wondered aloud as he tailed me into the kitchen.

"Aw, c'mon, pull the pinecone out of your ass. I brought you some beer." He held up a six-pack of beer, his version of a belated get-well card. Even more annoyed, I put the bottles in the fridge. As many times as I commiserated with Steve over drinks after work, you would have thought he'd have remembered that I didn't like beer, was allergic to it in fact.

The package was short one bottle, which Steve had already opened and was chugging as he helped himself to some pizza. Would you like some pizza? I started to ask, but then figured, why bother? I shook my head instead, grabbed my plate and wine, went into the dining room to eat.

Steve was right behind me. "Heard you talked to the lieutenant today."

"Yeah, and got a whole load of South Bureau shit dumped in my lap." I took a sip of my wine, hoping it would remove the bitter taste still in my mouth from the morning's meeting.

Steve said, "I've known Mike Cooper for a long time . . ."

"So have I."

". . . and he doesn't mean any harm. He's just one of the old dinosaurs in the Department."

"Yeah, a *Tyrannosaurus rex*. The man is dangerous, Steve."

"He's got to be, working gangs. You remember what that's like, Charlotte."

"Sure I do; it'll eat away at you if you're not careful. That's why most cops don't stay with CRASH more than a few years. But you should have been on that bus, Steve. Cooper was sure 'nough 'round the bend. That physician happened to be on the receiving end of a stockpile of anger Cooper's been storing up for fifteen, twenty years."

"Well, if you don't want that anger directed at you, I suggest you make some kind of peace with him about Friday."

It was a bit of advice I really didn't want to hear. We ate in silence until I asked if there were any breaks in the Lewis case.

"What case?" he snorted. "There are no witnesses, no weapon," he ticked off on the fingers of one hand. "All we've got is a body. Under the circumstances and based on Lewis's history, trying to get to the bottom of this one is going to be Heartbreak Hotel."

"Whether we like the victim or not, we've got an obligation to find out who did him." I was a little more emphatic than I would have liked, but I was hoping Steve wouldn't notice.

He did. "I don't need you to tell me how to do my job, Detective." Steve's voice dropped a few decibels. "But just between you and me—aren't you glad he's gone? Lewis was nothing but another piece of trash that made your life a misery. I *hate* niggers like him and the rest of his shit-for-brains homies on the streets these days."

"How can you say something like that, Steve? Have you looked in a mirror lately? Isn't you calling somebody a nigger kind of like the pot calling the kettle black?"

"I am nothing like these monkey-assed motherfuckers . . ."

"But you *are* black," I reminded him. "How would you like to be called out of your name like you did just now?"

"My *mother* was black, I'm . . ."

"What?" I prodded.

"*Different*," he said finally. "Like you. With your looks and education, you don't *have* to be black. You could be whoever and whatever you want."

"Black is what I am, Steve, what my parents are. I can't change that. I wouldn't want to."

He shrugged. "Well, you can keep all that 'Say it loud, I'm black and I'm proud' crap. I don't need it."

If I ever needed a sign that I shouldn't have gotten involved with Steve Firestone, that was it. Curious now, I asked, "Did you talk like this around your mother?"

Steve's neck and face began to flush a fascinating pinkish red. "My mother and father split up when I was ten," he said through compressed lips. "I didn't see a lot of her after that." He reached for his beer. "Dad got custody of me. My mother got the house in the Valley and the Cutty Sark. And the bruise collection." His voice echoing slightly through the upturned amber bottle. "She fell a lot when she drank."

I shuddered, suddenly chilled to the bone. It felt as if someone were walking over my grave. Steve caught my reaction out of the corner of his eye, bowed his head, left hand over his heart, and genuflected broadly with the beer bottle in his right. "Well, exc-u-u-u-use me, my Nubian queen."

I wasn't sure if he was being sarcastic or condescending or what. But letting him know my true feelings about his behavior was not in my best interests, especially given the favor I needed. I went to the kitchen and brought back two slices of pizza, a peace offering. "What about Dr. Mitchell? Is he a viable suspect?"

"I think there's something there." Steve mumbled around a mouthful of pizza and gulped it down. "Although his co-workers at the hospital say he's a pillar of the community, a couple of months back Cortez found an assault-with-a-deadly-weapon beef filed against him by his wife that subsequently got dropped."

"She gonna check into it?"

Steve rolled his shoulders. "With everyone in our section as overworked as they are, she's doing triple duty and so is everyone else. No telling when we'll be able to dig any deeper on Lewis."

With our normal caseload plus the riot-related deaths we

had picked up, I was sure everyone in RHD was up to his ass in alligators. I offered to help out on the Lewis case.

"Not with your conflict of interest," Steve replied. "Plus, with you being out on an injury, Stobaugh would have my shield if he found out."

"So I'll do it behind the scenes," I countered. "I can stop by the apartment buildings near the stand, see if any wits come forward, and turn over my findings to you."

"Uh-uh. It's still too hot down there to be interviewing anybody."

"Whatever you say, boss." I knew I was lying, and Steve should have, too. Going into a rough neighborhood had never stopped me when I needed to interview witnesses. It especially wouldn't this time.

I tried another approach. "You know, I went to high school with the guy who's head of Mitchell's medical group. I ran into him at the hospital Friday night, and he gave me his card. I'm sure I could get some information about Mitchell's background under the guise of catching up on old times without it raising Stobaugh's suspicions."

Steve still looked skeptical.

"I'll pass on anything I find to you, and once I'm released to return to work, maybe I can be a backup resource. I just don't want us to let this one go so fast."

Steve stared at me as if I were one of those street-corner preachers, totally sincere and totally insane. "You've really got a bug up your ass about this one, don't you?"

"Wouldn't you?"

He threw up his hands in defeat. "If you feel you need something to do, be my guest. Stobaugh's already made it perfectly clear he's not that enthusiastic about this one—it's just not one we're likely to clear." He pointed a piece of pizza my way. "I still got a problem with you pursuing this. You're way too close to be objective."

I touched Steve's arm. "I want the truth about Lewis. And the truth is always objective. I promise I'll be discreet. If I can prove Lewis did my family in the process, then it's worth the trouble. And the risk."

"If it gets back to Stobaugh that I knew what you're doing, both your and my ass will be in a serious wringer. You'll report everything you find directly to me?"

I raised my unencumbered left hand solemnly. "Scout's honor."

"Okay," he conceded finally. "We could use the help."

Steve went into the kitchen for another beer. I followed him and sat down to sort the mail the housekeeper had left stacked on top of my Cinque Lewis binder on the breakfast table. A few minutes later he came up behind me and startled me by lightly stroking my hair. I jumped up and stood in the doorway.

"What's the matter?" he asked.

"Don't go there, Steve."

I moved left, so did he. I feinted to the right, and there he was. Finally he placed himself directly in my path. Beast heard our moving feet and came to scope out the situation. He stood close to my side, staring intently at Steve's leg like it was a smoked beef bone he just needed the go-ahead from me to tear into.

"Look," I mumbled, "I need to feed and walk this dog, take a pain pill, and get some sleep, especially with my doctor's appointment tomorrow."

"So what are you, one of those females who gives a man a little taste but won't let him enjoy the full meal?" Steve took a step toward me, growling my name in a piss-poor imitation of Barry White. He was stopped by a real growl coming from somewhere around his kneecap.

I moved around him and whistled. Beast bulldozed his way past Steve as if he wasn't there and stood at my side, begging for pizza scraps. "Seen the family lately?" I had found out quite by accident that asking Steve about his estranged family was a surefire way to ruin his day. It was the first time I had used the knowledge deliberately.

And to obviously good effect, by the look on his face. "They're okay now, but they were so scared I had to go down there and calm them down," he said, avoiding my eyes.

So that's why his machine had been on since Friday. Knowing Steve, if he was staying with his ex and kids, I was quite sure he wasn't sleeping on the sofa. And if he was going to Hump City with the ex, what was he doing sniffing around me? I considered this while I busied myself with the dog and finally decided it wasn't worth thinking about. "Come on, Beast, let's walk Detective Firestone to the door."

Steve didn't move immediately. Beast stood in the middle of the kitchen and gave him a tight-jawed stare as if to say, *Time's up, asshole. Didn't the lady ask you to leave?*

We waited until Steve drained his beer. He moved to put the bottle on the back porch for recycling. Beast responded with another warning growl. I took the bottle away from him. "Don't worry about the trash. I'll dispose of it when we get back."

As chilly as I was with Steve, I was plenty hot when I returned from my walk and itching to talk to Katrina. She wasn't at home yet or in her office, so I tried her cell phone and caught her at the YMCA downtown.

I could hear my best friend huffing and puffing on one of the treadmills we usually walked together three times a week. *Wheel of Fortune* was playing on a TV in the background, and I could imagine her special carrot-and-wheatgrass juice blend in a bottle somewhere nearby.

"He sounds just like some of these sorry-assed brothers I've been dealing with," she huffed. "Where does he get off thinking he can shack up with his ex for three days, not even call you to say 'Hello, dog, how you doing?' and then come over to your house with a six-pack of beer, rub up on you, and get hot pussy like it's running out the tap?"

I winced, not at Katrina's par-for-the-course bluntness, but at her on-the-money read of Steve Firestone's behavior. I just hoped there was no one in the gym who knew she was talking to me.

"And you *know* what it is," she said. " 'Once they get black, they can't go back.' "

"Get it straight, Katrina. He never, as you so crudely put it, 'got' any, at least not from this black woman."

"You know what I mean! From what you've told me, boyfriend's got some more-than-skin-deep identity problems. But if he can beg up on some punannie from you, he's got the best of both worlds. He gets to keep nice blonde wife in the suburbs . . ."

"Jessica's a brunette," I corrected.

"What*ever* . . . and then he can come to the 'hood and get buck wild with you whenever he wants."

Mrs. Franklin's comments about Steve cruising my house came to mind. "It's not about that," I argued as much to convince myself as Katrina. "We work together, for heaven's sake!"

"Don't kid yourself, girlfriend! I've seen his type before, on both sides of the color line, and as far as I'm concerned, he ain't nothing but a beer-guzzling, kinky sex-loving wannabe. And, frankly, if I gotta eat 'em, baby, I prefer my Oreos with milk, thank you!"

Katrina had taken on that tone that told me she was getting wound up to really preach. But I lost the thread of what she was saying as my own peanut gallery piped up. What *was* the deal with Steve, anyway? Maybe talking with him about work as much as I did was a sorry substitute for the kind of soul-mate relationship I had with Keith. Maybe he was confusing my interest in the work with an interest in *him*. But after tonight it was pretty clear Steve wanted to use me as a way station on the road to reconciliation with his wife. And even clearer that continuing to see him in anything other than a business setting was a very bad idea.

Katrina was still going strong. I decided to change the subject by telling her I had run into Aubrey Scott.

"Class of sixty-seven, the brainiac on the basketball team, right? Ooh-*wee,* what a Dark Gable he used to be! I bet he's bald now and a hundred pounds overweight!"

Katrina, who could have joined me in singing backup for Chubby Checker in junior high school, still did regular battle with the scales over that last fifteen pounds, so everyone looked heavy to her.

"Uh-uh. Brother is still fine, maybe even better looking than he was then."

"What's he doing? Did you get his number?" Katrina was

single again, after a tempestuous, three-year marriage to a record producer she met at the Playboy Jazz Festival. Since she was hitting the gym five days a week, I assumed she was getting ready for the hunt for Mr. Wonderful Number Three.

"I've got his card. He's head of an emergency medical group now."

"Is he still married to that leprechaun-looking girl—what was her name?"

"Janet Murphy, and I don't know."

I shook my head and laughed at myself.

"What's so funny?" Katrina asked.

"Nothing. It's just that . . . I haven't felt this way in years."

"Felt like what?"

"Like maybe I should actually use a card a man gave me."

"Well, it's about damn time!"

"Katrina, he's probably still married to Janet Murphy and has a passel of kids."

"You'll never know unless you *dial them digits*!"

As I was hanging up the phone, my hand swept Aubrey's card off the nightstand and onto the floor. I picked it up and felt the same tingle as I had talking to Katrina.

Why would I have that reaction to Aubrey Scott after all these years? There was a risk-free way of finding out. I placed the card near the telephone, a reminder to call Dr. Aubrey Scott tomorrow to talk about his knowledge and opinion of his colleague, Dr. Lance Mitchell.

CHAPTER 9

A CLANDESTINE MEETING ADDS SPICE

Once called Santa Barbara Avenue, the street where Cinque Lewis's body was found had been renamed in 1968 in honor of Dr. Martin Luther King, Jr. Funny how streets renamed to commemorate a man of peace were usually the rowdiest in the city. Someone had spray-painted the name Rodney over Martin's on the street sign at the corner where the taco stand stood. It made me wonder how many cities in America had a street named after a black man that *didn't* commemorate his violent death or ass-whipping.

I parked my car in the glass-strewn spot where Dr. Mitchell's Infiniti had been Friday night. I noticed how far away he had parked his car from where he was delivering the medicine—at least a half a block. No way would I have parked a fifty-thousand-dollar car so far away from where I needed to go, whether I was going to get some burritos later or not.

A couple of young Latinos—maybe late teens to early twenties, wearing highly polished Stacey Adams wing tips, flannel shirts, and Gap chinos doing some serious hang time around their behinds—were standing on the concrete steps of 1559, the brick apartment building closest to the stand. The black bandannas sticking out of their pockets and "MLK" tattoos on the side of their necks and hands told me they rolled with the Muy Loco Killers, the dominant gang in the area.

"Who got smoked?" the big one asked when I told him I was investigating a homicide.

"A man by the name of Robert Lewis." I produced the Polaroid from the crime scene and an earlier photo of Lewis from my murder book. "His street name was Cinque. Either of you seen him hanging around anywhere?"

The other kid, on closer inspection, appeared to be black and Latino, with a gap in his mouth where one of his front teeth had been. "I ain't never seen him." Snagglepuss handed the photo to his obese partner.

Gordo agreed: "I 'ont think he was from none of the sets 'round here."

Residents of the nearby buildings weren't any more forthcoming. Hurrying to work or hustling their children to the school bus, most of them were immigrants and probably illegal from the averted looks I got when I told them I was with *la policía*. All they wanted was to put me and the violence of the past few days as far behind them as possible. I ended up back on the steps with Gordo and Snagglepuss. I was just getting their names—Hiram Rubio and LaJohn Myers—when a disheveled black male opened the foyer door. He was muttering to himself and twisting the frayed edge of a once-green letterman's sweater that engulfed his thin frame like a big blanket. Embroidered on the big H at the pocket was the year 1966. No way did this man graduate then; he was seventy if he was a day.

"Why 'ont you ax ol' Riley in number fourteen what he seen?" LaJohn suggested. "His windows face the stand."

Riley's eyes, brown irises rimmed in milky blue, darted about, then rested on a spot somewhere above my head. He took my card and looked past it to the street beyond. "I see everything that happens in this neighborhood, Detective. Name's Jerry Riley, but they call me the Sentinel."

"Like the black newspaper?" I asked.

I wasn't sure why Hiram and LaJohn started tittering until Riley's hostile eyes turned and lasered through the boys, then zeroed in on me. "No! Like my namesake, the prophet Jeremiah, God set me to stand guard over the nations and kingdoms, to root out, and pull down, and destroy, and to throw down the evils of the world."

There wasn't a hint of humor on the Sentinel's face or in his fire-and-brimstone voice. My horoscope in the paper that morning predicted a clandestine meeting would add spice, but I wasn't expecting this.

"Okay, Mr. Sentinel, were you on duty Friday?" I left my notebook in my purse; I sensed the chances of getting anything useful from this old man were slim to none.

"That was the third day the streets ran with the blood of our warriors," he intoned. "I had taken up my position on the parapet—" an ashy finger pointed up to an iron railing surrounding the building's rooftop, "—when I saw the armored land carrier arrive." He gestured down the street. Hiram and LaJohn hooted and pounded each other's shoulders.

"You mean the police bus?"

"No, it was a black armored *land carrier* with little windows in the sides. The enemy forces inside had on shiny helmets and carried ray guns. They approached a young warrior king and tried to subdue him, but he fought back valiantly."

I had a hunch he was describing the Mitchell situation. I asked if the warrior king was driving a car.

"*X-wing fighter,* Detective. It was a white metallic X-wing fighter."

Maybe the old man was having a *Star Wars* flashback. Or just maybe he was describing Lance Mitchell's Q45. As I got out my notepad, I could hear Grandmama Cile's chastising voice in my head: *Never judge a book by its cover.*

"The warrior king had emerged from his fighter," the Sentinel continued, "and had spoken to one of his subjects in a ringing declaration of peace and prosperity. When he returned, the invaders tried to cut him down and make slaves again of our race!"

"Where did this speech take place?" The old man pointed to the left, in the direction of the stand. My heart fluttered. "How was this warrior king dressed?"

The Sentinel frowned, his hands trying to sculpt what was in his mind's eye. "His raiment was the green of the whispering pines, and he wore an ebony coat made of the skins of animals proud to be sacrificed for such noble shoulders."

Mitchell had been wearing dark green scrubs and a black leather jacket. If my semicoherent witness was to be believed, then Lance Mitchell *had* been with another man, most likely Cinque Lewis, behind that taco stand. I handed the Sentinel the Polaroid of Lewis. "Was the warrior king with a man who looked like this?"

He brushed off my question and the photo. "In the sorry history of our tribe, the enemy has always tried to destroy the New Zulu Nation of God." He clutched LaJohn's arm. "They tried in Watts, and now they're at it again. But you cannot surrender. You are God's chosen people!"

LaJohn tried to throw the old man off by circling his arm. "Bet' keep yo mu'fuckin hands offa me, ol' man!"

The Sentinel reached out for me. "The enemy aliens can take them prisoners, torture them, even kill them with their lasers, but the New Zulu Nation of God will not surrender!"

I backed him up by dangling the Polaroid in front of his face again. "Mr. Riley, did you see this man at Mel's Tacos with Dr. Mitchell?"

Suddenly Riley's head snapped back like a boxer on the wrong end of a Muhammad Ali combination. "Doctor? I'm not going to any doctors!" He hurried away from me, up the steps and into the apartment building's foyer, where he started pacing in a tight circle, talking to himself. The loose thread from his sweater got caught in the door, and I could see it pull at the old man's sleeve before he broke free and stumbled down the hallway toward the stairs.

Neither young man was laughing now. "You shouldn'a said nuthin' 'bout no doctors, Five-oh," Hiram chided. "The Sentinel's a regular in the loco ward out at the VA. He *hates* him some doctors!"

"Where'd he go?"

"Probably up to the roof or out the back door," LaJohn replied. "It'll take him a while to chill out. Maybe you should come back tomorrow."

I spent a good hour searching the area for the weapon and even retraced our path down King to the foul-smelling doorway where I huddled with Mitchell, waiting for Cortez to bring help.

Nothing. Nada. Zip.

Out of the corner of my eye I could see a black-and-white pull up alongside me. The window slid down, two men whistled, then one of them said, "Hey, mama, you got some fries to go with that shake?"

I could feel my neck getting hot. Was this what female citizens had to put up with on the streets? I whipped around to give them a good piece of my mind and found myself scowling into the faces of Chip LeDoux and Darren Wright, the Southwest Division uniforms who were my escorts to the hospital Friday.

I could tell Darren had made the comment from the way he was leaning across the mobile digital terminal, his wide brown face creased by a big, mischievous grin. LeDoux was riding shotgun, the bulky Kevlar vest squeezing his midsection, making him look like the Officer Teddy Bear toys they sell at the Police Academy gift shop. I noticed above the bandage on LeDoux's arm the edge of a tattoo and a quintet of five-year hash marks on his shirt sleeve. Given the amount of gray in his black mustache and close-cropped hair and the leathery crinkles around his blue eyes, I was betting he was more than halfway to number six. Almost thirty years on the job, God bless him.

"Wha's up, Detective Justice?" LeDoux smiled.

"Not much, fellas. Just making another sweep of the area for the weapon in that Lewis homicide."

Wright, a little younger and trimmer than his partner, his bald head gleaming like Charles Dutton's, leaned across the terminal again. "You ain't got no business out here alone, Detective."

The drawl in his stern voice made me think of my Texas-bred neighbor Mrs. Franklin. "These gangs out here have no fear of cops at all since the riots. Besides, if that gun was out here, the patrol unit for this area would have picked it up by now."

"I thought this was your area."

"Naw, we've got a sector up in Baldwin Hills," LeDoux explained.

"Not a bad way to wait out your retirement," I joked. Baldwin Hills was just north of my parent's house, in another one of L.A.'s Negro golden ghettos. A few car burglaries, some breaking and enterings—B&Es—nothing too rough. But why were they way over here?

Wright must have read my mind. "We're Code 7, on our way to grab some breakfast, when we spotted you. Would you like to join us?"

I hated to say no to that big smile, but I really had no interest being in a quasi-social setting with a cop, even one as cute as Wright. But it made me wonder if Darren Wright was single, and whether my girlfriend Katrina might be interested.

"How's it comin' with the investigation?" LeDoux asked.

"Slowly, but I was just talking to a potential witness who may have seen the whole thing go down."

"That so?" Wright asked.

"Yeah. Old guy in the building next door by the name of Riley. I thought I was getting somewhere until he upped and ran off when I said the word *doctor*. Couple of MLKs in the building say he's a got a season's pass to the psych unit out at the VA."

LeDoux and Wright looked at each other solemnly for a moment, then busted out laughing. "Sounds like you're getting kind of desperate, Detective, goin' after the schizos," LeDoux teased, shaking his head.

"Well, if you or the unit that has this sector see him today, would you call Steve Firestone at RHD?"

"We'll put the word out," LeDoux promised, making a note on his clipboard in a cramped, southpaw scrawl. "He'll turn up somewhere."

"Heard in roll call that guy Friday was one of those fugitive radicals from the seventies," Wright said.

"Well, he ain't gonna be no fugitive no more," LeDoux joked. "Somebody ran that old boy to ground like a rabbit in huntin' season." He half-laughed and drew a bead with his finger, turned, and squeezed off an imaginary shot at his partner's head.

"That shit ain't funny, man." Wright had quickly lost his smile. Maybe he heard the undercurrent in LeDoux's joke, too.

LeDoux punched him playfully in the shoulder and laughed. "Just kiddin', man. My partner here is a little cranky, Detective. Let us go so I can get some caffeine into him."

I let my hand rest on the car door and peered inside. "Hey, if I didn't say it before, thanks for having my back last Friday. I haven't had a chance to send out my thank-you notes."

"Think nothing of it," Wright smiled. "We gotta take care of our own."

"And we'll find that old man for you," LeDoux assured me, "even if he is nuttier than a fruitcake."

As they drove away laughing, I realized I felt kind of silly making such a big deal about Riley, but my gut told me there was more to his words than met the eye. *Never judge a book by its cover.* And I wasn't going to let two cynical patrolmen turn me around, good-natured though they may be.

I checked my watch. Almost nine. Not a bad time to take a ride to the beach.

Driving to the Marina has always been a weird experience for me. I could never go there without thinking of a sliver of sand a few miles south called Dockweiler State Beach. Beginning at the end of Imperial Highway, the southern end of Dockweiler was where my parents used to go as teenagers and was one of the few beaches open to "colored" in their day. They took us there one Sunday for a picnic, before it was swallowed up by LAX in an eminent-domain grab. Matt and Joymarie's beach was deserted now, part of a condemned stretch of no-man's land under the airport's flight patterns, permanently blanketed by engine noise and lethal mists of jet fuel.

I remember riding back from Dockweiler Beach that day to our house on the Eastside, through swampland and fields of celery, wild mustard, and fennel. That swamp was now called Marina del Rey, a Fantasy Island for upscale runaways, running from the bad weather back east, bad air in the valleys, or a bad marriage right in their own backyards. And, in keeping with changing times, black folks populated the Marina now like they did Dockweiler in my parents' day—strolling along the channels and shopping centers as if it were the only beachfront property open to them. There was even a soul food restaurant in a shopping center across from where Aubrey worked, although, truth be told, it was frequented as often by whites as blacks.

CaER was located on the second floor of a wood-sided office building. I waited in the lobby until a door opened and Aubrey walked briskly to the receptionist's desk. He was dressed in street clothes—a white linen shirt, a long drape of taupe gabardine slacks, tasseled brown loafers, and no socks. Only the stack of files in his arms and the redness in his eyes hinted that Aubrey Scott was more than just another well-heeled buppie on his way to some celebrity gym or lunch at the Brentwood Country Club.

He ushered me into his office and settled me into a chair. "Make yourself at home. I'll be right back."

Aubrey's office was dominated by a high-tech glass and polished-steel desk on which sat the CaER name and logo in Lucite, a Nikon camera, slide projector, and a big pile of folders and reports. There were books on emergency medicine, medical group management, and mergers and acquisitions on wall-mounted shelves to the right of the door. The wall on the left was dominated by a huge tropical seascape that appeared to undulate toward me. The other two walls were floor-to-ceiling windows that looked out on the shopping center that housed that soul food restaurant to the west and a condo development to the north. I didn't see any photos of his wife, kids, or a girl-friend on Aubrey's desk or on the shelves. None of a boyfriend either—these days a woman would be a fool not to consider all the possibilities.

Aubrey returned and sat behind his desk, but reached out to me with a smile. "So are you back at work?"

"Officially, no—not until I get a clean bill of health from the doctor. Which I hope to do today."

"So is this an official or unofficial visit?"

I tried to suppress the color I could feel rising to my cheeks. "A little bit of both, I guess." I paused a moment and cleared my throat before explaining I was helping out on the Cinque Lewis murder and just wanted to ask him a few questions. "We know that Dr. Mitchell was off duty when we encountered him on King Boulevard . . ."

"That's right. Lance had pulled four consecutive twelve-hour shifts at the hospital, and the strain was getting next to him. I finally told him he needed to go home and get some rest."

I could relate to that. "So what time did Mitchell leave?"

"About three thirty, a couple of hours before the others. But after almost forty-eight hours, I wasn't going to hold that against him. Lance and his staff had put forth a Herculean effort. I knew my instincts about him had been right."

"What do you mean?"

"We brought Lance into the group as a partner just about two years ago. He'd been in L.A. for a number of years, though, knocking around in a bunch of ERs with a group called Valley Emergency Medical Care Partners."

I asked Aubrey why Mitchell joined CaER. "A couple of reasons. For one, we're the fastest growing emergency medical group in the state." Aubrey sat up a little straighter in his chair, transformed by my question into CaER's publicity director. "We got that way by specializing in inner-city areas, offering a higher level of sophisticated care than ER docs who work those carriage-trade markets."

"Beg pardon?"

"You know—soccer injuries, skateboard accidents, the occasional heart attack—suburban stuff. Definitely *not* what you see in an inner-city hospital. We provide skilled professionals like Lance with the means to practice the highest level of emergency medicine without all the administrative or political hassles, and for a decent wage."

Very decent, if Mitchell's car was any indication. "You said there were two reasons he came to CaER."

The features of Aubrey's face shifted into something harder, less open. "I don't feel comfortable discussing Lance's personal business."

"If we're going to get to the bottom of what happened out there, we need to find out everything we can about Dr. Mitchell," I reminded him.

He was still uneasy. "Well, I doubt that this would be helpful."

"Does it have anything to do with the assault on his wife?"

Aubrey seemed relieved I had brought it up. "Lance's wife is a class A bitch. That whole assault nonsense was her just trying to get even. She had jumped in front of his car to stop him from moving some things out of their house in Beverly Hills, then lied and swore he tried to run her over." Lance had been trying to leave his wife for a long time, Aubrey said, before he made his final escape on Valentine's Day to a house the couple still owned in Baldwin Hills.

"Brotherman's timing was not the best," I noted. "So they're not final yet?"

Aubrey shook his head sadly. "They'll be fighting over practice values and real-estate appraisals for years."

"Sounds like the missus is a serious gold digger."

"You'd be surprised. You ever hear of Holly Hightower Mitchell?"

"You mean Dr. Holly, the relationship expert?" Now that *was* a surprise. My grandmother listened to her radio show all the time. "Isn't Dr. Holly getting a divorce kind of like the cobbler's children having no shoes?"

"That's how she took it. More than the insult to her ego is the effect the split could have on her syndication deal. One hundred and ten stations tuned into a divorced 'Love Doctor'?" Aubrey threw up his hands, palms to the ceiling. "But I can't see what that would have to do with the LAPD's investigation."

"Now that you've explained it, probably nothing," I conceded. "I'm just trying to get a feel for Lance Mitchell, figure out why he would take such a chance out there on King Boulevard. We've talked to the patient and the hospital staff, so his alibi checks out. I'm just wondering if there was some other reason he'd go out of his way to deliver some medicine to a patient."

Aubrey perked up at that. "What kind of medicine was it?"

"Something called Cardura, I think."

"That's a hypertension medication," Aubrey explained and sat back in his chair. "Knowing how devoted Lance can be to his patients, that doesn't surprise me."

I asked Aubrey why he had loaned Lance money that day.

"He hadn't been able to get to a bank, and I just gave him some cash rather than see him risk going to one of the ATM machines around the hospital. Lance does dumb shit like that sometimes. Thinks he's invincible."

"Borrowing a couple of hundred dollars just seems odd if all you're going to do is drop off some medication, grab a burrito, and go home," I noted. "Is there any other reason Dr. Mitchell would have been over on King near Vermont?"

It turned out patients from that neighborhood were sent to California Medical Center a lot. "Maybe he saw a kid he knew out there about to torch a building or something and tried to stop him," Aubrey said.

"Or maybe he saw a kid having a beef with the victim."

Aubrey frowned. "That's possible, I guess, but if he did, wouldn't he be needlessly putting himself under suspicion by not telling the truth?"

"Sound like something Dr. Mitchell would do to help a kid in trouble?"

He shrugged. I intentionally let the question hang in the air, the silence stretching out a bit, until Aubrey stepped in to fill it. "Is there anything else you want to know?"

"Anything else you want to tell me?"

"Not about Dr. Mitchell."

For a moment I thought the sun must have broken through the coastal haze, because I swear I could feel the temperature change in Aubrey's office. We sat for a minute regarding each other, Aubrey's smile seeping into my pores and warming me like his hand on my shoulder did Friday night.

"So how's Janet?" I tried to distract him with an unexpected question like I had with Steve the night before.

This man didn't even blink. "I wouldn't know. We've been divorced for years."

"Oh, I'm sorry." It was the first out-and-out lie I told Aubrey Scott.

"I'm not. It was the best decision I ever made." The smile again, briefly, then a cloud passed over his face. "Perris told me about your husband and daughter."

I nodded, wondering just how much my brother had blabbed in the ER Friday night.

"That must have been rough. Was it an accident?"

Thank God Perris didn't tell him everything. "In a way," I said with an odd sense of relief.

Aubrey nodded, thankfully letting it go. "You ever remarry?" he asked.

"No. You?"

"Nope. Despite rumors to the contrary, being married to a doctor isn't all it's cracked up to be. Especially an emergency doc. Most women just don't understand that removing a splinter from a construction worker one minute and trying to stuff some kid's intestines back in his body cavity the next might make me a little jumpy by the time I get home. And not that interested in going to some Westside hair-tossing restaurant or charity ball."

"Been there, done that," I laughed. "Being a cop is hell on your private life, too, especially if you work Homicide. Most men don't understand the long hours, getting paged in the middle of the night, just when they might have had something else in mind."

"Been there, done that," he agreed.

"They expect you to drop your career at the door and be

totally tuned into them—dinner on the table and decked out in a black negligee."

"Hmmm . . . that could be interesting," he said.

You sure left yourself open on *that* one, I chastised myself. I decided to shine it on, and the warmth his comment stimulated in me somewhere below my waist.

I was saved by a knock at the door. Before Aubrey could answer, Lance Mitchell walked in, wearing an oversized purple and black nylon sweatsuit, an *Arsenio Hall Show* baseball cap pulled low over his eyes, and preceded by Aubrey's very flustered assistant. "Hey, man, have you still got my camera . . . ," he said from behind her.

"I told Dr. Mitchell you were in a meeting," the assistant began, "but he . . ."

Mitchell's confident bop was stalled when he saw me sitting in Aubrey's office. "Charlotte just stopped by to say 'hi,' " Aubrey explained. "She's on her way to a doctor's appointment."

"Looks like she already has one," Lance mumbled and turned to Aubrey. "Where have you been, man? I've been calling your house since Friday!"

"You could have left a message with the service. I've been trying to reach *you*."

"I'm off until tomorrow. I didn't think I was obligated to check in with you, too," he said testily, with an uneasy glance in my direction.

"Of course you're not." The tone in Mitchell's voice brought out an edge in Aubrey's, too. "But after everything that went down, I was just concerned . . ."

"I didn't mean to jump down your throat, man," Mitchell apologized. "I decided to stay with a friend for a few days. After someone stole the keys out of my car Friday night, I didn't feel comfortable going back to my house until I could get the locks changed."

"Well, you should have said something," Aubrey replied. "Do you need to talk to me privately? We can step outside . . ."

"No, it's nothing like that. I just wanted to get my partner's distribution check."

Aubrey nodded to his assistant, who left the room and returned with a long blue envelope.

"Did you take out the two hundred I borrowed?" Lance asked as he slit open the envelope.

Aubrey waved him away. "Don't worry about it."

Mitchell's eyes darted from me across the desk to Aubrey and back again. "Dr. Scott and I were just catching up on old times. We went to high school together," I explained, hoping the half lie would put him at ease. "How are you?"

"Fine, especially after I got past your partner. That Detective Cortez is something else."

"She does her job," I said cautiously.

"But Sandra Douglass, does hers *better*." He laughed bitterly. "I guess all lawyers aren't like that shark my wife hired."

I was beginning to get a feel for the war brewing between the Drs. Mitchell. In the awkward silence that followed, Mitchell asked Aubrey if I told him why my partner was so interested in whether he knew the man at the taco stand. In an attempt to cut him off at the pass, I quickly gave Aubrey the abridged Cinque Lewis story.

"Doesn't sound like a revolutionary to me," he said.

"He wasn't," I replied. "Far as I'm concerned, he was a drug dealer and a murderer."

Maybe I said it a little too forcefully because I saw a funny look pass between Aubrey and Mitchell. "But from what Ms. Douglass tells me," Mitchell added quickly, "Lewis was also the primary suspect in the murder of your husband and child."

With Sandra Douglass's mother and mine serving together in the same social clubs—most notably the Bench and Bar Mother's Guild, L.A.'s black matriarchs' bragging-rights club—there was no way she wouldn't have heard the full back story on Cinque Lewis. But the way the intimate details of people's private lives got dissected by the L.A. niggerati still made my skin crawl.

A gasoline truck rumbled past in the street below us. Inside, it was so quiet I could hear those rats pissing all over that cotton, just like my father always said.

"I . . . I . . . didn't know," Aubrey stammered. "Perris never mentioned . . ."

"That's why I'm not working the Lewis case—conflict of interest. That and my injury." I gestured toward my restrained arm and turned so I could see Mitchell's face. "I think my superiors are concerned I'd want to pin a medal on whoever did Lewis instead of investigating the case."

Mitchell's face was stone-cold. "Or look the other way."

This brother needed a *major* attitude adjustment. But before I could think of a good comeback, he had turned to Aubrey. "You haven't forgotten about the TAGOUT reception tonight at Spiral West, have you?" He hefted the Nikon on Aubrey's desk. "And don't forget to bring my camera." He checked the display on the top of the camera. "I've got about a dozen exposures left. Take some shots for the group's newsletter."

"Isn't TAGOUT that tagging crew?" I asked. "You're involved with them?"

"They prefer to be called 'writers' or 'aerosol artists,' " Mitchell replied, setting the camera down with a little laugh. "We're putting on an art exhibit of some of our at-risk youth's work and giving a scholarship to one of the kids in the program this evening."

"You mean *you're* giving a scholarship."

Aubrey turned to me. "Lance donated most of the money himself for one of the kids to attend CalArts, including room and board."

I made some approving noises—they were talking about a good chunk of change. Aubrey looked across the desk at me, eyebrow raised. "Would you like to go? I could pick you up."

"A cop is probably the last person those kids will want to see tonight." The same could be said of Mitchell, from the look of him.

"I think young people need to understand that not every police officer they meet is out to get them," Aubrey countered, ignoring the face Mitchell was making. "Sure wasn't the case for Lance."

The intensity of Aubrey's smile made me fumble through my purse for no reason. "I don't know. I'm not into high-profile events like that."

"Don't push her, man," Lance cut in. "If she's not interested . . ."

"It's not that . . ."

"If you're not working the case," Aubrey prodded, "why can't you go?"

He had a point, at least on the surface. Plus I could use the opportunity to learn a little more about the increasingly jumpy Lance Mitchell. "Okay, I surrender. What time?"

"I've got it down here for seven, and the awards presentation is at eight." Aubrey looked to Mitchell for confirmation. "Right, Lance?"

Mitchell was staring out the window. "Oh, yeah . . . that's right."

I jotted down my address and phone number and gave it to Aubrey. "How about I pick you up at a quarter to seven?" he asked.

"Okay," I said, mentally scanning my wardrobe for something to wear that might not look too gruesome with a sling.

CHAPTER 10

ANOTHER ONE BITES THE DUST

After my doctor's appointment, I called Steve from my cell phone. I was surprised to catch him at his desk, even more surprised at the pout I could hear in his voice. "I don't have time to play games, Justice," he groused.

Maybe he was still pissed about what happened—or rather didn't—last night. Whatever the reason, I decided to overlook his funky attitude and stick to the business at hand. "The doctor sprung me, no pun intended," I told him. "Limited duty for ten days, then, depending on how I feel, I can come back full speed after that."

"Good. You'll be back in the office tomorrow?"

"If you'll convince Stobaugh to let me work with Cortez on the Lewis case."

Steve mulled it over for a bit. "I *could* put in a good word for you with the lieutenant. But what's in it for me?"

"How about I clear up all our ninety-day reports?" Our captain had been on a new campaign to get our progress reports on open murder investigations filed in a more timely fashion. It was a challenge that I knew was near and dear to my promotion-driven lieutenant's heart and therefore Steve's and mine.

"Not good enough," he said.

"What then?"

He lowered his voice to a whisper. "You know what I want."

I felt my chest tighten. No way was I going down that road, I didn't care how hard Steve tried to force it.

"Why don't I just take this up with Lieutenant Stobaugh?"

"He won't like you going over my head."

"He'll like it even less if I tell him the quid pro quo you want in exchange for letting me work the Lewis case."

That shut him up. "You want to hear the rest of my news?" I asked sweetly. More silence. Good. "I talked to an old man in the apartment just west of the scene who I think saw something." I related my encounter with Jerry Riley into the silence at the other end, stressing my hunch that, beneath his disjointed gibberish, the old man may have seen Mitchell talking to Lewis prior to the murder.

Steve let out a little half laugh in spite of himself. "What's the New Zulu Nation of God he was talking about, some new gang? Mandingo their mascot?"

I clenched my teeth so hard I could taste my fillings. But I wasn't rising to the bait. "I *told* you Riley had some mental problems. But even so, he did describe a man dressed like Dr. Mitchell who appeared to be talking to someone *before* we arrived on the scene."

"Did you show him the photo of Lewis?"

"I did, but he freaked and ran off. Maybe Cortez can try him again later today or tomorrow. Just be sure she doesn't mention doctors. It makes him *real* agitated."

"Probably just some nut case burnt out on too much Thunderbird," Steve concluded with a laugh, "but I'll have her check him out. But I still don't approve of you endangering yourself on the streets without adequate backup." Steve lowered his voice again. "I want you live and well to take care of that unfinished business we've got."

I ignored the urge to get him straightened out right then and there, and told him instead about my conversation with Aubrey

Scott and the fact that Dr. Mitchell took off a couple of hours before his shift was over.

I could hear the scratching of Steve's pen again. "Your doctor friend give you any potential motives for Mitchell doing Lewis?"

"Not really, but I think Dr. Scott was holding something back. He really got lockjaw when I started asking why Dr. Mitchell joined their medical group. Said something about not getting into his personal business."

"Probably got something to do with the domestic beef. A lot of couples go through that, so I don't know why it'd be such a big deal."

"I don't think that was it," I said, wondering if Steve was talking about Lance Mitchell or his own situation. "I think Mitchell may have left some dirt behind him when he split from his old medical group."

"Anything else?"

"Dr. Scott let something drop that made me think Dr. Mitchell is the type who'd intervene if he saw a kid he knew in some kind of trouble."

"That's a good way to get shot."

"Or end up shooting someone yourself."

Steve's silence told me he was thinking. "What's your spin on it?"

"Dr. Scott said Mitchell has treated a lot of these kids in the ER over the last two years, so maybe he did see something go down on the street with a kid he knew. He's also connected to TAGOUT's antigraffiti program, which is chock full of reformed thuglettes. He's involved in a reception tonight for some kids in the program, so I'm gonna go and check it out, if that's okay with you."

"What time's the reception?" he asked.

"Seven. It won't take more than a couple of hours, Steve."

He finally relented. "But just don't go charging off and get your ass caught in a wringer," he warned. "Stobaugh's made it crystal clear he wants me as primary on this one. He said he wants you to be strictly a backup resource."

So Stobaugh had already given Steve the go-ahead for me to

work the case—even if it was just as a resource—and here he was trying to get me to sleep with him in exchange for him "putting in a good word." I could think of a few good words I'd like to put right where the sun doesn't shine.

"Just think of my going out tonight as a date, Steve," I said sarcastically. "A girl *can* go out on a date if she wants to, can't she?"

Before Steve could come up with some wiseass reply, I gave him a taste of the dial tone.

See how you feel. That's what Dr. Mostafavi had said as I left his office earlier that afternoon. "What you've been through in the last few days is like being in a war," the orthopedic surgeon had told me. "Your three days on the street put you through more physical and emotional trauma than most people will ever experience. You're only human, Detective Justice, not some kind of crime-fighting robot. Use the shoulder injury as an excuse to catch up on your paperwork, and then see how you feel about jumping back in with both feet."

Like elevator music, Dr. Mostafavi's words stuck with me as I turned on the stereo in the living room and sat down at the breakfast table to finish reading the *Los Angeles Times*'s account of the Apocalypse Chronicles.

A radio station reported on a young black entrepreneur who had organized a bus tour for downtown bankers to see the damage in South Central firsthand. While it sounded like postmodern bwanas on a ghetto safari to me, his and other efforts were being heralded as if they were the Second Coming, complete with inspirational oratorio: *L.A.—The Cleanup Continues.*

The *Times* took up the hallelujah chorus and had moved from reporting on the devastation to the city's efforts to dig out from under. While charts and maps in the paper showing the affected areas made it clear South Central Los Angeles had suffered most dramatically, the paper seemed bound and determined to find multicultural "good news" stories all over town of people helping each other, come what may.

The whole thing was bizarre, like one of those movie musicals of the forties, designed to cheer up the folks at home while distracting them from the war raging on a not-so-distant shore. But in a corner of page 1 was an article by that redheaded reporter from Friday afternoon. It initially caught my eye for the wrong reason—I thought it was about Cinque Lewis—yet I realized as I read that it was actually much closer to the not-so-upbeat heart of the matter.

Another One Bites the Dust: Gang Founder's Death Marks End of an Era

BY NEIL HOOKSTRATTEN
TIMES STAFF REPORTER

While most of the world was transfixed before its televisions on the afternoon and evening of April 29, LAPD officers in the Crenshaw District were making a grim discovery that may raise as many fears about the direction of gang activity in Southern California as the beating of Reginald Denny.

When the decomposing bodies of 33-year-old Royals founder Demetrius Octavius Givens and another man were discovered in a graffiti-strewn, vacant Crenshaw Boulevard storefront on Wednesday—several hours before the first blow was struck on Florence and Normandie—LAPD officials recognized that the end of an era had arrived. An era that Big Dog, as he was known among hardened gang members, had dominated with an incongruous mixture of Afrocentric self-determination and brutality that has made the Royals one of the most feared gangs in the nation.

Givens, who had been missing since April 22, was an O.G.—a term commonly used to denote a gang's original gangster or veteran—of the deadly Lucky Ones faction of the Royals, which he founded in the late 1970s. The Lucky Ones run roughshod over an area popularly known as the Jungle, which in the 1960s was a middle-class apartment development designed to serve the then-growing population of airline pilots and flight attendants but is now home to some of the most notorious drug dealers in the city.

Givens embodied a vision of gang life that was, in the beginning, as much about community pride—"standing up for the 'hood"—as it was about the rock cocaine the Royals would come to distribute, or the drive-by shootings and violence that have often followed in the wake of their drug-dealing activities.

"Big Dog was always stressing to the little homies that you got to be about more than hangin', [gang-]bangin', and slangin' [selling rock cocaine]," lamented Franco Donovan, aka Little Dog. Little Dog knows firsthand the importance of Big Dog's message. Once one of most feared lieutenants in the Lucky Ones, Donovan is a casualty of one particularly vicious gang vendetta last March that left his mother, two sisters, and three of his children dead and him confined to a wheelchair. . . .

I got up from the table to get my notebook from my purse and started making a few notes.

For all of the death and destruction he left in his wake, Big Dog had earned a grudging respect from other cliques, or "sets," of Royals and not a few of his former enemies. Edward Carmichael, a former key lieutenant in the Lucky Ones, said, "Anyone who takes up the gang life knows you live by the Uzi, you die by the Uzi. Big Dog played a rough game. He had to know that it was only a matter of time [before he'd be killed]. But," he conceded, "it's sad to see a brother with so much potential go down that way."

Members of Deathstalker sets were more sanguine about their rival's demise. "It's just another motherf——bites the dust, far as I'm concerned," laughed an unidentified red-and-black–shirted young man, his words a profane paraphrasing of a once-popular rock song.

LAPD officials refused to comment on the case, stating only that Big Dog's death had all the markings of a turf dispute or a drug deal gone wrong. The graffiti-covered storefront where Big Dog and another lieutenant, June Bug Morrow, 26, were found—bound at the wrists with steel wire, bullets through their heads—was located in Deathstalker territory. Former gang member Carmichael, who "retired" from the Lucky Ones to establish Peace in the Streets, a nonprofit gang intervention program in 1988, tried to play down the implications of their deaths, saying his organization has "been working hard to hook up a gang truce that would have made something like this unnecessary."

Public announcement of funeral arrangements for Demetrius "Big Dog" Givens are being withheld, LAPD officials said Monday, to prevent further bloodshed or reprisals.

Big Dog's days had been numbered just like Cinque's, ever since I encountered him as a smart-mouthed drug runner while I was working patrol in Southwest Division. Even though the Royals had flourished in the rock cocaine business where Cinque's Black Freedom Militia had floundered—thanks to a better distribution network of gang members/dealers and more capital to get started—it didn't enhance Big Dog's life or increase his life span.

Another one bites the dust indeed.

My eye fell on the bulging blue binder I had lugged home from the office yesterday, resting on the edge of the breakfast table. I started to open it to double-check on Cinque's known enemies when I was reminded of Dr. Mostafavi's parting words.

See how you feel.

I sat for a long time and considered what lay between those blue covers. Other than pulling out the extra photos of Lewis I kept in the front, I hadn't actually read the murder book in years. Yet I knew I could recall almost every detail by heart. But, memorization aside, I had never let it touch me inside.

See how you feel.

As I opened the binder, the black Xeroxed letters of the copy came off on the inside of the blue plastic cover. Some of the detail on the picture did, too, leaving a reversed ghost image on the plastic that stared up at me from the left, its faded original echoing the same vacant, deadly gaze on the right.

It was a picture of a nineteen-year-old Cinque Lewis, his face adorning a be-on-the-lookout notice—BOLO, we called it—issued by the Department. Although Lewis was an American black, he had deliberately scarred his face like some of the Africans I had met in college, I guess in a misguided attempt to identify with the Motherland. The faded Xerox image made the scars appear hazy and indistinct, much as they were on Lewis's face Friday night.

I flipped to the Unsolved Murder Investigation Progress report and read the BOLO.

Name:	Robert Anthony Lewis
AKA:	Cinque
Last known address:	Trudy Mitchell Lewis Forrest (Mother) 4329 3/4 S. Kenwood Avenue Los Angeles, CA 90037
Wanted for:	Questioning in the double homicide of Keith Eric Roberts, 34 (78-592), and Erica Justice Roberts, six months (78-593)

Similar state and FBI wanted notices were included with the press releases toward the back of the book. Those pages were yellowed, too; the last official notice on the Lewis case was over twelve years ago.

Other addenda in the binder included background information on the Black Freedom Militia and a few declassified reports I
had managed to get from the Department's old Public Disorder
Intelligence Division. PDID was created by the Department in the
seventies to monitor terrorist organizations that were considered a
threat to the public safety. The Black Freedom Militia, like the
Black Panthers or the former Ron Karenga's US organization,
would have qualified for—and gotten—PDID scrutiny.

I hadn't known it at the time, but the PDID's surveillance of
Cinque Lewis's group had begun some months before Keith and
Erica were killed. A police informant had apparently infiltrated the
Militia in November of 1977. There were reports of his meetings
at their headquarters on Crenshaw Boulevard and conversations
with a number of members. The notes indicated the informant's
street name was Q-Dog.

Hel-*lo*! Why had it never occurred to me that Big Dog and
Q-Dog could have been the same person? If so, maybe
Demetrius Givens was the one who set up Cinque for a fall all
those years ago. From the age given in the article, I figured
Demetrius Givens would have been about nineteen in '77, just
the right age to have been susceptible to that kind of "power to
the people, off the pig" rhetoric. And if he really had other things
on his mind—like dealing drugs—he could have watched and
learned from Cinque's mistakes, stepped in after he disappeared,
and taken over his contacts.

The reports on the Militia's activities dried up after Cinque
disappeared, and became more focused on other gangs as targets of
opportunity. The Department and the city paid dearly for that
error in judgment. By the time I got to the Southwest's gang table
in '83, Big Dog Givens and the Royals were so firmly entrenched
in the drug scene, they had surpassed all the other gangs in their
involvement in drug trafficking and violence against their enemies.

Maybe PDID convinced the homicide detectives working
Keith and Erica's murders they were chasing their tails because
they knew Cinque had been dispatched by Givens. What if Givens
had assigned some underling to do the deed for him only to be

sadly—and fatally—surprised in that building on Crenshaw when he and June Bug found themselves staring down the barrel of an old rival's gun?

Dr. Mostafavi had said I should see how I feel, but as I pulled out some extra photos of Lewis from the binder, all I felt was relief. Relief that Lewis and Demetrius "Big Dog" Givens had finally gone to their Maker. Relief they couldn't kill somebody else's child, or husband, or brother.

But as I got my things together to go out again, there was something else I was feeling. A hollowness inside me, a void that was usually filled with a cold, dry rage. A sudden thought flared up in my mind: With Cinque Lewis dead, who was there left for me to hate? If the hate I felt for him was gone, would some other feeling slip into my dreams to take its place?

CHAPTER 11

GANG WAR, ETERNAL PEACE

South Bureau's headquarters always put me in the mind of a speakeasy. If you approached it from the small substation inside Baldwin Hills Crenshaw Plaza, you would think it was merely one of those community policing centers where patrol cops fill out forms or wolf down a hurried lunch from Mickey D's or the 7-Eleven. But behind the door in a corner of the mall was one of the LAPD's larger operations, complete with over a hundred employees and its own homicide, CRASH, and traffic tables.

I hadn't been in the Bureau's offices in a few months, and then it had been to attend an organized-crime/gang task-force meeting that had drawn detectives from jurisdictions all over the county. At the time, Mike Cooper's presentation on L.A.'s major gang factions and too numerous wars had appeared reasoned and knowledgeable. Knowledgeable enough to get him placed on an intra-agency Gang War Task Force. But high-profile assignment notwithstanding, maybe the everyday conflict between being a hard-charging, paramilitary-trained police officer and working with a unit euphemistically called Community Resources Against Street Hoodlums had gotten next to Cooper, transformed him into the bitter, cynical little man I had seen on the bus last week.

I was hoping Stobaugh had spoken to Dreyfuss, and he in turn to Cooper, about last Friday. I needed some information, and I didn't want Cooper's attitude standing in the way of me getting what I needed.

Dreyfuss was out, but I found Cooper over in the South Bureau Homicide bull pen, two butterfly bandages on his pale right cheek. I could see behind him a wall display of ties on a nearly seven-foot wooden tie rack. Whenever South Bureau homicide detectives got promoted, they had to sacrifice a tie with their name and date of promotion on it. I had dug one of those long-forgotten, God-awful Brooks Brothers woman's ties from the bottom of my scarf drawer to add to the rack when I got promoted. I couldn't even see it on the crowded tie rack now.

Cooper was bragging to some of the homicide detectives about an alleyway encounter with a crack-addicted prostitute. "Strawberry offered to blow me right there if I wouldn't run her in."

"What did you do?" one of the detectives asked.

Cooper stepped back, legs spread, hips thrust forward. "Made her face the nation," he proclaimed, slapping hands with a few male members of his audience, "and it don't increase the population!"

A couple of the Bureau's male and the few female homicide detectives had made themselves scarce in anticipation of Cooper's punch line, nodding hello to me on their way out the door. I imagined my sister detectives in the Bureau's in-house gym, taking turns at the punching bag and visualizing Cooper's face making contact with their gloves.

"Hey, Mike," I called out, "can we talk for a minute?"

Cooper strutted over with a smile and stage-whispered in my ear, "Am I going to need witnesses? I wouldn't want to be accused of sexually harassin' one of the Department's *finest*."

Cooper's slicked-back, mousy brown hair reminded me of the old Brylcreem commercials. *A little dab'll do ya!* "No need for all that, Mike. Just you and me."

Cooper's eyes widened as he played to his audience. "You

heard her, fellas. Just me and Detective Justice." As he directed me across the hall to his office, he whispered in my ear, "I may even enjoy this."

Cooper had gotten much worse since I'd had any significant contact with him. I sat down in a burgundy chair by his desk and steeled myself not to gag on the words I was about to say. "Look, Mike, I came over to talk because I want to put Friday behind us. A lot of things were said and done in the heat of the moment that shouldn't have gotten as far as they did."

He nodded his head vigorously. "You got that right."

"There's nothing personal here, Mike," I rushed on, wanting to get this over with as soon as possible. "We've always worked well together, and I want to keep it that way."

"Long as you understand it wasn't some antiblack thing out there, Justice. That motherfucker was out of line, and I wasn't havin' it. It woulda been the same no matter what color he was."

I shrugged, wondering if Mitchell's dark green hospital scrubs would have said "doctor" instead of "Mandingo-assed motherfucker" to Cooper if his skin had been white, or if Cooper would have automatically assumed a white man would have been trying to steal that car.

"You've always been able to take the heat," Cooper was saying, "but if you've gotten soft like the rest of them RHD divas and don't have the *cojones* to kick a little ass when necessary or stand up under a little good-natured kiddin', then you ain't gonna make it in this man's police force."

Cooper leaned back in his chair, as satisfied with his little speech as a pig in shit. He lit up a pipe, forbidden inside the building, reared back in his chair, and blew smoke in my direction. He was clearly enjoying every minute of watching one of RHD's elite eat crow. For me, smoking the peace pipe with Big Chief Mouse Dick was just a means to an end.

Determined not to play into his little power game, I casually looked down at his desk. Under a piece of glass that acted as a wipeable blotter were pictures of Cooper posing with his marksman awards, an inspirational poem about the Green Berets, and a variety of pictures of a tawny-skinned blonde woman in a nurse's uniform and two brown-haired girls that I assumed were his family.

"Yep, those are my angels." His face softened a bit. "Oldest girl is nineteen now. Wants to be a marine biologist. The baby is twelve. Wants to be a cop like her dad."

I was hoping not *just* like her dad.

After a little more small talk about his wife and kids, his precious Harley, and the crapper the city was in, I steered the conversation around to the Cinque Lewis homicide. "Finding that lowlife sonofabitch behind that stand surprised me and Burt as much as it did you," he admitted.

"Anybody on the Gang War Task Force come up with a theory on where Cinque's been hiding?"

"Uh-uh. Cortez called today, said the lab rats are gonna run a check on his clothes, fibers in his pockets, everything, to try and figure out where the hell he's been all this time."

Cortez and her divided loyalties. Still, the Gang War Task Force, including Cooper, had a need to know. "How closely are you following this one?" I asked.

"If Cinque Lewis's reappearance is a signal of the resurgence of the Black Freedom Militia, I'm gonna be all over this case" was his clipped response.

"Don't go getting all worked up, Mike." I lightly punched Cooper's forearm. I didn't need him angry and uncooperative at this point. "What I meant was have you had time to check on the Militia with any of the other agencies."

He relaxed a little, the color receding from his cheeks. "Outside of the Department, I've checked with the surroundin' counties as well as the California Gang Investigation Association. None of them has heard of anything on the Black Freedom Militia since heck was a pup. How's it going with the suspect?"

"Mitchell? We didn't hold him. Word is he's one of those salt-of-the-earth, conscientious types—on the board of TAGOUT, the whole nine. Even giving a full scholarship to a reformed tagger tonight, over at that art gallery in Santa Barbara Plaza."

"Spiral West?" His tone was disdainful.

Mine was noncommittal. "I think so."

"This is the kind of shit that bothers me," he said with considerable bite in his voice. "All Reggie Peeples is doin' over there is pumpin' those kids up with a bunch of false hopes. Nobody wants those cave scribblings hangin' in their house."

I could have mentioned Jean-Michel Basquiat or Keith Haring, the New York graffiti artists whose "cave scribblings" were raking in a fortune, but what was the point? "Well, Dr. Mitchell sounds like a true believer. Enough to put his time and money where his mouth is, way I heard it."

"Sounds like a real Father Teresa to me," Cooper murmured while drawing tight little spirals on a notepad.

"That doesn't mean he didn't have a motive for doing Lewis," I pointed out.

Cooper's doodles grew larger, big loops and arrows practically spilling off the paper. "Could be Lewis was gettin' in the way of Mitchell convertin' kids to the straight and narrow path," he suggested. "Maybe the good doctor did the public a service by poppin' that zit."

The notion seemed to cheer Cooper up considerably, but his face soon grew serious. "You should be glad Cinque's out of the way." His small eyes were intense. "To take your old man and kid out like that, just wipe out your whole family." Cooper glanced down at the pictures of his smiling daughters and shook his head in a show of what I took for genuine sympathy. "I don't know if I could have coped with it as long as you have."

For all of his racism and misogyny, Mike Cooper was also a man the world would say had strong family values. It was a combination I'd encountered a little too often in the LAPD to consider it an aberration any more.

"What's the word on that Lucky Ones O.G. who got popped . . ."

"Big Dog Givens? Yeah, 'cept he wasn't so lucky this time around." Cooper's pun was delivered without a laugh. He sucked on his dead pipe. "He was a smart little bastard, or so he thought. Got so he was runnin' crack all over the county."

"When did he come on the scene, Mike?"

"Late seventies, early eighties, out of those apartments on Nicolet in the Jungle. He and Carmichael started stealin' cars and dealin' drugs, and pretty soon they were shootin' high school kids at Dorsey and Manual Arts that wouldn't join up with them. By the time we finally popped him the first time for possession with intent to sell, he had an organization rumored to be three thousand strong—and that was ten years ago." He sighed. "Givens's death is gonna set off a power struggle in Royals' cliques all over the county."

"Problem is sometimes innocent people get killed in the crossfire," I noted.

"That's always the problem," Cooper agreed. "If it was just these knuckleheads blowin' each other away, I wouldn't care. But invariably it's some old man or some mother's son who's a straight A student on his way to Stanford who catches the bullet. Protectin' them is what keeps me doing this job." He stood up abruptly. "Speakin' of which, I gotta git."

I walked with Cooper to the parking lot. "Where are you headed?" I asked.

"Big Dog's funeral."

"Maybe I'll go with you."

"Why bother?" he asked sarcastically.

"I was going through the old case file on the Roberts murders." Saying it out loud made me catch my breath for a moment; it was unnerving referring to Keith and Erica so matter-of-factly. "There may be a connection between Big Dog and an old informant on the case."

Cooper shrugged. "Suit yourself. They're plantin' him over at Eternal Peace." He snorted in derision. "All I can say is it's gonna be a whole lot more peaceful without that sonofabitch to contend with."

Although living, breathing blacks had moved into the surrounding neighborhood in the sixties, Sunnyslope Cemetery/Mortuary's discriminatory policies had kept our dead out until the early seventies. But with white flight decreasing the target market, as it were, Sunnyslope had determined that they needed to change with the times and—since black-on-black crime presented a major growth opportunity through the end of the century—get the money while the getting was good.

Consequently, in addition to the gone-to-glory members of my grandmother's church and the better-known members of L.A.'s niggerati now interred there, Sunnyslope and its Eternal Peace Chapel had become quite accustomed to accommodating a gang clientele. So Royals, Deathstalkers, Muy Loco Killers, and the rest congregated regularly in the chapel and at the graveside before expensive rare wood and metal caskets or—on two *Jet* magazine-reported occasions—a gold-plated coffin and a Mercedes sedan in which the dearly departed lay in splendiferous, dearly-paid-for peace.

Taking to heart the old Biblical adage *For unto him who is given much, much is expected,* Sunnyslope's flush-with-cash owners had thought of every convenience—and precaution—to make each rite of final passage a peaceful one, including installing a metal detector at the chapel entrance and, when public safety dictated, asking off-duty LAPD officers to augment the cemetery's private, discreetly armed security staff. Obviously the extra measures weren't required for the violently deceased—who flowed through Sunnyslope at a rate of about two or three per week—but for the family and aggrieved friends who turned out for the services, armed to the hilt and looking for trouble.

Edward Carmichael, the gang truce activist pictured in the *Times* article that morning, stood at the cemetery gates in a purple Minnesota Vikings jacket, passing out Peace in the Streets leaflets to the arriving caravan of cars so expensive, so luxe, that to see them all in one place was a sure sign of only one of two things—the annual meeting of NFL owners or a Royals funeral.

Carmichael had stuck a leaflet through my car window before he realized I was behind the wheel and tried to snatch it back. "I ain't wasting this on you."

I won the tug-of-war and put the flyer on the passenger seat. "We all want peace, Ed."

His eyes were cold: "So you say."

I parked my lowly red Rabbit between a seven-series Bimmer and Cooper's Department-issued Ford, and rejoined Carmichael at the cemetery gate. "I like the purple, Ed. New fashion statement?"

"Purple means power and royalty, Detective. Red plus blue. Deathstalker and Royals." He extended a lavender sheet to an entering car. "It's all there in your flyer."

I glanced at the sheet, which contained pictures of children killed by stray bullets, a plea for a gang truce, and the Peace in the Streets address and phone number. "Ed, you've been in the mix for a long time. When was the last time you heard about Cinque Lewis or the Black Freedom Militia?"

He regarded me suspiciously. "Why do you ask?"

"He's popped up again."

Carmichael paused a second before handing a flyer to the driver of a tricked-out Bimmer. "Dead or alive?"

"Interesting you should ask. Dead, as a matter of fact."

I saw his shoulders slump a little. "Why am I not surprised?"

"What's that supposed to mean, Ed? You seen him lately?"

A car slowed in front of us. The driver, a Royal I busted years ago when I was in Southwest, saw me, bared his teeth in a gang snarl intended to intimidate, and sped away.

Carmichael threw up his hands in exasperation. "You're blocking me, Detective! I can't be seen talking to you. Ruins my credibility."

The way he was angled away from me and wouldn't look me in the eye suggested his reticence to talk was about more than me ruining his rep with his homies. He knew something about Cinque Lewis. "When *can* we talk, Ed?" I pressed.

"Call me tomorrow. Number's on the flyer," he mumbled as he hurried away to another arriving mourner, flyer in hand.

Inside, the Eternal Peace Chapel was awash in a sea of button-downed white shirts, crisply creased and cuffed blue jeans, and blue denim jackets, the official formal wear of the Lucky Ones Royals. I noticed a number of royal blue kuftis atop the shaved and cornrowed heads, marking this funeral as a high-profile occasion.

Mourners from other Royals cliques were there, too. I was surprised that so many of them were still alive, if you could call it that; more than a few had to be lifted and passed through the metal detectors by friends. Their wheelchairs were politely but thoroughly checked by a wary security staff used to firearms being concealed even under a sheepskin cushion intended to prevent pressure sores.

The chapel was filled with hardened faces I recognized from both sides in L.A.'s bloody gang wars. Played off against the royal blue of the gang members was a tide of uniformed and moonlighting LAPD officers—Chip LeDoux, Darren Wright, plus at least a dozen brothers I knew from the local chapter of the National Organization for Black Law Enforcement—prominently and grimly stationed at the entrance and back of the chapel. Cooper, although in civilian drag, was no less somber than our navy-attired colleagues. The only ones smiling were the mortuary staff, situated in a corner by the door, serene in the knowledge they would eventually get a fair number of those in attendance, on both sides of the aisle, one way or the other.

Darren Wright nodded his head in my direction and eased over to me at the back door. "Anything shake loose on that case, Detective?" he whispered out of the corner of his mouth.

"Not yet."

"I didn't know you knew Big Dog."

"I didn't. I'm just tagging along with Cooper."

He nodded, then said, "I noticed you don't wear a wedding ring."

"And?"

"Well," he stammered, "I just thought if you weren't seeing someone you might want to have dinner with me on my boat sometime. I've got a forty-two footer docked at the Marina, and I can throw *down* on a grill."

I turned to face him. "I'm flattered, Darren." And I was. Wright seemed like a righteous brother and wasn't hard to look at either. Good-looking, well mannered, and cooks, too? I *had* to mention him to my girl Katrina. "Unfortunately I'm just getting into something . . ." It was my standard line for brushing off cops, but I surprised myself by picturing Aubrey Scott as soon as I said it.

Wright gave me a lopsided smile and threw up his hands in mock surrender. "No problem. Just asking."

Mike Cooper had made his way to the front of the chapel, where he embraced a plump woman I assumed was the dead man's mother and sat down to talk with the wheelchair-bound Little Dog Donovan. Both of them seemed at ease with the little man, almost friendly.

Wright nodded in Cooper's direction. "That's one dedicated cop." Although his face was noncommittal, there was a bit of a sneer in the uniform's voice.

"Are you being facetious?" I asked.

He shook his head. "Don't let Cooper's rough talk fool you; he's very committed. Always comes to these bangers' funerals, trying to get these kids to straighten out their lives. More than you'd catch me doing, that's for sure."

Never judge a book by its cover, I could hear Grandmama Cile say. And as hard as it was to admit, Cooper *did* have some redeeming qualities, even if they were wrapped in a combative, abrasive little package.

I excused myself and made my way over to the other side of the chapel, where I saw Fred Stoppard and Neil Hookstratten from the *Times*. "I've been meaning to call you guys to say thanks for being my personal ambulance Friday night."

"My pleasure, Detective," the photographer smiled. "Reminded me a little of the old days."

"You ever miss us, F-Stop?"

He smiled at Hookstratten and shook his head, a red mane rustling around his head. "Only until I get my paycheck every month."

"By the way, Hook, did I leave something in your backseat Friday?"

"Like what?"

"Uh . . . my black notebook." I was glad the lie came to mind so fast.

"Haven't seen it." He unearthed a set of car keys from a pocket and tossed them to me. "My car is parked by the cypress trees at the end of the lot. Feel free to take a look for yourself."

I checked the back seat of the Taurus thoroughly, but outside of a cartridge of used film and a package of breath mints in the cushions, which I returned to Hookstratten with his keys, there was nothing. No smoking gun hidden in the cushions to link Mitchell to Lewis.

"I gotta let you search my car again sometime," he joked as he pocketed the items. "You do a better job than the car wash."

I shushed him, concerned we'd draw attention to ourselves. He moved away a bit to interview a young woman while F-Stop started snapping pictures with a telephoto lens.

You would have thought the mourners would have objected to the whirring motor drive on F-Stop's camera. But the people assembled in the chapel that afternoon didn't seem to notice, more intent on their grief—or making sure they were all *seen* to be visibly shaken by Big Dog's death. I wouldn't have been surprised if some jealous rival from within his own organization was the shooter. The wheelchair-bound Little Dog, still talking to Cooper, was off the list; wouldn't have had the physical ability to tie the two men up, although he could have ordered the hit. Maybe it was the good-looking, bronze-skinned brother in the front row, the one with the azure-blue embroidered kufti on his head who was comforting a keening female Hook said was Big Dog's girlfriend.

"Second in command to Big Dog," Hook noted the bronze Adonis, whose name was Trig. "Not as smart as the Dog, but twice as ruthless. I wouldn't be surprised if Trig started making his move to fill Big Dog's shoes soon."

And Big Dog's bed, too, the way he had his arm around that young woman.

The congregants had just finished mumbling their way through the Lord's Prayer. I took advantage of the awkward pause to slip into a back pew. While an almost-attractive young female—made less so by straw-blonde hair that was dyed, fried, and laid to the side—read the acknowledgments, I took the opportunity to read the order of service printed in the program.

Grandmama Cile, by virtue of her age and temperament the most frequent funeral goer in the Justice family, would have been appalled. Not that she would object to the order of service, but at the names of the people participating, not to mention the selection of music. The towheaded Celica Davenport—her mother must have gone into labor in a Toyota—was followed by Little Dog and Trig, whose remarks were blessedly brief.

A slight-built young man of not more than fourteen, listed in the program as Too Smooth Sanders, shyly approached the microphone. As he took his place at the front of the chapel, I could read the words "Royals" and "Big Dog" artfully cut into his head, a personal tribute to the deceased. And while Grandmama Cile might have hoped for something more traditional (even "Rock of Ages"—though in bad taste, considering the dead man's profession—would have sufficed), no one was prepared for Too Smooth's musical homage to Big Dog by way of Marvin Gaye, another brother brought low by drugs.

Too Smooth's solo selection, "Inner City Blues," delivered a cappella with an icy-veined plaintiveness, reflected Marvelous Marvin at the height of his genius, when he captured the pain of my youth and evidently that of this congregation as well. By the recessional, when Too Smooth cried out the refrain of the song I had played in my car just a few days ago, I was forced to acknowledge the connection between me and these young men and women. Eastside or Westside, South Central or South Bay, there were things that bound black folks together beyond the superficialities of skin color or hair texture. It was memory and culture resonating from within, from the way we grieve to the music that had everyone bobbing their heads in the chapel's late afternoon gloom.

But in the chapel that day I came to believe there was something more, something so universal that it could blow you away from the hilltops of View Park or the blacktops of Watts before you knew it. Could take your breath away on the ninth green of the Brentwood Country Club or crush you in a county jail cell. Whether it was in a driveway or behind a taco stand, in a hospital bed or hanging from the magnolia trees of history, death was the same for everyone. Catching us unawares or unprepared, but catching us all just the same.

The thought gave me a chill so thorough I had to leave before the services were over and the mourners moved on to the adjacent cemetery. As I made my way to the door, F-Stop and the others were capturing the Kodak moment, catching the Royals flashing signs in unison to Gaye's haunting and prophetic words:

Makes me wanna holler,
Throw up both my hands . . .

CHAPTER 12

PICASSO WITH A KRYLON CAN

Getting ready for the art exhibit that evening, a thousand thoughts jockeyed for position in my mind, not the least of which was . . . I actually had a date! Not an extension-of-work dinner with one of the three or four deputy D.A.s or firemen I'd dated over the years, but an honest-to-God, put-on-your-high-heeled-sneakers date. And even though my ulterior motive was to dig up as much information as possible on Dr. Lance Mitchell, I was going to do it in the company of one of the finest men I'd met in my whole life.

It took me forever to decide what to wear besides my usually conservative *Cagney & Lacey* drag. Indecision was making me slow as a turtle with constipation and just about as snappish. I was almost at my wit's end when I ran across my black silk jumpsuit with a low-cut buttoned front. It wasn't exactly new, but Aubrey had never seen it. I threw it on, a green silk blazer over it and threaded a silk scarf in a kente print fabric under the jacket collar. The back of my closet yielded some mock lizard pumps with a gold buckle on the instep. Matching gold earrings and a medium-weight gold herringbone necklace warmed up my sallow skin. The blue sling was definitely a fashion "don't," but I dutifully put it on and gauged the effect in a mirror.

I needed help.

My neighbor Odetta Franklin was only too glad to come to my rescue and had the truly inspired idea to make a sling out of my scarf. She had tied it in place and had me sitting in the kitchen while she bumped some oomph to my hair with a large curling iron she'd brought with her when Beast started barking and the doorbell rang. While Mrs. Franklin went with the dog to the door, I rushed to remove the hair implements from the kitchen and to the bathroom to finger comb my hair.

Mrs. Franklin came into the bathroom and whispered in my ear, "Now, baby, that one out there is a *keeper!* I got me a *good* vibe about him!" She gave me a thumbs up and patted my shoulder as I walked to the living room to collect my date.

I had to collect myself when I saw Aubrey Scott sitting in my living room that night. His pecan-hued face and hands stood out in delicious relief against a black cashmere sweater and matching wool pants. He sat on my black leather sofa, taking a picture of Beast, who sat posing with a chew toy in his mouth.

Before I flipped out into some romantic/domestic fantasy, I had to stop and get a grip. This was a business obligation for him and a chance for me to check out Dr. Mitchell on his home turf. Nothing more, as much as the woman in me might wish otherwise. And nothing less, as the cop in me knew full well.

My ham of a dog showed Aubrey his profile, which was dutifully captured on film. "You two are a mess!" I laughed. "Don't use up all of your film on him."

As if he knew I was talking about him, Beast insinuated his muzzle into Aubrey's free hand. "It's okay. I like dogs."

The boxer, leaning into Aubrey's massaging fingers, was having a canine-style orgasm. "Well, he sure likes you."

So do you, the voice in my head reminded me.

Aubrey rose from the sofa, his legs long as ever. "You look great, Char." He fingered the silk of my makeshift sling. "Pretty."

Mrs. Franklin stood peeking into the living room. She clattered her curling iron, a polite way of getting my attention. "Oh, I'm sorry. Mrs. Franklin, this is Dr. Scott. Dr. Scott, Mrs. Franklin. Aubrey and I went to high school together."

He took her hand. "Pleased to meet you, Mrs. Franklin."

"Please call me Odetta, Dr. Scott."

"Only if you call me Aubrey," he smiled back.

"Well," she cooed and patted her dreads, "I best be gittin' outta here. So nice to meet you Dr. . . . Aubrey."

Once Mrs. Franklin left, Aubrey seemed a little at odds with himself, pacing in my living room, sitting down on the sofa, then springing up to look at a photo on the mantle. "I need to get something off my chest before we go," he said at last.

"Sure." I made my mouth smile. He's seeing someone. I should have known it.

"I told you this morning there were two reasons Lance joined CaER. I didn't think the other reason was relevant to your investigation, but when you told me about Cinque Lewis, it made me wonder . . ."

"Told you what? About him being a revolutionary?"

"No, the part about his drug dealing. See, when Lance was with that medical group in the Valley, they had to let him go because of a drug problem."

"What kind of drugs?"

It turns out Mitchell had gotten strung out behind a variety of prescription painkillers, including the same one he had prescribed for me. "It's not a problem if you're careful how you take it," Aubrey assured me in response to my alarmed expression. "But it started affecting Lance's work to the extent he was writing scripts for patients who came through the ER and then getting them filled for himself. When the hospital he was assigned to found out, they blew the whistle on him and the senior partner at the group had to let him go."

Mitchell had been real jumpy on King Boulevard that day, in the ER that night, as well as in Aubrey's office earlier in the day. Maybe Mitchell had started dipping into the goodie jar again.

Maybe he got something more than Mrs. Rucker's heart medication from the pharmacy that night. Or had met Lewis to score some street drugs.

"But he went to Betty Ford and had been clean for six months when he came to us," Aubrey was saying. "He's an excellent doctor, and even though I had to fight my partners to bring him in, I don't regret it. He's been a great addition to the group."

"So why tell me all this now? Wasn't the medication he took to that patient for hypertension?"

"It was. I just didn't want to feel like we were keeping any secrets from each other."

The truthfulness shining in Aubrey's honey-brown eyes made me feel like two cents for the half lie I was perpetrating about our date. In the uneasy silence, Beast started rubbing against Aubrey's leg, shedding tan hairs all over his pant leg.

"We'd better go. This dog will have you playing with him all night. And Aubrey?" I put my free hand on his forearm, felt the strength of the muscles there. "I appreciate you being honest with me."

Even if I couldn't be just yet, I wanted to add.

Reggie Peeples started Spiral West Gallery almost thirty years ago in tribute to a group of socially conscious East Coast black artists who came together in concern over their role in the civil rights movement. Founded on the eve of the March on Washington, the original Spiral group—which included artists like Romare Bearden, Richard Mayhew, and a dozen others—lasted only a few years and had only a couple of New York shows, but its namesake gallery out here had been limping along since 1963.

In the seventies and eighties Spiral West attracted some of the best artists of the day but had recently fallen on hard times, economics and disposable income being what they weren't in the black community. My father was one of a group of neighbors, friends, and core clients who tried to keep the man we kids called Uncle Reggie and the gallery going, buying a Charles White drawing or a Betty Catlett sculpture from time to time. And even though I just finished paying for a Betye Saar collage that hung in my bedroom, our support was but a few drops in a very large and too-often-empty bucket.

But Uncle Reggie wasn't exhibiting African-American fine art that night. The current show was called ART HURTS: VISIONS FROM YOUNG LOS ANGELES AEROSOL ARTISTS. Printed on the front of the program distributed at the door was a poem that set the tone:

> Does man love Art? Man visits Art, but squirms.
> Art hurts. Art urges voyages—
> and it is easier to stay at home,
> the nice beer ready . . .

The poem was "The Chicago Picasso" from Gwendolyn Brooks's "Two Dedications." Picasso with a Krylon can was more like it, I thought as we stood watching the crush of people standing behind the roped-off door. And the voyage Aubrey and I were about to undertake looked more like Mr. Toad's Wild Ride at Disneyland than anything resembling art.

It was a madhouse. The Beef Brothers, a black-owned security company hired to work the event, had their hands full and had called on the traffic unit that worked the area for an assist. But the unit was busy, so Chip LeDoux and Darren Wright had rolled by instead. And were standing around milking the easy assignment for all it was worth.

We stood outside for a moment talking to Wright until Aubrey remembered his assignment to get pictures of the event for his medical group's newsletter. "I should get a shot of the crowd, too." He took the lens cap off the camera and pointed it toward the entrance. "This is a trip!"

Wright offered to help. "That way you can both get in the picture."

I heard the whir of film being advanced in the camera. "That's okay, this'll do," Aubrey said, waving him away.

As we went into the gallery, Darren Wright gave me a smile and thumbs up as if to say, *No hard feelings.* What a nice brother. Too bad I hadn't invited Katrina; it would have been interesting to see if they would have hit it off.

It looked as if the gallery had been turned inside out, the graffiti that usually covered the outside of the building now on canvases displayed on its interior walls. As Grandmama Cile would say, *If the walls could talk.* If they could, my guess was they'd be screaming, *Who the hell put this shit up in here?*

Some of the guests were equally outdone by the turn of events. Business leaders of every color, shape, and size stood in little clumps of twos and threes, hoping their sincere blue suits would camouflage them from art so angry it seemed about to jump off the walls and kick their butts. Moving among them were quite a few members of the press plus film producers and television weasels, scurrying about in search of heroes for their special Los Angeles Uprising Editions or a movie of the week. Trailing them were the celebrities—black and white, known and wannabe— eager to see and be seen doing *something* meaningful, Edward James Olmos and his push broom having taken the early prize in the roll-up-your-sleeves activism sweepstakes.

The minority community and business leaders allowed to pass beyond the gold-rope barrier were the genuine article, if black and Latino L.A. could be said to have such a thing. I saw at least a dozen bankers I recognized from both white- and black-owned banks plus community organizers including Ed Carmichael of Peace in the Streets. There were a couple of local doctors in attendance, and some well-known lawyers—including Sandra Douglass, Mitchell's recently acquired attorney—were also in the mix. They were all milling about, trying mighty hard not to appear outraged by tagging they worked overtime to remove from their fences and buildings, now pulling down more money than many of them made in a week.

Once inside, Aubrey went to get us something to drink while I wandered over to talk to Carmichael. "You keep showing up like a bad penny, Ed."

"Look who's talking." He offered me a half smile and grudgingly extended his hand.

"What brings you out tonight?"

"You gotta show your support for the ones trying to make something out of their lives," he replied, gazing with a fair amount of pride at the TAGOUT artists.

I pulled Carmichael aside ostensibly to admire a painting, but really so we could talk without ruining his image with his homeboys. "You got a funny look on your face when I mentioned Cinque Lewis this afternoon, Ed. Did he reach out and touch?"

Carmichael, pretending to study the painting, whispered out of the corner of his mouth: "Lewis came by my mom's crib on the twenty-second, looking for me. She told him to catch me at the office, which he did, but I didn't have a lot of time to spend with him." Carmichael was in the middle of putting the finishing touches on a gang peace summit between Big Dog Givens's clique of Royals and some Deathstalkers scheduled for that evening. "So glad as I was to see him, I had a lot on my mind. I'm kinda sorry now I didn't take the time, especially since Big Dog didn't even show up for the meeting."

"What did Lewis want?"

"Said he heard about this group that worked with kids that was supposed to be so righteous, and he wanted to know was the folks running it legit."

"You expect me to believe he's been gone all this time and he comes back to ask you about TAGOUT? Did he want to know about anyone in particular?"

"Just Peeples and that doctor on the board. Said he read about them in an article in the *Sentinel*."

Something did run in the *Sentinel*, "but it wasn't an article," Reggie Peeples explained when I caught up with him. "It was a photo from our fund-raising luncheon last month."

He led me to the back room where he pulled a large glossy photo out of a manila envelope. The photo was one of those unimaginative, deer-caught-in-the-headlights shots that community newspapers are notorious for printing. This one featured

Reggie Peeples on the left, looking remarkably young for a man in his late sixties, standing next to two young men holding plaques. To the right of them was a slender woman with her arm around the taller boy, then Lance Mitchell leaning next to her. All of them, except Mitchell, were wearing TAGOUT T-shirts, the name spelled out in an artfully spray-painted design, the international "no" symbol through the word "tag."

The date the photo ran in the paper was April 22. So Cinque Lewis picks up a copy of the *Sentinel* to catch up on what's happening with black folks in the city. He runs across the photo of Reggie Peeples and Lance Mitchell and immediately pays a visit to a former homie to get the lowdown on TAGOUT. And later that same day Big Dog Givens punks out on a big gang summit meeting, drops off the face of the earth, only to turn up a week later, dead in a vacant storefront on Crenshaw.

As Arsenio Hall would say, *Things that make you go "hmm."*

As we returned to the gallery, I saw Lance Mitchell on the other side of the room having a private tête-à-tête with the shorter kid in the *Sentinel* photo, who this time was wearing paint-splattered overalls and clogs. "That's Gregory Underwood," Reggie explained, "the kid getting the scholarship."

Reggie was filling me in on Underwood's background when the room fell quiet. I looked around in time to see Councilwoman Moore standing at the door with a full complement of ass kissers and flunkies. Earnestine Moore wasn't called the Queen of the Council for nothing. A six-foot diva with a shock of prematurely gray, immaculately coifed hair, Moore had made such inroads into the City Council since riding in on a pro-black vote twenty-some-odd years ago, she not only knew where all the bodies were buried but who did the deeds. Spiral West sat in her district, and there was no way a photo-op like this could go down without her bejeweled fingers in the middle of it.

Neil Hookstratten appeared at my elbow. "She really knows how to make the grand entrance, doesn't she?"

"Puts Jessye Norman to shame," I whispered back. "What brings you out tonight, Hook? Doesn't the *Times* have an art critic?"

"I'm here to do a story on Dr. Mitchell for the Metro section. What about you?" He eyed me hungrily, like pearls—or some newsworthy tidbits—were about to fall from my lips.

"Date." I was relieved when Aubrey arrived, plastic punch glasses in hand, to bolster my alibi. I introduced them and told Hook that Aubrey was CEO of the medical group where Dr. Mitchell worked.

Hook handed him a card. "We're doing an article on Dr. Mitchell and his work with youth—you know, giving back to the community and all. Would you be available for an interview?"

While the two of them worked out the details, I gratefully escaped to the opposite side of the room to get a little closer to Dr. Mitchell. He and the other kid in the *Sentinel* photo were standing next to a sniffling white man and his taut-skinned wife who were admiring the painting they had just bought. "I'm glad you snapped this up, *liebchen*," Taut Skin praised her husband. To the kid, she said: "You're going to be bigger than Basquiat one day, young man . . ."

The painting was actually quite good—reminded me of a tortured El Greco landscape or one of Archibald Motley's later works. The signature scrawled in the corner of the sold canvas read Peyton Bell. A tall, handsome, chocolate-syrup-colored kid in a fresh box-cut hair style, Peyton's quiet manner was more in tune with his well-heeled patrons than his hip-hopping friends.

Gregory Underwood and a couple of other kids joined us. "Mack P, who hooked you up, man . . ." Underwood capped on Peyton's black sport coat and matching slacks, ". . . yo' mama?"

"Aw, man, you know how that is" came the barely audible answer. I followed Peyton's embarrassed gaze toward a slender, conservatively dressed thirtyish female with a that-short brown Afro and reddish skin tone the old folks called "mariney." It was the woman standing next to him in the *Sentinel* photo, albeit in a more animated pose. That night she had a glass of wine in one hand while the other gestured excitedly at another one of her son's paintings for the benefit of a couple of skeptical community leaders.

Mitchell threw his arm around the young man and held him

close. "Mr. Peeples says he's sold three of your paintings. That should help with tuition."

"I'm gonna give that money to my mom," Peyton whispered. "She's gone through a lot raising me. She deserves it more than I do."

"But what about your education?" Taut Skin's husband asked in a thick German accent. "You *are* going to art school?"

Peyton seemed on the verge of tears. "I don't know."

I was hoping he would; I liked this soft-spoken, talented kid.

As the older couple moved away, I noticed Jamilla Brown sashay into the gallery, trailed by a prison-buffed young man someone said was Donnie Watson. While I might not have recognized her without her hospital lab coat, Jamilla's liberation-colored nails confirmed her identity better than a fingerprint. Her skintight miniskirt and black leather bustier were making another, more overt statement.

"Oo-ooo, *we-eee*!" Underwood called out in a deep voice, leaning sideways around the group of kids. "Lookit the junk in her trunk!"

Jamilla started in our direction, then changed course when she saw Mitchell moving toward the buffet table in the middle of the room. They stood for a moment in a heated conversation which seemed to revolve around her attire. The exchange was not lost on her date, whose face clouded over as he tried to play off the situation and saunter over to join us.

First in the ER, now here. Even though she was a little rough around the edges, I wasn't sure why Mitchell had such a bee in his bonnet about Jamilla. Peyton Bell was watching them, too, an unreadable look veiling his thin face. He finally walked over to them and pulled the physician aside, where they began their own anguished conversation.

Underwood sighed and turned his attention to the swarming activity in the gallery. "Y'know, wit' all these rich muthafuckers up in here, I feel like we sellin' out. I 'on't know what my homes would say if they could peep this, us in here playin' kiss ass with Dr. M and these Oreos!"

"You'd better be thankful you've got Dr. Mitchell, Gregory." Peyton's mother came up, put an arm around the boy, and introduced herself to me as Raziya Bell.

"I bet he's saved as many brothers by gettin' us scholarships and jobs as he has in that ER," Watson added. "Me included."

"How's that?" I asked as Aubrey came up and snapped a photo of our group.

Watson's rock-hard brown eyes wavered for a moment. "Dr. Mitchell helped me get a job at the hospital. First-for-real gig I ever had. Now I been promoted to pharmacy tech II. I owe Dr. M some heavy props!"

I wondered if payback included free samples from the pharmacy's controlled-substances cabinet.

Just then Jamilla Brown stepped over, wine glass in hand, and aimed one of her lacquered fingernails at me. "I know you . . ."

Mitchell was right behind her. "Not here, Jamilla," he warned.

"Oh, yes, right here and *right now!*" The young woman's head swiveled and craned ominously. "You got your nerve!" She angrily threw Mitchell's hand off her arm. "Uh-uh, I ain't having this 'ho' from five-oh comin' up in here after the way they treated you last Friday."

At the mention of the police, everyone remembered they had somewhere else to be. Right then. Mitchell apologized to me and yanked the fuming Jamilla off to the side. Aubrey steered me away from the spot where Jamilla had dropped the turd in the punch bowl and stood with his arm around my shoulder, pretending to show me some art.

"Charlotte, I see you're doing well tonight." Sandra Douglass's words were directed to me, but her wet, glossy lips were taking in Aubrey in a long, who-have-we-here pucker.

I half-heartedly introduced Lance's attorney to my date. "Sandra is an old friend of the family—we go back to Jack & Jill."

"Girl, don't remind me!" Sandra's laugh tinkled over the crowd as she flipped her warm-brown hair in my face. "That kids' club was fifteen years ago." She insinuated her fingers on Aubrey's forearm, and squeezed. "I've moved on to much more adult activities." Another squeeze of Aubrey's arm.

Something about the lilting tone Sandra had adopted for Aubrey's benefit made me remember why we used to call the girls that went to Bishop Conaty High School "Pico pickups." I felt like sticking a pin in her surgically enhanced breasts. "Come on, Sandra, you must be slipping in your dotage," I said. "You were in Jack & Jill thirty-five years ago if it was a day."

Sandra twisted her mouth and shot me a look so lethal I was half-sorry I wasn't wearing my Kevlar vest. But she was only thinking of a snappy comeback. She settled on asking me about the awkward moment with Jamilla Brown.

"One of those silly kids screamed on Charlotte about being a cop." Aubrey still had his arm around me, God bless him.

"Well, that's one of the problems when you work on the wrong side of justice . . . no pun intended," she smirked. "Seriously, Charlotte, if you ever decide you want to leave that cesspool downtown, I might be able to throw you some part-time work as a private investigator in our office." She gave Aubrey another long look. "Think it over."

"After I'm done with your client, maybe I will," I smiled sweetly.

"Why so sad, everyone?" As if on cue, Raziya Bell reappeared and dragged Aubrey and me away to look at Peyton's paintings. She pointed out every aspect of her son's work, her skin barely able to contain her pride. Peyton, however, had made himself scarce after his conversation with Mitchell. "He's really been distraught since the uprising," she confided, her face lined with worry, "especially when he heard there was only enough money to award one TAGOUT scholarship. He's worried to death there won't be enough money for him to go to CalArts this fall."

So that's what I was picking up, now able to put the boy's downbeat manner and brooding looks at Mitchell in context. "But hasn't he sold enough art tonight to help out with his tuition?"

"I sure hope so," she sighed. "My husband and I have both taken extra jobs to get the money together, and we're still several thousand dollars short for the first semester's tuition, not to mention room and board." She wrung her hands as if she could squeeze the money from them. "Yusef would have been here, too, except he couldn't get time off from his second job. If I didn't help out at the gallery, I wouldn't have been here tonight myself."

We both nodded sympathetically. Then Aubrey excused himself, walked over to Mitchell, who was talking to Hookstratten, and whispered in his ear.

It was about eight thirty when Uncle Reggie stood in the middle of the gallery, his bald head gleaming, and tried to quiet the audience. Finally, Gregory Underwood's baritone went out through the crowd—"Yo, Brother Reggie is tryin' to speak!"—which did the trick better than a bullhorn.

"Thank you, thank you, for coming out tonight and lending your support in our greatest hour of need. For those of you who don't know, I'm Reggie Peeples, owner of the Spiral West Gallery but, more importantly, Chairman of the Board of TAGOUT. And now, let me introduce Dr. Lance Mitchell, Vice-Chairman of our board."

Mitchell made some introductory remarks and then presented each young artist where he or she stood and led the applause for them all. Peyton Bell had returned and was standing uncomfortably next to Gregory Underwood. Then Mitchell motioned for Underwood to come up to the microphone. The other boy smiled for his friend and stood back to give him the spotlight. Not content, Mitchell kept motioning until Peyton realized he, too, was being singled out.

"What's going on?" I asked Aubrey, who was back at my side, camera ready.

"You'll see," he promised and moved away to get an unobstructed shot.

"When TAGOUT began to raise money to fund a college scholarship," Mitchell was saying, "they came to me and California Emergency Medical Group for help. For me, the opportunity to support the artistic growth of a young person was an attractive proposition." He clasped Underwood and Peyton around their necks. "But the chance to support *two* such young people was irresistible." He smiled through his choked-back tears. "Gregory Underwood and Peyton Bell are two artists who have transformed their pain into something greater, the stuff from which they'll make great art. It is TAGOUT's pleasure to honor them tonight."

Peyton's amazement was captured by Aubrey on film, while his mother just about ripped the sleeve off my blazer. The boy's eyes widened as Mitchell handed him a check. Mitchell then gave an envelope to Underwood, which contained a check the boy excitedly waved at his friends in the crowd.

The audience, like Peyton Bell, was also moved, seemingly by two very different emotions. They went in two directions, some to mob the boys and Mitchell, others to snap up the remaining works of art.

Aubrey reappeared at my side. "After listening to the kid's story and talking to Lance, I decided CaER could afford to make a bigger donation. Good thing I had my checkbook with me."

Mitchell must have tipped off the press about Aubrey's generosity, because Neil Hookstratten and some other reporters were headed our way. Aubrey placed a hand on the small of my back and steered me toward the door. "Let's drop this film off and get some dinner, " he whispered. "I'm starving."

CHAPTER 13

THE HUNTER
GETS CAPTURED
BY THE GAME

After a week of smoky nothingness the stars had returned, scattering their blessings across the night sky like a sigh. Even though I had gone to the gallery opening partially to check out Mitchell, I had actually enjoyed myself. Not even Sandra Douglass or Jamilla Brown showing their asses could diminish the encouragement I felt seeing young artists trying to make chicken salad from the chicken shit of life in L.A.

Beast stood behind my chain-link fence, a steel-jawed sentry under the starry sky, trying to decide if Aubrey's car was friend or foe. The familiar sight of my leg emerging from the passenger's side door was his all-clear signal, and he began to prance a canine welcome in the driveway.

We stood on my front porch. "Thanks for a great evening, Aubrey. The exhibit was . . . interesting, and dinner was great."

"Is that all?" he asked.

I could feel my face grow hot. "And I enjoyed the company, too." I turned to open the door. "You want to come in for a minute? I can make you some coffee."

You don't even know where that coffeemaker is, the voice in my head chided me.

"I don't drink coffee. Do you have some te

"Sure." I gave thanks to a God who under
ness. "Come on in."

As I let the dog in the back door and put on the κ
could hear Aubrey walking around. "Where did you get the John
Biggers lithograph?" he called out from the dining room.

"*Shotguns?* It was a Christmas present from my parents last
year. They bought it from Spiral West."

I got the napkins from the sideboard in the dining room and
gazed at the lithograph above it. "I love the way the women stand
in front of their narrow little shotgun houses, carrying the smaller
houses in their hands."

The kettle called me, and I headed back to the kitchen.
Aubrey followed me and watched while the hot water worked its
magic on the dried herbs and leaves.

"Can I see the rest of the house?"

"Sure. I can give you the nickel tour, but there's not a lot
to see."

Aubrey brushed past me. "People's homes say a lot about
them, whether they know it or not."

The heady aroma of the herbal tea and Aubrey's cologne
mingled with the warmth radiating from his body, temporarily
throwing me for a loop. "What did you say?"

"I like your kitchen," he said. "You must be some cook—
you've got all the gadgets."

"Not really. My mother keeps giving me these appliances I
think in a misguided attempt to domesticate me." And impress
potential husbands, I didn't say.

He took his time inspecting the rest of the kitchen, soaking it
all up the way I had the paintings earlier that evening. The air in
the room soon took on a fragrant, disorienting electricity.

"What about the rest of the house?" he asked.

I shook off the spell and walked him through the laundry
room to the main hallway.

"Is this your bedroom?"

"Mm-hmm." I turned on the light. Beast plopped down on his

d by the door, looked at us quizzically, then dropped off to sleep.

Aubrey was staring at a collage opposite my bed. "I like this."

"Me, too." At first it was hard to understand the hold Betye Saar's *Letters from Home/Wish You Were Here* had on me, but it had haunted me from the moment I first saw it at Uncle Reggie's gallery. It was as if the artist had made art from the scraps of my life. The envelope at the top of the collage reminded me of letters I used to get from my Aunt Winnie, my mother's sister, and my uncles when I was little. The old photograph in the middle looked like a picture I had of my father with his brothers and sisters in Arkansas, and I was the solitary woman in the high heels at the bottom of the canvas, walking down a long, rough road. And while I was probably reading too much into it, the blue collage spoke to me of southern roots and the disconnected loneliness that was peculiar to L.A.

I didn't notice Aubrey had entered the closed office across the hall until it was too late. I stood uneasily in the dim light from the hall as he took in the orange and brown Marimekko-covered futon, a man's sweater draped across the office chair, the broken eyeglasses on the desk. He sneezed in the dusty stillness of the room. Reaching for the tissue box, he almost knocked the photo off the desk. I dove for it and anchored it to my chest. Beast came running, ears up and ready for trouble. I tried to turn on the light, but the bulb sputtered, then went out.

There was sad acknowledgment in Aubrey's eyes. "This was your husband's office, wasn't it?"

I put the picture back on the desk; Keith and Erica's smiles drifted back to us in the half light from the hallway. My family had been trying to get me to clean this room out forever, but I never seemed to get around to it. The last time I tried, six years ago, I was stopped by the smell of Aramis that permeated Keith's sweater and his smudged fingerprints on his eyeglasses. They were the last bits of him I had, and I couldn't bring myself to let them go.

"What's that?" Aubrey pointed to the package wrapped in faded Snoopy paper on the end table by the futon.

I fingered its curled pink ribbon, faded now to almost white. "It was a present my girlfriend Katrina had bought for Erica. She had given it to me the day we went to the library, the day Erica and Keith were . . . I never had a chance to give it to her."

I shivered; the room had gotten chilly. Aubrey drew me toward him, whispered in my hair, "Fourteen years is a long time to keep a shrine."

I jerked away and moved back into the bright hallway. "The tea's probably ready." I stood at the door with my hand on the knob. Aubrey eased by me and walked softly down the hall to the light of the living room, Beast trailing him like a guard.

I spent a few extra minutes getting the tea—and myself—together. Thankfully, Aubrey kept his distance in the living room, but I could hear him rummaging among the CDs. The stereo clicked on; the Funky Divas reached out to me in the kitchen and told me it was my life and I should live it my own way.

I had recovered by the time the tea was ready. Aubrey helped me with the tray while Beast lay on the carpet under the dining-room table, watching and dozing by turns. Aubrey sat on the leather sofa, one of the few new pieces of furniture I'd bought since Keith and Erica were killed.

"I never told you about what happened to my marriage."

I positioned myself on the edge of the sofa, unsure I wanted to play relationship show-and-tell at this stage of the game.

"Janet never saw me the whole time we were married. Even in high school, I was just a prize to her. Something she could brag to her girlfriends about: '*My* boyfriend is captain of the basketball team. *My* boyfriend's going to an Ivy League college.' " He purred it out in what sounded to me like a perfect imitation of how I remembered Janet Murphy's voice.

"But it couldn't have been all one-sided? I remember she had some pretty impressive tickets, too."

"Big breasts, big smile, big ambitions." There was something in Aubrey's voice I couldn't quite read. "I was the envy of all my friends. Even your brother," he teased with a sly smile.

"Perris was into *her?*" I couldn't imagine sexy Janet being interested in my goofy teenaged brother. In the background En Vogue, singing "My Lovin' (You're Never Gonna Get It)" seemed to agree.

Aubrey laughed, took a bite of Mrs. Franklin's pound cake. "We were all young and dumb back then. No one looked below the surface or saw anything beyond what was put right in front of his face."

"And Janet sure put what she had in your face," I smiled, remembering. "You really didn't have a clue, did you?"

"I guess not." He looked a little sheepish.

That was about par for the course in those days. Katrina and I called sisters who were fixated on ball players "tennis-shoe freaks," but there were all kinds of predators back then, including those who were obsessed with being what Grandmama Cile called "Mrs. Dr. Somebody." And while I was a little too young and too chubby to join the chase in high school, I watched the older girls from the sidelines, laying their sweet-smelling traps with feigned interest and butt-hugging minis. And all the while, the poor harebrained brothers thought because they were the hardlegs, they were in control.

The hunter gets captured by the game.

"When she told me she was pregnant, I didn't even question it," Aubrey was saying. "I knew I'd been dipping my pen in her ink—as Pop would say—and since she swore I was the only one, I stepped on up to the plate. Too bad she was more into my M.D. than m-e."

He shrugged and sipped his tea in the suddenly quiet room.

"Since we're playing truth or dare," I offered, picking at my cake, "I have a confession, too." I was afraid to look at him. "While Janet Murphy was scheming on you, there was someone else who was interested, too."

It took a moment for it to register, then Aubrey asked, "Are you serious?" He stared at me with what looked like real surprise, and shook his head. "Your brother kept telling me you had a crush on me. I thought he was just putting me on."

I shrugged it off. "You wouldn't have noticed a butterball like me."

"You still could have said something."

"Most girls weren't as bold then as they are now," I reminded him. "Remember the big party Katrina had the summer before you went back to New Haven? Losing all that weight had given me the courage to tell you how I felt. We were dancing by the pool. They were playing the Five Stairsteps' 'Ooh Child,' and you were singing in my ear."

" 'Ooh, child, things are gonna get easier,' " he sang. "I've always loved that song. It reminds me of my mother."

I remembered Mrs. Scott had died of cancer in the fall of that year. "Well, I thought you were singing to me. And I was all prepared to tell you how I felt, when Janet . . ."

"Cut in on us. Now, *that* I remember." He wagged a finger into the past. "She wasn't feeling well and wanted me to take her home. That was the night she told me she was pregnant."

"Maybe I *should* have said something."

We sat that way for a few minutes, our revelations swirling in the soft lamplight. Aubrey broke the spell. "Char, I can't call back the past. Even if I had known how you felt, I wasn't mature enough to do anything about it." He shook his head and told the ceiling, "I was so out of it then."

I swept away the crumbs and memories from my lap. "Well, it's all in the past now."

"That's what I was getting at earlier." He turned to face me on the sofa. "The past is gone—the good and the bad of it." He touched my hand. "You can't live in the past, Char."

I grabbed my empty teacup and quickly poured myself some more tea. This was not where I expected this conversation to go.

"I'm not saying this to make you uncomfortable," he hurried on. "I say it because I know. Living in the past will keep you from the present."

I hunkered down behind my teacup, wishing for my bullet-proof vest.

"I'm not going to bite you." He reached over and carefully pried the cup from my fingers. He bent down and peered into my face until my eyes met his. "This is your journey. You've got to make it in your own time. I'm just letting you know that you're not the only one who's had to make a new life for herself. Once you take a step or two, it gets easier, and pretty soon you figure out there *is* life on the other side."

I wasn't sure Aubrey was referring to my situation or his. He gathered up my hand in his and sat silently looking at it, turning it over slowly in his. "Giving Him Something He Can Feel" was playing on the stereo. Nervousness made me want to jump out of my skin. I tried a joke instead: "Taking my pulse on the sly, Doctor?"

"No. I'm just thinking how I enjoyed being with you tonight. And how I want to see you again." When he looked up at me, his face was serious. "That is, if our mutual fantasies and ghosts don't get in the way."

Still holding my hand, he turned it over and did a double take when he glanced at his watch. "Damn! It's almost one o'clock! I gotta go—I've got a staff meeting tomorrow. And you need your rest."

"Doctor's orders?"

"That's right." He led me over to the front door, bent down to whisper in my ear. "Dr. Feelgood."

My smart answer lay in my mouth, stilled by a kiss so soft that at first it felt like butterfly wings had fluttered against my lips. Soon he began to apply just a little pressure as he slowly kissed and sucked every inch of my parted lips before he introduced tantalizing bits of his tongue. My mouth began to feel like a hungry bird's, anxious for the delicacy being dangled in front of it.

His hands, both of which were holding my face, decided to divide and conquer. Dread flooded my pores. After his examination of me in the ER, I feared my body would hold no surprises, but Aubrey moved his right hand down my neck and to my shoulders as if he had never touched me before.

He took me by the shoulders and gathered me into him with a gentle but unrelenting pressure. Despite my immobilized arm, I could feel his heart pumping, and an insistent swelling pressing against my stomach.

This wasn't a make-out fantasy played out when I was

twelve, grinding my hips against the doorjamb in my bedroom, trying to imagine how Aubrey Scott would feel. It wasn't even the semi-safe slow drag we did at Katrina's party that long-ago summer. This was consensual fondling by two free, black, and over-twenty-one adults. And, good as it felt, it was scaring me to death.

It took all of the restraint within me to break contact. "Aubrey, I'm not sure we should . . ."

"Sshh . . . let me just hold you for a minute." His second kiss, slow and warm, melted into my bloodstream and did battle with the fear. He held me closer. "I'm not going to hurt you, Char."

We stood that way for so long I began to feel myself drift away. I barely noticed at first, but soon realized he was untying my sling. The silk fluttered to the floor, and he started undoing the buttons of my jumpsuit. His fingers unclasped my bra, slowly moved the lace aside until his hand cupped my left breast, and his fingers began making little circles around my nipple. I could feel it awaken and stiffen under his touch and a hot dampness gather between my breasts and legs. My blood began to tom-tom in my ears, and my knees started sending messages to my brain that they were about to give way.

Every so often the lights from a passing car bathed us in a blue-gray glow, allowing me to see in snatches that expression men have on their faces when they're single-mindedly engaged in the hunt. And I was lost at sea, unsure of my instincts, of what to do with myself. My left hand reached up to stroke his cheek. He caught it and slid it down his chest. I tried to unbutton his shirt, but he stopped me.

"Let's sit down," he whispered.

We stumbled to the sofa in an age-old dance step, my hands drawing him toward me by the belt buckle, his trying to keep up with my retreating nipple-hardened breasts. Once on the sofa, he eased the top of the jumpsuit off my shoulders. He hummed to himself as he gently took both breasts in his hands.

He bent to kiss them.

I knew I was lost.

I called Aubrey's name, my mind shrouded in fog, hoping to get a bearing. "Are you sure we should be doing this?" I moaned. "You don't even know me."

"I know what I see," he whispered back, "and I know what I want."

He kissed my nipples again, and I felt a warm, open wetness begin to flow through me. But something had shifted in the universe because the intensity of his touch ebbed and he stared up at me. "I could say the same thing to you, Char. Do *you* know *me?*"

I saw a break in the storm and stumbled toward it as best I could. "I know that everything I've seen of you these past few days is better than I could have ever imagined," I began and struggled to raise up on the sofa, "But I also think this is going awfully fast, Aubrey. Moving this fast could be dangerous for both of us."

Aubrey sat back on the sofa and regarded me for a moment before reaching into his back pocket. "If you're wondering about my health status, I've been celibate for the past year . . ."

I put my fingers to his lips. I didn't want to admit it had been even longer for me.

He unfolded a sheet of paper he pulled from his wallet. "I've got my last three AIDS test results . . ."

"Aubrey, as far as that goes, I'm negative, too. But you *know* that's not what I mean. "

He sucked my fingertips, sending electrical messages straight to my clitoris. "Then what?"

"God *knows* I want you, Aubrey." I brushed my fingers over his short, gloriously kinky hair and gazed into his eyes. "But how do I know you're not just taking pity on a poor sister who used to have a crush on you? I know about sympathy fucks and where they can—and can't—lead you."

He sat back on the sofa and looked at me long and hard. Finally he said, "Look, Char, I'm very attracted to you. You're smart, brave, principled, and *very* sexy." He ran a finger down my breastbone and sighed in confirmation of his own assessment. "But you gotta believe me, seeing you last Friday was like meeting you for the first time. I see you as you are today, not twenty-some-odd years ago."

His eyes traveled around my living room and toward the hallway leading to the back of the house. "But I'm not sure what you see. There are too many memories in this house. And as much as I'm attracted to you, maybe *I* need to be sure I'm just not another ghost come to life for *you*."

I closed my burning eyes and felt a scarred, parched desert of longing constricting my chest. I pushed him back on the sofa and struggled to kiss my way up his chest, until I found his mouth and drank deeply, hoping for salvation.

He must have sensed the drought in me. He kissed me.

Gently.

Slowly.

Deeply.

And pulled away. "I'd better go."

"What will my neighbors think?" I pointed to his awkward, stiff-legged stride. "At least stay until you can walk out normally."

He laughed a little. "Around you, woman, that could be forever."

My face grew hot, and I had to smile in spite of my disappointment. I got up and walked him to the door. "Maybe we'd better not try another good-night kiss."

Aubrey bent down to pick up my scarf at the door. He pressed it into my hand, wrapped his around mine, and pulled me to him. I stood molded against the hardness of him, quiet as a church mouse, afraid to start up again, afraid I'd be swept out on the sea flowing through me.

A pager vibrated between us. "Is that yours or mine?" I asked.

"I think it's mine." He laughed and checked the number on the display.

"Want to use the phone?" Anything to get him to stay.

"No, I'll get this in the car. It's my service; probably another crisis at one of the hospitals." He kissed me again, so softly I wished I remembered how to cry.

I went back inside and lay for a minute with my face buried in the warm, musky imprint Aubrey had left on my sofa. There hadn't been a man to leave that kind of impression on my furniture, my mind, or my body (come to think of it) in a long, long time. The scent of his cologne blended with the leather made me wonder if maybe one day something other than my job would be a reason to get up in the morning, maybe even be a part of my prayers at night.

I lay there giddy, touching myself in the places his hands had been, inhaling the possibilities for so long I embarrassed myself. Finally I got a grip and went to the bedroom to put on my sling. I cleared the coffee table and decided to make myself another cup of tea before going to bed. The clock on the microwave read 1:38; it would have to be herbal tea this time of night. I fired up the tea kettle and opened the door to let the dog out. When he ran bristling to the gate instead of to his tree in the back, I looked toward the driveway in time to see Aubrey's car pulling up.

Thank you, God. Maybe Aubrey decided his misgivings were bogus and was going to pick up where we left off (hope, hope). I checked my reflection in the bathroom and ran a comb through my hair before racing to the door.

Aubrey's face was rigid. "Char, can you ride with me over to Baldwin Hills?"

"What's the matter?"

"The service . . . a Sergeant Barnes called . . . he said . . . they just found Lance. He's dead, Char."

CHAPTER 14

TRASH OR TRADE?

When Baldwin Hills was developed, a lot of the streets were given Spanish names—maybe to honor the Mexican landowners who sold the property to real estate speculator Lucky Baldwin in the early 1900s, maybe to sucker the early Anglo buyers into thinking they were part of some romantic, early California past. So the streets were christened with exotic names like Don Lorenzo and Don Zarembo. Don Diablo and Don Quixote. There were so many that by the time black folks integrated Baldwin Hills in the sixties everybody just called the whole area "the Dons."

Lance Mitchell lived in a fifties-style ranch house at the end of a cul-de-sac on Don Alegre Place. Happy was not the word I would have used for the tired one-story structure with its faded paint job, white burglar bars on the windows, and crime tape stretched across the driveway.

Aubrey was so agitated after receiving the call from his service, he asked me to drive. "I'll catch up with you," he promised when we arrived, and stayed in the car while I made my way past the small clusters of neighbors in nightgowns and jogging suits.

Murders happened so infrequently in this neighborhood of doctors, lawyers, and community chiefs, yellow crime scene ribbon still drew a crowd. But unlike the people at the gallery just a couple of miles below us, these pajama-clad buppies weren't nearly as anxious to get a front-and-center seat for this show. They hung back, talking in twos and threes, about what interested them most—what this latest insult to the neighborhood would do to their property values.

Officer Darren Wright was handling it well, though, chatting amiably with some of the neighbors stirred from their beds by the flashing red lights on the murder van brought to the scene by the duty detective who responded to the call. Darren gave me a crooked smile and a brief nod, and recorded my name in the log as I ducked under the crime scene tape.

Lieutenant Tony Dreyfuss and a supervising detective from South Bureau were standing in the driveway, arms crossed and legs spread like two old-time sheriffs at the O.K. Corral. "I didn't call RHD on this one." Dreyfuss's shaggy mustache twitched suspiciously around the corners of his mouth, reminding me of Tom Selleck. "What are you doing here?"

Before he started stuttering, I told him how Aubrey got the call from the Bureau.

"Who from?" Dreyfuss wanted to know.

I read from my notes: "A Sergeant Barnes."

The two men frowned at each other. "I think somebody's yanking your chain, Justice," Dreyfuss said.

"Why's that?"

"Ain't no Sergeant Barnes in South Bureau."

"But there *is* a victim in there, right?"

Dreyfuss jerked his head toward the front door. "See for yourself."

Wright's jokester partner was stationed at the front door. "No rest for the weary, is there?" he asked. In this case, the saying was true. Chip LeDoux looked like he'd been dragged over five miles of bad road. First the crowd at Spiral West, now this. And he had probably handled a half a dozen other nasty calls since I'd seen him earlier this evening. Looking at his haggard face made me thank my lucky stars I'd gotten off the streets years ago.

I handed him a peppermint from the stash I keep in my purse to trick my nose at ripe crime scenes. "By the way, Chip, what does your last name mean?"

"Sweet, in French." He perked up enough to give me a wink and puckered his mouth around the candy. "Sweet as I can be."

So much for small talk. I saw and motioned Aubrey to the other side of the tape. LeDoux nodded and reintroduced himself. Aubrey was still too stunned to reply.

"What's the story in there?" I asked.

With Aubrey there, LeDoux lowered his voice and leaned into my ear: "Pretty gruesome. Looks like he snuffed himself."

His voice was extra-breathy in my ear. I stepped back and gave him my best don't-even-try-it glare. "Who caught the case?" I asked.

"Roxborough and Truesdale."

The names weren't ringing any bells. I handed him a couple of cards. "Would you tell them I'm here?"

"Can I keep one of these for myself?" LeDoux took the cards in his left hand, inhaled them, and held them close to his heart. "I may want to come and visit you sometime."

"Just tell them I'm here, okay, LeDoux?"

LeDoux gave me another wink and slipped inside.

"What was that all about?" Aubrey asked.

I shrugged it off. "Female officers are always getting that kind of gas from our male co-workers."

"And what does he think I am, chopped liver?" Aubrey's tone was indignant, and he had assumed that angry-black-man stance.

"Don't go having a testosterone surge on me, okay? He probably just assumed you were another cop."

"Which makes it okay for him to treat you like a piece of meat?"

"Believe it or not, LeDoux is relatively harmless. You don't want to see the real weasels."

When LeDoux returned, I caught a glimpse of a body hanging inside the house. Although the paramedics were there, they had not cut it down. Instead they were packing up their cases and talking to a male and female I assumed were the detectives. A few feet to the left the SID photographer had started taking pictures.

"Can either of you ID this guy?" LeDoux asked.

I looked at Aubrey's stricken face. "I'll do it," I told him.

"Detective Roxborough said to go on in."

I entered the parquet-floored entry carefully, walking as close to the wall as possible. There was an opening to a galley kitchen on the right with a breakfast nook beyond. A wet bar, stocked with expensive crystal glasses, was on my left. A dusty, rectangular glass-and-marble dining-room table was positioned at the end of the entry hall in an open dining area. Five silver-toned metal chairs surrounded the table, and atop it sat a pale green Chinese vase that crowded the hanging lamp suspended over it. Two shining, black lacquered pedestals flanked either side of the step-down entrance to the living room ahead of me, festooned with a second ribbon of yellow crime scene tape that separated us from the body.

Lance Mitchell hung awkwardly from the top of a door on the far side of the living room, suspended from a thick, twisted, gold-colored cord. The cord hadn't come from the blue houndstooth-check silk robe he was wearing. That belt was lashed around his waist in a half-hearted attempt to keep the robe closed. Neither the robe nor the paisley silk briefs peeking from underneath it were enough to ward off the chill of a May night in a city that most people forget had started out as a desert.

Two black detectives stood talking to the crime scene photographer a few feet away from the body. The female was sepia-toned, a little younger and shorter than I, maybe thirty-three and five-two to my five-five. Built like a brick house with a cute little pixie haircut and a trio of moles near her lazy right eye, she nodded in my direction. It was then that I recognized her as Billie Truesdale, the treasurer of the Georgia Robinson Association, a black female law-enforcement group. Her medium-brown partner was a good twenty years older, a little potbellied, and well endowed with an abundance of nose and an outdated Afro that started in the middle of his head.

He held up a gloved hand. "Jimmy Roxborough, Detective. And that's Billie Truesdale. You know this guy?"

I gazed up at Mitchell's bloated blue-black face. "His name is Dr. Lance Mitchell. He was an emergency physician at California Medical Center."

Billie's eyes independently searched my face. "What's your relationship to him?"

"He was being investigated in connection with a 187 that went down on King Boulevard last Friday." I referred to the notes I made before leaving my house. "Your Sergeant Barnes called the vic's employer, Dr. Aubrey Scott, to come to the house. Dr. Scott contacted me."

Roxborough turned to Billie. "Who's Barnes?"

Billie checked her notebook, her plucked eyebrows moving like two tiny caterpillars. "Beats me. Lieutenant Patel was the watch commander who called me. Now, Bansuela was the first detective on the scene. Could it have been him?"

Danny and I had partnered up during a good deal of my tenure at South Bureau. No way would I have misinterpreted his name, and the name Patel wasn't even close. Aubrey must've heard it wrong. But when I ducked outside to double-check, he was nowhere to be found. LeDoux said he walked down the street to get some air, and he'd let me know as soon as Aubrey returned.

"How did *you* get the call?" I asked the detectives when I returned.

Billie consulted her notes. "An anonymous male called nine one one from a phone booth on Slauson and Overhill down in Windsor Hills at one twenty-five, directing officers to the house. Because it was placed so far from the scene, the operator who took the call thought it might be a prank until LeDoux and Wright rolled up here and found the door ajar and the body hanging from the door. They called Danny Bansuela at one fifty-five and then established a crime scene."

I glanced at my watch. It was three thirty now.

"What makes this case special enough to get one of you Red Hot Dogs out of bed?" Roxborough had slipped and called RHD the nickname I knew got used behind our backs, but I didn't bother to correct him or even acknowledge the crack.

"My King Boulevard vic was one of those fugitive revolutionaries, wanted for a double homicide back in seventy-eight. Mitchell may have been the last person to see him alive." I saw no need to tell them the rest.

"You must have inherited that case," Roxborough noted with a smile. "You're too young for a case that old to have been yours."

"I'll take that as a compliment, Detective, but, yes, you could say that."

Billie's lazy eye focused with its mate on me for a moment, then she turned abruptly and went back to diagramming the scene.

Roxborough frowned. "Sorry you had to come out on a trash run."

I inwardly cringed at the use of the slang term for suicide, even though it was one I'd heard some homicide detectives use from time to time.

Billie put a hand on her partner's coat sleeve. "Why don't you get started with the photographer, Jimmy, and I'll talk to Detective Justice." She tossed me a brief smile. "I can't imagine a Red Hot Dog coming out this time of night just for the hell of it."

I exhaled a sigh of relief. If Billie knew the real deal about my underlying connection to the Lewis case, at least she didn't scream on me right then and there.

Roxborough pulled a toothpick out of his jacket pocket and started using it to direct the work of the crime scene photographer. "We're waiting for the coroner's investigator to cut him down," he said, "but I'm telling you, this is a trash run."

"I just saw Mitchell earlier this evening, and he didn't seem despondent or depressed to me. What makes you think he killed himself?"

"Take a look."

Between the flash bursts of the photographer's Nikon, I saw in fragmented snippets what Roxborough meant. The sixth metal dining-room chair, laying on its side beneath the body at the open door. Silver gouge marks from where the back of the chair scraped against the door. Other, smaller marks on the door that looked like scratches Mitchell might have made as he reflexively struggled against the rope in his last moments. Magazines strewn around the chair.

"This victim has got to be pushing forty, forty-five," I noted. "Don't you think he's a little old for this kind of thing?"

Roxborough bristled at that. "Well, it's either trash or trade. Somebody was getting their rocks off, that's for sure."

The photographer had zeroed in on the slick porno magazines scattered around the chair. Young black men wearing nothing but eight-inch, half-mast erections pouted up at us suggestively. The photographer took several shots of these and their proximity to the body.

I leaned in a little to get a closer look at Mitchell's neck. "What do you make of this cord?" I asked Billie.

"It's a little like the ones they use to rope off the crowds at the Academy Awards." She saw me make a note. "Is that relevant to your case?"

"Maybe. I'm just trying to get a fix on things here, see if they relate to our guy from last Friday. Where does that door lead?"

"Down the hall to the bedroom," Roxborough said. "It appears the deceased placed the chair against the door, worked the rope underneath and over the top of the door, and put his neck in the noose. Then all he had to do was start pulling the rope with one hand and choking the chicken with the other while he got off on the magazines."

Roxborough sighed and shook his head. "I've seen this kind of setup before. Crude, but it gets the job done. They say it's the greatest high on earth, but I'd rather get my jollies the old-fashioned way, you know what I'm saying?"

Billie ignored her partner and scowled up at Mitchell's swollen face. "It's a damn shame, grown man like this."

"Any evidence he might have had some company?" I asked.

"That's why I was saying to Jimmy earlier that it could be trade-related." Billie piped up, giving Roxborough a sidelong glance. She stepped over to the coffee table. "There are two wine glasses over here. The one with the white wine has a dark stain on it—probably lipstick. And there are a couple of bottles over there that have been opened recently."

"Any evidence of drugs? I understand the victim had a problem with prescription painkillers."

Billie shook her head, scribbled a note in her notebook. "You know if he lived alone?" she asked.

"Far as I know. His boss told me he was separated from his wife, and I haven't heard about any roommates."

"That's what the neighbors say, too," Billie said, "but we've requested a warrant to search the premises anyway. Don't want to step on anybody else's rights in case he was shacked up."

"I know we gotta follow procedures," Roxborough added, "but with a setup like this, he *definitely* lived alone."

"Even so," she warned, "I don't want any evidence to be thrown out later in court because we screwed up."

Roxborough rolled his eyes. "As if there was a crime committed here."

The argument I could feel brewing between Roxborough and Truesdale made my temple throb. "So lemme see if I'm following you here," I cut in. "The victim had a female over . . ."

"Or a man wearing lipstick." Billie pointed to one of the magazines across the room, which was devoted to the fine art of cross-dressing.

"Okay. They drank some wine and then what?"

Billie led me into the bedroom, which had several Japanese erotic drawings on the walls and was dominated by a black lacquered bed. She stood by the sliding glass door and directed my attention to a wet spot in the middle of the satin sheets.

"And then?"

"Got into some kinky games, I guess." Billie spoke with all the conviction of a black Republican trying to explain how trickle-down economics work in the ghetto. It may have been what she and Roxborough wanted to think, but I wasn't buying it.

"You may be right," I said as diplomatically as possible, "but this just isn't adding up for me. From what little I knew, Dr.

Mitchell fancied himself a real ladies' man. Even tried to hit on me in the emergency room a few days ago."

"Well, you never know about people," Roxborough argued. "He coulda been working both sides of the street. Just look at this place."

While the exterior may have been a little worn, the inside of Lance Mitchell's house was done to death. Art everywhere. Two fresh-off-the-showroom–smelling white silk love seats atop a thick, oversized Oriental carpet in front of the fireplace. Lamps with the designer tags still attached. "A young, impressionable kid could really get carried away in here, under the right circumstances," Roxborough's ample lips curled in contempt.

My mind went back to the reception, tried to reframe Mitchell's easy camaraderie with Peyton Bell and Gregory Underwood. Mitchell with his arm around Underwood. His long hug with Peyton. The thought of a grown man luring those barely legal young men here made my skin crawl.

LeDoux stood at the entrance to the bedroom. "Bansuela dropped off the warrant, Jimmy. And the SID guys are here." He handed the paperwork to Billie, who scanned it and nodded for the criminalists to get started. Herman Wozniak and another green-jacketed tech came in and started setting up shop.

"Your doctor is back, too," LeDoux told me.

Billie stripped off her gloves. "I'll question Dr. Scott. I need a smoke, anyway." She led me away from the suddenly active scene. "Why don't we get out of their way, Detective Justice?"

I watched Billie light up a cigarette in the driveway. As she shaved a few minutes off her life span, her skin took on a bluish cast in the swirling smoke and light fog that had settled in the hills. She stared off into the weedy garden for a moment before both eyes focused on me. "That double homicide in seventy-eight was your husband and child, right?"

I nodded, afraid if I opened my mouth she would hear my heart thudding.

"We heard about that case at the Academy," she remembered. "I always wondered what I would have done if it had happened to me."

"Now you know."

Billie nodded, stubbed out her cigarette in a flower bed, and walked over to where Aubrey was pacing up and down the sidewalk. After the niceties were over, she got down to the nitty-gritty. "Detective Justice tells me you received a call informing you Dr. Mitchell was dead. What time was that?"

Aubrey looked to me for an assist. When he saw no help forthcoming, he cleared his throat. "About one thirty. I had just left a friend's house."

The memory of Aubrey's pager vibrating between us caused a guilt-laden shiver to run through me, which I forced down with a dry cough.

"The operator at our service said Sergeant Barnes called notifying us that Dr. Mitchell was dead and for me to come to his house."

"Are you sure about the name?" I asked.

"Is there a problem?" he asked, confusion on his face.

"Does your service keep records of your calls, Doctor?"

Aubrey nodded again. "Have to, for malpractice purposes," he explained to Billie. "I can have them verify it, if you'd like."

"Don't bother." Billie's words were clipped. "Just give me their number, and I'll call them myself."

Aubrey was handing her a card when Roxborough came to the door, waving his hand. "Billie, Justice, get in here. We've got something," he said, and disappeared back inside.

I caught up to her just before we got inside. "Billie . . . Dr. Scott was with me tonight."

She nodded. "I thought it was something like that." And waited for more.

I moved closer and explained under my breath, "Aubrey's an old high-school friend. When Mitchell popped up in connection with the Lewis murder, I went to Aubrey for some background information on his colleague. He took me to an art exhibit earlier this evening, where I was checking out Mitchell. We went to my house afterward, and that's where he got paged."

She still looked skeptical. "I don't want my business all out in the street, Billie. I especially don't need Detective Firestone, my supervisor, asking me a bunch of questions about why I didn't call him soon as I heard Mitchell got popped. Can you help me out on this one?"

Race and gender notwithstanding, there was little reason for a South Bureau detective to cover for a Red Hot Dog. In fact, there was every reason for her *not* to be cooperative. I held my breath while Billie squinted at me in the fog. At last, she nodded. "If it was me trying to get to the bottom of who did my family, I'd hope someone would have my back."

But she lingered for another moment in the chill air, spat out a bit of tobacco, and fixed me with one steady eye. "Charlotte, your personal life is certainly none of my business. But don't let your hormones cloud your judgment. Think about it. There's no way someone from South Bureau would have left a message like that with an answering service. We'd have done the next-of-kin notification *after*, not before, we got to the scene."

I felt the blood color my cheeks. It was something that hadn't even occurred to me in my heated rush with Aubrey earlier that night.

"And how would some nonexistent sergeant have known to call Mitchell and Scott's answering service unless they knew the victim or searched the body?" she asked. "And none of our guys would even *dream* of touching a body until the coroner's office showed up."

I let that one hang in the air. "Mitchell probably didn't have time to buy a new wallet," I admitted. "His old one was taken into evidence in the Lewis homicide."

"Even if he bought a new one, do you think he's had time to fill out a next-of-kin card?" she asked.

Before I could answer, Roxborough stuck his head out the door again. "Let's cut the chitchat, ladies. This ain't no slumber party!"

Lance Mitchell's bedroom had been tossed. "The jewelry box on the dresser is empty," Roxborough noted, "and someone's been through the closets. Real neat job, though. Looks like they took their time. We'll need to get a property list from the next of kin and put a notice out to the pawn shops."

"The deceased's wife might be able to help with the list," I said, "but from what I've heard, don't expect her to be too cooperative."

Billie was impatient, pen poised: "Let's have her name, anyway." A homegirl-inflected "Uh, *uh*" escaped her lips when I told her Dr. Mitchell's estranged wife was the popular radio talk-show psychologist.

Even Roxborough was impressed. "The wife listens to Dr. Holly religiously." He pulled a cell phone out of his pocket as we walked back to the living room. "I'ma notify Press Relations downtown on this one right now, before all hell breaks loose."

I walked over to the open sliding glass door and looked across the patio and out onto the city. For Lance Mitchell, moving back to the Dons after Beverly Hills must have been a real step backward, making him sort of a downwardly mobile Jed Clampett. And somewhere in the hills of Beverly was Mitchell's estranged wife, Dr. Holly Hightower Mitchell. Given what Aubrey had told me, I wondered how she'd react when Detectives Truesdale and Roxborough did the next-of-kin notification later in the day.

I didn't hear Roxborough come up behind me. "This is some sick shit, ain't it?" It was more of a statement than a question.

"Yeah, but not for the reasons you think."

"What d'you mean?" he asked.

"I just have a bad feeling in my gut about this one."

"Is this one of those 'women's intuition' things?"

"Call it what you like, but something's just not clicking for me. Gives me the heebie-jeebies, you know what I mean?"

"Well, I'm putting my money on autoerotic asphyxiation, with or without an audience." Roxborough wore the determined look of a man who's made up his mind, regardless of the facts.

My throbbing temple had graduated into a full-fledged headache.

The telltale click-clack in the parquet hallway announced Mikki Alexander's arrival. The ever-stylishly-dressed coroner's investigator was trailed by two attendants bearing a gurney. And while she had the look of a supermodel coming down a runway, the dense layers of Halston and cigarettes that clung to her clothes suggested she'd just come from a ripe one. It was four forty-five.

"We gotta stop meeting like this, Detective," she smiled in an offhanded greeting. "Isn't this a South Bureau case?"

"This victim was a suspect in the Lewis murder."

Her eyes widened. "The guy from the situation Friday whose wallet was found under that body?"

I only had time to nod before Roxborough and Billie appeared. "What've we got here?" she asked them.

"Trash run, far as I'm concerned," Roxborough replied.

Roxborough, Billie, and Alexander studied the position of the body. "What time did you get the call?" she asked and listened to our description of the chain of events while she snapped on some latex gloves.

Alexander motioned the attendants over. One of them squatted down a little, gripped Mitchell around the hips, and held the body while Alexander cut the cord, leaving a tail of about eight inches from the knot around Mitchell's neck. Then his female partner eased the body to the ground, and Alexander carefully moved the rope aside with the eraser tip of a pencil and considered Mitchell's discolored face and the marks on his neck.

"Give me some light here," she asked. The female brought over a large flashlight and directed it toward Mitchell's head. Alexander examined Mitchell's neck and the cord. "It looks as if there are two marks here," she noted.

"Rope musta slipped before it took hold," Roxborough noted. "It happens."

Alexander hummed something to herself, then looked around the room. "It looks like a decorative rope of some sort. Anybody know where it came from?"

"Unh-unh," Roxborough said, "but we're looking."

Roxborough marched off to the bedroom to direct the SID techs. Billie got out her Polaroid and started taking pictures of Mitchell's face for ID purposes and handed one to me.

"How much longer do you need?" Alexander asked Billie.

"Maybe another couple of hours," she replied. "I want to go over the rest of the house a little more thoroughly, see if there's any other physical evidence or if it appears anything else was taken."

Mikki Alexander nodded. "We're gonna get started collecting specimens—scrapings from under the nails and the pubes."

Billie looked at Roxborough, who had rejoined us. "Great," she said to Alexander, ignoring Roxborough's yawning. "Get everything you can."

"At least you can do your job without worrying about dodging bullets like the other night," I said.

"Ain't that the truth," Alexander laughed.

"You gonna take a closer look at him in Processing later this morning?" I asked.

"Soon as I can," Alexander answered. "Got a messy one ahead of him. Family dead in the house ten days before anyone thought to make a missing persons call."

So that explained it. Everyone had ways of trying to disguise the smell from the ripe ones that gets into your clothes. A lot of cops use cigars. I burn incense in my car. Alexander used expensive perfume.

"Well this guy was a popular doc about town," I offered, "involved in a lot of activities in Councilwoman Moore's district. She's gonna be all over your boss like white on rice about this one."

"Thanks for the warning." Alexander pushed back a loose strand of hair with the back of her sleeve and considered Mitchell, her face strained. "Why can't we just get some John Does for a change?"

"It's pretty clear what we got here." Roxborough pointed his wet toothpick toward Mitchell's body. "Boyfriend brought home some trade, got carried away and choked himself out, then Sweet Cheeks made off with his shit. It's a slam dunk. So I wouldn't get too worked up over this one if I were you, Mikki."

Billie sneaked a peek at Alexander and me, gave an almost imperceptible twitch of her shoulders that seemed to say, *See what I'm up against?* The moment reminded me of a line from the LAPD's *Homicide Detectives Manual:* "A homicide detective carries a heavy responsibility when called upon to investigate a death, for he stands in the dead person's shoes to protect his interests against those of everyone else." As I gazed at Mitchell's body, I felt the silent plea of a victim who had no one else to speak for him. It was then that I became bound and determined to find out the truth about Lance Mitchell's death, even if I had to do battle with Jimmy Roxborough, Billie Truesdale, or Lieutenant Dreyfuss himself.

Alexander must have felt the call, too. She stared at Roxborough, then gazed down at Mitchell's blue-black face, and leaned over him as if she were making a promise. "If I do a little juggling, maybe we can examine him in Processing in a couple of hours."

"You ladies suit yourselves," he shrugged. "I'ma interview the neighbors, do the next-of-kin, then I'ma sign out to you on this one, Billie. I gotta meeting."

Billie Truesdale cut her eyes at Roxborough, then turned quickly back to the body. "Sure, Jimmy. I'll touch base with you later."

"Have fun, ladies," he smirked on his way out the door.

"You, too," Billie called after him. The sarcasm in her voice told me she was wishing him anything but.

I t was after five. Aubrey was still pacing outside the house. The other South Bureau detectives had left to take other calls. "I overheard the officers saying Lance's death was autoerotic asphyxiation," he whispered. "Is that true?"

"Why do you ask?"

"Because in the E.R, we usually see that kind of thing with adolescents, not grown men Lance's age!" Aubrey looked at me with a pained expression and shook his head. "This just doesn't add up."

And neither did Aubrey's story. While it was clear that the call he got was bogus, I couldn't decide if Aubrey Scott was trying to play us for his own reasons or if someone had set him up to find the body. The implications made my head hurt a little more.

A cab pulled up to the curb. "I knew you'd be a while," he explained, "so I'm going to go back to your house and get my car."

"I'm sorry about this, Aubrey . . ."

He started to say something else, then checked himself. He scribbled his home number on the back of his business card. "Call me if anything develops or if you think I can help."

He hesitated, then moved to kiss my forehead. I almost leaned into it before I saw Officer LeDoux looking our way. I stepped back and threw up a hand. "I'll talk to you later."

Inside, Alexander had made the incision and shoved a thermometer into Mitchell's liver to determine the time of death. Around her, people were busy collecting evidence. I stood off to the side, staring at Mitchell's dusty dining-room table.

Billie joined me, whispered: "Roxborough's got a girlfriend who lives down in Hawthorne. He ends up there whenever he gets a late-night call. Word is, he's been tipping on his wife like that for years."

Probably while the poor Mrs. Roxborough listens to Dr. Holly. Goes to show that just because you listen to the message doesn't mean you know what to do with it.

"You see the vase on this table?" I asked. "Wouldn't you say it's too tall to be sitting under that lamp?"

She looked at it again, hunched her shoulders. "So the doctor didn't have a good eye for decorating. A lot of men don't."

"That's not my point," I said. "Everything else in the house is exquisite. A little dusty, maybe, but the place reeks of good taste. That vase is out of place. And I bet you five bucks if you move it you won't find a dust ring."

"You're on." Billie had a SID tech carefully lift the vase. Sure enough, there was dust underneath it but the vase itself was clean as a whistle. Which is what Billie did. "Well cut me off at the knees and call me Shorty," she said under her breath. "Guess I owe you five."

"Have the guys check for pottery shards around those pedestals over there. I'm thinking there was a pair of them, and this one got moved after the struggle so no one would notice."

Billie went over to check out the black columns. "They've

been dusted clean, too." She looked around the rest of the house. "Only things in here that have."

"And there's another thing," I added. "If Mitchell was a chicken choker like Roxborough said, how could he jerk off with his underwear on?"

Billie's eyes darted over to the body in time to see Alexander pulling Mitchell's silk shorts back up. "Damn! I knew there was something off about the body."

"It's hard to concentrate when your partner's giving you static. But it ought to be a lot easier with Roxborough at his 'meeting.' " I patted her arm. "I'll call you later this morning to see if you found anything else."

"I'll call you from the morgue if they find anything significant," she promised. "And I'll call Detective Firestone in the morning and see if we can get you involved in the case as an RHD liaison." She fished a five out of her purse to pay off our bet on the vase and handed it over with her business card. "Although it might cost me a few bucks in the short run, I think I could use your help."

CHAPTER 15

DOWN HOME BLUES

By the time I got home at six thirty, I felt lower than a snake's hip. The sun peeking over the rooftops created an eerie backlight for Beast, who was standing in the driveway, staring in my direction. The only survivor of a mother-daughter homicide I worked back in '89, Beast had developed the ability to smell death. When I opened the back door, he stopped to snuffle me carefully at the top of the steps, gave me a sad, accusing look that said, *Where have you been?* and slunk away to his bed.

Although my nose was so dead I couldn't smell anything myself, I took the dog's hint, stripped in the laundry room, and headed for the shower to wash away the invisible blue funk clinging to me like a shroud.

I was feeling down because I believed we were being played. There was enough suspicious evidence at the scene to tip me off that Mitchell's "accident" just didn't ring true, I didn't care what kind of face Roxborough tried to put on it. But for the life of me I couldn't figure out how or why someone would kill Dr. Mitchell and then go to such lengths to implicate him in something as sordid as what I'd seen on Don Alegre.

I paged Steve when I got out of the shower to give him an

update, but after a half an hour, he hadn't responded. I should have gone on to sleep. God knows I needed it. But as I got into bed, something kept eating away at me, wouldn't let me rest.

It just didn't make any sense. Mitchell and Lewis, Lewis and Mitchell. A card-carrying member of the L.A. niggerati versus a pseudo-revolutionary gang-banger. A South Central homeboy versus a Westside buppie. There was nothing they had in common, no way their paths should have ever crossed. Except they had, somewhere on King Boulevard, and now they were both dead. Which made them connected, whether I liked it or not.

Eventually I got up and went in search of my personal book of fairy tales that, along with a warm glass of milk, might lull me to sleep. I settled for what my father called mother's milk for adults—a sea-scented twelve-year-old Bunnahabhain—and sat down with a finger of the single-malt Scotch and my cobbled-together murder book. I flipped to the Xeroxed police bulletins to get the name and address of Lewis's mother. Perhaps she could shed some light on her son's whereabouts all these years.

For the first time since pulling out Keith and Erica's murder book the day before, I realized Cinque Lewis's mother lived only a few blocks from where his body was found. I started to jot down the address and immediately felt like an even bigger fool for not seeing it sooner. Cinque's mother, Trudy, had at least two husbands by 1978, but it wasn't to learn her secrets of connubial bliss that propelled me out of my house and toward her South Central address like a bat out of hell. It was her maiden name—Mitchell—sandwiched between the string of acquired surnames that made me realize there may be more to the Lance Mitchell–Cinque Lewis connection than met the eye.

To hear some folks tell it, you would think the motto on the Statue of Liberty only applied to wide-eyed immigrants arriving on steamers from places like Germany, Ireland, or Russia. As I drove toward King Boulevard, I began to think a new statue should be erected right here—maybe downtown near the city's El

Pueblo de Los Angeles Historical Monument, where the first forty-four settlers, mostly nonwhite, set up housekeeping in 1781. Our statue would be a beautiful black angel—*ángelitos negros,* Angela Bofill once called them in a song—with inky, gossamer wings outstretched to enfold the new huddled masses. The El Salvadorans and Eritreans. Koreans and Costa Ricans. Guatemalans and Guamanians. *Los ángelitos negros* could be installed all over the city to commemorate the flux and flow of the new Angelenos that heralded the browning of America.

Take Kenwood Avenue. Before the Watts riots, the street was solidly black and resolutely middle-class. Schoolteachers and postal workers. McDonnell Douglas aircraft mechanics and beauticians. Some of them were still there, still driving the Buick deuce-and-a-quarters and Oldsmobile Delta 88s that once upon a time announced they had *arrived*, had it made in the shade with lemonade. By 1992, though, these same black folk were outnumbered by new immigrants from every conceivable Spanish-speaking country and a good number from the Pacific Rim as well. But unlike the flighty whites of the fifties and sixties, ready to move at the drop of a property appraisal, a lot of these black folks, uprooted once from Texas, Georgia, Mississippi, or Arkansas, had made it perfectly clear that they weren't going, as Grandmama Cile would say, "Another futher, brother."

I suspected the old woman sitting in the flower-choked courtyard of the Kenwood Garden Apartments was like that. A currant-colored giant with stockings rolled down below her knees, she looked as if she'd been planting her yellow vinyl-covered dinette chair in that garden every morning for the past fifty years. Z. Z. Hill crying the blues from her kitchen window further staked her claim to the property, and was engaged in a boom-box battle of the bands with N.W.A.'s "Straight Outta Compton" and Kid Frost's "La Raza" blaring from the cluster of one-story bungalows in the rear.

Her name was Mrs. Sparks.

"Why y'all wanna talk t'Trudy now?" she asked, frowning at the business card I handed her. "You police dogged the poor woman to death. Whatchu want—" she chewed out the words with some tobacco, spat them into a Maxwell House coffee can for punctuation "—t'pick over her bones?"

"I'm sorry, Mrs. Sparks. I came to tell her that her son was found dead last Friday night. I didn't know she'd passed away. Mind if I sit down?"

She grudgingly indicated a matching chair on the opposite side of the coffee can. I moved the chair back a little further from her makeshift spittoon, just in case she missed—accidentally on purpose.

"Trudy been gone almost nine years." Mrs. Sparks sat staring in the direction of the garden, her dark slab of a hand busy gathering her bosom together. "She was a 'Bama girl, just like me." She interrupted her reverie to ask how Cinque Lewis died. She listened grimly to the details, her lips pulled tight over teeth I was sure weren't hers. "Mmph, mmph, mmph. Bobby loved that taco stand, ever since he was a li'l boy. And t'think he went back there t'die."

"Had you seen him in the last few days, Mrs. Sparks?"

Her eyes flickered but stayed focused on her flowers. "Cain't say as I have."

The old woman's response took me back to childhood and one of my grandmother's sayings: *Ninety-nine lies may save you, but the hundredth will give you away.*

I tried another approach. "You said you and Trudy were from Alabama. Do you know if she had any other relatives out here, anyone else Bobby might have stayed with, somebody we could notify?"

She moved about in her chair, her eyes still on the garden. "They didn't have no blood kin out chere. I 'ont rightly know 'bout who's left down home."

There went my "Cinque Lewis and Lance Mitchell as kin-folk" theory. "So you were just friends?"

"Chile, sometimes friends are better'n family," she laughed a little, a rich, rumbling sound cut off abruptly by a wave of remembered grief.

Thinking of my homegirl, Katrina, I knew she wasn't lying about that. But I also knew, if she really believed what she was saying, Mrs. Sparks was bound to know something about Cinque Lewis, her 'Bama girl's son.

"Well, you sure are right about that." I tilted back in my chair to chuckle along with her. "Did you and Trudy come out here together?"

"Unh-unh. See, I was a good twenty years older'n Trudy, more her mama's age. Me and Mr. Sparks come out chere in forty-two, a full four or five years 'head of Trudy, her mama, 'n' them. Everybody from down home knowed we owned this property and all, so me and Mr. Sparks had us a steady stream of folks comin' from all over the Black Belt. So many folks from home lived in these apartments over the years, we started t'call the place 'Down Home Out West.' "

As a child, I'd heard my father's friends joke that L.A. was just another term for Lower Alabama. Looking into the past with Mrs. Sparks, I finally understood why.

"Now Trudy's people was from Three Notch, outside of Montgom'ry. Mine was from Perdido, a li'l dent in the road named after the river what runs through the place. Town used to be so small and so poor there wudn't even colored and white drinkin' fountains when I lived there. Ev'body just drank from the river."

"Sounds like my father's description of Charlotte, Arkansas," I chimed in. " 'A pinprick near the grease spot of Batesville' is what he calls it."

She laughed again. I leaned forward in my chair, pressing the advantage. "We're trying to find out what happened to Trudy's son, Mrs. Sparks. Maybe if we can figure out where he's been all these years, it'll lead us to his killer."

"Hmph! What happened t'Bobby is he broke his mama's heart, is what happened." She reached across me for her chaw can, spat into it, and sat back in her chair. "Shee-it, Bobby Lewis had his mama's nose so wide open it was a cryin' shame. Woman worked *two* jobs tryin' t'he'p that little one-arm bandit. And how do he repay her? Spoutin' all that 'Black Is Beautiful' mess on the one hand and then takin' the life of another woman's husband and baby on the other. The only killer here is Bobby. The day he shot that man and his baby, he put a bullet in his mama's heart, too . . . it just took her longer t'die."

Trudy died three years to the day after her son disappeared, Mrs. Sparks told me. That made it May 10, the same date that Keith and Erica were killed.

Sweat started to prickle my armpits, despite the coolness of the early morning garden. My discomfort did not escape the old woman. "You okay, Miss Detective?"

Unto thee will I cry, O Lord my rock. You will *not* lose it in front of this woman, I warned myself. "I'll be fine."

Mrs. Sparks disappeared inside, reemerging with a small drinking glass decorated with once-bright yellow lemons. She pulled up her chair and patted my knee while I gulped the water. "Now you gotta tell Jeannie what's troublin' you, baby."

The droning of a bee struck me as extraordinarily loud until I realized it was my ears ringing. Mrs. Sparks studied my face, as if she could read my sorry history seeping from my pores. "You pregnant, darlin'?"

"No, ma'am," I answered from what seemed like a great distance. "I finished my childbearing a long time ago."

"Boy or girl?"

"Girl. Twelve this month." If she had lived, my voice echoed in my head.

"That's a nice age for a girl. Still tomboys, a lot of 'em, but with just enough womanliness peekin' round the edges for you t'know they gonna come into they own someday. It was that way with Bobby's girlfriend, Candy, but she was much older when she went through that phase. Even though she was twenty-two, she was just sorta out there, y'know, not knowin' which way t'go. But she was a sweet li'l thang, 'neath all that wildness. In the long run she made it up t'Trudy for all the pain that no-count son of hers brung her. After he left, her and Trudy was like Ruth and Naomi out the Bible, them two was."

"Are you talking about Sojourner Truth?"

"Hmph! I never did call her by that ign'ant, made-up name Bobby give her. Her mama named her Candy, and that's what I call her."

She had used the present tense. "So you're still in touch with her?"

Mrs. Sparks smoothed down her apron and got to her feet. "Look at me, I'm fo'gittin' my manners. Can I getchu some more water or sum'm?"

I stopped her on her way to the door. "Where is Candy now?"

The old woman's eyes fluttered as if she were awaking from a dream. "Candy? Shoot, after Trudy passed, she went back to school, met a nice fella, and moved away. I encouraged her, too—she had t'get on with her own life, make a fresh start. Except for a Christmas letter and a birthday card the first few years, I ain't hardly heard from her. But I 'ont blame her. She had t'do what she had t'do."

"Where is she, Mrs. Sparks?" I asked, my voice a little sharper.

"I 'ont know!" The old woman changed direction, and moved toward the garden, deadheading roses and trimming the stalks on the spent delphinium and salvia blooms with some cutting shears she produced from a pocket in her apron. She had completely forgotten about getting me some more water. Her behavior reminded me of another of my grandmother's sayings: *When falsehood walks, it goes astray.*

I joined her in the garden and turned over a rock with the tip of my shoe. Ants scurried everywhere. "If you kept her letters, Mrs. Sparks, the postmarks could help us find her. She might be able to lead us to Bobby's killer."

Mrs. Sparks let loose a laugh that ran helter-skelter with the ants among the flowers. "You know, Detective Justice, my eyes is so old, I could barely read them cards, never mind the envelopes. But I sho will look through my things and letchu know if I finds som'm. I sho will."

I stood gazing into the tangled mess of Mrs. Sparks's garden. I wasn't going to sweat an eighty-something-year-old woman over her sudden and convenient lapse in memory or for doing the Butterfly McQueen "I don't know nuthin' 'bout birthin' no babies" on me. But I had to admit it annoyed me to think this old woman would try to pull the okeydoke on me.

I could ask her to come downtown for questioning, but I knew with a woman like Jeannie Sparks, that wouldn't get me very far. Or I could try working her mind, far more effective a tactic with a person her age. "Well, if Candy calls, let her know I came by, would you?" I gave Mrs. Sparks my card and whispered: "They've got Bobby's body down at the morgue. The county's gonna have to cremate him if some of his people don't step forward."

My words had the desired effect. Mrs. Sparks's shoulders drooped as if they were carrying the weight of the world. "Trudy would just turn over in her grave if she knew her baby was gonta be burnt up 'stead of put in the ground. She always wanted to bury Bobby with her. Even bought a double plot out at Sunnyslope for when the time came."

I left her to mull it over in the garden. Walking toward my car, I considered how Mrs. Sparks sounded more like Mrs. Franklin or Grandmama Cile than a landlady. A woman like that would have stayed in touch with Candy, and the younger woman didn't sound like the type who would just up and abandon someone who obviously cared for her so much.

I waved at the old woman and pulled off, hoping for two things: one, that the thought of her best friend spending eternity separated from her only child would prey on Jeannie Sparks's mind. And two, that Mrs. Sparks would do the right thing and put me in touch with Candy Grant, aka Sojourner Truth.

I paged Steve and left my cell phone number with a 911 flag after it, our code for urgent. I was heading west on the Santa Monica Freeway toward home by the time he got back to me.

"So what the hell happened?" he asked after I told him Mitchell was dead.

"It looks like autoerotic asphyxiation."

"No shit!"

"But too much is off about this one, Steve. Gave me the hee-bie-jeebies." I told him about my suspicions about Mitchell's "accident." "Mikki Alexander's gonna take a look at him in Processing later this morning if she can."

Steve swore again. "Stobaugh's gonna chew my ass out when he finds out you were at that scene instead of me or Cortez."

"I think I've got that handled." I told him about Billie Truesdale and our connection through the Georgia Robinson Association. There was silence on the line. "You know, the black female law-enforcement group. Named after the first black woman cop in the LAPD."

Still no response. Jeez, even Stobaugh knew about the GRA. "Anyway, I told her I was in kind of a delicate situation with the Lewis connection and all. Bottom line is I think she'll cover for me. Better yet, she's going to call you to request I act as an RHD liaison on the Mitchell case."

After I gave him Billie's number, he asked, "So how was your date?"

"So why didn't you answer your page?"

"Is that a note of jealousy I hear in your voice, Detective?" he asked.

"Hardly. Let's get real clear on something, Steve. You and I are *co-workers*, not lovers. If you want to reconcile with your wife, that's your business. And if I want to go out on a date, that's mine. *¿Comprende?*"

"Jessica and I were married for six years," he whispered. "You just can't expect me to give her the cold shoulder when she calls up in distress."

Damn, was he calling from her house now? That was probably why he didn't answer my page. Thought I was calling about something other than work. Half-Negro, *please,* I wanted to say. I settled for, "Let me know when you speak to Detective Truesdale, okay?"

"I'll stop by your house later," he said.

My pager went off in my purse. "I gotta go, Steve. And don't bother stopping by—I won't be home."

"Don't play me, Detective!"

"Don't play *me*," I snapped and cut the power on the phone.

The page was from the morgue. They must have found something on the Mitchell homicide. I circled the cloverleaf at La Brea to get on the eastbound Santa Monica Freeway and punched in the number. Billie Truesdale came on the line within a half a ring.

"How long will it take you to get down here?" she asked.

Hurrying up the morgue's receiving dock and through the linoleum-floored lobby, I entered what reminded me of an odd but peaceful nurse's station. But instead of nurses bustling about, there were mortuary attendants behind the curved morgue desk, talking quietly with the coroner's investigators and criminalists about their kid's new braces or their dog's hip surgery. And unlike a hospital, the sickly sweet, still smell of death, instead of being isolated to one or two rooms, was everywhere. It worked its way into conversations, papered the walls and coated the floors, added a sad patina to the metal desks and cabinets scattered about. Not even the teeming fish tank in the lobby, installed by the staff as some sort of olfactory camouflage, could fool the senses about what went on in that place.

Billie was waiting for me in the Processing Room with Mikki Alexander and a coroner's criminalist, François Ha. François was a medium-height, well-built male of Chinese and French-Canadian heritage who had the rugged good looks of a lumberjack or a Eurasian Marlboro man, even though he'd lived in L.A. for fifteen years. His Timberland boots, corduroy pants, and blue flannel shirt, while out of place for L.A. in May, were perfectly suited for the chilly morgue air.

"There are two sets of ligature marks on the victim's neck," François began. "That can happen in a suicide, if the rope slips." A lock of dark hair fell over one eye as François waved Mikki Alexander, Billie, and me in for a closer look. "But based on the position of the body as it was photographed and diagrammed at the scene, the hanging groove should have been angled low from the front of the victim's neck to a higher position toward the back, consistent with the rope being pulled up and back when someone hangs himself."

François pointed to a faint mark on Mitchell's neck. "The groove should also be quite wide, given the thickness of this cord, and show some of the cord's detail." François was speaking rapidly, his words tumbling over each other in his excitement. "One of the marks on the neck—see here, and here—match the cord. But this wasn't what killed him."

François was getting so animated he was practically hopping from foot to foot, which made him look like he was practicing to enter a logrolling contest. "Slow down, François, and run that by me again." I squeezed the weariness from my eyes and looked again at Mitchell's neck.

"Whatever killed this man was pulled straight back from behind the victim, not up and backward." The criminalist pointed to a more pronounced mark, lower and darker than the first, that cut horizontally across Mitchell's neck. "And I'd wager a bet that, from the angle of pressure of the ligature, your choker was a leftie."

"You mean someone strangled him and *then* hung him to make it look like autoerotic asphyxiation?"

"This is what I suspected at the scene," Alexander explained to Billie, "but given the static I was getting from your partner, I decided to examine the body in a better light and confer with François." She held up Mitchell's right hand. "See the marks on these two fingers? The victim struggled with whoever strangled him, and these fingers got in the way of the ligature. He has some old scratches on his face, too, probably from the fight last Friday, but some of these are fresh."

"Are we looking for one assailant or two?" I asked.

"One person could have done the job," Alexander released Mitchell's hand and turned to me, "but he would have to have been pretty strong. Didn't you say this victim may have murdered or been the last person to see that other guy we picked up Friday night?"

"That's right," I nodded and held her eyes in mine. "Incredible coincidence, isn't it?"

Alexander looked at François. "A little too incredible for my liking. Cassie Reynolds has got the Lewis autopsy tomorrow," she informed us. "We'll talk to our boss, see if she can be scheduled to do this one right after. It would help having her on both cases."

I walked out of the Processing Room and outside to the receiving dock. After a few minutes on the phone, Billie joined me and lit a cigarette. "You were right about the vase," she said. "Although the killer or killers had vacuumed, the SID guys found a few pottery shards in the carpet and near where the body was hung."

"The killer had time to vacuum?"

She nodded. "Weird, isn't it? And now with what François is telling us, I've got Roxborough back over there with a crew from SID, checking for additional evidence of a faked suicide. I hope this taught him a lesson about leaving a crime scene."

"Did you catch him in midstroke with his Hawthorne honey?"

"I hope so," she laughed.

I drove back home, thoughts clogging my brain like the traffic on the Harbor Freeway. Mitchell had been strangled, his death made to look like an autoerotic sex accident. What would the killer have to gain from that kind of cover-up? Was there some message he was trying to convey about the victim, or, in the panic of the moment, was it the first thing he—and I was sure it was a he—thought of? And what kind of person would have kinky sex on the top of his mind—was he a boy toy or someone more meaningful in Mitchell's life?

I was so tired I couldn't make heads or tails of anything. And although it was ten by the time I got home—time most people were up and at it—I decided to lie down and try to get some sleep.

My telephone, however, had something else in mind, interrupting my restless dreams every half an hour or so. The first couple of times I half-listened for a voice on the answering machine, but the caller always hung up. After the third time, I turned off the ringer, but I could still hear its insistent clicking even in my sleep.

A little after four it clicked again. I yanked the receiver off the hook and barked out a hello, ready to cuss out Steve Firestone or whoever it was on the other end of the line. I was surprised to hear Aubrey's voice. "Did I call at a bad time?" he asked.

"No, no, it's okay. How are you?"

"About as well as can be expected. Detective Truesdale called the office early this morning to get Holly's home number, which meant my assistant had to call me and I had to tell her what happened. Since then, it's been nuts—calling the other partners to let them know, meeting with the staff here, telling the people at the hospital. Have you found out anything more?"

"Detectives Truesdale and Roxborough would know more than I would."

"You're probably right." I could hear Aubrey breathing into the silence on the line. "Char, I don't know quite what went down between us . . ."

"Things were just going a little too fast, Aubrey."

"I wasn't talking about *that*." There was bristling frustration in his voice. "Detective Truesdale's already called the answering service. It was just the way I told her . . . the service confirmed a male called in at one twenty-seven this morning and said he was Sergeant Barnes from the Sheriff's Department . . ."

I rose up on one elbow in the bed. "That's *exactly* what the man said?" I sat up and started to hunt for Billie's card on the nightstand.

"Yeah. Why?"

"Nothing." Where was that damned card?

"So you don't have to think of me as a suspect any more."

I heard the hurt tone of his voice. "Why would you say that?"

"I saw your face when I was talking to Detective Truesdale at Lance's house. You didn't believe a word I said."

"That's not true!" I protested with all the conviction I could muster.

"Charlotte, you don't have to lie to me. Not ever, okay?"

Ninety-nine lies may save you. The silence this time was mine.

"Can we go somewhere and talk?" he asked.

"I was actually taking a nap."

I could feel Aubrey sizing up my answer, him checking *me* out for the telltale lie. "*You* said I needed to get some rest," I reminded him.

He asked if I'd join him for an early dinner. I was about to beg off when my inner voice told me, *Go on and go, girl*. I reluctantly swung my feet onto the floor. "Okay. Pick me up around five."

I sat for a moment, thinking about what Aubrey had just told me. L.A. was a crazy quilt of a town—a hodgepodge patchwork of neighborhoods, some of which called themselves "Los Angeles" but in fact weren't in the city at all. My parent's home in View Park was like that, as was Windsor Hills and Ladera Heights—Los Angeles addresses but located in unincorporated zones outside the city limits and thus serviced by the Los Angeles County Sheriff's Department. Baldwin Hills, while just spitting distance away from the others, was just the opposite—within the city limits and therefore in the LAPD's jurisdiction.

So a "Sergeant Barnes" of the L.A. County Sheriff's Department calling to notify Aubrey about a death in Baldwin Hills was about as phony as Naomi Campbell's flowing tresses. But our caller didn't know that. The error was our first real, albeit tiny, break in the case, and I hurried to call Billie.

The South Bureau detective had her own news to share. "Roxborough and company hit the jackpot on their second pass of Mitchell's place. They found some decorative rocks in the flower beds near the sliding glass door that had been disturbed and not by any of the victim's shoes."

"Why's that significant?"

"The next-door neighbor said Dr. Mitchell's gardener just installed them earlier in the day. And while there was no residue from the white-powder coating on the rocks on any of Mitchell's shoes or the soles of his feet, there was all this dust from them in the carpeting and inside the vacuum-cleaner bag."

"No chance the gardener cleaned up behind himself before the murder?"

Evidently not—Roxborough had gotten the gardener's

number from one of the neighbors, called, and found out he didn't have a key to the house. "And that's not all the guys found," Billie said. "There was a gun hidden in the toilet."

Unusual place for a civilian to keep a gun. And it was a .38, the same caliber as the one that shot Lewis. "You think they can have the results from ballistics in time for the Lewis autopsy tomorrow?" I asked.

"I doubt it, but I can ask. By the way, I've already spoken to Firestone on the liaison thing, so hopefully I'll be hearing back from him soon."

"What did he say?"

"He wasn't too encouraging, but he said he'd pass the request along to your lieutenant."

He'd better, I thought as I put down the phone, or there'd be hell to pay.

CHAPTER 16

UP CLOSE AND PERSONAL

Kind of down-at-the-heels now, Crenshaw Boulevard had been my generation's street of dreams, a paler version of what Central Avenue had been for my parents. The original Baldwin Hills Shopping Center at Crenshaw and what was then called Santa Barbara Avenue was the place to go for school clothes, while Maverick's Flat and The Total Experience night clubs farther south on Crenshaw played host to everyone from Harold Melvin & the Blue Notes to Gladys Knight & the Pips. A dream world in the sixties and early seventies, the way Crenshaw declined afterward was part of the black middle-class nightmare. The Black Freedom Militia setting up shop in an abandoned storefront on the boulevard was only the icing on a rotting cake that included the demise or relocation of too many small businesses, the exodus of white-owned car dealerships to the suburbs, and the black musical acts to newly integrated clubs in Century City, Hollywood, and bigger venues like the Greek Theatre or the Universal Amphitheatre.

But for every business lost, there was another to take its place, including Coley's Café, a Jamaican restaurant down the street from the place where I got my first Afro haircut. Just walking into the gaudily decorated space with Aubrey and inhaling the mélange of spices made me wish I was in the islands.

"I had an emergency meeting with management at the hospital today," Aubrey was telling me. "Everyone is very worried about the Lance situation."

I took a swig of Ting soda, one of the best things to come out of Jamaica, next to jerked chicken and reggae. "I'm sure. A sudden death is always a terrible shock."

"I wish that was all that was bothering them." He dug into his jerked chicken. "Somehow it got out that Lance's death was part of some kinky sex-for-hire scandal."

"You didn't say anything to anyone, did you?"

He almost choked on his food. "That would be the *last* thing I'd repeat, even if I heard it from the coroner himself! It probably came from one of the EMTs at the scene. You know the motto of some of those guys is 'Gossiping for Dollars.' "

I wasn't surprised, especially after the paramedic who leaked a story to one of the tabloids about a celebrity's up-close-and-personal encounter with a small rodent a few years ago. Rumor had it the guy put a down payment on a house in Las Vegas on the fees paid to him by the *Clarion* alone.

"What makes it even more damaging," Aubrey continued glumly, "is that it's threatening to derail a deal I've been negotiating for over a year with the hospital's parent company to acquire our medical group."

Aubrey seemed so troubled, I decided to risk Billie's wrath and tell him we believed Mitchell had been murdered. "This is not for public consumption, though," I whispered. "We hope to throw Lance's killer off as long as we can."

"That's probably not going to do us a lot of good." Aubrey had also lowered his voice as a dreadlocked couple sat down at a nearby table. "The hospital's CEO got a call this afternoon from the *Clarion*, nosing around for a story. They said they were told 'by an anonymous source' that Lance's death was autoerotic asphyxiation. Another one called ten minutes later, asking the same questions."

"Those rags are sniffing around because of Dr. Holly. I'm sure they all want the exclusive on that one: 'Love Expert's Husband Dies in Sleazy Sex Scandal.'"

"Whatever the reason, management at the hospital has called in an outside PR firm to do some crisis management. And they've called off the acquisition of our group until this whole thing blows over." A thought flickered across his face. "Perhaps you could encourage Detective Truesdale to work with us on this one, maybe clue hospital management in on what's going on. It could really be helpful to us."

"I'm sure she'll be cooperative. You should talk to her."

He grew uneasy, a third grader squirming in his seat. "I don't think Detective Truesdale likes me too much. Are cops always as suspicious as she is?"

"In homicide, people lie to you all day long. Being suspicious grows on you almost like a protective covering. I'm afraid it comes with the territory."

He took my hand. "Well, since I passed inspection with Detective Truesdale, do you think you and I can get squared away, too?"

I started to object, but Aubrey gently yet firmly squeezed my hand until I was quiet. "Don't explain," he said simply. "As you said, it comes with the territory."

I held my breath through the awkward silence until it felt safe to ask if anyone had a chance to tell Reggie Peeples and the TAGOUT kids about Mitchell's death.

Aubrey released my hand and signaled our waiter for the check. "I called over there today. Uncle Reggie was pretty shaken up. He and Mrs. Bell were getting the kids together over at the gallery this evening to give them a chance to vent. They were all real close to Lance."

The porno magazines around Mitchell's body were of young men, roughly the same age as those in TAGOUT. Lance Mitchell's interest in them being anything more than paternal seemed completely out of whack with the picture Aubrey was painting, but I'd been proven wrong before.

I felt a gentle squeeze of my hand again. "You still working, Detective?"

I squeezed back. "Not really. I was just wondering how these young people are going to deal with someone so close who *wasn't* a banger lost to them like this."

"I don't know, but I'm sure Uncle Reggie and Mrs. Bell will handle it."

"Do you mind if we swing by there?" I asked. "It's not far away."

"Will we ever have a date without business interrupting?" he asked.

I tensed up for a moment, thinking we were headed down the same road I'd traveled with other guys I tried to date, guys who felt my work crowded them out of my life. Then I saw the mischief in Aubrey's eyes. "Oh, is *that* what this is?"

He tickled the palm of my hand, brought it to his lips. "Our second, if you're keeping track."

"Would you mind?" I said, mesmerized by the feel of his lips on my hand. "It won't take long."

He shook his head and gave me a devilish smile. "I don't know about you career women. But I guess I can handle it one more time."

Red eyes and swollen faces turned our way as we entered Spiral West. Reggie Peeples was there with Raziya Bell, who was sitting on the floor, comforting her son, Peyton, Gregory Underwood, and a couple of the female artists I saw last night. Gregory Underwood was the first to turn away. "What's five-oh doing here?" he complained to the adults.

"The term is *police*, Gregory," Uncle Reggie said, glaring at Underwood as he got to his feet to greet us. "What can I do for you, Char . . . Detective Justice?"

Aubrey stayed out in the main room with Raziya and the kids while Uncle Reggie and I went into his private showing room in the back. The remnants of the reception were still evident—plastic glasses, empty wine boxes, and several of those black plastic trash bags. "This must've been quite a cleanup effort last night, Uncle Reggie."

"Raziya and I were here until almost two," he sighed. "We even started packing up some of the paintings to ship to the owners." Several canvases in various stages of completion confirmed their efforts and were stacked next to wooden shipping crates, rolls of bubble wrap, and heavy-duty shipping wire.

He offered me a seat in a worn, hide-covered wicker chair and sat down heavily in its mate. "Lance was like a son to me." The old man's mustache twitched, his cork-colored face contorted from the effort to hold back his emotion. "Do you know what happened yet?"

"That's why I'm here. I've gotten some information that I need to check out with you." I showed him the Polaroid of Lewis taken at the scene. "Have you ever seen this man?"

He looked the photo over and winced. "He seems kinda familiar. Who is he . . . or should I say was he?"

"Robert Lewis. Went by the name of Cinque back in the seventies."

"This was that guy from that Black Freedom group that killed Keith and Erica?" Reggie nodded along with me, the light bulb now on. "I remember the name, of course, and his picture from the papers, but he looks a lot different than I remember." He handed the photo back with a rueful smile and a swipe at his bald head. "But I guess we all do, don't we?"

"Did he show up around here or contact you in any way?"

"Why would he?" he asked, alarmed. "I was never into that wild-eyed Negro mess. You know me better than that, Char!"

Actually, I did. Uncle Reggie had been a neighbor and friend of our family forever. A decorated Korean War veteran, he was one of the stalwarts of the black community, had been ever since I could remember. He was committed, honest, always trying to help someone in need.

"I'm not accusing you of anything, Uncle Reggie. We have information that Lewis was making inquiries about TAGOUT, and specifically about you and Dr. Mitchell, shortly before his death, so we've got to check it out. Why do you think he was asking around about you?"

He looked a little befuddled. "Hell, I don't know. I don't ever remember meeting the cat."

"It may have had something to do with that photo of you, Dr. Mitchell, and the kids taken by the *Sentinel* at the fund-raising luncheon."

Uncle Reggie's gray mustache twisted around on his face. "I don't know why." He pulled out the glossy photo from the night before, turned it over, and handed it to me. Although I saw nothing more than when he had first shown it to me, I asked if I could keep it. "Sure, baby, if you think it'll help," he replied.

"Where were you on Friday afternoon, Uncle Reggie?"

His face clouded over, and he drew himself up, his feathers ruffled by my question. "With my wife and mother-in-law," he replied, his mustache compressed into a pout. "Your aunt Faye and I had to go pick up Mother from the nursing home on Thursday because the rioting had knocked out the electricity. I spent all day Friday setting up a hospital bed in our spare bed-room."

"So, to your knowledge, Cinque Lewis never came by here or called on Friday?"

He shook his head emphatically. "Not on Friday or any other day, at least not when I was here. But Raziya works a couple of evenings a week. Maybe she talked to him."

Away from the kids, Raziya Bell seemed more openly upset about Dr. Mitchell's death. I showed the teary woman the photo of Cinque Lewis. "Did this man ever come by the gallery?"

She stared at the crime scene photo as if she were going to be ill. "I'm sorry." She sat down in one of the chairs, her eyes welling up again. "I've never seen a dead body before."

"I'm sorry to upset you, Mrs. Bell . . ."

"Please, call me Raziya."

I pulled the Xeroxed photo taken from my murder book. "This one is pretty old, but you can see a little better what he looked like."

She stared at the first photo, then the Xerox, then back again before shaking her head. "What do you want from me, Detective?"

"Robert 'Cinque' Lewis was a radical with the Black Freedom Militia and a fugitive for a number of years until he resurfaced recently, asking around about TAGOUT, Reggie, and Dr. Mitchell. Shortly after that, he was murdered. Did you receive any calls from someone by that name or anybody unfamiliar asking a lot of questions?"

Her face seemed lost in concentration. "We've gotten a lot of calls in the past month," she finally said. "First it was RSVPs for the exhibit. Some of the callers were from as far away as New York City and Germany. Then after the uprising, we got even more calls from people concerned about the gallery or asking if we were still having the event. I wouldn't have known if this one man called or not."

"Did you record messages for all the callers?"

She dug a message pad out from under a cluttered desk. "If they wanted someone to call them back, I'd jot it down." She thrust the pad at me. "But a lot of them didn't, so after a while, I didn't bother writing down the names."

I went through a month of messages, but saw nothing that would have suggested a call from Lewis. I had just given her a card when we heard a loud voice and a thud against a wall. "I'd better get back out there," she frowned. "The kids are really taking this hard."

All eyes were on Raziya's son, Peyton, who must have been the source of the outburst. Raziya went to him, sat down and put her arm around his shoulder, and whispered something in his ear that seemed to calm him down. I sat down in the semicircle between Uncle Reggie and Aubrey. "For those of you I didn't meet last night, my name is Charlotte Justice, and I'm a homicide detective with the LAPD. I want you to know how sorry I am about Dr. Mitchell." I locked into four pairs of angry, mistrusting young eyes. "I know he meant a lot to all of you."

Gregory Underwood's face was drawn, sullen. "What do you want, Detective Justice?"

"You here to spy on us some more?" Peyton added.

"I need your help," I explained. "Do any of you know where Dr. Mitchell went after the opening was over?"

Underwood looked at Peyton, then reluctantly spoke up. "Me and Mack P went to the Cheesecake Factory in the Marina to celebrate. Dr. M rolled through there for a hot minute, picked up the tab for our dinner, and booked."

"What time was that?"

Underwood turned to Peyton again. "'Bout nine thirty. He didn't stay more'n fifteen minutes, though."

"Have any of you seen this man?" I passed around the crime scene photo. "His name was Robert 'Cinque' Lewis."

Each of the four kids stared at the photo, frowned, came up with blank looks. Oddly, none of them were as shocked as the adults had been to see a photo of a dead body. But perhaps it wasn't so odd, given the harsh reality of their young lives.

"He lived in Los Angeles about twelve years ago," I continued. "Started an organization called the Black Freedom Militia."

I watched their faces closely for a reaction. Nada.

"I've got information that he was asking around about TAGOUT and may have been looking for Dr. Mitchell when he was killed last Friday night."

Peyton reacted immediately. "He wouldn't have hurt him!"

"Yeah, Dr. Mitchell wasn't like that!" one of the Latinas added tearfully.

"No one is accusing Dr. Mitchell of anything. We're just trying to find out if Lewis tried to contact him."

"But if this brother died on Friday, what could he have to do with what happened to Dr. Mitchell last night?" Underwood asked.

"We don't know," I admitted. "That's what we're trying to find out. Perhaps we could start with where each of you were Friday afternoon."

The two girls in the group had alibis for Friday afternoon—taking care of younger siblings off from school or watching television and talking to friends on the telephone about the riots.

Peyton and Gregory were at Spiral West with Raziya. "With the schools and my office closed because of the rioting, I thought it would be a good opportunity for the boys to finish up their paintings and help me get the gallery together for the exhibit."

Peyton Bell's mother was with them most of the time, except for when she went to buy some gasoline around four, about the time we were arriving at the taco stand.

"Do you remember what time you got back?" I asked.

"It was around five. The lines were awful."

I nodded, remembering the long lines I'd seen at the few gas stations open in the neighborhood.

"I probably can find the receipt with the time on it if you need verification," she offered.

"Why you acting all nicey-nice with this cop?" Peyton's eyes were a hurting, wet red. He tried to get up, but his mother's grip on his shoulder kept him bound to the floor.

Uncle Reggie held up his hand for silence, looking sternly at Peyton and the others in turn. "I know how you feel about the police, but, remember, Detective Justice was the one who saved Dr. Mitchell from the cops who wanted to thump him last Friday. I've known this lady since she was knee high to a jackrabbit. She's good people, and she wants to find out what happened to Dr. Mitchell as much as we do. Dr. Mitchell helped all of you, now it's your chance to return the favor."

"Thanks, Uncle Reggie," I murmured and handed out my cards. "I'm reachable anytime, 24/7, at the pager number," I told them.

As Aubrey and I got up to go, I noticed the larger paintings, which had been taken down and were waiting to be crated up for delivery. Peyton Bell's mural that I had admired last night still dominated the room, a big red "sold" tag plastered in the left corner. I remembered how Mitchell had convinced Aubrey to ante up at the last minute to make sure this kid could go to college, too.

Raziya Bell sat before the painting, comforting her son. They looked as if they had lost their last friend in the world. Maybe they had.

y adrenaline level took a nosedive when I got back into Aubrey's car. Although it was only nine o'clock, I was nodding by the time we got on the Santa Monica Freeway and was getting some of that good, drooling-out-of-the-corner-of-my-mouth sleep when I was startled by a nudge from Aubrey. "You know somebody who drives a black Corvette?" he asked.

Steve Firestone was parked in the driveway behind my Rabbit. He got out of the car, dressed in casual clothes and a Dodgers baseball cap, like he had just come from a game. We met at the sidewalk, exchanged terse greetings. Steve looked Aubrey up and down. I didn't offer any introductions.

"Can I talk to you for a minute?" Steve asked.

"Sure." I stood on the lawn, left arm crossed over my sling. "Go ahead."

Aubrey backed away. "I think I'll be going, Detective."

"You don't have to," I said emphatically and gave Steve a stern look. "This shouldn't take too long."

Aubrey's eyes shifted from me to Steve. "I gotta be getting home anyway," he said again and took another step back. "Thanks for the public relations advice."

I watched Aubrey get into his car. "Any time."

I had dropped my purse inside the door, let Beast in, and was filling his dish with kibble when Steve called out from the living room, "Was that the new boyfriend?"

I stood in the archway. "I'm not even going to dignify that with a response."

"I'll take that to mean yes." He stood up, shook out the crease in his khakis, and gave me a tight smile. "You know you can't just treat me like this."

"Treat you like what?" I didn't try to keep the irritation out of my voice. "Listen to me carefully, Steve: I have never, repeat, *never* slept with a member of this Department. It's just not worth jeopardizing my career to lay down with you or anybody else." I moved for the door. "So unless you have something work-related to talk to me about, you're wasting my time."

Steve walked to the door, put a hand on my arm. "How will you know unless you give it a shot?" he asked.

"Let me try saying this a little differently: you and I don't have a relationship, Steve, and we're not going to have a relationship. Furthermore, I think you've just been trying to line me up as a bed warmer in case things don't work out with your wife."

Maybe I had gone too far with that last bit, but I was way past caring. Steve Firestone had really pissed me off.

He grabbed me by the waist. "Come on, Charlotte, let's cut to the chase. You know I still want you."

I tried to pull away. "As what? An insurance policy?"

He grabbed me by the left side of the neck and gave the right a hard, sucking kiss. The more I pulled away, the harder he drew me in.

"Step off, Steve!" I elbowed him as hard as I could in the ribs and stooped down to get to my purse. "Have . . . you . . . lost . . . your mind?"

He gripped my shoulders and pulled me upright. A shooting pain ran down my right arm. "You *want* it rough, don't you?" His breath, hot in my ear, reeked of beer. "Yeah, maybe you're one of those women who likes a man to take control."

Suddenly a blur crossed my vision. It was my boxer, who flew by me with a snarl and backed Steve into a corner, his jaws locked onto the sleeve of his windbreaker. Steve stepped back with a scream and tried to get to his gun.

I reached in and hauled the dog back by his collar. "Beast! Off!"

There was a knock at the door. "Miz Charlotte, you home?" It was Mrs. Franklin. "I wasn't sure if that was Beast or the TV," she called through the door. "I just wanted to stop by and get my cake plate."

I yanked the door open. Odetta Franklin was wearing a pair of hooded sweats with a bib apron over them. One hand was under her apron while the other was motioning me to come outside. "Baby, them little heathens down the street was playin' in yo' yard again and broke one of yo' sprinklers." She took my good arm and dragged me outside. "Lemme show you which one."

I held Beast by the collar and grabbed my gun-heavy purse on my way out the door. "And let me give you that money I owe you, Mrs. Franklin."

My neighbor stood close to me, restraining the dog and showing me a perfectly fine sprinkler in a corner of my yard. A moment later Steve appeared on the front porch, fingering the rip in his jacket sleeve. "That damn dog of yours is dangerous."

"Only when he's provoked."

Steve looked from Mrs. Franklin to me and started toward his Corvette before stopping and snapping his fingers. "Before I forget, Big Mac called a joint meeting tomorrow at nine for RHD and South Bureau detectives working the Lewis and Mitchell cases. Stobaugh wants you there." He delivered the news cool as a cucumber, as if we'd been having a polite business discussion instead of a vicious struggle. "Try to be there on time."

Mrs. Franklin put her arm around me and held me still until Steve's black car rumbled away into the night.

I was still trembling with rage by the time we got into my house. "That asshole!" I went to the kitchen and fed Beast a couple of peanut-butter biscuits as a reward for a job well done.

Mrs. Franklin started making tea. I sat in the dining room beneath the row of solemn women in the Biggers lithograph, holding their homes in dark, work-roughened hands. "I tole you there was somethin' off about him, lurkin' around like that," Mrs. Franklin called out from the kitchen. "I picked up on it right away."

"How did you know to drop by when you did?"

She returned with two mugs of tea and the bottle of Cragganmore, which she proceeded to pour liberally into our mugs. I did not protest the way she was wasting good Scotch.

"It was sorta slow at Sister Odetta's today." She took a big sip from her mug and sighed. "So I lays down in the back to rest my eyes. Had this dream about you bein' surrounded by dead snakes that kept tryin' to bite you. It was so real I had to go to my dream book and see what it meant."

Snakes. I shuddered at the imagery, but the black women in the lithograph seemed to be hanging on Sister Odetta's every word.

"The dream book said it meant you will suffer from the malice of a pretended friend. When I saw the three of you standin' in the yard when you first drove up, I didn't like your body language, so I decided to keep my eyes peeled. Then when Dr. Aubrey left and that other one didn't, I thought I'd just come on over with Beulah." She reached under her apron. "Did I overreact?"

I stared, slack-jawed, at the Colt .45 she placed on the table. Should I have scolded my neighbor for carrying a gun or be grateful she had my back? "No, Mrs. Franklin," I finally said. "I don't think you overreacted at all."

CHAPTER 17

POST TIMES

There were seven of us sardined around the conference table in Captain Armstrong's office on Thursday morning. At one end our captain was talking to Lieutenants Stobaugh and Dreyfuss about the upcoming LAPD Night at Hollywood Park. Lexington-born and -bred until his family moved to Los Angeles during World War II, MacIverson Armstrong came from a long line of horse breeders and had the ponies in his blood. Engravings of thoroughbreds decorated his walls, along with a dozen photos of him posing with the Metropolitan Bureau's Equestrian unit and standing in the winner's circle at Santa Anita, dwarfing jockeys like Willie Shoemaker and Eddie Delahoussaye.

Gena Cortez sat beneath the picture of Armstrong and Shoemaker, in the middle of the table directly across from me. A dusty blue murder book sat open before her, and she was making notes in a small notebook. As she closed the binder, I noticed "ROBERTS, K & E, 78-592–3" printed on a square of white paper inserted in a pocket on the book's spine. Cortez gave me a weak smile, averting her eyes as she slid the binder across to Billie Truesdale, who sat next to me. Steve Firestone sat at the other end of the table, biting a hangnail and staring out the window. The epitome of the well-dressed RHD detective, he wore a starch-stiff, long-sleeved white shirt and rep silk tie held in place with an LAPD tie pin. He had barely spoken to me when I came into the office that morning, which was fine with me. He could rot in hell for all I cared.

Like Steve, I had dressed conservatively for the morning's meeting. While I knew instinctively what had happened between him and me the day before wasn't my fault, I had selected a cream-colored shirt with a high collar to cover the faint hickey Steve had put on my neck and a boxy beige pantsuit that called no attention to my figure or anything else. I felt as if I were virtually fading into the room's cream-colored walls, which was also fine with me.

Everyone came to order when Captain Armstrong cleared his throat. At six-six, and about two-ten, with a thick mane of silver hair, Armstrong was the last of a dying breed, still holding firm Chief Parker's thin blue line. And with forty-two years on the job and nineteen at the helm of RHD, he had earned the respect of LAPD homicide detectives everywhere, even the hard chargers of South Bureau. Big Mac, they called him, as a sign of deference and respect. But for others, me included, another nickname applied that I thought better suited his pony-loving, hobnobbing style, one that went with his initials—Captain MIA.

"I just wanted it to be clear to everyone at RHD *and* South Bureau that I consider these cases to be very special circumstances," he said. "And I don't mean just because of the connection to Detective Justice." There was a slight dip of Armstrong's patrician head in my direction.

He pulled off his tortoiseshell cheaters and pointed at each of us in turn. "The way I see it, we've got several opportunities here. One, to clear the Lewis case. Two, to nail the sonofabitch for the Roberts family murders and clear two more cases. And three, to find out where this bastard's been hiding since nineteen seventy-*fucking*-eight. If there's an underground escape route for the likes of Lewis, I want us to be the ones to find out where it is and plug it up before the FBI or some other agency does and makes us look like fools—or some of these other low-life thugs figure out how to access it."

Tony Dreyfuss broke in. "We understand how important the Lewis case is to the Department, sir. But with all due respect, South Bureau's first priority has got to be the Mitchell murder. Councilwoman Moore's office and his attorney, Sandra Douglass, are all over me like a cheap suit, demanding we devote every available resource to this case. And we can only hold the press at bay for so long with a one-liner about a suspicious death."

The tabloids must've called Lieutenant Dreyfuss's office, too, not to mention the always-persistent Neil Hookstratten of the *Times*. I half-raised my hand. "Excuse me, Lieutenant," I broke in, "but I think the reason the captain brought us all together is because the two cases *are* connected. According to Ed Carmichael of Peace in the Streets, Lewis surfaced about a week before he was killed and went to Carmichael asking questions about the gallery's owner, Dr. Mitchell, and the TAGOUT program. And according to a witness—" I heard, and pretended I didn't, the noisy scraping of Steve Firestone's chair, his audible sigh "—Dr. Mitchell was either at the scene talking to Lewis Friday afternoon or in the vicinity when Lewis got popped."

Stobaugh frowned down the table. "We got a statement from this witness, Firestone?"

"Not unless you're willing to check into the funny farm to get it." Steve sat back in his chair and cracked a small smile. "But I'll let Detective Cortez explain."

Cortez squirmed in her seat and glanced at me from under her dark lashes as if to say, *Don't blame me, I didn't want to do this.* "Jerry Riley, the witness in question, suffers from schizophrenia," she began. "After Detective Justice's first, er, encounter with him on Tuesday, he became progressively more agitated. The building manager said he got so bad by Wednesday they had to have him admitted to the VA psych unit out in Brentwood. I've called his doctor out there to see if they'll let me interview him, but they're not budging. They've got him on a seventy-two-hour hold. No visitors, no exceptions."

I could feel myself recede further into my clothes. Did my questions press Mr. Riley too far and into an inpatient unit, mumbling his *Star Wars* visions to whoever would listen? God, I hoped not.

"It's not a lot to go on, Captain," Stobaugh acknowledged before Armstrong did it for him, "but we'll stick with it nonetheless."

Armstrong compressed his mouth in a thin, mirthless imitation of a smile. "Cinque Lewis was a drug dealer when the Department last had contact with him. Any evidence he was trying to use these juveniles in the TAGOUT program to rebuild his distribution network?"

"If he was, he was doing it without the knowledge of Reggie Peeples, the owner of the gallery," I replied. "He and the staff said Lewis hadn't contacted anyone there."

"People *say* a lot of shit," Steve said, not quite under his breath.

I tried to ignore that end of the table and concentrated on making my case to the senior officers in the room. "I've known Reggie Peeples practically my whole life. I know he's struggled for a long time with Spiral West, but he's not the kind of man to run drugs to make ends meet. And if he were, wouldn't Peeples have been the one to meet with Lewis instead of sending an emergency-room physician?"

"But didn't you say at the scene that Mitchell had a drug problem?" Billie asked.

"Yeah, but that was prescription painkillers. That's a whole different kettle of fish than street drugs. Plus his boss said he was clean."

"The way that fool was behaving Friday night, I wouldn't be surprised if he was on *something* again," Dreyfuss pointed out and turned to Billie. "Check it out with his friends and associates at the hospital, and see if they can expedite the toxicology results from the post. And let's get Cooper to check into whether any of these TAGOUT members have gang affiliations or a drug history."

I offered to provide Billie with the brochure from the art show, which included the names of TAGOUT members. "There's something else you might want to check into with Cooper, too." I told her my suspicion that the recently deceased Givens may be the same person who ratted out Cinque Lewis's Black Freedom Militia to the Department back in the seventies. "Maybe Lewis found out it was Givens who set him up all those years ago and came back to get revenge."

Captain Armstrong had turned to Lieutenant Stobaugh to review staff deployment on the cases. Stobaugh leaned forward in his chair, eager to redeem himself and his team after my overzealous presentation of Jerry Riley as a witness. "I've assigned Firestone as primary on the Lewis murder investigation with Cortez and Justice providing backup. Detective Cortez will stay on Mr. Riley and try to hustle up some leads among Lewis's old gang connections. Detective Justice will lend assistance to them and be a resource, given her knowledge of the case file. And, with your permission, I'd like to grant South Bureau Homicide's request for Detective Justice to act as liaison to them on the Mitchell case. We need to coordinate our investigations as much as possible."

Armstrong squinted over his cheaters at Steve. "You've been awfully quiet, Detective Firestone. Can you afford to spare Detective Justice on this one?"

"Fine by me," Steve mumbled around his hangnail a little too petulantly for my taste. But Armstrong didn't seem to notice. Maybe I was just being overly sensitive.

After giving us his initial perspective and expectation of the outcome, our captain had rapidly lost enthusiasm for the details and was surreptitiously peeking at a *Racing Form* hidden in his paperwork. He rose abruptly from the conference table, our signal that the meeting was over and he was on to more important matters.

"Let's ride this one into the winner's circle," he said. Or, on second thought, maybe it was just time for Captain MIA to make a call to one of the Las Vegas sportsbooks. He gathered up the papers under his arm. "I smell a winner here."

I waited until we were in the parking lot before confronting Steve. "So when were you going to tell me I had the liaison assignment?"

"It had to be cleared with Armstrong."

"But you knew Stobaugh was going to request the assignment. He wouldn't have done it without talking to you."

Steve's face was a blank mask of indifference, but I could see the anger smoldering in his hazel eyes.

"The least you could've done was say something. You're supposed to be my supervisor, Steve."

"I've been thinking about that," he said. "Maybe it's time we make a change."

"That'll look just great in my jacket right before my promotion review."

He shrugged. "Your choice, Charlotte. It didn't have to be this way."

"What is this about, Steve . . . if you can't have me in bed you don't want me on your team?"

As I was unlocking my car, Steve put a hand on my arm. "Listen, Charlotte, I . . ."

I jerked away. "Maybe I should warn Gena Cortez about what to expect working under you. And maybe Lieutenant Stobaugh, too!" I opened the car door and put it between us. He turned four shades of red, spun on his heel, and walked quickly to his car in the next row.

"Hey, Steve?"

"What?"

"Touch me again, and I'll blow so many holes in you, you'll look like Swiss cheese."

They had held up the autopsy until we arrived. Lewis's freshly washed body lay waiting for us on one of a half-dozen stainless-steel autopsy tables in the room, naked as the day he was born.

Dr. Cassie Reynolds, a whisper of a woman, no more than five feet two, walked into the suite with a scowl showing on that part of her face not covered by the blue paper mask. "We're squeezing a lot in here today for your benefit, Detectives," the medical examiner grumbled behind the mask, "so we don't have a lot of time to be wasting!"

I adjusted my breathing mask, checked my watch. It was only a little after ten. Reynolds sounded exactly like Ted Receiros, the county's chief coroner. Dr. Receiros was a maniac about punctuality. As if the dead had a schedule to keep.

As we took our places against the institutional tan-colored wall, Reynolds started examining the body while Humberto Peña, a Department tech on the case, stood nearby. Blonde curls poking from underneath her surgical cap and a reedy voice may have made Reynolds seem a little like Shirley Temple, but Cassie Reynolds was all woman and all business.

The wall felt cold against my back, but no colder than the vibes I was getting from Steve. We stood listening silently to Reynolds, several awkward feet from each other, all our usual jokes and banter idling somewhere in the backs of our throats.

"The body is that of a well-nourished, thirty-three-year-old black male with white hair and green eyes," she began. She rolled back Lewis's right eye, the only one left intact. "No, check that, brown eyes."

I leaned away from the wall in time to watch her peel off a contact lens from Lewis's pupil. Firestone's thick eyebrows shot up above his mask despite his nonchalant pose against the wall.

Reynolds moved around to the left side of the body, where Lewis's prosthesis had been removed. "You guys ever seen one of those bionic arms?" she asked. "They can run as much as forty thousand dollars plus the cost of the surgery to prepare the arm to be fitted with it."

Peña, short, dark-haired, with the whitest teeth I'd ever seen, brought over an open file for us to read. It was a report on the device Lewis wore. "The prosthesis is a battery-operated electric arm composed of fiberglass and steel with a silicone glove," I read. The attached photos showed it had been peeled like an onion, the skin-colored, glovelike covering slipped off the pale inner shell and metal framework of the device. The inner workings of the arm resembled something out of that *Terminator* movie. In a close-up shot they had taken, the name "Hoggman-Dorrangle, San Jose, California," and the six-digit serial number were visible on the interior of the wrist of the metal frame. Reynolds explained that manufacturers keep a list of the licensed prosthetists who buy their equipment, who in turn keep records of the patients whom they outfit with limbs containing the numbered parts. "He should be easy to trace once you get that prosthetist's name."

I held up one of the photos and signaled to Peña. He nodded, and I slipped it into my pocket.

Reynolds had moved up to Lewis's face. "He's got these funny little scars on his cheeks," she told Steve, "although they've been mitigated somewhat by plastic surgery. Was he an African trying to assimilate?"

"Gang initiation, back in the seventies," I replied. "Can you tell how long ago he had the plastic surgery?"

"Not with any accuracy. But it looks as if it was some time ago. This is odd, too." Reynolds's already-high voice had gone up another half an octave. "The face and extremities are blue-gray in appearance . . ."

She swore softly. I checked to see if Steve heard. He had and had come off the back wall to see what was up.

Reynolds and Peña were standing over Lewis's head. "I don't know how she missed this," she whispered to Peña, obviously upset. "Would you get that wire we were looking at last week? And get Alexander, too, will you? Here," she motioned and reluctantly stepped aside. "You need to see this."

The thin straight groove around Lewis's neck was unmistakable. Lance Mitchell's neck bore the same groove, although someone tried to disguise it after the fact to look like autoerotic asphyxiation.

Steve found his voice: "Strangulation was the cause of death?"

Reynolds gave a quick bob of her curls. "There's enough cyanosis in the victim's face and body, and petechiae—you know, those little hemorrhage spots in the eye—to indicate it, yes."

"So he was strangled, then shot?" I asked. "There were *two* killers?"

"I'd say so," Reynolds replied. "From the trajectory of the bullet through Lewis's head and the angle at which it hit the wall, the shooter would have to have been standing next to the victim, shooting straight across, not shooting down from a height above the victim's body. And the mark from his neck suggests the same thing—he was strangled from a standing position."

This was a new wrinkle, one that took a moment to digest. "So one person stood behind him, strangling him," I began, "while the other came up and shot him for good measure?" It seemed like a lot of anger for two people to be carrying. "Where's his wallet?"

Reynolds waved me toward a table where Lewis's personal effects were displayed. I peered at Mitchell's wallet in the bright lights and opened it up. The cash he had borrowed from Aubrey and his driver's license were gone, but a handful of credit cards in his name were there along with a fistful of receipts and some of his business cards.

I considered the pictures of the body taken at the scene and realized what had bothered me that night when Steve had first shown me the wallet. Lewis had crumpled down on his left side when he fell, his left arm pinned beneath him like a boxer gone down for the count in an old cartoon. Yet in the picture of the wallet's position, it peeked from under Lewis's left shoulder as if it had been tucked under him rather than had fallen with the body. I wondered if anyone on the scene noticed it that hectic Friday night. As far as I was concerned, the whole thing pointed in only one direction.

Someone had planted that wallet under Cinque Lewis's body after he was killed. Someone who wanted to set Lance Mitchell up for the murder.

But I just couldn't wrap my mind around the notion that Reggie Peeples was involved, regardless of what Steve had insinuated in Captain MIA's office. Lance Mitchell was a key fund-raiser for TAGOUT, someone that Uncle Reggie should have wanted to keep around as long as possible, not frame for a murder.

But I had to face the facts: Cinque Lewis had been asking around about Reggie Peeples, Lance Mitchell, and TAGOUT a week before he was killed. Maybe Lewis did reach Mitchell and set up a meeting. Maybe Mitchell took reinforcements with him,

Peeples or one of the kids. For some reason they argued, maybe struggled, and one of them ended up strangling Lewis while the other one shot him. Afterward, they got scared, split up, and Mitchell ran smack dab into us on the street.

Had Lewis tried to get back into the business by approaching them about using TAGOUT as a front for drug dealing? There was certainly no evidence of it from what I saw at the gallery during the opening or last night either. But what if they were already running drugs, as a way of raising money for the organization? Those high-powered bankers and entertainment types at the reception would be a built-in market. Maybe Lewis had set them up in business and later started jacking them up for more money to remain their silent partner. But the two hundred dollars Mitchell had borrowed from Aubrey Friday afternoon would only be a drop in the bucket, hardly enough to buy a man's silence. And it still didn't explain why Lance Mitchell's wallet would have been planted on Lewis's body after the fact.

Peña returned with a length of steel wire in his hands, which he passed to Reynolds. She carefully slid it close to Lewis's neck. "Just what I thought." She nodded grimly. "Your killer was a southpaw, too."

As was Mitchell's murderer, according to François Ha, the coroner's criminalist. Was Uncle Reggie a lefty, too? "What is this?" I asked.

"Shipping wire, the kind they use for heavy-duty cargo boxes." Peña spoke with a soft Castilian lisp. "It's very similar to wire used to bind the wrists of Givens and that other O.G. in that Lucky Ones hit. Our guy here was a *vetrano,* too, wasn't he?"

"He was a founder, an O.G. all right, but the Black Freedom Militia was more like one of those Panther offshoots."

Peña shrugged. "Either way, *muerte es muerte,*" he said under his breath.

"But this one didn't die easily," Reynolds noted. "You can see where the victim was cut by the wire here, and here."

I made a note while peering at marks on the body's right fingers and hand that Reynolds indicated. Lewis had obviously struggled with his assailant. And while it should have been caught at the scene or in Processing that night, under the circumstances last week I wasn't surprised it had been missed.

Cassie Reynolds, however, didn't look very forgiving. She straightened up, stretched her back, and asked with a little more force where Mikki Alexander was.

"Cassie, I hope you won't sweat Alexander over this," I said. "How many bodies did you have in here over the past week? Fifty, damn near sixty? You guys would have to be infallible not to miss *some*thing."

"There was no way she could have caught this at the scene," Steve agreed, much to my surprise. "We couldn't roll the homicide van to the scene in all the chaos, so we didn't have adequate lighting. And in addition to the darkness, Alexander was trying to do her job under cover from the National Guard. Hell, I was nervous out there, and I had a gun. Far as I'm concerned, the whole thing was above and beyond the call of duty. I don't want to see her get punished for making a small mistake under the worst of conditions."

Plus, Mikki Alexander had moved heaven and earth to get these two postmortems scheduled together. Steve and I both knew jamming her about an error on the Lewis case that was caught anyway would only make her regret having worked so hard on our behalf. And be unlikely to do it again.

The medical examiner allowed herself a tight smile that gave me hope she might let the new coroner's investigator slide. She turned and pointed to Lewis's head. "There's a one millimeter gunshot entry wound at the right temporal bone about three millimeters behind the right ear." She put down her ruler and checked her measurements against a photo from the case file. "There's no blackening around the entry opening, and the entrance wound is star-shaped with flaps directed outward from the skull. The muzzle of the weapon left a clear and distinct imprint on the victim's head. It was a contact shot, right against the skin," Reynolds summarized. "You should be able to get a good match on this one, if you've got a weapon."

Thanks to the .38 Roxborough had found at Mitchell's house, we might.

Reynolds had selected a scalpel from the tray and started to make the Y-incision in Lewis's body—cutting from each shoulder to the middle of the sternum and across the midline—that would end up making him look a little like a butterflied crustacean, his internal organs to be removed, examined, and catalogued.

I stepped outside to check my messages and make a couple of calls. There was one from Aubrey about Lance Mitchell's funeral arrangements. Next I called Hoggman-Dorrangle in San Jose to find out where Cinque Lewis had his fancy arm made. They checked their computers and gave me the name of a prosthetist in Las Vegas, who in turn told me from the serial number the device was fabricated in 1983 but he couldn't remember the name of the patient. He agreed quite readily to check his records and get back to me as soon as possible with a name and an address.

A couple of hours later, Steve Firestone had been replaced on the back wall by Billie Truesdale, who had joined me for the Mitchell post. It was late afternoon by the time Dr. Reynolds finished. She had confirmed what Mikki and François Ha had told us the day before—that Mitchell was strangled by a left-handed person using the same kind of ligature that killed Lewis and was then hung to make us think it was some kind of masturbatory sexual "accident."

Billie and I stood on the morgue receiving dock talking about what our next moves should be when my stomach started growling. "Let's grab a burger at Teddy's," I suggested. Teddy's, down on Eighth Street near Wall, was an old diner run by an even older interracial couple, Theodore and Helga Roosevelt. "And, naw I ain't no Rough Rider!" the elderly black man would yell out at least once a day to the Asian and Latino garment and floral workers studying for their citizenship exams and the police officers from Parker Center and Central Division who came to sit cheek to jowl on the worn red vinyl stools or in the equally decrepit booths. Watching Teddy sling hash, flip burgers, and shoot the shit about life in L.A. was one of the benefits of working downtown.

Billie and I found a booth in a corner and ordered double chili cheeseburgers. "My daughter would love this place," Billie said.

For an awful moment I felt the hole, the space where Erica had been. Billie must have seen it on my face. Her own instantly registered her embarrassment. "Oh, God, Charlotte, I'm sorry."

My face felt like lead, but I was able to keep up the smile. "Hearing about other people's children doesn't usually bother me. It's just lately . . . what's her name?"

Billie pulled out a photo from her wallet. A toddler the color of elm bark with little braids held by a rainbow of barrettes smiled up at me, breaking my heart. "Turquoise," her mother beamed. "I adopted her a year ago. She's three now."

"You adopted her by yourself?"

"Couldn't wait forever for some dream lover to come along and sweep me off my feet in order to have kids. In our line of work, you see too many children needing homes. I eventually had to do something about it, even if I don't exactly fit the Huxtable model."

That one statement spoke volumes about Billie Truesdale. "Love is all that counts," I said carefully. "And I can tell Turquoise is getting plenty of that from her mom."

Billie nodded and looked relieved. "I love her to bits," she admitted.

Helga shuffled over with our drinks. "Well, she's gorgeous." Despite my words, I was surprised at the thorny vines of envy constricting my heart. I took a deep breath and shook them off. "What did you dig up on the kids in the TAGOUT program?"

"Gregory Underwood has a bunch of minor beefs on his record consistent with being a tagger—misdemeanor vandalism of bus shelters, trespassing in a bus yard, misdemeanor possession of marijuana, that kind of stuff. Fairly minor, but it establishes a pattern."

Underwood's record was by far the most extensive of any in the TAGOUT group, but his running buddy, Peyton Bell, was right behind him. "It's a damn shame, really," Billie said. "Kids come from these difficult home situations, don't know which way to go. Too often it's toward the gangs."

I pointed out that Peyton Bell seemed to have a pretty solid home life.

"He does now, but who knows what his life was like before he was adopted," she replied.

According to the court records, Billie said, the Bells had adopted Peyton almost seven years ago. "He must've been ten or eleven at the time," I pointed out. "Kind of old for an adoptee."

Billie agreed. "No telling what kind of foster-care situation he was in. I really admire people who adopt older children; there aren't enough of our people doing it. But the problems they can open themselves up to . . ."

Helga arrived with our food. I took a bite of my burger and caught the juices dribbling down my chin with a napkin. "What else have we got?"

"Not a lot. We know Mitchell's autoerotic accident was a setup, and then there's that bogus call to Dr. Scott. Now if you ask me, the caller was one of two things." She ticked off the possibilities on her French-tipped nails. "Either a witness to the killing or an accomplice who dropped a dime on his partner for some reason. But either way, it's gotta be someone who knew they could get in touch with Dr. Scott through Mitchell's exchange."

I pulled out my notebook and went down my list. In addition to Underwood, Peyton, and Reggie Peeples, all of whom had seen Aubrey with Mitchell at the gallery along with a hundred others, it included everyone who worked in California Medical Center's ER plus administration, the CaER staff, even his estranged wife. "We could narrow it down if we had that tape," I sighed.

"*Voilà!*" Billie pulled a cassette out of her purse along with a small recorder. "Picked it up today. I've listened to it, and I don't hear anything remarkable, but the voice may mean more to you than me."

It didn't. Just a man who sounded like he was three sheets to the wind, slurring his words from a phone booth. People seemed to be walking by him, and I could hear the noise of cars starting up. "What was the caller's location?" I asked.

"A phone booth at the corner of Slauson and Overhill, in Windsor Hills."

"That's in the County Sheriff's jurisdiction," I frowned. "If that's the same person that called Dr. Scott's exchange to drop a dime on Mitchell's murder, saying he was from the Sheriff's Department would have been a logical mistake. Sheriff's deputies roll through there all the time, checking on the businesses and La Louisiane, that Creole restaurant near the corner. There's a phone booth next door there. One was probably rolling by when our tipster called."

"So what . . . our caller goes out for gumbo after finding a dead body?" Billie asked. "That's pretty cold-blooded."

"You and I have both seen worse," I reminded her. We ate our burgers in silence until I asked her if she'd heard from Aubrey Scott.

"No, but the public relations director at the hospital called. Wanted to know when we're releasing details of Mitchell's death to the press. I told her the notices should go out today. I won't be surprised if the television stations pick it up by this afternoon."

"Are you calling it a murder?" I asked.

She shook her head. "Suspicious death for now. I want whoever did Mitchell to think we're still scratching our heads."

"Any word on the gun yet?"

"Untraceable. No serial number on it, and the prints have been wiped clean."

No breaks there. I started flipping through my notes. "So where do you want to begin?"

We agreed I would go back to the office, set up some meetings with the staff at California Medical Center who knew Mitchell, and have Cortez dig a little deeper on the kids' alibis. "I'd like you to be involved in as many of the interviews as possible since you've met these folks," Billie said. "That's an advantage."

She sucked noisily at her straw. "I overheard Reynolds telling Humberto Peña they'd gotten some pressure from Councilwoman Moore's office to release the body for the funeral. You hear anything about when the service is gonna be?"

"Dr. Scott called to say it's Saturday at two."

"Did he now?" There was a twinkling question in her eye I decided to ignore. "How come so quick?"

"I guess Dr. Holly doesn't care if his friends and family can make it or not."

Billie clucked softly. "Too bad his mother or somebody else can't make the arrangements."

"She's still his wife," I pointed out. "And you know how *that* goes."

Billie nodded. "Do I ever."

"You wanna go?"

She bobbed her head again. "If I can get a baby-sitter. I'm sure it's going to be a real show."

CHAPTER 18

IT MUST
REALLY HURT
WHEN YOU
LOVE THEM

"If it had been left to his wife, the poor man would have been buried in a cardboard box. And after all he did for me during the Uprising! Brought me my medicine, right to my front door." This denture-clacking pronouncement was made by a white-haired matron who turned out to be Mrs. Doxie Rucker, the woman to whom Lance Mitchell delivered the hypertension medicine last Friday afternoon.

"That casket musta been the cheapest one they had in stock," her bewigged friend replied, her white dress and black bow tie a stiff polyester twin to Mrs. Rucker's. "And they've got the nerve to advertise her radio program 'Dr. Holly Would Like You Should!' I wouldn't treat a dog like this!"

Their man-made fibers rustling, the women continued to clatter and chatter in the next-to-the-last row of the chapel, just in front of Billie and me. They reminded me of the little ladies from my childhood church who sat in the front pew to catch and comfort those overcome by the Spirit during call to prayer at the altar. But many of them had another job—that of professional funeralgo-er. I knew this because it was a role Grandmama Cile took on from time to time, albeit in natural fibers and more colorful drag. But these ladies didn't wear the maroon pocket square that would identify them as members of my grandmother's church. I was relieved because these two certainly had neither my grandmother's style nor the Allen A.M.E. Church spirit in their hearts that Saturday morning. And it was a shame because, if any place should have stimulated the peace that passeth all understanding, it would have been Crenshaw Boulevard's Angelus Funeral Home, the mortuary with the old motto "an institution as distinctive as its name."

A sixties design by black architect Paul Williams, one of the distinctive embellishments he and the owners dreamed up for this building was to lay out the night sky in lights on the chapel ceiling, faithful in position and intensity to what one could really see if you looked up on a spring night in Los Angeles—that is, before smog and the city lights got in the way. But these electrical heavens were controlled by a bank of rheostats at the front of the chapel that could simulate the dark night of our grieving to the bright dawn of gone-to-glory joy. A tall, handsome young man in a dark suit manned the dials and divided his time between the lights and consoling the family, who remained obscured behind a screened-off viewing/seating area on the right side of the chapel.

Other mourners were less reticent about making their presence at the funeral known or their feelings about Dr. Lance Mitchell's death.

"Do you think Dr. Holly knows about *her?*" Billie whispered and jerked her chin toward Minda Santiago, the Filipina nurse who had helped Dr. Mitchell reset my shoulder that Friday night. Black-haired and petite to the point of waifishness, the young nurse sat in the fourth row on the left side of the chapel, dabbing her eyes with a lace-edged handkerchief.

It was the same handkerchief Nurse Santiago had used when Billie and I interviewed her the day before about her relationship with the deceased.

"Lance was unhappy long before he left his wife," Santiago had explained over coffee and teary regret in the ER staff lounge that day. "I wasn't the first."

She had twisted that handkerchief like a tourniquet around her fingers during our entire interview. "But I loved Lance," she had insisted. "And I thought he loved me. So much so, I left my husband to be with him. But I found out the hard way you can't be somebody's Band-Aid love."

"The wife is always the last to know," I said in response to Billie's question. "Mitchell probably kept his hospital love under cover, no pun intended. Just as well since it didn't work out."

Santiago's disappointment at the demise of their affair had not diminished her respect for Dr. Mitchell, especially during the riots. "He worked so hard," she had said in our interview. "I was glad he got away early. Whoever called and convinced him to leave was a real godsend."

Although Santiago didn't get her name, she believed she would recognize the woman's voice if she heard it again. I pointed in Mrs. Rucker's direction. "After the service, let's get Santiago to verify that it was her on the phone."

Billie nodded and looked around at the well-dressed crowd. "I haven't been to a buppie funeral and feed for a while," she whispered. "Do you think the widow will have it catered?"

"If how the funeral is being handled is any indication, I'd say the repast would more likely be Colonel Sanders than duck à l'orange."

The sanctuary was sparsely decorated, with only two sprays of gladiolas on either side of the bare casket. All of the other flowers sent by his friends and colleagues had been banished at the widow's request to an anteroom outside the sanctuary. Good thing the media, both respectable and not-so who had gotten wind of Dr. Mitchell's funeral, had been restricted to outside the building. They would have had a feeding frenzy if they had seen the bargain-basement send-off Dr. Holly had cooked up for her estranged husband.

It was bad enough as it was. Circling in the parking lot were the usual complement of media types—Neil Hookstratten of the *Times*, a guy from the *Sentinel*, plus a couple of local television reporters. A crew from *Hard Copy* was filming the arriving mourners like it was a Hollywood premiere and fighting with a freelancer from the *Clarion* for the choicest comments. The tabloid's exposé-style headline on Dr. Mitchell's death had run in its Thursday editions and brought out the freaks and the faithful, eager for a glimpse of radio's number one black psychologist in her hour of grief. Dr. Holly was so outraged by the coverage, she had insisted the mortuary staff screen the attendees, checking off names at the door like it was some exclusive Hollywood party.

Not everyone was upset with the tabloid coverage. The sensational articles had amused the hell out of Sidney Hairston, the black ER nurse who had fitted my sling at California Medical Center. The bottle blond-haired man had been laying in wait for us outside the staff lounge where we had interviewed Minda Santiago.

"All this talk in the rags about a gay sex scandal? Honey, please!"

Never judge a book by its cover, my grandmother's voice reminded me. I had asked him whether he thought it was possible that Mitchell might have been bisexual or gay.

Puffy-eyed, fortyish, and attired that day in bright orange scrubs that did nothing for his looks, Hairston had pursed his generous lips demurely and leaned forward in his chair. "Miss Thing," he had said, his voice all low and this-is-just-between-us-chickens confidential, "if Dr. Mitchell was family, I would have known it, no matter how hard he might have tried to hide it. I can smell a mile away someone who's trying to pass."

Hairston demonstrated his abilities by inhaling deeply in both our directions, lingering a nanosecond longer than necessary when he got to Detective Truesdale.

I saw Billie wince a little. This guy was a real jerk. My mother's brother, Uncle Syl, was gay, and I had a number of gay friends, both in and out of law enforcement. I knew none of them cared to be "outed" by some self-appointed member of the sexuality police, whether they were open about their preferences or not.

"Do you have any *concrete* knowledge about Dr. Mitchell's private life, or are we just going on your keen sense of smell?" I had asked, not even trying to keep the contempt out of my voice for Hairston's little stunt with Billie.

"He was an unrepentant nookie man, much to my chagrin." Hairston had sighed the sigh of a man who had tested the waters and found them too cold. "When he found out I was gay, he was *too* happy. Told me that left the playground at the hospital wide open for him."

It was Hairston's contention that Minda wasn't the only hospital staff member, married or single, who "Lance Romance put on the examination table," as he had so quaintly put it. But for someone who so obviously liked to dish, Hairston had been sketchy on names. "Oh, I think they'll make themselves known," he had predicted archly. "Just check out who does what at the funeral tomorrow."

So Billie and I had taken a position in the back of the sanctuary to do just that. To see which women came in crying, which ones had a few tearful moments alone with the casket before the services began, and which ones got tight-jawed when they did. Five women fitting the general profile of a Mitchell conquest came into the chapel and had their moment at the casket, but it was the last of them who silenced the crowd when she strode up the aisle to say a private good-bye.

The church sisters could barely contain themselves. "Do you see that, Sister?" Mrs. Rucker whispered behind her Angelus Funeral fan.

" 'Deed I do," her companion ogled. "Councilwoman Moore come to pay her respects. Your doctor must have really been an important man. And look . . . the poor woman is so overcome, she almost knocked those children over."

The children Earnestine Moore nearly flattened on her way to her seat were Donnie Watson and Jamilla Brown, who seemed as stunned by the councilwoman's behavior as they were by the shock of their benefactor's death. "That young woman is the phlebotomist I mentioned to you," I whispered, "the one Mitchell helped get the job but then hassled all the time."

"Could she have been angry enough to have her boyfriend waste him? He's big enough to have done the deed by himself."

Jamilla and Mitchell's argument at the gallery *had* been pretty heated. "Maybe. According to their department heads, they've both been out sick since Mitchell's murder."

"They look perfectly fine to me," Billie said. "Let's be sure and talk to them before they leave today."

After a few moments together at the casket, the young couple joined the TAGOUT kids on the right side of the chapel. Aubrey was among them, talking quietly with Underwood and one of the girls from the gallery on his left. Sandra Douglass was sitting on Aubrey's right side, in a fitted black suit and hat that were more of a looking-for-a-man outfit than something an attorney would wear to a client's funeral. Behind them were Reggie Peeples with his wife, Faye. The sag in Uncle Reggie's shoulders made him look as if Mitchell's death had left him permanently deflated. Next to him was Raziya Bell. She was pretty broken up, too, crying softly but steadily on the shoulder of a male I assumed was her husband.

I pointed her out to Billie. "Mitchell was a real benefactor to her son, Peyton. He's the slender, dark-complexioned boy sitting over there with the other kids."

Billie's eyebrows started doing the caterpillar. "The way girlfriend is crying makes me wonder is that all."

"What do you mean?"

"Don't forget our boy Mitchell was quite the lover."

"But she's the mother of one of the kids!" I whispered. "Don't you think that's a little *too* messy?"

"It would be for me," Billie replied. "But I'll tell you like my father told me: Ain't no telling what can happen when the little head starts doing the thinking for the big head."

The artificial sky lightened a bit above us, and the organist began playing the processional "Peace Be Still." The minister read the Lord's Prayer. Of course that was the moment my pager decided to go off, making Mrs. Rucker and her sidekick turn and give me the evil eye. I ducked into the lobby to call the number on the LED display.

It was Mrs. Sparks. "You got t'promise me you won't mistreat my baby." I could hear the choked-back emotion in the old woman's voice. "She was just tryin t'make a new life for herself. After all that grief Bobby caused her, you cain't fault her for that."

As I suspected, Mrs. Sparks had known where Candy Grant/Sojourner Truth was all along. "She gave me one a'them one eight hunnert pager numbers so I could always reach her if I needed to," she confessed. "I called it yesterday. She said she'd get in touch wichu soon as she could, and Candy don't make no promises she don't keep."

I could hear papers rustling in the background. "She tole me not to tell you, but she go by a different name now. I got it right chere."

When I returned to my seat, I started to tell Billie what Mrs. Sparks had said, but was shushed by the old women in front of us. I made a face at the back of their heads, got out my notebook, and scribbled out a note. Billie read it, quickly scanned the chapel, and gave me the thumbs up.

Dr. Holly Mitchell stood in the half light of the pulpit. A stunning woman with long, chestnut brown hair and skin the color of dawn, her publicity photos on the sides of buses and on billboards all over town did not do her justice.

The assembled group leaned toward her as she began to speak, as if they were straining toward their radios to catch her special brand of morning drive time, cut-to-the-chase advice to the lovelorn and life-battered on a hundred and ten radio stations across the USA and parts of the Caribbean.

"Lance's mother, sisters, and I thank you for your letters, cards, and calls offering your condolences and support," she read, her Bausch & Lomb blues reaching through the crowd, drawing them in as much as her low, sultry voice. "What is clear to me in your outpouring of affection is how completely Dr. Lance Mitchell spent his life servicing others."

Maybe Billie and I were the only ones who caught Dr.

Holly's slip of the tongue because there was a general murmur of assent from the congregation while a few people began to cry more audibly, among them Jamilla Brown, much to her boyfriend's dismay.

"Servicing the needs of others was at the core of Dr. Mitchell's being," Dr. Holly continued, "for better or worse."

Billie and I drew in a breath, looked at each other, and then at Dr. Holly's hardened face. Aubrey turned from his seat near the front and caught my eye as if to say, *What did I tell you?*

"It didn't matter if it was the President of the City Council…," Dr. Holly paused to stare at Councilwoman Moore, who gave a regal, if wary nod of her head, ". . . a group of self-proclaimed 'aerosol *artistes*' . . .," with a wave of her hand Dr. Holly included and dismissed the TAGOUT group, whose bowed heads snapped up sharply at the slight they thought they heard, ". . . or the co-workers with whom he was so *intimately* involved . . ." She eyed the part of the chapel where the hospital staff sat and zeroed in on Minda Santiago and a few other women, which caused "that bitch" to audibly spill from the lips of more than a few. "Anyone could call on Lance for help at all hours of the day or night, and did. That's how Lance was. It's what made you *love* him, *serve* him, and *mourn* him with us here today."

The openmouthed organist had to be nudged by the young man at the light switches before she struck up a few chords. As the lights came up, the flustered soloist began to sing:

> *May the words in our mouths*
> *And the meditations of our hearts*
> *Be acceptable in Thy sight,*
> *O Lord*

"Did you hear that?" Doxie huffed. "I'm listening to Dr. Laura from now on. That Dr. Holly is evil personified."

"Well, you know what they say," her friend replied. "Evil deeds are like cheap perfume—they'll funk up a room every time!"

At an appropriate interval, Billie and I approached the cur-
tained-off area, introduced ourselves, and expressed our condolences to Dr. Holly, who sat batting her store-bought eyelashes at
the mortuary attendant. Lance's mother and sisters, seated directly
behind her, were alternately preoccupied with their own grief and
with what looked to me like an urge to slap the living hell out of
Lance's not-quite-grieving widow.

Dr. Holly managed to dredge up a few crocodile tears for our
benefit. "Please forgive me, Detectives," she said between little
forced gulps of air. "Much as I hated that man, here I am crying
and carrying on. It must *really* hurt if you love them."

Lance's mother jumped up as if she'd been shot from a can-
non and stalked out of the enclosure. His sisters stared at Dr. Holly
in drop-jawed disbelief before gathering their things to join their
mother.

"We can see you're upset . . ." Billie began.

"Upset?" she said. "No, I was upset when Lance told me I just
wasn't 'sexually adventurous' enough for him. I was upset when that
bastard came home smelling of other women. I was upset when his
drug habit made the tabloids and the ratings for my show went into
the toilet all over the country. This is *nothing* compared to that!"

Billie had begun to ease away. "Perhaps we could make an
appointment to see you on Monday," she suggested. "We just have
a few questions to ask you."

Outside the enclosure, the mourners were taking their last look
at the body and speaking to Lance's family in the first row. "Let's do it
right here," Dr. Holly suggested. "Mama Mitchell and the wicked sisters of the East are receiving the condolences for the family just fine.
God knows none of these people want to talk to me."

I'd seen all sorts of responses to grief, but Dr. Holly's took the
cake, as my grandmother would say. I glanced at Billie, who
seemed as uneasy about interviewing her right there—practically
at the deceased's coffin—as I was.

Billie took a deep breath and sat down next to her while I
took a seat in the row behind them. "We have reason to believe
your husband may have been murdered," she began gently.

Dr. Holly fixed us with a steady, dry-eyed gaze. I'd seen women display more emotion on learning there was a run in their pantyhose. "Detective Roxborough said it was sexual misadventure," she finally said and sniffed. "That was so much more fitting for Lance."

"I beg your pardon?" Billie asked.

"Lance Mitchell wasn't faithful to me for more than a month during our entire seventeen-year marriage," she spat out with considerable force. "I tried to ignore it, lose myself in my work, but it only got worse. As long as he was discreet—you know, kept it restricted to those once-a-year, boys-only 'getaways' where everybody knows the girlfriends are flying down to meet them, or a sudden, can't-be-missed, out-of-town 'medical' conference—I was willing to go along."

Dr. Holly's eyes glittered with a steeliness that made the temperature drop ten degrees inside the chapel. " 'Go along to get along,' isn't that how the saying goes? And after all, as my agent said, how many people would listen to a Love Doctor who can't keep her own man?"

She yanked down the jacket of her black and red Chanel suit, causing the heavy gold buttons to clatter and echo slightly off the walls of the enclosure. "And when I told his doormat of a mother what was going on, you know what that cow said? 'You got to take the bitter with the better.' As if being in a loveless charade with a pill-popping skirt chaser was the price you had to pay to have a man!"

She practically sneered at Lance's mother, who was weeping into her handkerchief as Sidney Hairston approached her to pay his respects. "That may have been what she had to endure with Lance Senior, but *I* wasn't having it. So I took the bitter and made it better all right. Dusted off my pride, got me a good lawyer, a facelift, and tummy tuck. Then I restructured my show from goody-two-shoes 'Love Doctor' to taking-no-prisoners, radio-shrink-from-hell and never looked back."

Dr. Holly twisted up the memorial program like she was wringing Lance Mitchell's neck. The surprising strength in her hands reminded me of what Aubrey had said about how furious Dr. Holly had been when Lance had moved out. Gazing at those hands, I wondered if they were strong enough to choke her husband.

Or sign the check to have someone else do the deed. "Did you know any of the women he was seeing?" I asked.

Her laugh reeked of bitterness. "Oh, Detective, there were so many, I couldn't keep track. One little floozy came to the station, into my place of business, rubbing his indiscretions in my face. After some of the things she said, I wasn't surprised at all to hear about how Lance died."

"The apparent cause of death may have been just a smoke screen," Billie noted. "The medical examiner thinks your husband was strangled, then hung to make it look like autoerotic asphyxiation."

Dr. Holly's eyes grew wide. "Do you think it was someone trying to damage my career?"

What a piece of work! Her husband is strangled to death, then implicated in a gay sex scandal, and she thinks it has something to do with her. I was getting a faint inkling of why Lance Mitchell packed up his bags and walked out on the lovely Dr. Holly Hightower Mitchell.

"Did your husband own a gun?" I asked.

"Not while we were married." Her mouth was a thin, hard line. "If he had, I might have used it on him."

This woman didn't seem to care *what* we thought of her relationship with the deceased. But she did have an alibi for Tuesday evening. "I was giving a talk at a dinner of my sorority's alumnae chapter at the Century Plaza Hotel. Afterward I had a drink with some of the sorors in the bar." She leaned forward to stare at the assembled mourners, who were still making their way up to the casket. "So if it wasn't me, Detectives, who could it have been? Everyone else thought the man walked on water and talked to God."

"You mentioned your husband's drug habit earlier," I said. "Was it just limited to prescription drugs?"

"As far as I know."

"Do you know if he was using again?"

"Not to my knowledge, but you must remember, Detective Justice, I tried to know as little as humanly possible about that bastard. Do you think he was killed over some drugs?"

"Robbery may have been a motive," Billie said cautiously. "It appears his jewelry case had been emptied. You wouldn't happen to know what items they may have taken?"

"They probably got that gold Rolex watch I gave him for our tenth anniversary. There would also have been a gold Patek Philippe watch and some jade and diamond cuff links we bought in Hong Kong last summer."

"Anything else of value that might have been stolen?" I asked.

"I hope they didn't take my celadon vases," she said indignantly. "Bastard snuck them out when he left. I tried to block his car, but he got away. They were worth six thousand dollars apiece!"

"Would you happen to have any photographs of the items?" Billie asked.

Holly Mitchell hoisted a perfectly shaped eyebrow in Billie's direction. "Why would I want anything that related to that weasel in my house? What he didn't take I burned the day that lying bastard left. It made quite a pretty fire in the fireplace, too."

She glanced down at the picture of Lance Mitchell on the cover of the memorial program. "A Life of Service" the caption under the picture read. "Yeah, but service to whom?" she asked softly and shredded the program into little pieces.

CHAPTER 19

A MEETING
IN THE
LADIES' ROOM

Aubrey was among the men shouldering Lance Mitchell's casket down the aisle. I acknowledged his brief smile but kept my eye on the other mourners moving out of the chapel; I didn't want to lose Cinque's girlfriend, Sojourner Truth. I spotted her moving into the vestibule and yanked at Billie's sleeve. "I'll take her. You be sure it wasn't Mrs. Rucker's voice Minda Santiago heard on the phone."

I caught up with Councilwoman Moore and Raziya Bell, who were asking an attendant for directions to the ladies' room. "Good idea," I said, falling in behind them. "Too much coffee this morning."

Raziya and I waited in line while Councilwoman Moore used the vacant stall. After she emerged and Raziya went in, the councilwoman glanced at me out of the corner of her eye, then started finger combing her thick hair and reapplying her lipstick.

"It was a lovely service, wasn't it?" she said and kissed at the mirror. "All except for that dreadful woman's comments. No wonder poor Lance dumped her."

I had to remember to close my mouth as I watched the councilwoman primp in the mirror and head out the door. Just goes to show you—Lance Mitchell's string of women knew no boundaries.

Billie entered the lavatory with Minda Santiago in tow. She gave me the thumbs down, as I expected: Mrs. Rucker was not the woman who telephoned Lance at the hospital the night Lewis died.

"Where did you grow up, Raziya?" I asked over the partition.

"On the East side, Forty-seventh Street," she replied.

Minda frowned, closed her eyes, and cocked an ear toward Bell's voice.

The toilet flushed, then Raziya said, "But that was when the streets were safe to walk and the walls weren't covered with graffiti."

Minda opened her eyes and nodded. I motioned her to leave us alone, something she seemed only too glad to do.

"I spent a few years in that neighborhood myself until my family moved to the West side," I said as Raziya emerged from the stall.

Billie introduced herself and leaned on the sink while Raziya Bell washed her hands and I planted myself at the outer door. "I grew up in South Central, too," Billie said to no one in particular. "My folks were *real* radicals, though, not like my buppie partner here. Charlotte, I bet you grew up reading those little Golden Books and Martin Luther King," she teased. "At our house it was Chairman Mao's Little Red Book and *Soul on Ice,* all the way." She turned to Raziya. "Now I *know* you read Eldridge Cleaver."

Raziya straightened up and stared at us, her hands dripping water on the tile floor.

I studied her reflection in the mirror. "*Soul on Ice* would have been okay for a young radical back in the day, but what did you read to the children in the Black Freedom Militia's alternative school?" It took effort to keep my voice at a normal pitch. "Ann Petry's book about Harriet Tubman? Or maybe Sojourner Truth's memoirs?"

Raziya was rubbing a paper towel to shreds that speckled her dark suit like snow. "I was going to come to you, I swear . . ."

"Mrs. Sparks said you'd make yourself known to us when you had the opportunity." I came off the door and poked her in the shoulder. "But we need to talk now, Candy, or Sojourner, or Raziya, or what*ever* your name is."

Breathe in, my little voice reminded me. *Don't blow this.*

Raziya looked alarmed. Billie inserted herself between us and sent me back to my post with a warning glare. "You'll have to excuse my partner, Mrs. Bell. Detective Justice gets a little worked up sometimes."

Billie's lilting voice alerted me she was setting Raziya up for nice cop/bitch cop. There was no doubt about which role I would play.

"Raziya's an African name, isn't it?" Billie asked pleasantly. "What does it mean?"

"Sweet one." Her voice was just above a whisper. She cleared her throat and said, "I had it legally changed when Yusef and I got married. Seemed a logical progression from Candy." Her eyes wavered behind tears, her mouth twisted into the fragment of a smile. "Mrs. Sparks liked it, too."

"What does your husband have to say about your past?" I spat out.

Billie nailed me with another scowl.

"Yusef knew that I had been involved with the Black Freedom Militia. He had flirted with the Panthers himself, so it was no big deal. But I never told him the whole story."

"You mean like what Cinque Lewis and your gang did to my husband and daughter? Or have you forgotten the two people your ex-boyfriend shot to death?"

Raziya's eyes were blank for a moment, then widened slowly as my words sank in. She tried to speak, her mouth forming O's like a fish in a restaurant tank. Soon the tears started falling, streaking her makeup and splattering the countertop, reddish-brown drops mixing with the black of her mascara.

It took a while for her to wind down to little sobs and hiccups. Finally she said, "When I saw how much you had enjoyed Peyton's work that night at the exhibit, I thought, 'She's probably got a child, too.'" She started to reach out to me. "I'm so sorry." When I drew back, she dropped her arms sadly. "I feel like this is all my fault."

I backed her up against the counter with an outstretched arm. "What do you mean, 'your fault'? Were you in the car that day, too?"

Raziya's spine seemed to collapse, and she leaned against the countertop for support. "I might as well have been. I was the one who gave your husband information about the Militia. If I hadn't, Cinque would never have gone after him."

In the beginning, she explained, "Sojourner Truth" had been Cinque Lewis's chief lieutenant. "But he moved me aside, started meeting more and more with his male lieutenants in what they called the Inner Circle and leaving me and the other sisters completely out of the loop."

"Sounds a little sexist to me," Billie murmured.

Raziya's mouth worked itself into a sad half smile. "That's how a lot of the brothers in the movement were back then. A female, no matter how bright, had a certain place. And I had come from a home that was so chaotic, any kind of structure—even a bad one—felt like an improvement to me. And when Cinque picked me to run the alternative school, I felt special, like maybe I could make a difference for the first time in my life."

I was reminded of something Keith once told me about the woman in front of me: *One of the most dedicated sisters I've ever met.*

She brushed at the paper lint on her skirt. "So I turned a blind eye to being excluded from the meetings. I was just getting over it when Q-Dog told me about Cinque hooking up with this other sister. Q-Dog said that because he told Cinque he was wrong, they were keeping him on the outside looking in, too."

She stared at a spot on the floor. "Cinque and the Black Freedom Militia were my life. When I found out he'd excluded me from the Inner Circle *and* was sleeping with another woman, I felt like I'd been played for a chump the whole time. So when Professor Roberts came to an orientation meeting and I found out about the book he was writing, I just told him everything."

Keith had told me about Sojourner's revelations and, later, how Cinque had barged into his office, yelling and screaming about the "bitch traitor" who was trying to ruin his organization's good name. How Lewis had first tried to appeal to his sense of racial pride—"rich professor like you should be supporting the community instead of tearing it down, writing books about us for whitey"—then had attempted to extort money from Keith, and finally had threatened our lives when Keith wouldn't cave in.

But this story Raziya was weaving was something else entirely. "Do you mean to tell me you set this whole thing in motion because you were jealous of another woman sleeping with your *man*?" I could hear myself shouting, my voice echoing off the tile, but I couldn't help it. "Don't you tell me some stupid bullshit like this is why my husband and child were murdered!"

Someone was trying to get in the bathroom, but I leaned against it with my full weight. "It's out of order!" I yelled.

Raziya stood, flushed and wet-faced, against the far wall. "I'm so, so sorry," she half-whimpered. "I was only twenty-two, but Cinque had thrown me away for a seventeen year old like I was an old shoe! I thought I was going to die!"

"Were you involved directly in the Militia's drug dealing?" Billie asked.

"That was handled by the brothers in the Inner Circle," she explained. "But we knew. We sisters told ourselves they were like black Robin Hoods—you know, selling drugs to the rich to feed the poor. And Cinque said since their customers were just rich white college kids and record executives, they didn't matter. Only black lives mattered."

Long as it stays over in that part of town and doesn't affect me and mine. It was a refrain I'd been hearing a lot lately from some other parts of town, and it didn't sound any better—or any truer—coming from Raziya Bell than it did from folks in the suburbs.

I could feel the lavatory walls closing in on me, and it was taking everything I had within me not to draw my weapon and blow this woman to bits the way her sorry-assed boyfriend had my family. She must have read my mood because she refused to look at me and started talking exclusively to Billie. "I eventually came to understand how wrong we were. I think Bobby did, too. After he left L.A., he would write to me, telling me what he saw in places like San Francisco, Omaha, or Kansas City. Cocaine, and then crack, creeping into the cities and the suburbs."

"How was he able to stay underground for so long?" Billie asked.

"Safe houses with a network of sympathetic revolutionary groups in the beginning. When those became too risky, he hid out among the homeless. Even worked in some soup kitchens and for a while in a program for the handicapped. Then, in eighty-two, he wrote to me about a man who offered to set him up with a new identity, but the paperwork and some surgery he'd need would cost five thousand dollars. He needed the money bad, and we were the only people he could turn to. So Mama Trudy and I sent him every dime we had to Las Vegas in care of a friend of his named Rodney Langston."

Mitchell must've used the money for the surgery on his arm and the plastic surgery on his face that Cassie Reynolds had commented on in the postmortem. But she had also said that prosthetic arms like the one Cinque Lewis had could cost as much as forty thousand dollars. Even after the surgeries and the new ID, how could a man on the run have been able to come up with the rest of the money inside of a year to buy that arm?

Raziya Bell didn't know, but she did notice how Bobby's letters changed after they sent the money. "Before, he kept writing and saying how he was going to send for us soon as he got established. But after we sent the money order, we got fewer and fewer letters. After a few months, they stopped altogether."

It was losing her son a second time that contributed to the decline of Bobby's mother's health. "Mama Trudy had started having heart problems before we sent the money," Raziya explained. "I tried to tell her she was going to need the cash for herself, but she insisted on sending it to Bobby anyway. She ended up having a heart attack, then a series of strokes. She finally passed in eighty-three. I tried to reach Bobby through Mr. Langston at the post office box in Las Vegas, but the letter came back 'moved with no forwarding address.' "

It took Trudy's death for Cinque's girlfriend to wise up. "It finally dawned on me how much Bobby had used us, taken what little we had and left us high and dry. So after Mama Trudy died, I went back to school to finish my degree. I met Yusef that next year."

Her face softened at the mention of her husband. "Yusef was honest and kind. He loved me not for what I represented to some movement or what I could do for him. He wanted to do for *me*. We got married a few months after we met and adopted Peyton in eighty-five." Her eyes refilled. "I love my husband very much, Detective Truesdale. I shared as much about my past as he needed to know, but I don't want all of this to come out. It would destroy his faith in me."

"Was Peyton your and Cinque's son?" Billie asked.

"Heavens, no!" Raziya's eyes widened again, and she got all jumpy and startled like the ants underneath that rock in Mrs. Sparks's garden. "We adopted him."

Something was still bothering me, though. "How did Cinque Lewis find you?" I asked.

"He saw my photo in the *Sentinel*."

So it wasn't Uncle Reggie or Lance Mitchell in the photo who had attracted his attention. Cinque Lewis had seen the face of his former lover and comrade staring up at him in a black newspaper and decided he wanted to see her again. Back down memory lane, or was it something more?

"Did Peyton know about your relationship with Cinque Lewis?" I asked.

Again the wide eyes. "Why do you ask?"

"Just answer the question, Mrs. Bell!" Billie said sharply.

Billie's change in tone made the other woman fidget and

look away. "No! And if you think Peyton killed him, you're barking up the wrong tree. He and Gregory were both at the gallery with me that day."

"What about when you went to the gas station?" I reminded her.

"This is *my* shit!" she insisted. "It doesn't have anything to do with Peyton!"

A line of a Shakespeare play ran through my mind: *The lady doth protest too much, methinks.* I watched Raziya Bell take a breath to steady herself and ask Billie what would happen next.

"That depends," Billie replied and glanced over at me.

"Depends on what?" Almost against her will, Raziya looked my way.

"On you getting real with us instead of dancing around the edges," I said. I got up in her face. "Now I'm going to ask you again, and this time I expect an answer—*did Peyton know about your relationship with Cinque Lewis?" Could he have killed Lewis?*

My question set off a struggle within Raziya Bell, one that showed all over her face. She looked from me to Billie, hoping for a reprieve but realizing neither one of us was budging until we had an answer. Finally she shook her head and said something, so softly I couldn't hear her.

Neither could Billie. "Run that by us again, please, Mrs. Bell."

She repeated, this time a little louder, "Peyton was Bobby's half brother."

Cinque Lewis having a half brother wasn't in any of the reports in my murder book. Billie and I exchanged a look. At last things were falling into place.

"Peyton was only five when Bobby disappeared," Raziya explained, "but he was old enough to understand, old enough to see how much his brother's lies hurt his mother and me."

With Bobby in the wind with her hard-earned money, Raziya devastated for a second time, and her health failing, Trudy knew provisions would have to be made for her younger son after she died. "There was no way I was ready to take care of a child, so

Mama Trudy asked Mrs. Sparks to be Peyton's legal guardian, then went to court to make it official before she died."

After Trudy's death, Mrs. Sparks thought it was best for Peyton to continue to live in the apartment he had shared with his mother and Raziya. "He needed the continuity, and having to look after a growing boy made me get myself together," Raziya admitted. "I had to act like a mother, even if he wasn't my blood." She took a second job and went back to school to get her bachelor's degree. When she met and married Yusef, Mrs. Sparks said it was time to make it official and went back to court with the couple to help them adopt Peyton. "Luckily, we were able to convince the courts that I had rehabilitated myself and, together with Yusef, could be a good adoptive parent to Peyton."

Raziya had stopped looking at either me or Billie in the face, a sure sign she was withholding something. "That's a lovely story Raziya, and really I'm touched," I said, "but my question still stands—did Peyton know his brother was back in town?"

She stood for the longest time with a thousand-yard stare in her eyes before slowly nodding her head. "I told Peyton after Bobby called the gallery and offered me money for his tuition. Bobby said it was the least he could do after all the pain he caused us."

All Bobby wanted in exchange was to see his little brother. But Raziya was skeptical, she said, and suspected Lewis of promising the money as a way of getting back in their good graces. "I told him I'd have to think about it, talk it over with Peyton."

According to Raziya, Peyton was torn—excited about the possibility of getting the money for school, but unsure about whether he wanted to see his half brother. "Finally, I decided to talk it over with Dr. Mitchell," she said. "He cared so much about Peyton, I knew he'd have some good advice for me."

Mitchell offered to go instead of Raziya or Peyton to see if Lewis was on the up-and-up. "And if he wasn't, Dr. Mitchell said he'd tell Bobby that Peyton didn't want to see him."

"Did Dr. Mitchell ever say what happened?" Billie asked. "Did they ever meet?"

"I don't know," she replied. "I called him all that weekend, trying to find out what happened, but he never answered my pages. And when Peyton talked to him at the TAGOUT exhibit, Dr. Mitchell told him that when he got to the taco stand, Bobby was already dead. Peyton was so upset—about never getting to talk to his brother, about not having enough money for school—it was a real blessing when Dr. Mitchell's medical group put up the extra money for Peyton's scholarship."

Thanks in no small part to Aubrey's last minute donation. I watched Raziya dampen a paper towel to blot her face and reapply her makeup with a shaky hand. "So what happens now?" she asked. "Will I be arrested?"

"We'll need to get a statement from you," I replied, "about Cinque Lewis and what you know of his activities. And we need to talk to the boy, too." Good as her story sounded, I still wanted to be sure Peyton's feelings were torn by a longing to see his brother—not a desire to even the score for the pain Lewis had caused the women Peyton loved.

"I'll tell you everything I know, but can we do it later?" she asked. "I just need a chance to talk to Yusef alone. I've got a lot of explaining to do."

We arranged for Raziya and Peyton to make their statements at South Bureau on Monday morning. I was just giving her my card when there was a knock at the door.

"Babe, did you fall in?" came a deep male voice through the door. "We're about to leave for the cemetery."

"Coming, honey," she called out. "I was just getting myself together." To us she whispered, "Can I go now?" She scribbled her address and phone number on the back of a business card. "Here's my home address and phone number." She showed us her driver's license as proof, "Just so you won't think I'll run away."

I studied her business card; it said she was director of community arts education at one of the downtown museums. I took it and considered the woman before me. Could I trust Raziya to come in and not disappear like her former boyfriend? After overcoming her naïve faith in the Black Freedom Militia and her lousy choice in men, Raziya Bell seemed to have turned her life around. While no one could just ignore the fact that she had aided and abetted a fugitive, Captain MIA and the D.A.'s office might be willing to work out a deal in exchange for her information on the underground network that managed to keep Cinque Lewis hidden all these years.

"I swear we'll be there, Detective," she promised on her way out the door. "I owe you at least that much."

CHAPTER 20

FAMILY

The hearse had already left, and most of the mourners had followed the motorcade to Sunnyslope Cemetery. A red-eyed but composed Raziya and Yusef Bell stood in the parking lot talking to Aubrey and Sandra Douglass, while Peyton stood with Jamilla Brown and Donnie Watson, staring at their shoes and otherwise avoiding each other's eyes as only teenagers can.

"You think we're doing the right thing waiting until Monday to talk to the Bells?" Billie asked.

"I think so. Raziya Bell is too dedicated to her family and TAGOUT to cut and run. Plus she's got to be smart enough to know that if she doesn't show up with the boy, it'll cast even more doubt on him. I don't think she'd do that to a kid with so much promise."

"You believe her story?"

"I do, and I don't. The part about what happened within the Black Freedom Militia and Cinque being on the run sounds plausible. But who was this guy who offered to help Lewis to create a new identity? And did this man also give him forty thousand dollars for that arm? That story may have worked on Raziya, but I'm not lining up to buy that wolf ticket."

"I'm hip," Billie agreed. "But what about the boy? Do you think he's involved with Lewis's murder?"

"I don't think so." I dug out my notebook. "Cortez interviewed Underwood yesterday and pulled the phone records from the gallery for that Friday afternoon. Underwood claimed he and Peyton were at the gallery all afternoon. And the phone records show that between three and four they placed two calls to other kids in TAGOUT, three to CalArts, and another one to a party supply store on Melrose. The boys were definitely there."

Cortez had also confirmed with the other kids in the group that they had talked to Underwood and Peyton that afternoon, and the school's admissions and art department offices had confirmed that Gregory Underwood called the school about his scholarship. "And a clerk at the supply store remembered Peyton calling at five to confirm his mother's order for the reception, just about the time we were rolling down King Boulevard toward that taco stand. The gap in between the calls wasn't enough for either Peyton or Underwood to slip out, kill Lewis, and be back by the time Raziya returned."

We watched as the Bells and Peyton got into their car and pulled away. Before Jamilla and Donnie could do the same, I made a beeline over there to introduce them to Billie as the lead investigator in Mitchell's death. "We came by the hospital on Friday to see you, but you were both out sick," I explained. "Do you have a minute to talk now?"

Donnie Watson seemed uncomfortable. "Does it have to be right here?" he said, glancing around.

"You could always come to the station, if you'd prefer," Billie replied.

Their fear about going to a police station hovered in the air like pollen floating from the neighborhood trees. I put my arm around the young man. "It won't take long. Why don't you come inside the chapel with us?" I suggested. "Jamilla can wait in the lobby until we're ready for her."

Donnie reentered the chapel with us, which was fully lit now and quite ordinary-looking. He warily adjusted his large frame into the wooden pew in the back while Billie asked him how long he'd known Mitchell.

"'Bout two years." The curved ceiling of the chapel made his voice echo and boom. "Ever since he patched me up over at California and convinced me to give up tagging and go back to school. He even helped me get a job at the hospital as a pharmacy technician. I owe . . . owed Dr. M a lot."

"You said that at the gallery the other night," I said. "What do you mean, 'owed Dr. M a lot'?"

Donnie raised his face up to the ceiling, a trick I'd used many times to keep people from seeing my tears. It didn't work any better for him than it did for me. "I woulda been just another dead nigger if Dr. Mitchell hadna been there for me. He saved my ass, more than my own blood woulda done. I had three brothers and an uncle who rolled with the Lucky Ones. I'da never have gotten outta that set alive if it hadna been for Dr. M."

"Did Dr. Mitchell ever hit you up for any favors after you started working at the hospital?" Billie asked.

Although he didn't move his head, I saw a sinew pop out in Donnie's neck. "Like what?" he asked.

"Like filling special prescriptions for patients," I said, keeping my eyes on his upturned face.

He looked dead at me, his eyes were still fighting tears. "Only that one time, during the uprisin'. He needed a prescription filled for some Cardura for an old lady that come into the ER. Because of the problem we was havin' gettin' medication, we wasn't supposed to dispense medicines to any more outpatients, but he asked me to hook her up."

A breach in hospital policy, but hardly a criminal act. "Where did you and Jamilla go after the exhibit was over Tuesday night?" Billie asked.

"Over to Phillip's in Leimert Park to get some rib tips and potato salad. We took it over to where she lives with her granny," he explained. "She just got out of the hospital with a heart attack."

I suppressed a smile. Although I was sure they meant well, the famous barbecue joint's pork ribs and mayonnaise-laden potato salad was the *last* thing Granny needed for a heart condition.

Donnie said he dropped Jamilla at her grandmother's house around ten and went to his apartment in the Jungle, where he lived alone: " 'Cept for when Jamilla can sneak out to spend the night. Which is kinda easy, 'cause her granny cain't hear shit."

Donnie explained that, from the time he called her to come over, Jamilla could slip out the back door and be at Donnie's apartment in the Jungle in less than ten minutes from where she lived in Windsor Hills.

When Billie caught my eye, I knew what she was thinking: Windsor Hills was the location from which somebody dropped a dime to 911 on Lance Mitchell's murder.

"Why did Dr. Mitchell give Jamilla such a hard time Tuesday night?" I asked.

His thick neck disappeared in his shoulders. "Dr. M was fair, but he could be a mu'fuckah if he thought you was goofin'. Jamilla tole me Dr. M said she wasn't livin' up to her potential, said he was gonna ride her until she got it together or quit."

"That'd make me mad, somebody ragging on my honey all the time," Billie said.

Donnie did the turtle neck again. "It bothered me a little," he admitted.

"Did it bother you a little Tuesday night?"

He shook his head. "Jamilla was the one who was gettin' on my nerves. I tole her after the exhibit she was buggin'. It was embarrassin' the way she was goin' off on Dr. M. He didn't do nuthin' to deserve all that."

Not surprisingly, Jamilla didn't appreciate Donnie's opinion and was pretty pissed off, he said, when he dropped her off at home. It was the first time in a week he spent the night alone.

Billie escorted Donnie outside and returned with the young woman. We spread ourselves out a little in one of the pews. Jamilla sat midway between us, fidgeting and licking her dark-colored lips.

Her account of her activities after she and Donnie left the gallery were consistent with the young man's, even down to the order from the barbecue stand. A little too consistent for me. "And what did you do afterward, Jamilla?" I asked.

She edged away from me on the pew and licked her dark lips again. "I talked to my granny for a while, then I went to bed," she said and looked at me sideways while she chomped on her gum.

"What time was that?" I asked.

She shifted and chomped again. " 'Bout ten thirty."

I moved with her. "Donnie tells us you're real good at making those midnight creeps," I said. "I was thinking maybe you slipped out."

She moved a little farther away from me and started chewing furiously. "Not with my granny just out of the hospital. Besides, Donnie and I had a fight after the exhibit. I didn't want to see him."

"I was thinking about somebody else."

"Like who?" She moved again.

"Like maybe Dr. Mitchell," I suggested.

She moved farther away from me again, almost sitting on top of Billie. Jamilla looked from one to the other of us, her face all frowned up. "Don't even try it, child," Billie said irritably. "That lipstick you're wearing is the same shade you left on that wine glass at Dr. Mitchell's house."

I knew she was guessing, but from the way Jamilla's hand flew up to her mouth, Billie's bluff had worked. "Why don't you just tell us about you and Dr. Mitchell, honey," I said, slipping into the nice-cop role.

Jamilla sat for a long time, her face working in several directions at once. "Come on, Jamilla, we don't have all day!" Billie snapped.

"Give her a minute, Detective Truesdale." It was a relief to be the nice cop this time. "Jamilla's going to cooperate."

"She better make it quick, before I charge her ass with murder!"

That did it. "I didn't kill him!" she exclaimed. "I went to his house that night, but I didn't kill him!"

I placed my hand over hers. "Why don't you tell us what happened?"

"Me and him was tight," she began. "But then he dissed me for this Filipina nurse in the ER. I was so upset I couldn't concentrate at work or nuthin'. But instead of Dr. M cutting me some slack, he started gettin' all up in my face about me not doin' my job."

"You mean you had an affair with Dr. Mitchell?" Billie asked.

She nodded her head, sniffed a little, smacked her gum. "I've always vibed with men who was older'n me."

Old enough to be her father, she should have said. Looking at Jamilla's low-cut blouse, skirt that barely covered her crotch, and fishnet stockings, I could just about guess what Mitchell saw in her. "How did you two get together?" I asked.

"I met Dr. M at a career day my senior year in high school." The young woman—whose nails were black, I guess in deference to the deceased—started to cry. "He got me interested in health care. He helped me to get a scholarship to Drew. I thought he was interested in *me*, and he was until that skanky-assed Santiago came along!"

Billie dropped her head as if she were speaking to the floor. "Girl, if I was your mama, I'd whip your butt! I bet you were the one who went to Dr. Holly's radio station, bragging about your affair with her husband, weren't you?"

She nodded and snuffled way in the back of her throat. "But he hated her! Tole me all the time about how she didn't understand him, didn't know how to sex him up right."

And Jamilla clearly thought *she* did. As I observed her cocky posture, hot-to-trot drag, and too young eyes, I wondered where in the world this child's parents were. A mother to show her there were other ways of getting attention and respect, a father to tell her she was valuable far beyond the size of her ta-tas or the tricks in her sexual repertoire. I was surprised she wasn't pregnant with Mitchell's child. Funny how some things hadn't changed all that much since I was a teenager. Girls still trying to catch a man using their body as bait, just like Janet had done with Aubrey. And still ending up the same way—with no man and no self-esteem.

"If you had broken up, why did you go to Dr. Mitchell's house that night?" I asked.

"I tole Dr. M at the gallery that night if he didn't stop treatin' me like shit I was gonna go to the hospital CEO and tell him how he had me up in the doctor's sleepin' room lickin' the Reddi wip off of him. That made him real nervous, so he agreed to meet me at his house after the exhibit to talk."

According to Jamilla, they had met at Mitchell's house at eleven. "Did this 'talk' you had involve sex?" Billie asked.

She bobbed her head, snuffling back more tears. "I figured if I really rocked his world, he'd *have* to come back, y'know? So after Donnie took me home, I put on my leather and lace, y'know, and went over there to really try and turn him out. But afterward, he wanted to give me money, like I was a 'ho' or somethin'. I was so mad, I threw it in his face and got the hell out of there. I started to buy some gasoline and burn his house down. But then I decided to slash his tires."

"Now that's original."

Jamilla ignored Billie's sarcasm and spoke to me. "But when I got to there, I decided to see if I could get inside and fuck with some of that fancy pottery he was so proud of."

"What pottery?" I asked.

"Them big-ass jars he kept on them stands," she replied. "He was always goin' on and on about how expensive they was. So when I tried the front door and found it unlocked, I figured I'd tip on in and knock them over. But one of them was already broken . . . and Dr. M's body was hangin' offa that hallway door."

After discovering Mitchell's body about one, Jamilla "freaked," drove around for a while, then headed for home, stopping along the way and asking a man coming out of La Louisiane's to make the call to 911 and Dr. Mitchell's exchange. Then she hightailed it back to her grandmother's house, put on her pajamas, and woke up the old woman, complaining of a stomachache to give herself an alibi.

"Please don't tell my granny about me and Dr. M," she pleaded. "She's a born-again, always on me about staying a virgin."

Jamilla's granny must have been deaf, dumb, *and* blind to have believed there was still a chance of that. Or maybe just too busy

quoting Scripture to see how hard her granddaughter was struggling to be accepted, even if it meant giving away little bits of herself to men like Lance Mitchell. Sure, he helped Jamilla Brown
with her career, but he helped himself to her body and warped her
young mind in the process. And even though he was the victim of
a murder, I could not forgive him for the crime he perpetrated
against this girl.

"Your boy Mitchell sure got around," Billie said as we watched
Jamilla and Donnie get into his tricked-out black Maxima. "You
believe her?"

"It's a little too wild to be made up. Jamilla Brown doesn't
strike me as having that kind of imagination."

Billie jotted down the car's plate number. "I'm going to see if
one of the neighbors saw Donnie's car at Mitchell's that night. I'm
still not ruling out Donnie knew more about Jamilla's relationship
with Dr. Mitchell than he's letting on."

I nodded, watched Donnie peel out of the parking lot.
"Much as I dislike Dr. Holly, if she had to put up with that kind of
shit in her marriage, I understand why she's bitter."

"Hmph," Billie snorted, "but that shit usually cuts both ways.
We just haven't heard what dear Dr. Holly was up to all those
years. Given how she was falling all over that young mortuary
attendant, I bet it was plenty."

"You think that's important to the case?"

"It is if we find out she got some strong young thing to jack
up her husband." Billie flipped her notebook closed. "But I'm
putting my money on the kids. I'll try and get by Mitchell's place
tomorrow, do some more field interviews with the neighbors.
Maybe they saw Jamilla or Donnie coming or going from the
house. I just want to be sure she was alone or that Mr. Muscles
didn't follow her over there, peep their sex show, then kill Mitchell
afterward."

Aubrey's car was still in the lot, but its owner was nowhere to
be found. Maybe he rode out to the cemetery with Sandra

Douglass. It was a thought that gave me a little pang of I wasn't sure what.

"You want to go to the repast?" Billie asked.

"It's your call, but I think we've gotten as much as we're going to for now. Besides, I don't want to have to arrest Lance's mother or sisters on a 240 when they kick Dr. Holly's ass later today."

"Misdemeanor assault, my ass. Thick as it was in there, I'd bet a week's salary it'd be an assault with intent to 187."

"Let's hope not," I laughed.

Billie laughed, too, and shook her head. "I'll see you downtown on Monday, then, for the Bell interviews."

Billie got into her car, a black Maxima a lot like Donnie's, and pulled away. I turned to go back into the mortuary to use the restroom and ran smack-dab into Aubrey.

"Hi," he said. "You done for the day?"

"Yeah. I think I've seen enough."

"That was some funeral, wasn't it? I was surprised to see so many people turn out on such short notice. Lance's family, friends, even some of the paramedics were here."

"It seemed more like a three-ring circus to me."

"Now you understand what I meant about Dr. Holly," he said.

"She's a real piece of work, that's for sure, but I've found there's always two sides to every story. Where'd Sandra go?"

"The cemetery, I think." Aubrey looked up at the sky, which was layered with high, gauzy clouds meandering toward the ocean. I could see their reflection in his sunglasses when he looked back at me. "Where are you headed now?"

"Home to walk my dog, get some rest, maybe order a pizza."

"How about a home-cooked meal?" the clouds in his eyes asked me.

"Offers of free meals always get my attention. You want to try out my KitchenAid?"

"Why don't I cook dinner for you at my house?" he suggested. "Say about eight? You still have the address?"

I nodded. "Should I bring anything?"

"Just your appetite." He leaned over and whispered in my ear. "Not unless you want to bring a toothbrush."

It was my turn to stare at the clouds.

By the time I ran a few errands and got my nails done, it was six fifteen, just enough time to walk the dog around the block, take a bath, and change before heading up to Aubrey's house.

Beast, however, had other ideas and wanted to engage me in a furious Frisbee session in the back yard. Fifteen minutes later, both of us exhausted, I trudged up the back stairs and into the kitchen. I gave Beast his kibble, went to the bathroom to fill the tub, then poured myself some good Chardonnay. I was just getting settled in the water when my pager went off. It was a number in Ladera Heights, another one of L.A.'s golden Negro ghettos.

"I just got off the phone with Sidney Hairston from the ER." Billie was so excited, she had skipped the hellos. "He was calling from Leo's Lair in Venice. Says he's met somebody he thinks can help us. You want to meet me out there?"

"I was just getting dressed to go out. You think leggings and a sweater are dressy enough for Leo's?"

Billie laughed for what seemed like a full minute. "Charlotte, I don't think anyone in that crowd is gonna notice what either one of us is wearing. I'll meet you there in a half an hour."

CHAPTER 21

INTO THE
LION'S DEN

There was a time, my uncle Syl once told me, when gay men in Los Angeles lived as much, if not more, on the margins as black folks. But if things got too hot, white gays always had the option to go back into the closet, back to passing themselves off as masters of the universe. Not so their black counterparts, who at the end of the day were still black, still on the outside looking in.

Leo's Lair was a club where a black gay man could have a drink, socialize freely, and not feel as if he would be looked down upon by some disapproving black homophobe or as if he were an extra-tasty treat for chocolate-addicted whites. Leo's had been around for almost twenty years, operating profitably and quietly from a nondescript storefront in Venice, thanks to a liberal business community and owner Georgina White's reputation for discretion. Uncle Syl said you might see anyone there, from the choir director at your church to the academic dean of a major university, but what went on at Leo's was kept strictly confidential, strictly in the family.

Johnny Hartman's rendition of Billy Strayhorn's "Lush Life" was playing on the club's sound system. Through the crowd I could see Sidney Hairston standing with Billie at the bar. "Well, aren't you a sight," he called out and considered me with a slightly tipsy but appraising eye. He made a sour face at the outfit I had put on for my date with Aubrey. "That's nice for an evening at home, but that drag will never do in Leo's."

He was right. The crowd that Saturday night was dressed and scented to the nines, even though there were still one or two men who were stuck in that seventies Village People leather rut. Hairston himself was wearing a gold-threaded white dashiki that accentuated his hair color and did an admirable job of hiding his middle-age paunch.

He pointed out an immaculately dressed, olive-skinned black male, his relaxed salt-and-pepper hair straighter than mine, who was whispering with an older woman in a booth marked "Private" in the back of the bar. "I bet you know him."

It would have been hard not to recognize Brett Stewart, co-anchor of *The Scene at Six*, a nightly newscast that gave the network affiliates a run for their money and had earned him three local Emmys in five years. The last time I saw him—minus the Hollywood-style sunglasses—was on the tube Friday night after I got home from the hospital.

"I was just telling Miss Billie that Brett's a regular, drops in almost every night after his newscast," Hairston whispered. "Folks here assumed they hadn't seen him this week because of the extended coverage during the uprising. But I overheard him say to Miss G there—she's the owner—that he's been home recuperating all week because he got roughed up by some trade he met in here on Monday." He glanced around the bar and lowered his voice even more. "Seems Brett took a boy toy home and ended up being tied up with some kind of noose around his neck that was made from the cords of his *own* living-room window treatments."

Hairston saw Billie and me exchange a look. "I was right, wasn't I?" he breathed. "I told Miss G that somebody I knew had a similar experience and *died* from it! Well, that just about did her in—there's *never* been that kind of trade in Leo's—and it got me to thinking that maybe this is some kind of serial killer. That's when I called Miss Billie."

"I was just asking Sidney if he thinks Mr. Stewart will talk to us," she said.

"He swore to Miss G he won't talk if it means he's got to come forward and testify in public or if it puts Leo's Lair in jeopardy. But I'm sure if I put in a good word . . ."

Hairston craned his neck around the crush of bodies, zeroed in on Miss G's table until he caught her eye. Georgina White, the owner of the club, a seventyish diva wearing a diamond ring big enough to have its own zip code, widened her eyes in a silent question, to which Hairston responded with a rapid nod. She spoke briefly to Stewart, patted his hand, then motioned us over to the booth.

Hairston ushered us over and gave Georgina a kiss on her heavily made-up cheek. "Darlings, these are the girls I was telling you about."

"You won't be showing your badges, will you, ladies?" Georgina White's voice was a whiskey-weathered drawl. Her concerned frown quickly changed up to a smile when a patron walked by. "Badges scare the customers away," she said out of the corner of her mouth and blew the man a kiss.

Hairston said, winking, "These girls have more class than that. They're *family*."

Billie didn't flinch at the label this time, which I also noted had served to put both Georgina White and Brett Stewart a little bit more at ease. If Billie was cool about it, so was I; I'd discovered a long time ago that there were all kinds of ways to pass.

"It's very important to us, Detectives, that you find whoever did this awful thing to Brett," Georgina said emphatically, patting the newscaster's hand again. "This is a reputable gentlemen's club. I won't have another of my children abused this way."

I remembered Uncle Syl saying that Georgina White had started the club in tribute to her son, Leo Junior, who had been killed in a gay-bashing incident twenty years ago in a bar in Hollywood. After her only son's death, Uncle Syl said, all of Leo's customers had become Georgina White's sons, one way or another.

After getting us some sodas, Georgina and Hairston excused

themselves, although she had to practically drag our self-appointed deputy away from the table.

"I watch your show regularly, Mr. Stewart," Billie said to the newscaster. "I always feel as if I can trust what you say."

"Thank you," he murmured, uneasy but flattered nonetheless.

"I guess the key word here is trust," she continued. "What we're about to share with you hasn't even been released to the press yet. We're trusting you to keep what we say to you confidential, and you've got to trust that we won't reveal anything you say to us in confidence."

"I can assure you, Detective, it's not a story I'm interested in covering for my broadcast." Brett Stewart's smile was pained as he turned a margarita glass slowly in his hands. "If I tell your secrets, that would be like telling my own, wouldn't it? And while I *am* ambitious, there are limits to what I'll do for ratings. My agent is positioning me for a run at one of the networks this summer. I'm not about to upset that apple cart."

Billie took a breath, then began to fill Stewart in on the relevant aspects of the Mitchell case. The newscaster listened intently, soaking up her every word and nuance. He seemed to be turning it all over in his mind, sizing us up before he spoke, his words coming slowly and cautiously, a real contrast to the rapid-fire, in-your-face style of the news program he anchored.

"Even after I got married, I kept my house in Baldwin Hills." Stewart had started twisting his wedding band, a quadrillion-cut sparkler. Seeing it reminded me that Stewart had recently married an up-and-coming model in one of those lavish, *People*-reported weddings just a few months ago that had featured the rings. "My wife Evie's in New York most of the time anyway, so we kept her place in the city, and I fly back and forth every other weekend or she comes out here."

"So can you tell us what happened?" I asked.

"I usually don't bring anyone home I meet in a bar," he began. "It's just too risky. But I was exhausted from the schedule we'd been keeping at the station, Evie was in Jamaica on a photo shoot, and I was lonely. I had stopped by to have a quick drink on

Monday around nine when this young man walked in. All I could think of was that he looked like a Hershey bar—chocolate brown and sweet as he could be. Soft-spoken and so polite, he had the bartender send a drink to me at the bar before he even approached me. He bought the second round, too, even though he barely looked old enough to be drinking himself, and began to tell me how much he had appreciated my broadcasts during the riots, how much he admired me, blah-blah-blah. Soon he was telling me how confused he was about his feelings about men and how he believed I might be the one to help him understand."

A halogen spotlight illuminated the slight bruising along Stewart's jawline and under his left eye, concealed pretty much by the glasses and some expertly applied studio makeup. "It's one of the oldest come-ons," he said, "and I was fool enough to fall for it."

Billie asked what Hersheyman looked like. "He was slender, skin color a deep, pure brown. Broad nose, beginnings of a beard. Cute. What else can I say?"

Hersheyman told Stewart he was twenty-three, but the newscaster thought he might be a "a few years" younger. Not that Stewart was going to card him. Not surprisingly, he didn't ask the boy's name, either.

Stewart removed the sunglasses. The spotlight caught little pinpricks of tears standing in his eyes. "If it hadn't been for a neighbor who heard me calling for help, I could have been tied up in that house for days. I had no idea he was rough trade!"

When they got to Stewart's house, the young man suggested they play a few dress-up games with Evie's clothes. Soon he had bound the newscaster into his dining-room chair and began to shout obscenities and slap him around.

When Stewart looked at us, there was more than the memory of that night in his eyes. "My face is my business, Detectives. I would have done anything for him not to have hit me in the face." He wiped his eyes with the back of an unsteady hand, put his sunglasses back on. "He took the rope from the drapes in the living room and made it into a noose. He put it around my neck and slung the other end over the bedroom door. He said he wouldn't hurt me, but then he started pulling the noose from behind and . . ." Stewart's voice hovered just above a whisper, ". . . jacking off to pictures of young boys in the magazines he brought with him."

After the guy left, Stewart started yelling until a neighbor heard him and called the police. "A couple of patrolmen came out. But I wasn't filing a report," he said. "I know how the media scan those things, hoping for a celebrity to trash. I wouldn't give them the satisfaction. But the cops took down his description and told me they would hold it and the evidence at the station in case I changed my mind and wanted to file a report later."

"Could we stop by your house to see where all this happened?" Billie asked. "It would really help us determine if the cases are related."

Another shaky breath rumbled through Stewart. He stood up and drained his glass. "Okay. You can follow me over."

Brett Stewart's house on Don Quixote was a study in contrasts. The exterior was a modern glass, steel, and concrete box, but inside the heavy wooden door was an ornately decorated, rococo-styled living room that looked as if it belonged more in the French Quarter than Baldwin Hills. The living-room walls were blood red with drapes at the window made of a heavy, Merlot-colored velvet, held back on one side with a long, swooping length of gold-colored rope. Billie extracted some gloves out of her pocket and untied the rope. She pulled the Polaroid that Alexander had given us out of her purse, compared it to the rope in her hand.

Whispered to me: "I'll bet you that five I lost to you at the Mitchell scene that this is the same rope." To the newscaster she said, "Can we take this with us, Mr. Stewart?"

"Might as well," he said. "My young visitor and the cops took the ropes used for the other tieback and the valance. The window just doesn't look right without them."

Absent its golden ropes, the window treatment looked like the curtain at a theater. Stewart looked at it sadly and gingerly fingered his bruised face. "I'm supposed to fly down to Jamaica to meet Evie tomorrow. What am I supposed to tell her?"

The truth, I hoped.

It was almost ten. Billie and I sat in my Rabbit for a minute before going our separate ways. My head was spinning, and I could feel a headache gathering strength just beyond my field of vision. "You think Stewart's playmate is the same guy who paid a visit to Mitchell on Tuesday?" I asked her. "The two men's houses are only a few blocks apart. Our guy could be working the neighborhood, sort of a Kinky Sex Bandit."

She nodded slowly. "You know, Stewart's description of his assailant sounded a lot like that Peyton Bell kid."

I had to agree. And as much as I hated the thought, I kept coming back to the way Mitchell hugged the boy at the exhibit and then got Aubrey to kick in the extra money for Peyton's scholarship at the last minute. People don't do things like that for no good reason. We just needed to figure out which reason was the truth.

I said to Billie, "Find out who rolled out to Stewart's house Monday night." I figured it had to be someone other than LeDoux and Wright; they would've said something if they'd taken a report on a similar scene just the night before Mitchell's murder, whether they filed it or not. "Even if we assume for a minute that Peyton was involved in Mitchell's murder, he's still got an alibi for Lewis. If you'll recall, Cortez said Peyton talked to someone from the party store at five. That was just a few minutes before we got to King Boulevard."

"But do we know the employee at the party supply store actually talked to Peyton Bell? What if Peyton slipped out while Underwood was talking to the college, had Underwood place the call to establish his alibi, and went to that stand? Just because his mother doesn't think he's capable of murder doesn't mean he didn't overhear her talking to Mitchell about meeting Cinque and decide to take matters into his own hands."

"He *could* have seen Mitchell and Lewis arguing at the taco stand and stepped in," I agreed. Based on what I saw of Peyton's outburst at the gallery Wednesday night, he damn sure was angry about something.

Remembering Peyton and his mother at the gallery that night

triggered another memory—the shipping wire I'd seen in Reggie's back room. "We should see about getting a warrant and going over there and picking it up," she said when I mentioned it to her.

"You know," I said, "this could fit. Maybe Mitchell wasn't just supporting Peyton's talent by arranging for that scholarship at the last minute—he was feeling guilty about what happened behind that stand and was thanking Peyton for saving his life."

"And maybe the scholarship was also a little reminder of how valuable Mitchell could be to the boy long-term," Billie added.

"Then why choke the goose laying the golden eggs?" I asked, feeling that familiar headache coming on.

"Knowing someone is out there who could tie you to a murder would weigh heavily on anybody's mind," Billie reminded me.

But enough to cancel your meal ticket?

We agreed we needed to interview Raziya and Peyton Bell sooner rather than later. Billie suggested we go there immediately.

I disagreed. "If he's guilty and Raziya's already told him we want to talk to him, he's already in the wind. Nothing we can do about that."

Billie could see my point. "But I can call her tonight, tell her I forgot my kid has a doctor's appointment or something, and we need to see them tomorrow. She'll buy that. And I can find out if Peyton's still around." Billie dropped her head on the dashboard of my car. "Damn, this day has worn me out. If you don't mind, I'm going to go home and kiss my sleeping daughter."

I checked my watch. "I don't blame you. I've got to be somewhere myself."

I didn't think I had any expectations of where or how Aubrey lived, but as I headed toward Hollywood, away from the golden ghettos of the black middle class, I was a little thrown off. But I was cool—didn't gawk too much at the houses as they got bigger and bigger, and had fewer and fewer bars on the windows. But when I followed the directions Aubrey had given me into the hills north of Los Feliz Boulevard, I was beside myself with curiosity.

After another five minutes of driving along the winding hill roads, I pulled up to a Tudor house just below the Griffith Park Observatory. I got out of my car and stood looking out on the view of life. The city lay at my feet, little grids of lights twinkling through the smoky haze, making a luminescent patchwork quilt of East Hollywood, Silverlake, and the city beyond. The downtown high-rises stood clustered in the distance, crowned by the blazing green lights of Library Tower. City Hall, the tallest structure in Los Angeles when it was built in the twenties, stood dwarfed in the shadows, a little apart from the rest of the downtown skyline. Despite all of its political intrigue and problems that loomed so large in my life, Parker Center wasn't even visible from where I stood.

Aubrey met me at the front door and kissed me lightly on the lips. "Where's your sling?"

"Special occasion," I said, and flexed my arm. I stepped back to take in the view again. "God, this is gorgeous, Aubrey. Makes you want to drop your troubles at the door."

"That's the whole point." He came up to stand with me on the front steps. "It's very soothing, after a long day of blood, guts, and corporate shenanigans, to come home to peace and quiet. Although you should have seen the view with the fires from the uprising last week—it looked like Beirut."

He led me down the front steps through a door so massive I thought it would take a battering ram to get it open. "Drink?" he asked as he took my purse.

"What have you got?"

"Pouilly-Fuissé, juice, iced tea, designer water."

"The wine sounds good."

"Would you like me to fix you a plate?"

"If it's not too much trouble."

While Aubrey was in the kitchen, I looked around his living room. It was as large as my living and dining rooms combined, with a massive stone fireplace on the left and a wall of French doors and windows leading to a deck and that breathtaking view on the right. A pair of forest-green sofas and a dark-green marble-topped coffee table sat in the middle of the room atop off-white

Berber carpeting. Even the walls were white, soaring up to a magnificent coffered ceiling with gray-colored beams. The paleness of the walls made the black baby grand piano stand out in relief against the picture window and cityscape beyond.

When Aubrey returned, I was sitting at the piano, fiddling with the keys. "Do you still play?" I asked.

He set a platter of grilled vegetables and little slices of rare grilled tuna on the coffee table. "That's what I was doing when you called."

"When do you find the time?"

"I usually try to play for an hour when I come home and a few hours on the weekend," he said. "It's part of my personal prescription for relaxation."

"Sounds wonderful. Do you still play in any nightclubs like you used to in college?"

"No, I'm too rusty—and too busy—to be on the club circuit. I just do this for my own amusement." Aubrey sat down next to me on the mudcloth-upholstered piano bench. "Want to hear anything in particular?"

"Are you so good I get choices? I *am* impressed!"

He blushed a little, took a songbook off the top of the pile on the piano, and started to play. "This is what I was playing when you called earlier."

It was a jazz piece, soft and lilting, flowing as effortlessly through his long fingers as prayers on the lips of the faithful. I moved over to the sofa, sat back in the pillows, and let the peacefulness of his playing carry me away. Eventually I came back to earth and nibbled on some grilled eggplant and tuna from the platter. "That's beautiful. You wrote it?"

Aubrey's face colored up, embarrassed. "I wish. I first heard it on a Dianne Reeves CD. I hunted all over town for the sheet music. Just got it today."

"What's the name of it?"

" 'Like a Lover.' "

A roasted asparagus spear called out to me from the platter. I dove for it, hoping the move hid the flush I could feel creeping up my neck to my cheeks. Oblivious, Aubrey continued to play. "The piano is one of the things that got me through the hard times in my life."

Partially recovered, I leaned back on the sofa and sampled the wine. "I always loved the sound of it, but I rebelled when my mother tried to force lessons on me."

"Most of us did," Aubrey agreed. "But my mom was a singer, so I had no choice. She got the fever as a child after seeing Marian Anderson in concert."

"Your mother actually *saw* Marian Anderson? That must have made quite an impression!"

"She had a tremendous influence on a whole generation of black women. Not just the opera divas like Leontyne or Jessye who came after her, but little black girls living in Missouri towns who first heard her sing on the radio. By the time my mother got to see Miss Anderson at a concert in Kansas City, Mom had been bitten by the singing bug so bad she traveled all through the South as a teenager, singing with a female evangelist on what she used to call 'the chitlin' and fried-chicken circuit.' "

His fingers hesitated over the keys, then curled up into a fist. "I shouldn't be doing this," he said and thunked the keyboard closed.

I joined him on the bench. "What's wrong?"

Aubrey was staring at the closed keyboard. "Lance's death is bringing up a lot of stuff, not just for the partners or the hospital, but for me personally, too."

"What do you mean?"

He gazed out the window, whispered, "I really don't want to burden you with my old baggage, Char. We're just getting to know each other again, and you've got enough of your own stuff to deal with without weighing you down with mine."

"I don't know if you noticed when you examined me, but I've got strong shoulders," I smiled and took his hand, "or at least one."

I waited while Aubrey tried to form the words. Finally he said, "When we found my mom . . . she was . . . like Lance."

"You mean she *hung* herself? I thought your mother died of breast cancer!"

"She *did* have cancer, but that isn't what killed her. That's just what Pop and I decided to tell everyone. It was . . . too painful otherwise." The tears I had seen in Aubrey's eyes the night Lance was killed were back, but this time they made sense.

"We didn't know CPR in those days," Aubrey's voice came out in a shudder as he grasped my hand, "so even though she wasn't quite gone, we couldn't do anything. It's one of the reasons I picked emergency medicine as a specialty. I wanted . . . I thought maybe I could save somebody else, even if I couldn't save her."

It was like listening to my own voice thirteen years ago, telling me why I wanted to be a cop. We sat on that piano bench quietly for a long time, holding hands and memories and long-buried pain between us.

Aubrey was the one to break the silence. "I feel like a real hypocrite, telling you the other night about living in the past and here I am confusing Lance's death for my mother's. I'm sorry," he sighed and squeezed my fingers. "The funeral today just brought it all back to me. I haven't even been able to bring the pictures I had developed from the TAGOUT exhibit into the house. Stupid, isn't it?"

I shook my head. "I understand completely."

And I did. It's so seldom that cops see the long-term consequences of violent death, even when they work homicide. You do the next-of-kin notification, see the disbelief on people's faces when you tell them their loved one is gone, maybe even go to a funeral, but you hardly ever see how that loss can consume a person, year in and year out. For a homicide detective, no matter how much you care, the dead inevitably get reduced to case numbers, files to be closed, numbers to be added to other numbers that go into some departmental statistical report, a scorecard. Unless you have your own grief to bear, you don't fully understand what those numbers mean to the people left behind, thousands of people whose lives and spirits implode, just crumple up and blow away like ash carried on a hot Santa Ana wind.

Aubrey had wandered over to the stereo and loaded up the CD changer. "I talked to your brother this evening," he said, his voice a little brighter. "He's coming over to shoot some hoops in the morning."

"Is he going to meet you *here*?" If Perris was coming over, I wondered if Aubrey's sly invitation to spend the night was even going to be a possibility.

"Yeah—I've got a court at the bottom of the property." He held out his hand. "Come on and I'll show you."

If my house was a nickel tour, Aubrey's was the ten-dollar, deluxe special. Tasteful, housekeeper-neat, and with a kitchen to die for, Aubrey's house told me this was a man at ease with himself and his surroundings. I poured myself some more wine and sat sipping it at the kitchen table, enjoying the view of what looked like a Frank Lloyd Wright house across the canyon and Aubrey's basketball court and lap pool below while he dished up some homemade blueberry cobbler to take downstairs.

Because the house was situated on a downhill grade, the three bedrooms and den, along with the pool and court, were on the level below us. The den, a long windowless room situated against the hillside, dominated the floor. An office and guest bedroom branched out from it. The closed door at the end of the hall I assumed led to Aubrey's bedroom. Curious as I was, I didn't dare ask to see it.

We sat on Aubrey's leather sofa and talked about our activities since high school, our families, friends, and life in general while we ate dessert and listened to a CD of Dave Grusin playing Gershwin. By the time Shirley Horn's seductive voice and piano began to play, I was leaning on Aubrey's shoulder, as comfortable with my face in the soft cotton of his shirt as I'd ever been in my life, telling him how hard it was to play Top Cop all the time.

"You just need some TLC. Here." Aubrey stretched out on the sofa and eased me down on top of him. His arms still around me, my head resting on his chest, he began to gently massage my shoulders and arms and caress the small of my back through my sweater, which sent little shivers dancing through me but made me hold myself very still, afraid to obey the insistent orders of my pelvis to shift and move.

Despite my own restraint, I could feel Aubrey stiffening beneath me anyway, the growing pressure making my own body begin to swell and ache. He reached down and undid his belt. I rose up a little while he pulled it from his pants and let it drop on the floor.

Aubrey's long fingers worked their way under my sweater, then followed the straps of my bra like they were reading Braille until they came to the hooks in the back. He started to unsnap them, which made me squirm and kiss his blueberry-stained lips in response to the fire he was stoking inside me.

He opened his eyes, focused them on me. "What are you thinking?"

"I think I want to see your bedroom."

"Come on," he said and led me by the hand.

Aubrey's bedroom was a deep green, a dark, comfortable cave that opened onto the hazy lights of Dodger Stadium, Silverlake, and the navy shadows of the San Gabriel Mountains.

I sat on the edge of the bed and watched Aubrey light votive candles for the nightstands and headboard, which gave the bed the appearance of a massive, linen-draped altar. The flicker of the candles made his body glow like copper as he removed his shirt, then took off his pants, exposing those impossibly long, delicious legs.

He moved to the bed and peeled off my outer garments leaving me in the black-lace-bra-and-thong set that had been languishing in the bottom of my lingerie drawer for the better part of a year, waiting for just the right occasion. Aubrey started humming along with a song Shirley Horn was singing—*You won't forget me*—humming that sent me straight through the roof when he started kissing his way down the length of my body.

"Good God, Aubrey, what are you doing?" I managed to get out.

"Working my way to heaven," he murmured as he slid the elastic from my waist.

I never knew a man to talk so much while making love.

He'd nibble the inside of my thigh and ask, "Does that feel good?"

"Girl, you need to quit!" he'd mutter as I let my nails trail over the length of his body and planted kisses from his collarbone to the cuticles of his toes.

There was no hurry, no rush, no case to discuss afterward or meeting to attend. Nothing but the slow, wonder-filled exploration of each other's body and feelings and desires.

And after we had kissed, licked, and teased each other to distraction, after the protection was in place, after that one, breathless moment when he entered me—AHH!—after all that, the orgasms caught me by surprise. First just a softening, a warm, wide welcoming in the center of my being, they soon quickened, then shuddered, then raged over both of us like a storm. Mine first, then his jolting me again, rolling thunder between my legs, electric blue jolts starting low and snaking upward, getting trapped somewhere between my eyelids and the scalp on my head, making my hair crackle, making me move beneath, then on top of him, with every bump and grind I'd ever practiced in my adolescent fantasies (rescue me!), seen on the dance floor or at the lusting edge of that basketball court of memory. The man sweat dripping from him to me and back again, the man smell egging me on (ooh chi-i-ild!), churning turning floating soaring—THERE!—in that space, *there* it is, that makes-me-wanna-holler, slap-somebody-cause-it-feels-so-good passion I knew was there, from the moment he swept back into my life eight days ago.

Later, while Aubrey slept, I lay in astonished wonder, soaking up every detail of that room in the sputtering candlelight. The mahogany bed. Our colognes and body odors, rising up in fragrant waves from the soft linen sheets. Dog-eared copies of *Care of the Soul* and *Love Is Letting Go of Fear* on the nightstand beside me. The peace I felt being with this man, the first I'd known since . . .

Don't even think it, I cautioned myself.

. . . the first I'd known in a long, long time.

The stereo system was finally sending that Dianne Reeves song Aubrey had played earlier our way. When I heard the lyrics to "Like a Lover," I wondered if they might remind him of me. The thought made me afraid, afraid that by even thinking such a thing I'd be setting myself up more than I already had, packing my bags for some romantic fantasy trip I'd probably end up taking alone.

I tried to detach myself from my fantasies and fears long enough to hear Dianne sing:

Like a lover the velvet moon
Shares your pillow and watches while you sleep
Its light arrives on tiptoe
Gently taking you in its embrace
Oh how I dream I might be like
The velvet moon to you

I lay in the dark, listening and feeling the emotions within me make my eyes burn and my throat ache with the effort to keep them at bay. I had forgotten what this feeling was, was afraid to name it, afraid that naming it could mean it could be taken away. But here I was, lying next to a man with whom I'd locked hands and leaped into the blue, and he was still here, breathing and warm beside me.

Maybe it would be different this time.

CHAPTER 22

A TOUCH OF THE BLUES

I was back home by ten that Sunday morning, an hour before Perris was due at Aubrey's house to play basketball. As good as I felt about what was happening between the two of us, I had explained to Aubrey I wasn't quite ready to make an announcement to the world, especially to my nosy, sure-to-tell-my-mother big brother.

Instead I came home, put on some gospel music, popped some pain pills, and massaged my dog's ears while I went over my notes and interviews from the past week to see if there was really enough evidence to point to Peyton Bell as a suspect in Lewis's and Mitchell's murders. The problem for me was, all our theories and timelines aside, Peyton Bell just did not seem the type to commit murder. But my grandmother's adage was even more appropriate when it comes to murderers—you really couldn't judge a book by its cover. And a baby face or a quiet demeanor was no antidote against the rage in a person's heart. Sometimes it was just the opposite, as I had found out more times in my career than I cared to remember.

So I gave Peyton Bell the MOM test. Not a meeting with my mother, who could have cared less about the work I was doing, but

M-O-M—means, opportunity, and motive. And sad to say, despite his appearances, Peyton Bell got a high score against all three criteria—as good as anybody we'd encountered to date.

Means—he had access to packing wire in the back room of the Spiral Gallery, wire similar to that used in both killings, *and* I was sure he had access through his gang connections to an untraceable weapon in the Lewis case. *Opportunity*—the gap in time at the gallery between Underwood's last call to the college and Peyton's to the party supply store was enough for him—or even both of them—to have slipped out and done Lewis. There was a similar window of opportunity after Mitchell left the Cheesecake Factory after the opening when Peyton or Peyton and Underwood could have gone to Mitchell's house. And *motive,* the most damning of all—revenge in the killing of his half brother and the need to cover his tracks in the killing of Lance Mitchell, his benefactor but also a potential witness to the Lewis killing.

But luckily I had an ace in the hole, Jerry "the Sentinel" Riley, the old man from the apartment building who I was hoping was more coherent after his stay at the Brentwood VA hospital. If Riley could ID Peyton Bell, and Brett Stewart could place him at his house the night of Mitchell's murder, we might be able to shake something loose when we interviewed the boy later in the day.

I was just making a second cup of tea when my pager went off. It was Gena Cortez, calling from her home in the Valley. "I just got paged by the manager at Jerry Riley's apartment building. I asked him to call me when Mr. Riley turned up."

"Right on time! Can you get him over to South Bureau today? Detective Truesdale and I are interviewing a possible suspect . . ."

There was an awkward silence on Gena's end of the line. "What is it?" I asked. "Is there something wrong with him?"

"Afraid so. He jumped off the roof of his building early this morning."

I could feel my heart plummeting to somewhere around my kneecaps. "Who caught the call?"

"Danny Bansuela and Rhonda Deming are on the weekend

rotation. They said it was pretty cut-and-dried. Danny said they would send over a copy of their report if we wanted it."

Even though I knew my former partner and Detective Deming, both out of South Bureau, would write a thorough report, it wouldn't tell us what we needed to know most—what the Sentinel saw the afternoon of Cinque Lewis's murder. No one knew that for sure except Riley himself. And he was in no position to say. Not then, not ever.

As fruitless as it was, I felt like I ought to pay my respects. I felt responsible somehow, like I had set the wheels spinning in the Sentinel's head, wheels that spun him from a hospital to that roof and right off into oblivion.

The apartment building on King Boulevard was fairly quiet. Hiram and LaJohn, my homeboy informants, weren't around, but the manager, a shuffle-gaited elder the color and constitution of a dried twig, led me up to the roof and pointed out the spot where Jerry Riley had jumped.

A green thread was caught in the waist-high ironwork railing that surrounded the rooftop, the end blowing lazily over the edge of the building. It was from the Sentinel's letterman's sweater. The crime scene techs and the detectives must have overlooked it in their collection of evidence. I left it alone, thinking I should have them come back and take a picture of it, if for no other reason than to commemorate the sad spot where an old man finally decided he'd had enough of this sorry world.

Benjamin Gordon hitched up his old woolen pants—pants he probably filled out nicely twenty years ago—and lit a half-consumed cigar. A twig smoking a stump. "Jerry Riley was a scholar, you know. Never went to college or nuthin' like that, but read everythang in sight—history, the Bible, science, philosophy. Everybody round here knew, when his head was right, they could go to Riley and get the answer to any question under the sun."

I helped the old man back down the stairs. "What do you think made him go off the deep end?"

"Vietnam." We stopped at the landing while he coughed and caught his breath. "Riley lost his only boy over there. Wudn't never right in the head after that."

He stubbed out his cigar in a hallway ashtray, unlocked his door, and ushered me into the smell of frying chicken and Aretha Franklin singing "Mary, Don't You Weep" on the radio.

"Could there be any other reason?"

He fell into a gold-and-green–striped velvet easy chair, the unlit cigar jammed between his thin lips. "I think all this riot mess was preyin' on Riley's mind. Ever since it happened he was goin' on at me about how the enemy was goin' to wipe out the New Zulu Nation of God—that was his name for colored folks. Quotin' from the book of Jeremiah and everythang."

"Who was this enemy?"

"Anybody in a uniform. Riley hated two things in this life—uniforms and doctors. The uniforms came to tell him his son was dead, and the doctors locked him up in the VA psych ward and then threw away the key." His thin fingers wobbled through the sparse white hairs on his head. "Shame his last experience on this earth was with the ones he hated the most."

"What do you mean?"

He started to answer but was wracked by another coughing spell, which made his eyes water and seemed almost to break him in two. "First, he was out at the VA for damn near four days with them doctors. Then, even after he got home, they wouldn't leave him be. One of 'em was here this mornin'."

"Before or after Mr. Riley jumped?"

"Before. Fella from the hospital, just come by to check up on whether Riley was taking his medication."

"Did he give you a card?"

He shook his head. "Said he had run out of them, but he put his name down on a piece of paper." Mr. Gordon removed the cigar from his mouth, pulled out a blue-bordered handkerchief, and coughed up something I'd rather he hadn't. Then he reinserted the stogie between his teeth and started searching through his pockets. "Mrs. Gordon could barely make it out, the fella's handwriting was so bad. Typical doctor."

Mr. Gordon had gotten to his feet to continue his aimless

self-frisking. "Them detectives asked me for it, too, but I couldn't find it then either. But I *know* it's around here somewhere. Mrs. Gordon," he called out, "are you *sure* you didn't hide that piece of paper with that doctor's name on it?"

A querulous voice rose over the sound of chicken sizzling: "Quit accusing me of hiding things, you old fool! I *told* you to look in the breakfront!"

Mr. Gordon flung his hand impatiently toward the kitchen, shuffled to the tiny dining room. After several minutes, he found a scrap of paper and handed it to me. "Now what kind of name is that?" he moved in closer and pointed emphatically with his cigar.

I couldn't tell; the handwriting on the paper was almost completely illegible. The name scribbled on that yellow paper could have been Jones, or Johns, or Johnson. Yet something about it seemed familiar.

"How long after the doctor left did you find Mr. Riley's body?"

"'Bout a half an hour. Seen him lyin' between the buildings when I came from gittin' the Sunday paper."

"Could you describe this doctor for me, Mr. Gordon?"

"Well, he had on some a'them military pants and a shirt with that li'l blue 'gator on it. He was wearin' a baseball cap and dark glasses, so I didn't get a real good look at his face. Clean-shaven, though. Nice . . . Caucasian, but real respectful. Couldn't tell you much more than that."

I called Billie's house in Ladera Heights after I got home. There was a child's squeal of laughter in the background, then a splash of water. I felt I was intruding, just to tell her about an old man's death. But Billie didn't take it that way.

"That's a crying shame." Her voice told me she meant it. "Do you think his death was connected to our case?"

"I don't know, Billie. The old man had a history of mental illness. But he *was* the only witness to the Lewis killing."

I heard her tell Turquoise to get out of the pool. "Have you gotten a line on the officers who rolled out to Brett Stewart's house?" I asked.

"Not yet. I faxed a memo to all the watch sergeants at Southwest to mention it at roll call over the next few shifts, and I'm going to have the nine one one tapes pulled, too—see who picked up the call."

"Stewart's supposed to be in Jamaica with his wife," I said. "I'm going to call the station and his house, just to be sure he got away. If Riley's death *wasn't* an accident, I don't want our killer going after him next."

I asked her if we were set up for the Bells this afternoon. "Yep. I called her this morning, early. The boy answered the phone."

"At least he hadn't bolted; that's a good sign. What time's the interview?"

"She promised they'd be in after the late service at their church, around three."

We talked for a bit about strategy for the interview. I glanced at my watch; it was a little before one. "Would you mind picking me up?" I asked and told her where I lived. "My shoulder's bothering me a little."

"Too much party last night?" she teased. Before I could answer, a doorbell rang in the background. "That's my mother coming to baby-sit," she said. "I'm going to run by Mitchell's house to reinterview some of the neighbors, and then I'll swing by there—figure a quarter to three."

Much as I dreaded it, I paged Steve and did a good job of hiding my surprise when he called back ten minutes later with a "Wha's up?" like nothing had ever gone down between us.

"Something odd has come up on the Lewis investigation," I told him. "Cortez called to say our potential witness jumped off a building."

"That the old guy she was trying to catch up with at the VA, what was his name?"

"Jeremiah Riley."

Steve didn't seemed surprised, not even when I told him Riley had an early-morning visit from a VA psychiatrist. "But this doctor didn't have a card or any ID," I explained. "Gave the manager a scribbled-up piece of paper with a name on it that was pretty much illegible. Doesn't that sound odd to you?"

"No, it sounds like the Feds are making cutbacks just like us, and this poor bastard is just out there doing the best he can with limited resources." I heard a rustling in the background, then Steve's protracted sigh. "You're beginning to sound like the rest of these black people, hollering about one conspiracy or another."

"Just forget it, Steve."

"Why don't you talk to Stobaugh about it on Monday? I'm sure he'll be a sympathetic ear for you."

My antenna went up immediately. "Why would Stobaugh be so sympathetic to me?"

"He's just concerned, that's all."

"About Jerry Riley?"

"No, about you." A beat, then: "I am, too. You've been obsessed with this case since the very beginning, and it's not healthy. Even your reactions to innocuous events have been way off."

"I'd hardly call you trying to rape me as innocuous."

Another beat, then: "Look, we just had a misunderstanding, Charlotte. No harm, no foul. But if you try and make more out of it than it was, it's only going to hurt you, not me."

I heard, and questioned, the veiled threat in Steve's tone.

His response was quick. "What do you expect? With you threatening to go to Cortez and Stobaugh with your crazy story, I had to tell him the truth."

"And what would that be, Steve?"

"That you're so strung out on this case your judgment is impaired."

"And what—I *imagined* what happened Wednesday night?" For a minute I had the crazy feeling Steve was taping our conversation. "You and I *both* know what happened, Steve. I've got the bruises on my neck and Mrs. Franklin to prove it!"

"You probably got those bruises from that guy you were with," he said evenly. "I saw them when I dropped by your house to tell you about the meeting Big Mac called. And what did your neighbor see? Me coming out of your house, holding my sleeve and complaining about you siccing your dog on me is the way I remember it."

I could see Steve had been thinking about how to cover his tracks. "Fine, Steve, just forget it."

There was a pause on the line. Had he turned the tape recorder off or was it just the call-waiting signal on his phone? "I will, Charlotte" he said. "And I hope you do, too."

I was so furious, I had to do something, talk to *some*body before I burst. I tried Katrina, but my girlfriend was nowhere to be found. I started to call my father but decided against it—it would upset Matt too much and I couldn't risk him calling my godfather. Having a deputy chief, even one as loving as my uncle Henry, getting in the middle of my problems with Steve Firestone would be like the kiss of death for me with everybody at RHD.

Finally, I decided to go to the supermarket and pick up some groceries and a half gallon of ice cream for Mrs. Franklin, kind of a "thank you" for looking out for Beast and me.

"Child, you don't know how this takes me back," she exclaimed when she saw me on her doorstep. "You standin' there with that ice cream reminds me of Keith." She put a hand to her mouth. "And today of all days."

I had almost forgotten it was the anniversary of Keith and Erica's deaths. With everything going on, I didn't need the sadness I felt creeping up on me. She must have been reading my mind because Mrs. Franklin hugged me close and whispered, "You got a lot to be happy about, baby. And don't you worry—I'll be lookin' out for you and that dog long as I draw breath. That's what being neighbors is all about."

My cell phone rang as I was getting the groceries out of my

car. It was Perris. "I've been trying to reach you! Where are you?" he demanded.

"In front of my house." I heard the over-the-top big-brother tone in his voice and prayed Aubrey hadn't blabbed about my spending the night with him.

As I was getting out the double-bagged-for-your-safety packages from my car, I noticed a black car heading my way. I had to catch my breath, and for just an instant I could see Keith and Erica lying in my jacaranda-strewn driveway. I blinked and realized it was only Billie's Maxima. I shook it off and chalked my feelings up to a touch of the anniversary blues.

"I'm coming over there, Char. We've got to talk. I'm at Aubrey's, and he's got these pictures of cops that Mitchell took . . ."

"They're probably pictures of the cops in the altercation on Friday . . ."

My brother's voice was loud in my ear. *"Charlotte, will you shut up and listen to me for a minute?"*

Billie was walking up my driveway in a hurry. Whatever Perris was excited about would have to wait. "I gotta run, big brother. Someone from South Bureau is here to take me downtown." I said a hasty good-bye and clicked off the phone.

CHAPTER 23

NEVER JUDGE A BOOK BY ITS COVER

Billie's face was pinched, her eyes completely out of synch. "Let's go," she said.

I looked at my watch. "You're a little early. What's going on?"

Billie's fingers were clenching my car door so hard they looked arthritic. "We need to go *now*." She leaned toward me, a movement so slight I almost missed it, and said out of the corner of her mouth: "Please, Charlotte. He's got Turquoise."

From inside the car at the curb, I could hear the child's tinkling laugh and see her silhouette along with that of another, bigger head. "Can we just get in the car?" Billie urged.

I slipped my gun from my purse into one of the grocery bags and toted them over to Billie's car. Although my brain felt tight inside my skull, I forced my voice to be bright: "Good thing you caught me. I was just about to take some of these groceries over to my neighbor."

His face stretched into a smile as I got into the front seat. "Good to see you, Detective."

Mrs. Franklin's vision said I would suffer from the malice of a pretended friend, but I had no idea this was what it meant. He was wearing khakis and a burgundy Izod shirt that fit snug over his ample chest. With his clean-shaven face, Dodgers cap, and aviator sunglasses, I almost didn't recognize him. He was playing patty-cake with Billie's little girl like he was an old friend of the family. The only thing that suggested maybe he wasn't was the nine millimeter that lay across his lap.

I tried to ignore the handgun and made myself flash him one of my best smiles. "If it isn't sweet Chip LeDoux! This is a nice surprise, but I don't recall writing down my home address when I gave you my card."

"You didn't," he smiled. "Wright called me at home this morning, told me Detective Truesdale wanted to talk to the officers who rolled out to that news anchor's house. So I called Billie here and convinced her that my information on your 'Kinky Sex Bandit' was worth discussin' face to face. And, lo and behold, come to find out she's workin' the Mitchell case with you. I couldn't pass up the chance to see you again, and she was kind enough to oblige me."

Oh, dear God; now I knew which cops Lance had taken pictures of, probably minutes before we encountered him on King Boulevard that Friday.

Turquoise yanked at the sleeve of LeDoux's shirt. "Can we play patty-cake some more?"

"No, darlin', but you can sit on my lap."

Turquoise clambered happily into the patrolman's lap. He put his right arm around her and jiggled her up and down, causing the gold watch he wore to give off sparks in the afternoon sun. His left hand held his weapon, which also caught the sun in its deep, silvery glow.

"Now I know, Officer LeDoux," I forced a smile into his too-blue eyes, "you didn't bring your sweet self all the way over here just to see where I live."

"Call me Chip," he smiled back, but there was something disturbingly vacant in his eyes.

"So, what's up, Chip?"

LeDoux rubbed his gun thoughtfully against his cheek. "You girls have put us in a real bind. Me and Darren had no intention of writin' up a report on that news anchor. Faggot didn't want his big-bucks career going up in smoke. We could respect that." His mouth twitched upward, a grotesque, grinning mask. "Besides," he snickered, "as you know, the evidence came in handy later."

These are your colleagues, sworn to protect and serve, I thought with a chill.

Keeping my eyes on his face, I tried to size up the situation quickly. LeDoux was sitting in the middle of the backseat, over the car's transmission hump. I could see Billie's mind working, too, calculating whether she could grab the weapon from him in such close quarters. If she tried it, Turquoise would surely be hit, if not killed outright, and maybe one or both of us, too. As much as I knew it would be my first inclination as a mother, the cop in me said, *Don't risk it, Billie.*

But as hard as I was thinking, I was also praying frantically, the words rising up whole in my mind's eye as if it were 1978 again and I was on my knees, mumbling the psalm that kept me going after my family was killed: *Unto thee will I cry, O Lord my rock . . .*

LeDoux's smile dissolved as quickly as it appeared. "But then Darren called from the station, and I knew we were gonna be the ones with our careers in the dustbin if we didn't get this situation under control PDQ."

"It doesn't have to go down like this, Chip," I said. "What have you got—twenty-five years in the Department?"

"Twenty-seven," he corrected. "Joined up right out of 'Nam."

My mind was calculating furiously for the dates LeDoux would have been there, trying to fabricate some kind of connection between us. "I have a brother who was in Vietnam—Sixty-five to sixty-seven" was the lie I came up with. "Can't remember the name of his platoon."

"He wouldn't have been in my unit. I was Special Forces."

I caught a glimpse of someone walking on the sidewalk on the opposite side of the street, but I couldn't tell who it was. All my attention was focused on Chip LeDoux.

Who was saying, "But everybody in our unit had a second job, regardless of our rank or specialization." He formed a gun with his right hand, pointed a loaded finger at Turquoise's stomach, puffed out his cheeks, and blew in her ear.

Turquoise giggled. I could feel Billie flinch in the driver's seat and my stomach turn, but I swallowed down my fear and revulsion to concentrate on LeDoux.

Reminded myself to stay calm. Watched that left hand of his and said, "With your skills and discipline, you must have been in high demand when you got back stateside."

"Very high," he agreed. "I got a lot of respect in the Department for my talents when I first got back. And when Watts blew up, I helped to kick some serious butt to keep this city safe. I even got a commendation from Chief Parker. That put me on the fast track through most of the seventies. Brought down a lot of lowlifes, too, until they outlawed the choke hold. Then the job got real ugly in the early eighties, when the gangs started takin' over the streets with their drugs and drive-bys. And with the courts jammed up the way they were, you'd bust one of 'em in the mornin' and he'd be out by noon, standin' on the same gotdamn street corner, grabbin' his dick and talkin' about your mama."

Turquoise's eyes grew round. "Mommy, he said a no-no."

"It's okay, honey, Officer LeDoux is only playing. Be still and let grown folks talk."

Billie reached over her seat to soothe her daughter only to have LeDoux put the real gun in Turquoise's side. "Don't go trying something you'll regret later, Detective," he warned her.

Tears welled up in Billie's eyes. "Don't hurt her, LeDoux. She's just a baby."

"I've got an idea," I added quickly. "Let Turquoise take these groceries over to my neighbor. Mrs. Franklin will look after her so then the three of us can go somewhere and talk."

Billie's tears stimulated Turquoise's. "I don't want to go, Mommy," she whimpered. "I want to stay with you."

"See, she wants to stay with us." LeDoux bounced the child more vigorously on his knee, placed his lips close to her ear. "You can stay, angel, but you have to promise to be very good and very, very quiet. Can you do that for me?"

Turquoise nodded solemnly. LeDoux kissed her cheek and held her tighter, so tight I was afraid he would squeeze the breath from her.

I had to keep him talking, wait for an opening to get a clean shot. But how could I find some common ground with this man, what could I say that wouldn't push him over the edge, dragging all of us into the abyss with him?

I tried, "I was in the Southwest Division in eighty-three myself, gang table. Things were really getting ugly by that time. Sleazy lawyers getting their bottom-feeding clients off on technicalities . . ."

Forgive me, Perris.

". . . sometimes we couldn't get an arrest to stick to save our souls."

I struck a nerve; LeDoux's eyes connected with mine. "So you know what'm sayin'?" he asked.

"Absolutely," I nodded, and I did. For wasn't I, so full of hatred for Cinque Lewis and everything he represented for all these years, different only in degree from the wild-eyed man before me, a man who probably started out with a lot less anger than I had back then? There was one big distinction between us, though. I had tried to heal, find solace in the work, in the knowledge I was making a difference. And, ineffective as I felt at times, I had prayed.

But there was enough of LeDoux in me, in the icy fury I could see congealed in his eyes, beneath his reddened skin. Maybe by reopening my old wounds, I could make him believe I was more like him than different, kindred spirits, truly a brother and sister in blue. Maybe it would be enough, enough for him to let us live.

I took a deep breath to steady my nerves. "When I was with the Southwest," I began, "Royals and Deathstalkers were running the streets, polluting them with their drugs, and killing a lot of innocent people in the process. I lost my husband and kid in a drive-by, for Christ's sake! I wanted all of them dead."

That part was no lie, God forgive me. Except I wasn't willing to step outside the law to make it happen.

I held LeDoux's eyes: "And then they started the budget cut-backs. Fewer resources, these little pop guns they give us against the Uzis, and the lawyers tripping us up at every turn. How were we supposed to do our jobs?"

He was with me, his eyes deep blue pools of glistening rage. "It was just like 'Nam: 'Take care of this mess for us. We don't care how you do it, but just keep it away from *our* kids, and *our* homes, and *our* schools.' The brass had their goodies, their cushy lives behind the line. *We* were the ones out their dodging bullets, just like today. As if we don't have families we want to protect, too. And the money! Why did they think we'd keep riskin' our lives for that chump change they were payin' us? I'm drivin' a twelve-year-old Honda, and these little thugs are driving Bimmers and Benzes!"

"It ain't fair," I agreed, trying to convey empathy in my eyes when all I wanted was for God to strike this man dead.

Don't let him catch you judging him, I reminded myself. "So what did you do?" I asked instead.

"Went to the top, to the Big Dog himself." LeDoux was tickled by his own joke. "He had more than enough to share. There he was, richer than Rockefeller, and he expected to sell crack in *our* sector without giving us our props?"

"'Us' being you and Wright?" Billie asked.

"Darren wasn't up for it at first. But I made him see they owed it to us. Kind of a hazardous duty pay, y'know what'm sayin'?"

"You must have been upset when Big Dog got croaked," I said.

"That wasn't supposed to happen." The red in LeDoux's face deepened. "Me tryin' to keep three kids in private school and Darren with those payments on that sailboat. Doin' the Dog meant the end of our gravy train."

I could see worry creasing his forehead. He idly stroked Turquoise's hair. "My little one's got a learnin' disability. Do you know how expensive those special schools are?"

"Tell us what happened with Big Dog," I said softly.

"It wasn't intentional!" His eyes searched my face, then Billie's, begging for understanding. "We went to meet him at this building they use to store their drugs, and Givens started talkin' shit about how they didn't *need* our protection anymore, that they were too big for that. Can you imagine the balls it takes to get up in my face and front me off like that? After all that we did for him? Darren wouldn't have had to shoot him if Givens hadn't gone for his shit. And once Darren took the Dog out, his little partner, June Bug, had to go, too. We tied them up with some wire we found to make it look like a gang hit."

So that's why Givens missed the big gang summit. My stomach rumbled and my head began to throb. I ordered my face to be neutral. "You were lucky your partner had your back" was all I could think of to say.

"We look out for our own—even the ladies among us."

"How do you mean?"

"I was the one who kept you from crackin' your head in the ER."

So it was LeDoux's arm around me that night at the nurses' station. "I owe you twice, then." I couldn't bring myself to say the words "thank you" this time.

LeDoux nodded, a brief smile flitting across his face. "After we smoked Big Dog and June Bug, things got away from us. Like King Boulevard; that wasn't planned either. Darren and I had been lookin' all over for that white-haired sonofabitch ever since he ran out of that storefront on Crenshaw ..."

"Cinque Lewis was with Givens that day?" I asked.

LeDoux nodded. "Lewis musta been hidin' and watchin' us somewhere because we saw him slippin' out a side door as we were leavin'. We tailed him all the way over to the Coliseum, but then we lost him somewhere in them bungalow apartments. We kept lookin' for him, but he didn't surface until that next Friday."

Hiding out at Mrs. Sparks's house, no doubt. "So which of you killed him?" I asked.

"There was some baling wire from a television box somebody dumped behind the stand," he said. "Technique I learned in 'Nam—use whatever's at hand. Rusty nail, ballpoint pen, whatever. But the garrote was my specialty back then; I liked to feel their last breath when they went down. And they'd go down real quiet-like if you knew what you're doin'.

"Maybe I was a little rusty or somethin' 'cause this one wouldn't go down easy. Kept strugglin' and cursin'. But I held on, so by the time Darren popped him, he was already gone. But that didn't stop me from enjoyin' watchin' his body jerk one last time . . ."

I swallowed back the wave of nausea that ran through me. Not even Cinque Lewis deserved to die like that.

". . . or from picking his pockets," LeDoux was saying. "Lucky for us we did. That boy had five thousand dollars on him."

Peyton's money for school. So Cinque Lewis had been honest in his desire to help his half brother through college. My heart thudded when I realized I might not live to tell him.

But if I was going to die, I was going to die knowing the whole truth. "But why kill Riley, Chip? He was just a harmless old man."

He shook his head. "You told us yourself he made us. He had to go," he explained, "just like that doctor—he saw us cap Lewis. Even took pictures of it, for God's sake. We *had* to get our hands on those pictures. That's why we went through his glove compartment at the scene. Luckily in all the confusion, no one noticed. Then we saw you had him and tried to get him away from you . . ."

"*You* were the one who twisted my arm out there?"

"I'm real sorry about that, but we *had* to get that camera," he explained. "When you got away, Darren suggested we follow you to the hospital and intercept him. We almost had him, too, until his little co-worker volunteered to take him downtown."

A muscle tightened in LeDoux's jaw. "I coulda killed that little bitch." Then he laughed, a frightening sound that started deep in his chest and bubbled up out of his mouth to something just short of a cackle. "Thought about it again when she showed up at his house Tuesday night."

I took a closer look at the gold watch on LeDoux's arm. It was a Patek Philippe, the same brand Holly Mitchell said she gave her husband for their anniversary. No doubt Wright had the Rolex.

"So it was your and Wright's footprints outside Mitchell's house," Billie said.

"The dispatcher had us down as still workin' the scene at the gallery, so we had plenty of time to leave early and search the house. But we didn't find the pictures or the camera. We were in the bedroom when Mitchell got home, so we slipped outside and waited on the patio, hopin' maybe he had the camera on him. The girl showed up a few minutes later. We stood out there forty-five minutes, waitin' for him to finish boppin' her," LeDoux chuckled to himself. "Young girl nearly wore him out."

"Why didn't you just kill Jamilla Brown, too?" I asked.

"Outside of pissin' me off when she took Mitchell to Parker Center and makin' a nuisance of herself at Mitchell's house, she hadn't really done nuthin'," he conceded. "Mitchell was the rabbit we were huntin'. "

LeDoux half-laughed—more of a sneering sound really, just like the sound he made when he joked about Lewis to Wright and me on King Boulevard—and shook his head. "When he saw us in the bushes after she left, he got all indignant, demandin' to know what we were doin' on his property. But then he caught on to who we were and tried to get away. I still had some of that wire from the Lewis scene on me . . . he was dead before I knew it."

After LeDoux killed Mitchell, Wright took over. Afraid the coroner would discover the ligature marks and link the two killings, Wright went to their patrol car parked down the street and got the rope and magazines from their call to Brett Stewart's house the night before. "Darren said it made more sense to make it look like the doctor snuffed himself. With all that erotic art and shit up in there, it wasn't much of a stretch. And we knew Stewart wasn't going to file a complaint." He looked at the two of us as if seeking our approval. "I thought it was pretty damn creative."

"And then you turned around and answered the Mitchell call when it came in," Billie added.

"We were just gettin' in the unit when the call came, but we told the dispatcher we were just comin' off of a Code 7 at a greasy spoon down on Crenshaw and we'd go on up the hill and check it out. That extra fifteen minutes or so really helped. Gave us time to vacuum up the broken pottery and the dust from our shoes, and put the bag in the car before Bansuela arrived with the crime scene van. But we still didn't find what we were lookin' for."

LeDoux suddenly pointed the gun at me. "Where's that boyfriend of yours, Detective?"

I held my face perfectly still for an instant, then tried to register confusion. "I don't know what you mean . . ."

"Wright and I finally put it together today," LeDoux said. "That was Mitchell's camera your doctor friend brought to the gallery on Tuesday night. That's why we couldn't find it when we tossed his house." He shook his head. "And to think we almost had our hands on it that night."

"He had the film in the camera developed already, but you and Wright aren't in those pictures; I saw them myself," I lied. "And with no photos," I hurried to add, "no one could ever prove you killed Lewis."

A cold blue flicker flared up in his eye. "They could with what I've just told you."

I held his eyes in mine, tried to penetrate the core of his dark soul, make him believe I was on his side. "They won't hear it from me," I said flatly.

Billie, whose worried eyes hadn't left her daughter's face the whole time, nodded and whispered, "Or me."

LeDoux's dead ones told me he didn't believe a word we were saying.

"You did me a big favor whacking Lewis," I argued. "The bastard killed my husband and child. At least let me return the favor."

He tightened his grip on the gun. "Sorry, Detective."

"Take it easy, Chip," I said. "We're on your side."

His blue eyes told me he doubted that.

The child had begun to whimper. Tears fell freely from Billie's eyes. "Don't do this in front of the kid, Chip," I pleaded. "It'll ruin her life. Let her go over to my neighbor's, then Billie and I will go wherever you want."

LeDoux licked his lips nervously and glanced at his watch. "I don't think so. Wright's on his way to take care of that newscaster.

I'm gonna do the three of you, then we're gettin' on his sailboat and gettin' the *fuck* out of here!"

"Mommy, Mommy," Turquoise squealed and squirmed, her eyes big with fear, "he said the 'F' word!"

LeDoux cursed and shoved Turquoise off his lap, knocking her hard into the door. She cried out and grabbed at the door handle.

For a minute I thought she had opened the door and fallen out, then realized someone must have yanked it from the outside and removed her. The sudden movement distracted LeDoux for just a moment. It was just enough time for me to reach between my feet, grab my gun, get the safety off, and get a bead on him.

The shots from my weapon sounded like thunder in my ears and were intensified by the sound of another gun fired into the backseat from the open rear door. Then there was the blood, splattering like rain all over the back of the car, some of it even ricocheting off the right window and misting my face and arms.

Billie was nowhere to be found; her car door was open, and I could hear a muffled cry coming from somewhere in the street. Dear God, don't let her be hit, I prayed.

There was an odd sound coming from the backseat. Afraid at what I would find but as curious as Lot's wife at the Tower of Babel, I looked back. I had to be sure.

There was a gaping hole in the middle of his face, another in his chest. Blood was spurting everywhere, and he was jerking like a marionette caught up in his own strings. But it was just a reflex. Chip LeDoux was already dead.

Billie had removed her daughter from the line of fire and was crouching behind a tree with Mrs. Franklin, shielding Turquoise with her body from the carnage inside the car. I didn't breathe until I saw my partner and that child move.

I sat there breathing deeply, trying to calm myself, when the door on my side of the car opened and a hand reached in for me. Pulled me up and away from the blood and death, up out of the past. Wrapped me in strong arms. Held me warm and close until I dropped my armor.

Finally.

Gratefully.

And cried. Cried for all the times I couldn't, for the tears that had been burned from my soul by hate as strong as LeDoux's, hate that left me dry-eyed and angry at a world that would allow those I loved most to be cut down, and then left me alone, pretending to live without them. Cried for the love of a mother who didn't know how to show it. The love of a husband snatched away too soon. The love of a little girl whose scent and heft in my arms I could still recall whenever I looked into a child's eyes.

Aubrey Scott stood there holding me, unafraid of my pain, my blood-splattered clothes, my wild, wet eyes.

"Are you all right, Char?" he said loudly, looking into my eyes. "Are you hit anywhere?"

I shook my head gratefully. Out of the corner of my eye I could see Perris emerge from checking LeDoux's vital signs in the back seat, his .357 Magnum still in his hand. Perris placed his gun on the hood of Billie's car and walked around it to join us on the grass. He hesitated, stopping just short of where we stood. Struggled to say, "I tried to warn you, but you weren't listening . . . When you said a cop was picking you up, I didn't know what to think. And I couldn't be sure the black-and-whites would make it in time or if they'd even come, given what was in those pictures."

Sirens screamed in the distance as I told Perris about LeDoux's confession. "We gotta think fast," I told my brother. "If you get tagged as a cop killer, it could ruin your practice."

"I've got an idea." Perris flipped open his cell phone, his fingers a blur as he punched in a number. "This is Perris Justice," he said into the mouthpiece, "I've got a big one for you, but you've gotta get here quick . . ."

While Perris walked away, talking rapidly into the phone, I looked down the street to see three black-and-whites speeding toward us. I felt a chill and the hairs on the back of my neck standing on end. The voices were whispering in my ear again, but they were telling me, *It's going to turn out okay this time.*

Mrs. Franklin, Billie, and Turquoise came to stand with us, Billie clinging to her daughter as if she were a life raft in a storm at sea. Turquoise's face was streaked with gravel and tears, and Billie's wasn't much better. "I got a owie," the child whimpered, pointing.

"She scraped her knee." Billie was laughing through her tears. "That's all. It's just her knee."

I put my arm around Billie's shoulder and whispered to Turquoise, "Come on in the house. We'll put a Band-Aid on that owie. And after we get you patched up, how about a big piece of Mrs. Franklin's chocolate cake?"

CHAPTER 24

END OF
WATCH

End *of watch* is a term used to describe the end of an officer's shift. It's a time fraught with anxiety for families and loved
ones, for they never know when a cop goes out the door whether
he or she will return home whole and healthy, with his or her arm
in a sling, or not at all.

Billie and I were the lucky ones. We spent the hours before
our end of watch filling out reports and being interviewed downtown by the suits from Internal Affairs and then Press Relations,
who split us up and went over our statements about Chip
LeDoux's confession and the exchange of gunfire between him,
Perris, and me with a fine-tooth comb. And even then, there was a
lingering sadness among our colleagues and a hint of something
more troubling, as if they considered Billie and me more than just
the messengers bearing exceedingly bad tidings.

The officer-needs-help call that Perris and Aubrey made en
route to my house went out over the regular police frequency and
brought cops from Wilshire Division, where my house was located,
as well as South Bureau. It also sent Darren Wright, Chip LeDoux's
partner in crime, into hiding. Wright had last been seen at Brett
Stewart's house, peeking into the windows and telling the neigh-

bors that Mr. Stewart called reporting trouble at the address. When he found out Stewart had left the country to meet his wife, the neighbors said Wright left in a hurry, cursing at the top of his lungs.

The detectives from Internal Affairs assumed Wright had heard the call on his way back to the station house because he never went back there, not even to try and pick up his car. He just drove the black-and-white to his slip in the Marina and took off. It would be a week before his boat was found by the Coast Guard off the coast of Catalina Island, Wright inside, the back of his head blown away, a nine-millimeter sandwich his last meal.

They tell me Wright's casket was closed. Like his partner LeDoux, Darren Wright was buried quietly, without police honors, only a few family members and friends from the Southwest Division in attendance. Those were two funerals I was glad to miss.

Never judge a book by its cover. My grandmother's saying should have been stenciled on those two cops' headstones. It was fast becoming my personal mantra. It even applied to Sandra Douglass, the man-chasing, hard-as-nails attorney Perris had called from in front of my house. She was at my house fifteen minutes behind the black-and-whites to advise both Perris and Mrs. Franklin.

According to Perris, after they went downtown and she finished telling everyone from the Internal Affairs detectives on up of her plans to have Earnestine Moore call a press conference to expose the LAPD's role in the proliferation of drugs in the black community, they were more than pleased to have her input on a press release that would keep her clients' names out of the papers.

The first article that ran in the *Times* Metro section on Tuesday was short and sweet: "BIZARRE COP SHOOTOUT HAS AUTHORITIES BAFFLED." The story, which bore Neil Hookstratten's byline, was as close as anyone would get to the real truth of the matter for some time to come:

A twenty-seven-year LAPD veteran was killed Sunday as he held two LAPD female homicide detectives at gunpoint. Rudy "Chip" LeDoux, 49, had taken Detectives Billie Truesdale of South Bureau and Charlotte Justice of the Robbery-Homicide Division hostage in front of the latter's home in Los Angeles, and was brandishing his weapon at the officers when he was shot by Detective Justice.

An LAPD spokesperson said Monday that LeDoux, who was stationed out of the Southwest Division, "had been under tremendous personal and professional strain over the past few months" and was distraught over the disappearance of his partner, Darren Wright....

Wright's suicide was also duly noted in a follow-up story that made the whole affair, to coin one of my father Matt's phrases, as clear as mud.

While he dutifully reported what he was told at the press conferences, Hookstratten knew something was missing and had been dogging my heels for the real deal, even getting my unlisted number from some civilian snitch in the LAPD's Human Resources Department.

"Come on, Charlotte, you know the line the Department is putting down is as phony as a three-dollar bill."

"I got no comment, Hook."

"There's a rumor going around Parker Center that you were sleeping with both LeDoux and Wright, that the whole thing was some kind of romance gone sour."

"Who told you that lie?"

"You know I can't reveal a source, Detective." There was an overly long silence on Hook's end of the line. "We can help each other out, Charlotte," he finally said. "If there's something amiss in the Department, let me be the one to break the story. I *will* find out what's going on, with or without your help. But if you help me, maybe I can help you. You never know when having a reporter from the *Times* on your side can come in handy."

Hookstratten was only the first of a slew of calls, so many I eventually had to change my home phone number. Billie and I, Perris and Mrs. Franklin, even my parents were being dogged by reporters from the *Times,* the *LA Weekly,* and the tabloids, all hoping for an exclusive interview to follow up their lead stories: "JUSTICE SERVED BY FEMALE DETECTIVE IN COP KIDNAPPING," and the one that had everybody buzzing, even in the midst of the rebuilding efforts, "FUGITIVE REVOLUTIONARY'S DEATH SPARKS LAPD INQUIRY."

Once the press got hold of the story, things got real crazy. Raziya Bell retained Sandra Douglass, who stormed into a joint meeting with Tony Dreyfuss and Captain MIA with a list of quid pro quos a mile long for the information her client would give. But just when it looked like her lengthy negotiations with the Department were going to ruin our chances of learning the whole truth about Lewis's life underground, I got a call from the Vegas prostheticist with a lead on our fugitive.

The man for whom the prosthetist fabricated the arm was listed as Rodney Langston in his records—the "friend" to whom Raziya and Mrs. Sparks had sent the money for Cinque's surgery and new ID. Seems Rodney/Cinque had the surgery in Vegas, then left for a small Alabama resort town called Perdido Beach, about fifty miles downstream from Mrs. Spark's hometown. There he'd built a new life for himself, complete with a wife and kids and a business manufacturing pickled okra and other condiments. According to the Perdido Beach Chamber of Commerce and the local sheriff, "Rodney Langston" had been a model citizen and a leader in the community.

Never judge a book by its cover. Whether for purposes of revenge or something else, Lewis had been in that warehouse with Big Dog Givens, and the LAPD and the Feds from the Drug Enforcement Administration wanted to know why. So Mike Cooper and a DEA agent were planning a trip to Perdido Beach to get some background on Mr. Langston and his business ventures.

Lieutenant Stobaugh let me know I was welcome to tag along if I wanted to. "God knows, you've earned the right on this one," he said.

Even Steve had to agree with that.

It was tempting but ultimately an invitation I declined. Cinque Lewis was dead, which was all I needed to know. It was time for me to get on with my life, to shed the blues I'd been living for a much happier color.

I decided to start with a vacation. I didn't think I'd be missed. Captain MIA and Lieutenant Stobaugh were happy, at least on the surface. I had closed out five murders, so everybody's statistics were looking good. But in the process the LAPD had another scandal to deal with, which only fanned the flames of the Department's critics and made the incoming chief seem like more of a savior than he really was.

My sudden fame hadn't won me any new friends in the Department, either. Sure, some of my colleagues would sidle up to me in the parking structure or the women's room to say what a great job I'd done. But then these same people would avoid me when I walked through the offices or down a hallway. The whole thing made me a little sad. Sad, but not surprised.

But after a month of cold shoulders, I was getting so uncomfortable that I was considering leaving the Department for the first time in my career. I was sitting at my desk one Wednesday, completing yet another report on the Lewis case and feeling the chill in the air all around me, when I got a phone call from Uncle Henry.

"The Christopher Commission laid the groundwork in identifying the bad apples, and your work in exposing LeDoux and Wright is another important step," he reminded me. "We got a new broom that a lot of people are hoping will sweep clean. So hang in there, Goddaughter. I'm not in a position to promise you anything, but you could be an important part of the new chief's team."

"Thanks for the vote of confidence, Uncle Henry. I'm grateful." But not convinced it was reason enough to stay in the Department. "Just give me some time to sort things out, see how I feel, okay?"

The following Saturday night, Aubrey and I went to a barbe-cue at the Nut House. My whole family was there, including Grandmama Cile and my sister Rhodesia, who were wearing identical T-shirts that proclaimed, "I'M TIRED. I'VE BEEN BLACK ALL DAY!" and talking about making a documentary on the rebuilding efforts.

Grandmama Cile presented a T-shirt to me and reached up to give me a big, Charlotte, Arkansas–style hug. "My grandbaby is out there kickin' ass and takin' names!" she crowed.

"Really, Mother Justice!" Joymarie scolded. "What your grandmother means is that we're all so very proud of you."

My grandmother harumphed by my side. "Said it the way I wanted to the first time."

My Uncle Henry was there, chewing on his stogie, playing bid whist by the pool with my father Matt, Uncle Reggie, and girlfriend Katrina.

"Aubrey Scott!" my father Matt shouted. "Boy, git on over here!"

"Mr. Justice." Aubrey hugged and slapped my father on the back for a long time. Katrina eyed him appreciatively and mouthed a silent "Go on, girl!" in my direction.

Aubrey sat down with my grandmother to play a hand. Louise and the twins were splashing in the shallow end of the pool, while Perris sat in one of the chaise lounges, drinking what looked suspiciously like a glass of champagne.

It was. I knew the LeDoux shooting had taken its toll on my brother, but he had been talking about it more than I'd ever seen him talk about anything in his life, and we had gotten much closer in the process. I thought things were moving forward, not back-ward.

"This is just to celebrate my little sister's triumph," he reas-sured me when I questioned him about his drinking. "Besides, I had a problem with hard liquor, not champagne."

Louise heard him from the pool, her mouth set edgewise. My mother hovered, eyes wide with concern, and put more potato chips into an already-full bowl at his elbow.

"Just as long as you don't start backsliding," I warned.

"Don't you worry about me," he said. "You've got a vacation to think about. And while you're gone, Mother and I thought we could start getting that old room packed up for you, if you'd like."

"Thanks, but I'll do it when I get back," I smiled, took the glass out of his hand, and handed it to Joymarie. "I think it's time."

Perris took Aubrey and me to the airport on Sunday morning. On the way, I asked my brother to make a couple of stops. A few minutes later, I found myself not more than a hundred steps from the Eternal Peace Chapel, two mixed bouquets clutched in my sweating hand. I had never been able to bring myself to visit the gravesites after Keith and Erica's funerals, so I was surprised to see how well maintained the graves were. A man on one of those John Deere lawnmowers passed between the flat markers, mowing the grass to a bristly green stubble that tickled my kneecaps through my linen pants as I knelt and made my nose itch.

The granite markers looked good, their blue-gray color still as peaceful and strong as the day I picked them out. "Keith Eric Roberts, August 19, 1943–May 10, 1978" and "Erica Justice Roberts, November 10, 1977–May 10, 1978," I read, the stone beneath my tracing fingers cool and smooth to the touch.

I placed the flowers in a nearby holder, opened the bag I brought with me and pulled out a copy of the Metro article from the Times about Cinque Lewis's death. I placed it on the grass and placed Keith's broken eyeglasses on top. I pulled out the sweater next, and thought I could smell just the faintest trace of Keith's cologne. The sweater would probably be picked up by one of the groundskeepers before the day was over, which would be okay.

I opened the gift that Katrina had given me for Erica the day she was killed. A pair of crocheted baby booties, the pink yarn still stiff and new-smelling. My heart caught in my chest, and I was overcome with the urge to stuff them into my pocket, but I ended up placing them on the pile, too.

I pulled out the old piece of paper from my wallet with the Twenty-eighth Psalm written on it in my grandmother's perfect handwriting. Instead of reading the whole thing, I let the words flow through my heart, then murmured the last lines aloud—*Save thy people, and bless thine inheritance: feed them also, and lift them up for ever*—knowing they were a benediction for me and my family, living and gone, as well as for Raziya and Peyton, Billie and Turquoise, for the city I loved and the Department I had served for most of my adult life. I refolded the prayer and placed it in the pocket of Keith's sweater. I hoped whoever got the sweater could use the blessing, too.

Aubrey was standing at the road, the car door open. When I walked up to him, he gave me a big, full-bodied hug, a hug that said no matter what, I had a friend, one who would stand by me.

"Are you ready to go?" he whispered and graced me with a gentle, understanding smile.

I looked back at the graves, felt a warm spring-turning-to-summer breeze on my cheek, smelled the grass-scented promise in the air.

Nodded, took his hand, and said, "I think it's time."

ACKNOWLEDGMENTS

The author wishes to express gratitude to the many friends and colleagues whose unconditional love and buoyant support were much appreciated during the writing of this novel. Special thanks go to James Fugate of Eso Won Books, who advocated for more about the Justice family after reading an epistolary story featuring them in the anthology *Merry Christmas, Baby*; Blanche Richardson of Marcus Books, who read an early version of the manuscript and gave valuable encouragement; Barry Martin of Book 'Em Mysteries, who was kind enough to be enthusiastic when he read the book's first chapter; and the family of booksellers across the country, who have been eagerly awaiting Charlotte's debut.

To family and friends who have put up with the author's mental and physical absence for much too long—thank you for providing the space for the author to bring Charlotte and company into the world. And thanks, too, to the writers who were supportive and welcoming of another sister into the literary family. Special thanks to Gar Anthony Haywood, who provided life- and plot-saving early advice; Valerie Wilson Wesley, whose "Go on, girl" enthusiasm was invaluable; Eleanor Taylor Bland, who listened to writerly woes; and Walter Mosley, who led the way for us all. And particular thanks go to Special K and Coach, literary and spiritual sisters who helped me more than they know and to whom I will be eternally grateful.

Profound thanks also go to the women and men of the LAPD, Los Angeles County Sheriff's Department, Los Angeles County Coroner's Department, and others in law enforcement, committed professionals who opened the doors wide, shared their stories, and corrected the author's exuberant errors. That said, and despite their best efforts to set her straight, the author bears total responsibility for Charlotte's thoughts and feelings and any inaccuracy of detail.

But ultimately there were three people who provided the most clear-eyed, cut-to-the-chase commentary and advice that were sorely needed—agent and ally Faith Childs, who always believed the author had something worthwhile to say; Gerry Howard, whose editorial insights and guidance (and discussions of Motown music) were most appreciated; and the author's husband, Felix Liddell, whose keen editorial eye coupled with loving concern and personal sacrifice will always be treasured.

Credit: D Stevens

ABOUT THE AUTHOR

PAULA L. WOODS is the editor of the acclaimed anthology *Spooks, Spies and Private Eyes: Black Mystery, Crime, and Suspense Fiction of the 20th Century*. She lives in Los Angeles with her husband and her boxers. Her e-mail address is DetJustice@aol.com.